Claudia Gr[...]

The Murder of Mr. Wickham

Claudia Gray is the pseudonym of Amy Vincent.
She is the writer of multiple young adult novels,
including the Evernight series, the Firebird trilogy, and the Constellation trilogy. In addition, she's
written several Star Wars novels, such as *Lost Stars*
and *Bloodline*. She makes her home in New Orleans
with her husband, Paul, and assorted small dogs.
You can keep up with her latest releases, thoughts
on writing, and various pop-culture musings via
Twitter, Tumblr, Pinterest, GoodReads, Instagram,
or (of course) her own home page.

claudiagray.com

Also by Claudia Gray

THE MURDER OF MR. WICKHAM

THE Murder OF
Mr. Wickham

Claudia Gray

VINTAGE BOOKS

A DIVISION OF PENGUIN RANDOM HOUSE LLC

NEW YORK

Library of Congress Cataloging-in-Publication Data
Name: Gray, Claudia, author.
Title: The murder of Mr. Wickham : a novel / Claudia Gray.
Description: First edition. | New York : Vintage Books, 2022.
Identifiers: LCCN 2021038035 (print) | LCCN 2021038036 (ebook)
Subjects: GSAFD: Detective and mystery fiction.
Classification: LCC PS3607.R38886 M87 2022 (print) |
LCC PS3607.R38886 (ebook) | DDC 813/.6—dc23
LC record available at https://lccn.loc.gov/2021038035
LC ebook record available at https://lccn.loc.gov/2021038036

Vintage Books Trade Paperback ISBN: 978-0-593-31381-7
eBook ISBN: 978-0-593-31382-4

Book design by Steve Walker

vintagebooks.com

Printed in the United States of America
12 14 16 18 20 19 17 15 13 11

For Paul Christian,
most ardently admired and loved

The Murder of Mr. Wickham is set in 1820, at the very end of the Regency period. Jane Austen's novels were published within a few years of one another—in the case of her first three books, many years after they were written. This obscures the fact that her writing spans nearly the entire Regency period, during which manners and fashions altered. So while we can find hints that different books came earlier or later, the only one of Austen's novels that can be specifically dated is *Persuasion*, which takes place in 1814 and 1815.

I've taken advantage of the lack of dates, assigning a time frame to the principal events of each of the other novels, as follows:

> *Pride and Prejudice*: 1797–1798
> *Northanger Abbey*: 1800
> *Emma*: 1803–1804
> *Mansfield Park*: 1816
> *Sense and Sensibility*: 1818–1819

This involves a *little* cheating—there are definite suggestions that *Emma* would probably come later and *Sense and Sensibility* earlier—but not much.

I've also drawn from one of my favorite Austen adaptations, the 1995 film *Sense and Sensibility*, to fill in one important detail that is mystifyingly absent from the book itself: Colonel Brandon's first name. As in the movie, he is called

Christopher, and for clarity's sake, his ward is likewise known as Beth.

In a handful of places, I have used the word *Gypsies* to refer to Roma people/Travelers. This was the word used in Regency England and is probably the only terminology the characters would've known. It is my hope that these few brief mentions are not unduly hurtful and that the content of the book reflects no harmful stereotypes.

THE MURDER OF MR. WICKHAM

June 1820

The marriage of Mr. and Mrs. Knightley of Donwell Abbey had been a surprise to those who knew them best and not in the least surprising to those who knew them hardly at all.

"But they've always been at odds," protested her sister, Isabella, a tactful and soft-spoken creature, as soon as she read the letter with the news.

"You mean they fight like cats and dogs" was her husband's blunt reply. Since he was not only brother-in-law to the bride but also younger brother to the groom, he'd observed their bickering at length, and with some exasperation.

They were both correct—partly. Emma Woodhouse and George Knightley had disagreed about many things: the need for a gentleman to dance at parties, the propriety of arriving in a carriage rather than on horseback, and, above all, the matrimonial prospects of everyone around them. Emma's wishful thinking had often led her into error, but in the end she didn't hesitate to make the most unlikely match of all: her own.

Yet the regular people of the village of Highbury were far less astonished. Mr. Knightley was the wealthiest, most eligible man of the parish; Emma Woodhouse the wealthiest, most eligible lady. Such individuals seem to fall in love with each other quite often. Why should it be shocking that this rule would prove as true in Highbury as anywhere else?

What everyone would have agreed on, if asked, was the happiness of the marriage. For sixteen years now, they had lived as man and wife. Emma Knightley had borne her husband two fine children, a daughter named Henrietta, who arrived on their second anniversary, and a son called Oliver, who followed five years later. By now they were well settled into Donwell Abbey, the picture of family harmony . . . though not today.

"Why should a man not invite guests to his own home?" Knightley said as he stood at the sideboard, making his plate for breakfast. "Darcy and I were great friends at Oxford, and he is a man of considerable estate. Why then should he and his wife be unwelcome at Donwell?"

"Oh! You insist on misinterpreting me," Emma replied, in no good temper. "It is not that Mr. and Mrs. Darcy are not welcome here on principle. It is that you have invited them at the same time we have other guests!"

"Cannot Donwell offer beds and shelter to all? Are we so impoverished that a houseful of guests will bankrupt us?"

Emma gave him a censorious look—one she had learned from his own face, long ago. "My point is that we can hardly do credit to so many guests at once."

Knightley sighed. "So perhaps it is *you* who should not have invited your cousin—"

"But Brandon is recently married, and I hear his young wife is singularly charming. We must meet her, mustn't we?"

"Or the daughter of that wild lady novelist you befriended in Bath—"

"Catherine Tilney is not the least bit wild, nor are her books. She is an entirely respectable woman and the wife of a clergyman. Her daughter Juliet is so isolated up at Gloucestershire—she should improve her acquaintance with the greater world."

"Or our tenants. Who ever imagined inviting tenants to stay?"

Now Emma knew herself to be on firm ground. "Anyone who heard of the dreadful state of Hartfield would insist that we owe our tenants a decent place to await repairs!"

(Her elderly father had refused any changes to the house in his last years, even those most conducive to safety.)

This, Knightley paused to consider. "In that case, I take your point. It is only one large repair—"

"A staircase collapsed." Emma folded her arms across her chest for emphasis, though her argument needed none.

Slowly Knightley nodded. "This summer is too hot for any additional discomforts to be borne. Are they not enduring enough already? Besides, Captain Wentworth and his wife seem both amiable and intelligent. Their greater acquaintance I anticipate with pleasure."

At a moment like this, Emma would never fail to press her advantage. "And who was it who invited his relations to stay?"

"My invitation was an open-ended one, however. I could scarcely have anticipated that Bertram would bring his wife to see us *now*."

Having won a few points, she thought it wisest to move on. She was not one to lament long over difficulties, relishing challenges as she did. "We must make the best of it. Instead of a few guests, we shall have a proper house party. That will be just the thing."

"Even if it is not 'just the thing,'" Knightley said, "a house party is what we have, and we must make the best of it."

⁘

If Emma and Knightley's marriage had been surprising to some, the announcement of the engagement between Elizabeth Bennet and Fitzwilliam Darcy had been astounding to all.

At the time it was well known in Elizabeth's community that Darcy was a proud, disagreeable man, so impressed with his own wealth and estate that he rarely even deigned to speak at social occasions. It was equally well known in Darcy's set that Elizabeth Bennet was a mere country girl with no relations of worth, no dowry of any use, and thus no hope of ever marrying well.

Had it not been for Mr. George Wickham, they probably never would have discovered each other's true natures—or even their own. They certainly wouldn't have spent the last twenty-two years happily married.

Well, Elizabeth Darcy thought. *Twenty-one years happily married.* This last year didn't count.

She sat on her bed, staring at the dress her maid had laid out for her. It was yellow, Elizabeth's favorite color. No doubt that was why it had been chosen. The shade was an attempt to help her make this transition from black, gray, and lavender.

It's been eight months, she reminded herself. *Time to leave mourning.*

With that she got to her feet. In the moment before she would have called for the maid, however, Darcy walked in.

He looked much as he ever had. Men's attire did not alter as much upon entering or leaving mourning. For her husband, little had changed. Sometimes it seemed to Elizabeth that he had been completely unaffected by last winter's tragedy.

Whereas she felt entirely transformed from a cheerful, spirited creature into her own shadow. Passive, insubstantial, darkened.

No wonder she and Darcy had had hardly anything to say each other any longer.

"Not yet ready," he said. From many husbands this comment would have been barbed. From Darcy it was merely a statement of fact, without judgment. "If you would rather we left tomorrow—"

"No, no," Elizabeth insisted. "They must already have our letter. It would be impolite to arrive late." If only she hadn't agreed to this—a house party made up of people she didn't know, spending weeks away from her own home! At the time, she'd thought a change of scenery highly advisable. It would take her out of herself, allow her to see a county she'd never visited before, and introduce her to a host of new acquaintances. (Elizabeth felt that new acquaintances generally fell into two categories: those who were worth knowing and those who provided constant sources of amusement.) Now that the time had come, however, the mere effort of preparing for the journey felt unconquerable. How much worse would the visit itself be?

Darcy's gaze had fallen upon her gown. He understood the significance of it as well as she. Without raising his eyes to hers, he murmured, "I have always found you beautiful in yellow."

Beneath the terrible cold that had settled over their marriage like winter snow, he was still her Darcy. Elizabeth smiled. For she who had once laughed every day, a smile now felt unfamiliar—but welcome. "Then I will wear it for you."

The tenderness in his answering glance filled her with something almost like hope. When Darcy opened his mouth to speak again, she leaned forward eagerly—only to hear a rap at the door, followed by the sound of hinges creaking.

"Mother?" Her eldest son, Jonathan, walked in. "Oh, forgive me. I don't wish to intrude."

"You are no intruder," Elizabeth said gently. "You never could be."

Truthfully, she already regretted the shift in her husband's demeanor: formal instead of familiar, distant instead of near. He had stepped back, almost as though to admit a stranger into the room. Jonathan brought this out in his father.

Or did his father bring it out in him?

More than once, Elizabeth had wondered how she could've birthed a son who made his father seem . . . informal. Easy-going. *Relaxed*, even. She'd always known that her liveliness softened her husband, improving his spirits; she had naively believed that their personalities would mingle in their children, producing the same result. Instead, her younger boys, Matthew and James, sometimes seemed to have all her high spirits (possibly doubled, in James's case).

But Jonathan—oh, he was both clever and civil, a dutiful son and a generous brother, their pride and joy. He was the very picture of his father at a younger age, if the miniatures at Pemberley told the truth, which made him an extremely handsome young man. The stiffness she had initially so disliked in Fitzwilliam Darcy—that was present, too. In Jonathan, however, this trait dominated his public character so much that she feared he would never learn from his father's example.

You little resemble your mother or your father in character, Elizabeth sometimes reminded herself. *So why are you so continually surprised by your eldest's demeanor?*

Sometimes Elizabeth wished for something—or someone—to finally change Jonathan in the way she had changed his father. But then she thought of her son, so honest and true and distinctly himself, and hated the thought that he might have to alter his character at all. If only she could change the world for him, so that it saw the Jonathan she knew.

But the world was not so easily transformed.

Jonathan said, "The valet wishes to take my trunk to the carriage. I felt that first I should ask you both if you are entirely certain I should come with you."

"Certainly you must," Elizabeth urged him. Traveling, meeting new people—surely that would help her son acquire more ease and improve his understanding. Living at Pemberley could induce a certain amnesia about the fact that the rest of the world wasn't equally as grand. "We've been looking forward to taking the journey together."

Jonathan bowed his head slightly. "My concern is for Pemberley. The elderflowers are about to be brought in for brewing, and someone from the household should be here to keep the ledgers—"

"Mr. Abbott has matters well in hand," Darcy said, a touch of severity in his tone. "I have trusted his oversight of these affairs for some years. Were you to stay behind to supervise him, he would take it as a sign of distrust, and thus the gravest insult."

"I—I had not realized," Jonathan said. Elizabeth saw a blush of mortification on his cheeks. "I never intended to malign Mr. Abbott."

Darcy made a sound that, from a lesser man, would've been a sigh. "Of course not. Though you remind me, I should speak with Abbott again before we depart. You should come with me, to better learn how much he does for us."

Jonathan made no visible move, but Elizabeth could see the shadows fall over him. Her eldest child strove to do right, to live up to the expectations set by his father and by society . . . and yet, despite his cleverness, it seemed there was always something he misunderstood.

Father and son walked out. The brief moment of intimacy Elizabeth had shared with Darcy departed with them.

❧

"Are you well?" Edmund Bertram asked, for the third time in as many hours. "The heat is dreadful. If you are fatigued, we can stop at a nearby inn."

His wife, Fanny, shook her head. She did not like to put others to trouble on her account, not even her dear Edmund. "No, no, I am perfectly well."

"I believe you would say that even if you had fallen and broken your head open."

Fanny managed to brighten for her husband. "Then I should be insensible, should I not?"

"Thus unable to say anything. I concede the point." Edmund had a small, neat smile.

She continued to stare out the windows of the carriage. Fanny had always found her greatest comfort in the natural world—in forests and fields, in tree and flower. Normally she would've had the keenest curiosity to observe the unfamiliar foliage, but today she could not lose herself in it. Dread gripped her in its claws, refusing to let go.

Fanny had always been a fearful creature. As a small child, she had been taken from her chaotic family home to live with her wealthier relations, Sir Thomas and Lady Bertram. The grandeur of their home and their manners had intimidated her from her usual quietness to absolute silence. Only one person had been truly kind and feeling to her: her cousin Edmund.

As they grew toward adulthood, Fanny's deep gratitude toward him had ripened into love. Edmund's concern and admiration for her had not. Instead, he'd fallen under the spell of a lively new girl in the neighborhood, a Mary Crawford. No amount of jealous chagrin could conceal the fact that Mary was bright, witty, musical, and at times deeply caring toward Fanny herself. But beneath this brilliant sheen, it was clear to Fanny that Mary's morals were not what they should be.

Edmund had failed to see this. He had remained oblivious to Mary's faults for many months, excusing what could not be ignored, while Fanny's spirits sank yet further. They had reached the threshold of an engagement—the proposal practically on Edmund's lips—before Mary had finally shown her true colors. And after that . . .

It was the "after" that Fanny didn't fully understand. Within the year, Edmund had recovered from his infatuation with Mary Crawford well enough to propose to Fanny herself. She'd accepted him with tears of happiness in her eyes. But even at the height of her joy, she remained aware that Edmund had never courted her as he had Mary. His face had never taken on that telltale mixture of delight and vulnerability, the one that told the world he was in love. Their daily routines had hardly altered. One day Fanny was his cousin; the next she was his wife, living at the vicarage with him much as they had lived together at Mansfield Park.

(The principal difference she could not speak of, could hardly think of, was that they lay in the same bed at night. What happened there . . . it was pleasure, Fanny couldn't deny that, but it remained a mystery to her. Something that belonged to the dark. Something God had willed between husbands and wives for reasons Fanny did not seek to comprehend.)

Surely it was wrong of her to wish for more. Edmund was her husband, the fulfillment of hopes she had never allowed herself to speak. Their living was modest yet comfortable. God had not yet blessed them with children, which after four years of marriage was worrying, yet Fanny still knelt in church with the serene conviction her prayers would someday be answered. She did not doubt that Edmund loved her.

But she didn't think he loved her as she loved him.

Surely it would take a love that great, that powerful, to face the problem tormenting her now.

Edmund spoke again. "You are very quiet."

Bowing her head, Fanny nodded. "It is my nature." Sometimes, in darker moments, she wondered whether Edmund ever missed Mary Crawford's quick wit—which, while occasionally unfeeling or even immoral, never failed to be interesting.

"That is true, but it is not the whole truth, Fanny," Edmund chided her gently. "Something has weighed heavily upon you these past few weeks, has it not?"

"No, no."

"A wife must be truthful with her husband." Edmund's voice had taken on the preachifying tones of a clergyman—unsurprising, given that this was his profession. "The sacred bonds of matrimony demand no less."

Fanny, deeply devout, generally enjoyed his sermons. Today, however, tears sprang to her eyes. "I am quite well; do not distrust me."

"I trust you above all other persons," Edmund said with great feeling. "Very well, Fanny. I will inquire no further for now."

For now. The words hit her like two strokes of the lash, or as she imagined a lashing would feel, from William's vivid description in one of his more troubling letters. Edmund would ask again, he would have to know, and yet he couldn't possibly know. How could she be true to both her husband and her brother?

William's most recent letter rested in her traveling case, bundled beneath Edmund's feet, painfully present—like a third person riding with them, staring at her, judging her every word.

∽

"Yes, that is better," said Marianne Brandon, gratefully breathing in fresh air from the newly opened carriage window. "Traveling in summer can be so odious. How lucky we are that the roads are not dusty."

Her husband wore the grave, concerned look he so often did when trying to take care of her. "You are not fretful about the sunlight, then?"

It took Marianne a moment to understand what Brandon meant. "I do not stoop, as some do, to ridiculing those who have become tanned in summertime. Perhaps it is not refined, but it indicates a love of fresh air and nature that I consider most pleasing. So why should I worry about becoming tanned myself?" She caught herself. Their marriage was still new. "But do you very much dislike when a woman is so tanned?"

"I feel as you do. Natural spirits should not be repressed," agreed Christopher Brandon. Was that a hint of warmth in his voice? If only she could tell. "Do not inhibit yourself on my account."

Marianne had had little intention of doing so. She only wished to know how her husband felt about . . . well, about *anything* in the world, besides herself.

Five months into their marriage, her husband remained closed off. Walled in. Far from her. This ran contrary to all her notions of matrimony, much less those of deepest love. How could a man come to her in bed at night and yet be unable to speak openly to her, without reserve? Marianne would once have believed that impossible.

Then again, so many of her beliefs about love had been shattered in the worst possible way.

Not quite two years prior, Marianne had met a young man named Willoughby who seemed to embody all her ideals about a romantic hero: handsome, dashing, passionate about poetry and art. Then it was revealed that Willoughby had trifled with and left pregnant a young woman—in fact, Colonel Brandon's cherished ward. Willoughby's aunt had disinherited him, and his romantic ideals were tossed aside in favor of another bride, one who came with a fortune of fifty thousand pounds.

Marianne's heart had been shattered. Worse, she'd indulged her own heartbreak to the point of weakening her body. When she caught a severe fever, she hadn't had the strength to fight it. So she had become terribly sick—so sick, in fact, that she very nearly died.

Her sister Elinor was always urging her to learn from this incident or that. From her illness, Marianne had learned two valuable lessons: that she had to govern her emotions, for both her sake and that of her family; and that Colonel Brandon, older and quiet as he was, had proved himself a man she could trust completely.

Couldn't trust lead to love? She had to hope so.

Elinor had finally come to have some influence over Marianne, and thus practical factors had been at work in her decision to accept Brandon's proposal. Colonel Brandon had a fine establishment and a good character. He was respected by his friends and cherished by her family. With such a husband, Marianne knew, she would always be treated with kindness and respect. It was too easy, she thought, to underestimate the value of feeling truly secure.

Still, she'd sworn long ago that she'd *never* sell herself into matrimony purely for wealth's sake. Marianne had accepted Brandon's proposal only after she began to feel toward him the emotions a wife should have for her husband.

She no longer held any scruples about his age (thirty-seven, a full eighteen years her senior), nor about his steady, taciturn nature, so unlike her own. Yet she remained aware that she had first fallen in love, not with the man himself but with his love for her. To be the subject of such gentle, unselfish devotion—to be protected so tenderly, and with so little expectation of reward—who could not be drawn to it? It was Brandon's love—the fervor of it real, if buried deep, like glowing embers within the ash of a fire—*this* was what had persuaded her to become his wife.

Greater understanding and intimacy, she felt, would awaken in time. Indeed, her tenderness for Brandon increased every day.

Yet after five months of marriage, he remained closed to her.

As a child, Marianne had always responded to a locked door by throwing herself against it. Locked hearts had proved more difficult.

〜

The word *retrench* suggests the admirable qualities of prudence and thrift. Yet it also suggests a downfall in circumstances, which however blameless is never admired. It was this condition that had befallen Captain and Mrs. Wentworth.

Their fortune of twenty-five thousand pounds had, almost overnight, vanished.

One might have expected the loss to weigh more heavily on Anne Wentworth. As one of the daughters of Sir Walter Elliot, she had been used to living very grandly in her youth. However, she'd never had any great taste for finery, and she'd spent happier hours in the humble homes of sailors than in the elegantly appointed Kellynch Hall of her childhood. When she married a naval man, she spent several years at sea with him and felt no sense of deprivation. A captain's quarters could be made comfortable and pleasing for a young family, even if no one would mistake them for grandeur.

It was Captain Frederick Wentworth who had been more discouraged by his changed circumstances. His wealth had not been inherited; it had been earned through valiant service to his nation. The getting of it had been his greatest pride, and the losing of it his greatest shame.

The pain was the worse for the shame being undeserved. By rights, it ought to have belonged to another—an individual who seemed entirely immune to shame's sting.

Thus, the collapse of the staircase at their temporary home was to Anne a small inconvenience, but to Wentworth, an outrage.

"Allowing tenants to move into an unsafe home—a home

on the verge of falling down around our ears!" Wentworth fumed as their lone manservant loaded the carriage. "It's unconscionable. No man of decency would ever let a house in such condition."

Anne replied, "No man of decency would ascribe to malice what is more easily explained by ignorance."

Chastened, Wentworth lowered his head. "Aye, we were told no one had lived in the house these two years. Mr. Knightley would not have known. But when I think of what might have happened if you had been on the stair when it fell—"

"I *was not*," Anne said firmly, but with a gentle hand on her husband's arm. She knew he could not bear the thought of disappointing her, or hurting her, again.

Though another was to blame for that . . .

"Thank God for you, Anne." Wentworth spoke in a low voice that betrayed much emotion. "I know not how I would bear it, without you."

"You need not know," she promised. "I will remain at your side as long as the fates allow."

It wasn't as comforting as she meant it to be. They both knew how cruel the fates often were.

⁓

"I do wish we'd been able to get you some new clothes," said Mrs. Tilney as she tied the ribbon of her daughter's cloak. "But you look very well indeed, my dear."

"Thank you, Mama," Juliet replied.

Juliet Tilney, having just turned seventeen, had become far more conscious of her appearance in the past year. As a younger girl, she had been more of a tomboy, one drawn to boys' games and fond of climbing trees. Her father had sometimes clucked his tongue at it, but her mother had always said that she herself was exactly the same when she was young. Had she not developed an interest in muslins and dancing—and handsome young clergymen—precisely when a girl should?

In truth, Juliet still liked boys' games, and she would have continued climbing trees if her gowns allowed. Unlike her mother, and for that matter most grown people, she didn't understand why she couldn't like muslins, dancing, *and* a rousing match of bowls. Perhaps when she was older, the answer would seem as self-evident to her as it did to everyone else.

Juliet was very well aware that she was being sent on this visit not only for a greater experience of the world but in the hopes of forming acquaintances who might, in time, introduce her to promising young men. Certainly she would be meeting very interesting people, at least according to the letter from Mrs. Knightley, which her mother had read aloud more than once. A captain in the navy—that sounded thrilling. A colonel who had served in the West Indies and could tell her so much about the greater world. The curate didn't sound that intriguing; Juliet was, after all, the daughter of a clergyman. But he was made up for by a Mr. Darcy, who owned Pemberley, an estate so grand that its fame had spread even to Gloucestershire.

And, of course, their wives. Juliet looked forward to meeting them, too. Interesting men tended to marry interesting women. If not, she had learned, it was a hint that the actual man might not be as interesting as his credentials.

"Surrey," said Mrs. Tilney thoughtfully. "You must tell me if it is a country of hedgerows."

Inquiries about landscape meant only one thing. "Are you thinking of setting a novel in Surrey?" Juliet asked.

"It's a possibility." Mrs. Tilney always envisioned a place in great detail before writing about it.

Juliet laughed. She admired her mother's boundless imagination, but it never ceased to amaze her how the ideas caught ablaze from the slightest spark. "Am I to be your researcher, then? To establish your next great adventure?"

Mrs. Tilney put one hand upon her daughter's cheek. "I hope the next adventure will be yours."

⁓

For the previous five years, Napoleon Bonaparte had at last been permanently contained on the island of Saint Helena. Though Britain, and for that matter all of Europe, still remembered his escape from Elba, no such revival seemed likely this time. The once-great Napoleon had grown older, and reports agreed that his health continued to decline. The wars that had so deeply scarred so many nations were over.

Other wars would come, of course. They might even arrive soon. But they would be wars like those of old, between known ruling families, dueling for long-defined territories. Never again, surely, could there be any conflict as shocking as Bonaparte's campaign.

The British navy had proved itself the glory of the nation and the triumph of the world. None could challenge Britannia on the seas—that had been demonstrated beyond any doubt. As for the British army in Europe, their victories, too, were celebrated. However, there was one class of military men who had failed to distinguish themselves in the wars: those of the militias. Napoleon had never mustered up the force, or at least the opportunity, to invade England. The thousands of young men who had joined the militias meant to protect against such an invasion had worn uniforms, drilled, been admired, and otherwise little inconvenienced. Some of these men simply felt grateful the invasion had never come. Others—less aware of the horrors of war, and more hungry for distinction—deeply regretted the peace.

Most regretful of all were the avaricious. There were prizes to be won in wartime that would otherwise be out of reach of the average man with his fortune to make.

But fortunes could always be made, if you had the will. George Wickham had learned that.

Wickham smoothed his waistcoat, ran one hand through his hair. Gray threaded through it now, and his waistcoat fit a little more tightly around his waist, but he still cut a fine figure of a man. He knew that from the interested glances he still won from women . . . even if they were older women now, and even if their glances came less often. If he were to marry again, he could wed more advantageously than he had before. Yet Wickham no longer needed to marry for money. Finally he had tasted wealth, and he didn't intend to live without it ever again.

In fact, his recent venture might still offer him a few hundred more pounds, if a certain Mr. and Mrs. Knightley of Surrey truly loved their family.

Chapter One

This is not like Northanger, Juliet thought, excitement mounting as her carriage drew closer to the great house where she
was to spend the next few weeks. *Donwell is a* real *abbey!*

It had no crumbling towers or Gothic eaves, but Donwell
Abbey wore its age more proudly than her uncle's home did.
As the carriage horses trotted closer to the front door, Juliet's
wide eyes took in stained glass windows, ancient craggy trees,
a chapel in the near distance, and a promising outcropping
that with luck would prove to be a gargoyle.

She took a deep breath and collected herself. Time for
enthusiasms and fancies later. First, she had to make a good
impression—to come across as dutiful, quiet, polite, and
accomplished. Juliet wasn't sure she *was* any of those things;
but she had to appear to be, or else no one would want to know
her. The governess had explained that often enough. What
she hadn't explained was the point of pretending to be something you weren't in order to draw people closer. Once they
got closer, they'd realize you were pretending, which seemed
to Juliet to defeat the purpose.

If she asked her parents this, her father would tell her she
was being silly. Her mother would give her one of those knowing looks that meant *The world is a ridiculous place, my child.
Make of it what you can.*

Juliet intended to make as much of the visit as possible. She
had long awaited her first true adventure.

———

There is nothing so invigorating to the established society of a neighborhood as a new acquaintance. The newcomer's family must be identified; he must be assessed as to character, person, and fortune; he must be asked to dinners and balls. If married, there will be a spouse and perhaps children to be met; if not, there are matches to be made. A newcomer provides a freshly sympathetic ear for tales of woe that have lost their powers over those who have heard the tales before; he laughs anew at jokes that had gone stale. He may even have stories of his own.

Yet it is not always as pleasant to *be* the newcomer. He is introduced to many people at once and struggles at first to correctly remember their names and situations. He is under constant observation—and well aware of it. While some thrive under such attentions, others find them disconcerting.

Most disconcerting of all? A gathering where nearly everyone is a newcomer to everyone else. Everyone is under examination; no one is fully at ease. Such was the state of the house party at Donwell as soon as the first few carriages arrived. But Emma Knightley was an exemplary hostess, who smoothly helped the first connections form.

"You are both great lovers of poetry, I understand," Emma said. "And novels, too. I fear I have never been a great reader myself—no matter how many lists of books I make."

Marianne managed not to scoff. Through her love for her new brother Edward, she had learned that it was possible to possess a fine soul and yet no feeling for poetry. However, as Emma wandered away through the gathering group, Marianne could not resist saying, "I cannot fathom looking at all the titles of the greatest novels and poems of our age and finding nothing of interest."

"Nor I," Juliet agreed, perhaps too heartily. "I spend half

the day reading, sometimes. My mother says she should scold me, except that she was quite as bad as myself at her age—and still is, to own the truth." Juliet was eager to like Mrs. Brandon, and to be liked by her. They were closest in age of any women likely to be present, with but two years between them. (Mrs. Knightley had a daughter near her own age, but the children of the household were visiting Brighton with family friends.) So Juliet longed for Mrs. Brandon to become her more particular friend at this gathering. Mrs. Brandon was very beautiful, and elegant, too, but not in the stiff, formal way Juliet despised. There was a fire in her, one too rare among Juliet's acquaintance.

Curiosity gleamed in Mrs. Brandon's eyes. "I have heard that your mother is an authoress herself, and that, if she is the 'Lady' on certain title pages, then some of her books are among my favorites."

Juliet wished she could enthusiastically agree. Yet propriety didn't allow a woman to acknowledge her own authorship, nor her mother's. This struck her as a rule both unnecessary and disagreeable, but her parents had trained her to follow it. "Oh, I could not say."

Still, she felt the flush of pride in her cheeks and was certain Mrs. Brandon saw it.

Mrs. Brandon's smile widened. "Regardless, I can tell that your mother appreciates the poetic and sensible. Who else would name a daughter Juliet? It is so lovely."

"Thank you." Juliet's unusual name had occasionally attracted unpleasant comment; it was neither biblical nor traditional and therefore suspect. Nor could Miss Capulet be considered a beau ideal for young women. However, Mrs. Brandon's admiration seemed sincere, so Juliet continued: "My sister is called Theodosia, and our little brother is Albion."

"How *splendid*." Mrs. Brandon's face lit up with delight, and Juliet knew them to be friends already.

At the other end of the drawing room, more introductions were being made. "Colonel Brandon, I understand you were some years with the army?" Emma's smile relaxed as her guest nodded. "Well! Then you must speak with our good tenant, Captain Wentworth of the navy."

Brandon and Wentworth exchanged a glance that no civilian could ever have interpreted. It was their mutual understanding of the ignorance of those who had never been in the military. Such persons made many strange assumptions, such as the idea that serving in the army and serving in the navy were just the same, save for one being on land and the other at sea.

In reality, the differences were many. For example, rank in the upper echelons of the navy was determined largely by merit; army officers were chosen for their wealth more than their ability. This meant that many army officers looked down on sailors as upstarts, too proud for their position in life. It also meant that many sailors assumed army officers were . . . well, the politest word was *blockheads*.

Neither Brandon nor Wentworth made such assumptions. Brandon was an astute judge of character; Wentworth's first impressions weren't infallible, but he knew good sense when he saw it in a man's eyes.

"When will you next be at sea?" Brandon asked.

It was an ordinary enough question to ask a naval man, so he wasn't prepared for the way Wentworth's jaw tightened or for the slight edge in the man's voice as he replied, "I had hoped to remain at home with my family for far longer, but our present situation does not allow it."

If Wentworth had once hoped for a longer stay in England,

then his fortunes must have taken a decidedly negative turn. Brandon knew some navy officers had lost the prizes won in war—the prizes could be contested, and ships once considered fair targets were later proved to be vessels with rights of passage. He would have thought such matters settled years ago, but he was no sailor.

"As yet I hope to settle my affairs in a more satisfactory manner." Wentworth did not sound like a man with much hope, yet grim determination underlined his every word. "If I fail . . . then I must put in for the next worthwhile ship bound for the Indies, and my wife and child must spend a year or more alone."

Brandon glanced over to his bride, Marianne. She was speaking animatedly with young Miss Tilney, her smile warmer to him than the fire in the hearth. He knew the cruelty of being parted from someone dearly loved.

"I served several years in the Indies," Brandon said. As deeply as he sympathized with Wentworth, he could in politeness offer no more than advice. Advice was better than nothing. "If you have not yet traveled there, I would be happy to answer any questions."

Wentworth smiled unevenly. "Indeed, I have several."

"Did I hear Mr. Bertram say that you have a brother in the navy?" Emma tried to make eye contact with Fanny Bertram, but the young woman ducked her head. "Mrs. Wentworth's husband is in the navy, too. A captain, no less!"

Fanny looked up immediately; any connection to William, however slight, drew her full attention—especially now. But she had little dreamed that she would find such instant, heartfelt sympathy as she saw in Anne Wentworth's expression.

"Where is your brother sailing?" Anne asked softly. "Have you heard from him lately?"

"Oh, yes," Fanny hastened to reply, "William is a very faithful correspondent. He is a lieutenant aboard the *Tiberius*, patrolling the waters around Saint Helena."

Anne's smile was as gentle as her eyes. "So long as the Corsican draws breath, we shall need ships in that sea—but I believe your brother is as safe as it is possible for a naval officer to be."

William was in danger as great as he could face in any battle. At least if a man survived a battle, he was then safe again . . .

Tears sprang to Fanny's eyes, and Anne squeezed her hand. "You are unwell. Let me fetch you a glass of wine."

It went against Fanny's nature to accept favors rather than perform them. She didn't drink much wine either, but if this would divert Anne Wentworth's perceptive gaze for a moment—"Yes, please. You are most kind."

Something about Anne's expression suggested that she understood the real reason Fanny had accepted her offer. She simply said, "Of course. I will return with your wine when the hour strikes." According to the finely gilded clock on the mantelpiece, the hour wouldn't strike for five full minutes yet; this was much longer than necessary to fetch the wine. Mercifully, Anne seemed to be giving Fanny a precious moment alone.

How good it felt to be understood!

Fanny was almost always shy of new acquaintance. Anne Wentworth, however, struck her as a person both genuine and sympathetic, someone who could be trusted. She felt grateful that this house party—a gathering large and unfamiliar, and therefore terrifying to her—had offered up one potential friend.

Still, she had nobody in whom she could ever truly confide.

By and large, the women of the gathering managed to speak easily among one another. When personal interests failed to align, they talked of their families. Emma found fresh reasons for laughter in all her children's games and fancies; Anne's voice became even softer as she spoke of the Wentworths' one daughter—a young girl named Patience, currently with family at Uppercross. Fanny took such a keen interest in hearing about the children that Juliet wondered if she were perhaps in a certain condition herself. The waistlines of dresses had inched lower in the past year but still allowed an expecting mother some months of mystery.

Juliet would've felt left out of a conversation so focused on the concerns of married women if it hadn't been for Marianne Brandon. Neither unmarried women nor new brides were expected to have babies or to have completely centered their lives upon children not yet born. Though they listened politely and spoke civilly to the others, they were able to have some private conversation about dresses. (Marianne had recently ordered her wedding clothes, and she was very amused to hear that Juliet's father was an expert on muslin, more than any woman either of them had ever met.) Tea was drunk and everyone smiled; yes, the house party was beginning well for the ladies.

The men of the gathering weren't as fortunate. No one disliked anyone else, but conversational topics were scarce.

"Surely you have excellent hunting on these grounds, Mr. Knightley," said Brandon. Almost any gentleman would have agreed that he did, or explained where better hunting was to be found.

Knightley instead shook his head. "I fear not, Colonel. Hunting has never been among my pursuits. Saves one the expense of beaters and dogs—though, of course, I have one dog regardless." He smiled fondly at the small black-and-white mongrel dozing in front of the fire. "Pierre earns his keep through extensive napping and by wagging his tail at amusing moments."

This won a small smile from Brandon, who valued tenderness, but provoked looks of consternation from the less sentimental Edmund Bertram and Captain Wentworth.

Other subjects proved equally uninspiring. Bertram spoke of his sermons with a piety that the others admired in the abstract but for which they could muster no evangelical zeal. Wentworth was disappointed to find none of them especially fond of fishing. Silences stretched between words to the point of awkwardness.

The house party was expected to last no less than one month. Knightley silently hoped they came up with something to talk about in that time.

Then his eyes lit upon Emma, who was laughing heartily with Anne Wentworth. His wife would find ways to make everything easy. She generally did. Few could resist Emma's charm; Knightley knew this very well, because he'd tried. Instead, he wore a rueful smile, and Emma wore a wedding ring.

Knightley predicted dinner would provide more to talk about, if only compliments for the white soup. Shortly before the meal, however, deliverance arrived in a much more welcome form. He brightened the moment he heard carriage wheels on the drive outside.

Only moments afterward, the butler entered the drawing room and announced, "Mr. and Mrs. Darcy of Pemberley, with Mr. Jonathan Darcy."

Knightley had seen Darcy only thrice since their Oxford days and not at all in the past decade. He felt a moment of surprise when he glimpsed the thin threads of silver at Darcy's temples, the hints of lines at the corners of his eyes. *No doubt,* he reminded himself, *you are doubly astonishing in this regard.* (Sometimes Knightley missed the fashion for powdered wigs, which had been so prevalent in their youth; they had so elegantly disguised an older man's graying hair or the loss of hair altogether.)

No changes of age could've kept the smile from Knightley's face. "Darcy! My good man. Thank goodness you made it."

"The weather does appear to be turning," Darcy said, casting a glance at one of the windows, through which the darkening skies could be seen. Yet he, too, was smiling. "It's a pleasure to see you, Knightley. You remember, of course, my wife."

Knightley remembered Elizabeth Darcy very well. He had met her only once, shortly after their wedding. Initially he'd been astonished that Darcy would marry with no regard for family or fortune—an imprudent match for a highly prudent man. However, after his first brief conversation with Mrs. Darcy, Knightley had completely understood. Yes, she was lovely, but loveliness was the least of her attractions. Her vivacity was the perfect balance to Darcy's somberness, and her strong character shone forth as brightly as her wit.

Elizabeth's face remained lovely all these years later, but her spark seemed to have faded. There was no feeling behind her civil greeting; it seemed to Knightley as though she was merely going through the motions, her mind somewhere else entirely. She never met her husband's eyes. Was there trouble between Darcy and his wife?

More likely she is understandably weary after travel, Knightley chided himself. *You're being as fantastical as Emma.*

And now he had the pleasure of meeting his old friend's son. "How good of you to join us as well, young Mr. Darcy."

Jonathan drew himself stiffly upright. Very stiffly. A footman would've been more at ease. "Your wife honored me with the invitation, sir. I would not decline."

Knightley had not been privy to this detail of the Darcys' invitation. Instantly his gaze went to young Miss Tilney, dark haired and pretty, sitting in the very chair that would present the best view to anyone walking into the room. His eyes met his wife's, and she ducked her head only slightly—not afraid to have her true intentions known.

Matchmaking again, he thought. *Oh, Emma!*

"I had of course hoped to have more young people here for you to become acquainted with," Mrs. Knightley murmured in Juliet's ear, as the party began the stirrings that would take them to dinner at last. "But Jonathan Darcy is said to be the best sort of young man. Diligent in his studies, heir to a great estate—and rather handsome, don't you think?"

"Rather," Juliet said, and was rewarded with a broad smile, as though she'd said something funny.

Really, saying Jonathan Darcy was handsome was about as noteworthy as saying that grass was green. Tall, with hair nearly as dark as her own, aristocratic bearing: Who *wouldn't* find him handsome?

Juliet wasn't sure she aspired to such an exalted match. She had only a small dowry to offer and had no intention of going through her life apologizing for the fact. Still, when she realized that etiquette demanded Jonathan escort her in for dinner, she felt a flutter of anticipation that must have pinked her cheeks.

They took their places to go in for their meal, last among the company. Jonathan stood next to her—so very tall!—and bent his arm for her to take. His forearm felt muscled and firm through the fabric of his elegant jacket, a detail Juliet had never before noticed about any man in her life.

"Do you fence, Mr. Darcy?" she ventured.

Jonathan half turned his head toward her in apparent amazement. "I beg your pardon?"

"I only thought—" Juliet knew she absolutely could not admit to being curious about his well-developed arms. "It is a common hobby among young gentlemen . . ."

Jonathan's fine, sharp features might easily have been chiseled from marble. "The time for dinner conversation is during dinner, is it not?"

Juliet snapped her head around to stare straight ahead. She hoped her pink cheeks from before would disguise any flush of indignation. What a prig! An *ill-mannered* prig at that. Weren't prigs supposed to at least pay attention to etiquette? That was the only good thing about them.

He thinks himself above his company, Juliet thought. *At least, above me.*

Oh, well. Whatever Mrs. Knightley had intended, Juliet hadn't come to Donwell Abbey to catch a husband. She'd come here to learn more about the world. So far she had discovered that young men could be both very handsome and *very* rude.

He'd got it wrong.

Jonathan often did. Sometimes he thought that people outside his family were a different species entirely—like the farcical men with backward feet described by Pliny the Elder. Why was it fairly easy to talk with Mother and Father, with his brothers, or even with the Pemberley servants, and yet so difficult to have a conversation with anyone else?

In his early life, he'd been surrounded only by those he knew and loved; this included the senior servants, who'd doted on him, and some few people from the nearby town of Lambton. Anyone he spoke with had to first be introduced, and in the warm sanctuary of his childhood home, there was seldom anyone who required introduction. Jonathan had felt some vague uneasiness about the idea of going away to school, but Father had assured him this was absolutely normal. Jonathan was told his schoolfellows would be nearly as close to him as brothers.

Instead, school had been a torment. The unfamiliar faces—new slang—uncertain hierarchy—all of it seemed designed to

confound and unnerve him. When his fellow students figured this out, they took it as license to give him no end of hell.
Jonathan had kept his head down as best he could and worked
hard to win the approval of the schoolmaster, the one person
he understood how to relate to.

His parents had assured him that his situation would be
better the next year. Then, that it would be better at university. Oxford *was* marginally better, mostly because the worst
teasing was now considered juvenile. But Jonathan still had
no better idea of how to talk to strangers than he ever had.

That was why the rules mattered.

Society had rules. They were sure, solid, unchanging. Steps
in a dance he had taught himself how to perform. Yes, others might find him . . . rigid, or even cold, if he stuck firmly
to conversing only within those boundaries. But they didn't
find him ridiculous. They couldn't say he was *wrong*. When
Jonathan followed the rules, he was safe.

He'd been counting on those rules to help him make the
better acquaintance of Miss Tilney, a rather pretty girl. The
rules were also meant to guide him past the moment when
she would take his arm—he did not like being touched by
strangers, though at least this was expected, so he could brace
himself for the contact. Instead, just as they had touched,
Miss Tilney had deviated from the rules and thrown him off.
He'd meant to nudge them both back to the safety of conventional times and means of expression. Instead—to judge by
the redness of her cheeks—he'd offended her. The only thing
worse than the fear of offending someone was the knowledge
that he already had. How on earth were they to get through
an entire meal like this?

Not one meal, Jonathan reminded himself. One month.
Surrounded by strangers. He'd thought it might be easier
spending time with people who were his parents' peers, rather

than his own; he had always related more easily to adults. So far he felt as wretched as ever. Glumly he looked forward to a long hour of strained chatter, sinking fear, and delicious food he'd be unable to digest due to the knots in his stomach.

Conversation was meant to be conducted with those on one's right and left, never across the table—save for those few pronouncements intended for all. Jonathan had hoped to be between two extremely talkative people. He had noticed that with such individuals, sometimes he needed to do no more than nod and occasionally murmur assent. Strangely, these same people were often those who spoke most warmly about him to his parents, who would pass along the compliments with the implicit suggestion that this—whatever he had just done—was precisely what he ought to be doing more of. Jonathan had not explained the paradox to them, primarily because he did not understand it himself. It appeared that people did not like to listen nearly so much as they liked to be listened to.

Unfortunately, at this dinner, Jonathan had been seated between the soft-spoken Mrs. Wentworth and the primly silent Mrs. Bertram. A long, awkward meal seemed to await.

However, no sooner had the first tureens been set upon the table than the butler appeared, looking discombobulated. "Mr. Knightley—a gentleman to see you, sir."

Knightley frowned, as well he might. "This is rather uncommon, Greene."

"Indeed, sir." The butler looked as though he would rather burst into flames than keep going, but backward glances indicated the man had little choice. "As I told him, but he's most insistent."

"Yes, I am," said a male voice as a shadowy form came forward from the darkness beyond to the threshold of the dining room. "Most insistent." He'd forced his way through, not even waiting for the butler to return, an act so impolite as to be alarming. Jonathan glanced at his father, who disliked rudeness nearly as much as he did himself.

But his father didn't look superior or displeased. He looked . . . furious. His mother, on the other hand, had gone ashen, so much so that Jonathan wondered if she would faint.

The man stepped close enough to be seen clearly. He was roughly the age of Jonathan's father, dressed in fashionable clothing—almost too fashionable, enough to be gaudy. His smile was mirthless and thin. Across the table, Jonathan glimpsed Anne Wentworth trying to catch the attention of her husband, who appeared to be broiling in the heat of his own fury.

Was it his imagination, or did this man look . . . vaguely familiar?

The man's smile broadened. "Well, well. It looks as though I have no shortage of acquaintance at table. What luck that we should all meet again."

Some of the others looked around in consternation, but Darcy simply inclined his head and said, in tones of pure ice, "Good evening, Mr. Wickham."

Chapter Two

Three times now, Fitzwilliam Darcy had believed himself permanently rid of the odious presence of George Wickham. Three times, he'd been wrong. The division eight months ago had seemed as though it had to be final, but no. Fate could be pernicious.

"Ah," Wickham said, strolling forward. "I see my timing is inopportune. In the city, you see, the fashion is for later dinners."

Knightley stood, pale and drawn. He looked as though he loathed Wickham as much as Darcy did. "You would not have been invited at any hour."

Wickham's smile widened. Somehow, in the heart of a confrontation, the man managed to seem even more at ease. "If I waited for an invitation to receive that which is mine in right of law—yes, Mr. Knightley, I imagine my wait would be very long."

Knightley's lips pressed together. Emma's face had flushed with ill-repressed anger. Nor were they the only persons agitated at the table: Wentworth's expression was dark, and his wife had tensed, as though she expected to have to fly from her chair to hold him back. Worst of all was dear Elizabeth, frozen like ice in her seat; her fingers were wrapped tightly around the hilt of her dinner knife. Jonathan's distrust of his uncle clearly warred with his concern for his mother.

As for the Brandons, the Bertrams, and the young Miss Tilney: they each appeared deeply confused by the sudden, severe deviation from common civility. Therefore, none of them had ever met George Wickham before. Darcy envied them the privilege.

A loud clap of thunder rumbled through the air, the house, the ground itself. In the next instant, raindrops began to pelt the windows and ground, striking the windowpanes until they rattled.

Darcy could've cursed aloud. To judge by the hoofbeats he'd heard outside earlier, Wickham had arrived on horseback rather than by carriage, and not even the most odious company would be thrown out in such weather. Particularly in such hilly country as this corner of Surrey—to attempt to ride in a severe thunderstorm risked the health and nerves of one's horse, and even one's life.

Wickham raised an eyebrow, as aware as anyone of the etiquette that imprisoned his hosts. "It seems I shall be staying for a while."

✍

"I fear we cannot accommodate you at the table, Mr. Wickham." Mrs. Knightley pushed her chair back as abruptly as an ill-mannered child. Jonathan would've been scolded for less, as a boy. She said, "Allow me to get you settled, and the servants will bring something up to you for dinner." With that she strode out of the room. After a moment, Wickham inclined his head to the table—an ironical half bow—then followed her.

Had she done the right thing? The normal rules could not apply to such a situation as this. Jonathan would've resolved to ask his parents later had they not appeared so stricken. No, he would be left to interpret this for himself.

A silence followed, empty of words and yet suffocatingly

heavy. Finally, Knightley cleared his throat. "My dear guests, I must beg your pardon. The gentleman who has arrived is . . . no friend to this household. Yet there are matters between us that must be resolved."

"He seemed insolent in the extreme," said Mrs. Brandon, astonishingly forthright. "What a disagreeable person."

In any other circumstances, Jonathan might've found such a pronouncement rude; tonight, people seemed freed to speak their thoughts—and to the whole table, at that. Understandable, perhaps, but in his opinion it set a dangerous precedent.

"George Wickham is indeed disagreeable," Knightley agreed, "however skilled he is at pretending otherwise."

Brandon spoke for the first time at dinner. "Did you say— Mr. *George* Wickham?"

Knightley nodded. "A former army officer, who now fancies himself an arranger of investments. Bah! Investments that work to his own gain and everyone else's loss."

"Certainly to ours," Wentworth said, his voice hollow.

Jonathan saw Mrs. Wentworth wince.

But she rallied swiftly, turning to Darcy and asking very civilly, "How are you acquainted with Mr. Wickham, sir?"

"We grew up together in Derbyshire," Darcy said. Brandon's fork clattered against the dinner plate. Jonathan wondered—*How could anyone continue eating at such a time?* "He was the son of my late father's steward. As adults, our ways parted for many years."

To his surprise, it was Mother who spoke next. "Then Mr. Wickham married my sister Lydia."

And Lydia and George Wickham had had a daughter.

For a moment, Jonathan remembered Susannah so vividly that she might've been sitting at his side, giggling as she so often did, dark curls framing her round, smiling face. To him, she had been more sister than cousin. To his parents,

Susannah had been more daughter than niece. He knew himself and his brothers to be dearly loved, but he knew also that for many years his mother and father had longed for a little girl that never came.

Then, eight years ago, Susannah had been born—the belated first and only child of his aunt and uncle. Neither Aunt Lydia nor Uncle George had possessed much interest in the daily tedium of child-rearing; as soon as Susannah had left her wet nurse, she had been packed off to Pemberley for lengthy visits. Indeed, Susannah had spent far more of her short life in his home than she ever had with her parents. This suited everyone: Mother and Father, who doted on the child; Jonathan and his brothers, who were old enough to find her odd little ways amusing rather than irritating; Aunt Lydia and Uncle George, who showed no evidence of ever missing their daughter; and Susannah herself, who wept piteously before each of her journeys home and always ran back into Pemberley as fast as her small legs would bear her.

She would never run through the doors again.

❧

Of all the insolence, Emma fumed. *To present himself at our home, bold as brass, and at dinner, yet! On the first night of a house party meant to provide some cheer to the very people most affected by this vain, remorseless man—*

"I've never before been a guest at Donwell Abbey, Mrs. Knightley," Wickham said. Insincere courtesy dripped from his words like oil. "It seems a splendid old building of the best sort."

"I rather wish it weren't an abbey," Emma said, bustling upstairs as he trotted to keep up with her. Maybe he'd trip, fall, and break his head wide open. What good fortune that would be! "If my dear husband had instead inherited a castle, we might have had a dungeon."

Apparently Wickham did not feel so confident as to hazard a reply.

They reached the top of the first flight of stairs. Donwell, like many abbeys, enclosed at its center a chamber with a soaring ceiling that reached the height of its three stories. Other than the servants' back stair, this was the only path up or down within the house. The rooms below and above managed to be intimate despite the marble arches that framed every doorway and the thick columns that stood like trees growing in their midst—but no matter how much warmth or comfort Emma gave those rooms, none of them were ever more than a few steps from this cavernous space. It was one of the few aspects of her home that Emma didn't like—the way the vast corridors caught sound, echoed it, cast it about into strange corners and crannies, until it was hard to tell where the noise came from.

Emma dropped her voice to a near whisper, so as not to disturb her guests with any further evidence of Mr. Wickham's presence. "One of the servants will soon arrive to make up the room. Have you any baggage with you? Any other clothing?" Given that he'd arrived on horseback, this seemed unlikely, but politeness demanded she ask.

"I've only the small valise in my saddlebag, which I trust a servant will deliver to my room shortly. The rest of my things await me in London, ma'am."

She was too easily baited, too quick to react. "As do dozens of solicitors, I imagine."

Wickham drew himself upright, his insouciant grin even more maddening. "They may petition in vain. The law is very firmly on my side—as many other dozens of solicitors have explained."

"The *law*." Emma's scorn curdled her expression. "A few tricks of language that absolve you from your moral responsibility. You knew from the beginning that these investments were only ever meant to impoverish those who trusted you."

Mr. Wickham bowed his head slightly. "It pains me to trouble you further, Mrs. Knightley. Yet I must point out that the uncertain nature of the endeavor was made entirely clear to every investor—including your brother-in-law. He knew there were risks. He chose to take them. Not every risk leads to reward."

What was most galling was the fact that Wickham . . . wasn't entirely wrong. How could John have taken such a chance with his money? He was the younger son, yes, but his inheritance from his mother meant he was more than able to support Isabella and the children in comfort and elegance. There was no reason to aim at greater wealth.

Yet John had always taken some pleasure in knowing what other people didn't. Maybe, Emma thought, that had been the truest temptation—the desire to prove himself cleverer than those around him.

Instead, the result was ruination. Isabella's dowry alone kept them from poverty. Within a year or two they might be obliged to give up the house in London. Hartfield would await them; the Wentworths' tenancy was for only one year. But could John and Isabella even afford to keep up Emma's family home?

With such thoughts in her head, it was difficult for Emma to remain civil. Best to end this encounter as quickly as she could. "Up the stairs, second door to the right," she said. Putting Mr. Wickham on the second floor would keep him away from the rest of her guests, which would be a benefit to all. "You can leave Donwell at first light."

"You are generosity itself, ma'am." The mockery in Wickham's voice provoked Emma almost past reason—oh, if she could just push him over the rails, send him toppling down to—

Emma caught herself. Without another word to Wickham, she hurried back downstairs, and to her guests.

❧

Certain mishaps befall every dinner party. Gravy is spilled, seating arrangements prove awkward. An adept hostess, and congenial guests, can smooth away such small imperfections and allow the party to proceed pleasantly.

There was no smoothing over the sudden appearance of Mr. Wickham.

After the first heat of indignation had cooled, eating was concluded in awkward half snatches of conversation. No amusement was to be had. However, Marianne Brandon suspected the women's conversation afterward would prove far more interesting.

As the ladies took themselves into the drawing room, young Juliet Tilney took a seat close to Marianne, which allowed Marianne to lean in and murmur, "How terribly shocking. I quite pity our hostess and the other guests."

"Mr. Wickham seems to be quite a wicked man," Juliet replied, her voice lowered. "How could so many respectable people have been deceived as to his character?"

The face of John Willoughby flickered in Marianne's mind like a magic-lantern vision, shadowy and ephemeral. "Not all wickedness reveals itself immediately. Sometimes it masquerades as charm in the beginning. And the masquerade can be more convincing than you would ever dream."

Juliet glanced away, as though to avoid seeing something that couldn't be acknowledged in polite society. No doubt

Marianne's tone of voice had betrayed more than she'd intended. She no longer loved Willoughby; her heart belonged to her husband. But some of the wounds Willoughby had inflicted still bled fresh from time to time.

Marianne sought a glimpse of her husband as the men vanished into the next room to smoke their cigars. But Brandon was well out of earshot, and that rather priggish Mr. Bertram was chattering on to him about something or other as Knightley led them from the room. As Marianne watched, she realized that her husband was not at peace. His countenance was troubled, his gaze dark. Was he—angry? Sad? She couldn't read him well enough to know, not yet.

Maybe not ever.

"One wishes to know more of what Mr. Wickham has done," Juliet said, her tone even more hushed than before. No sooner had she spoken the words than her cheeks flushed. "Though I suppose that is gossip, and not a worthy topic of conversation, especially as it would disquiet our hosts."

"Of course one cannot pry, but—it is impossible not to *want* to know," Marianne admitted. "If only we had some other way of finding it out! Sure as anything, the men are talking about it over their cigars and brandy. *They* have the privilege of direct questions. *We* are trapped within etiquette."

Juliet's gaze sharpened with curiosity. "Or are we?" she asked.

Then Mrs. Bertram took her place near them. Though she showed no signs of intruding upon their conversation, she wouldn't have been able to help overhearing—and, Marianne suspected, disapproving.

Back to polite murmurings over tea and cake. With a sigh, Marianne prepared herself to ask about the weather in Northamptonshire. Again.

❧

"G——d wretched business," swore Frederick Wentworth as his host Mr. Knightley lit his cigar. "Why must the man demand his pound of flesh?"

He had *sworn*. Actually taken the name of the Lord in vain! Jonathan Darcy's cheeks flushed. Yet none of the other men in the room showed any signs of surprise, and disapproval flickered on Mr. Bertram's face alone. How could that be?

Jonathan turned the puzzle that way and this in his head before remembering a social rule that perhaps explained it: Wentworth was a naval man. Sailors were famed for their salty language, ashore as well as at sea; but it was excused as an incurable element of an otherwise noble profession. Derbyshire had not offered many chances for Jonathan to meet men of the navy. In future, he resolved, he would not be so easily shocked.

By now, his father had begun to speak. "Mr. Wickham believes himself to be wronged by the world," Darcy replied, "though precisely when, and in what manner, any objective observer would find difficult to identify. He forever seeks revenge for this wrong, against society as a whole, and in particular against whatever unfortunate persons find themselves in his company."

Mr. Bertram must have been bewildered by the turn the evening had taken, and the group's animosity toward a total stranger, but he maintained decorum as he took a thoughtful puff on his cigar. "An investment scheme, you said?"

"One in which I entrusted my prize money from the wars," Wentworth replied. His expression was dark, and while he restrained his temper, he could not hide it.

Prize money, Jonathan mused. For men of the navy, this could make the difference between a life of privation and near gentility. During introductions, it had been mentioned that Mrs. Wentworth was the daughter of a Sir Walter Elliot, and therefore of high birth. Perhaps the prize money was all that had allowed Captain Wentworth to marry so well. Now, instead of providing his wife with the elegant existence she was no doubt used to, he had impoverished her.

No—George Wickham had. Every dark thought Jonathan had ever entertained about his uncle flickered through his brain, and those thoughts were many.

"My brother, John, was also among those swindled by Wickham," said Knightley. "The promises made were very great, as were the assurances given. It seemed that many of the highest in the realm endorsed Wickham's scheme—even an earl was counted among their number."

"Which earl?" Jonathan asked. His aunt Georgiana was married to the earl of Dorchester—Harold Bellamy, known to his young relations only as Uncle Harry. But then he felt silly. Had his uncle been mixed up in such a mess as this, surely his family would already have heard of it.

Knightley simply shrugged. "The name escapes me. When I first learned of the entire affair, I looked him up in some friends' copy of *Debrett's Peerage*, but I confess that detail has seemed less important, compared to the fate of my brother and so many others afflicted by Wickham's connivance."

An awkward moment of silence followed, broken by Bertram. "I was taken aback, at first, that you had not your own copy of *Debrett's*. Most genteel homes have." Though only a clergyman, Bertram was the most nobly born of those present, the son of a baronet. Jonathan's parents had shared this fact with him, that he might understand the rules of precedence. "But too keen an interest can be taken in such things. Often it amounts to no more than vanity."

"I have always maintained," Knightley said, "that any relations near enough for me to be moved by their births, deaths, and marriages will undoubtedly write to inform me themselves."

Darcy spoke then. "Your brother has a list of all Wickham's investors?"

Knightley shrugged. "That I do not know. Perhaps it is somewhere in my own papers. The temptations for my brother's investment matter far less than the effects of it."

Colonel Brandon, who had been standing slightly apart from the rest, spoke at last. "It sounds as though this Mr. Wickham has been of disreputable character for many years."

"Since birth, perhaps," Darcy said, "though I came to recognize it only during our university years." Jonathan thought his father sounded tense. Then again, he had always sounded this way when speaking of Wickham, even in the days when Wickham was still Aunt Lydia's husband.

Knightley was staring pointedly at Wentworth. Why? Wentworth realized it the same moment Jonathan did: the man was gripping his cigar so tightly that it had been bent. Glowing ash fell beside Wentworth's shoe, singeing the carpet black.

つ

This, Fanny decided, *is what comes of associating with immoral persons.* Sitting primly at the edge of the room, she listened as Elizabeth Darcy spoke to them all. Her speech was far too free, but enlightening.

"They say one cannot choose one's family." Elizabeth attempted to smile, putting on a lightness of spirit that fooled no one. Her fingers kept worrying the embroidered handkerchief she held, which hinted at her inner agitation. "Not even one's family by marriage. Still, like anyone else, I had hoped my sisters would choose well. They all did, save for Lydia."

"Your sister is . . . ?" Emma Knightley tentatively began.

"Dead these three years."

Fanny was shocked at how coolly Elizabeth said this. As little as she liked Julia and as much as she abhorred Maria, she'd been raised with her cousins almost as siblings, and their deaths would prostrate Fanny with grief. Wouldn't they? Suddenly she entertained some doubts on the matter. Fanny consoled herself with the knowledge that Edmund would surely be sad, and her beloved husband could not be in pain without Fanny feeling it also.

Elizabeth continued: "That, at least, was no fault of Mr. Wickham's. But he did not distinguish himself as a husband any more than he did as a soldier."

To speak so of family—even by marriage, even someone so disreputable as Mr. Wickham appeared to be! Fanny could scarcely hide her blushing. She did not think Elizabeth Darcy an immoral woman; there was something of decency and character in her demeanor, despite her words. But this was beyond countenancing. Perhaps the manners were very different in Derbyshire. Manners were not the same as morality, after all—

Fanny caught herself. Morality was proving more complex than she had ever dreamed it could be.

The men lingered so long over their cigars that the women were, finally, obliged to go up to their rooms unaccompanied by any gentlemen at all. Fanny found she didn't mind Edmund's absence. An hour to herself to think and pray . . . yes, that would suit her nicely, far more so than any other aspect of the house party so far. She made the obligatory murmurings about a lovely evening, turned down Emma Knightley's kind offer of the help of a ladies' maid, and went to her room.

Someone was already there.

"Oh! I am sorry—" Fanny began, at first certain she'd blundered through the wrong door by mistake. But she recognized her own lap desk, her own letters, and the man who sat there with them.

"Well," said George Wickham. He had one boot on the windowsill, leaning back in his chair. "An unexpected guest. What a pleasure."

Did this man honestly think she'd sought him out? Fanny summoned her courage. "I believe that this is our room, sir."

Wickham frowned, then snapped his fingers. "Ah. Of course. Mrs. Knightley must have meant for me to climb one additional flight of stairs, rather than referring to the ones we had already climbed. Please forgive my intrusion."

His smile was all politeness. No, manners and morality were not the same.

As he rose to go, Fanny darted to her lap desk, gathering it up, grateful that the letters in their little hutch seemed undisturbed. She breathed out a sigh of relief she wouldn't have felt if she'd glanced up to see Wickham's face as he left.

Foolish girl, Wickham thought, closing the door behind him, *to so readily betray that she has a secret.*

Chapter Three

Despite the fervent wishes of the hosts and invited guests at Donwell Abbey, the rain did not cease overnight. Indeed, it had redoubled its efforts, falling thick and fast, turning every road into an impassable slough. The state of the roads was confirmed by one lone servant, who'd made his way into Highbury early in the day in order to collect the post. Even then, he testified, it had been difficult going. (The horse had to be seen to with a brisk rubdown in the stables, while the servant himself was braced with a brandy.) Mr. Wickham couldn't have left if he'd wanted to, though he showed no such desire. The others who might have departed to escape his company were similarly trapped.

This news spread during breakfast. As the meal was served on a buffet with breads, meats, and cakes, different parties came and went, each discussing the information in turn.

"At least Donwell Abbey has a second floor to which Wickham can be exiled," Emma Knightley murmured beneath her breath to her husband.

Captain Wentworth (who was standing closer than Emma had realized) thought, *Would that the staircases here copied the one at Highbury and collapse so that that man could never come near us again—or, better yet, that it might fall on Wickham's head!*

Slightly later, Edmund Bertram attempted to make polite, tactful conversation. "It appears that our uninvited guest may be with us for quite some time. I suppose we shall all make the best of it."

Elizabeth Darcy sipped her coffee. "What, I wonder, is the best that can be made of Mr. Wickham?"

Edmund thought this might be satirical, and therefore improper, and decided not to pursue the subject.

Juliet Tilney came down late, partly in hopes of missing Mr. Wickham, more from an intention to avoid the younger Mr. Darcy. Naturally, she arrived in the breakfast room at almost the precise moment Jonathan did. To judge by the faint flush on his high cheekbones, he shared her displeasure at the meeting.

It is not so much that he's rude—though certainly he is!—but that everyone in the house knows he was invited for me, or I was invited for him. They can all see how little he thinks of me. It doesn't matter that I don't think much of him either—he's rich and I'm not, so everyone will assume I've set my cap for him. Juliet burned with humiliation. *This house party is meant to last a month, though. Maybe that will be enough time for the others to realize the real state of my feelings. Surely they can't fail to notice what an insufferable boor Jonathan Darcy is—*

"Good morning, Miss Tilney," Jonathan said as he began making his plate. His tone was . . . not exactly friendly, but not cold either.

Having braced herself for impoliteness, Juliet found herself at a loss to respond to courtesy. ". . . Good morning, Mr. Darcy. I trust you have slept well?"

Jonathan seemed hardly able to reply. "I—I would not have thought—yes, thank you."

Has he never had a conversation before? Juliet's contempt turned into wonderment. Did Jonathan's parents keep him locked in the attic of the famous Pemberley? That sounded like something out of a Gothic novel, but how else could he be so unfamiliar with the basic niceties of small talk? Or he could be a simpleton, in need of Christian kindliness and forbearance. His deportment seemed to indicate otherwise, but Juliet decided not to make any assumptions.

Perhaps it would be best to speak slowly and patiently. "I hope you enjoy your breakfast," she said, enunciating clearly. Then she walked to the farthest point of dining table, in hopes he would at least have the social acumen not to follow.

❧

It was some small consolation that, this time, Jonathan understood what he'd got wrong. Juliet Tilney had addressed him very simply, as though it were any other morning. No doubt she thought it was. Jonathan knew better.

A distance between his family and the Wickhams had always been maintained. His late aunt Lydia had been allowed to visit Pemberley only when his father was away; Wickham himself never crossed the threshold. Nor were Jonathan and his parents invited to the Wickhams; in any such instance, the invitation would've been immediately refused.

Yet when he'd been small, Jonathan had spent a little time with them when visiting his grandparents or his aunt Kitty and once even with his aunt Jane and uncle Charles. (Aunt Mary's home appeared as rigidly closed to the Wickhams as Pemberley. This caused no hardship, as Aunt Lydia had frequently, and vocally, made it clear she had no desire to go "anyplace so dreadful boring as Mary's house would have to be.") He could not exorcise their presence from some of his earliest, most fundamental memories. Despite the years that had passed and the damage that had been done—despite the aging that had rendered his uncle's face unfamiliar to him—Lydia and George Wickham were Jonathan's family, both bound to him and separated from him. Neither Jonathan nor his brothers were even allowed to mention their uncle and aunt's marriage in front of Aunt Georgiana. The connection had a wild, dangerous energy to it Jonathan had never fully understood.

Aunt Lydia had caught the smallpox three years prior, when Jonathan was seventeen years of age; it carried her off even before his mother received the first letter reporting the sickness. Mother had wept, and Jonathan had asked her why. She'd had enough respect for her son not to lie.

"I cry not for the woman your aunt became," she'd said, "but for the woman she might have been."

He had pondered over that until he thought he understood. Aunt Lydia had no learning to speak of, yet she had nonetheless possessed a quickness of mind. Though her temper was changeable and sometimes very bad, she'd also been capable of finding fun in even the smallest of moments. If she had married more wisely, her virtues might have eventually outshone her vices.

In some families, Lydia's death would have ended Wickham's relationship with the Darcy family. It had not. Instead, the relationship had become more entangled, more emotionally fraught, and finally poisonous.

Juliet Tilney wasn't prying; she'd meant only to ask a polite question. She couldn't have guessed that Jonathan had spent half the night lying awake, trying not to listen to the angry murmurs from his parents' room on the other side of his wall. That he'd sometimes thought one or both of his parents might be on the verge of ignoring all decorum—every rule of conduct Jonathan knew—and storming out of their room to confront Wickham in the dead of night. How often had he heard one or the other speak bitter words about Wickham during the sorrowful year past? He'd often wondered what his parents might do were they ever again in the presence of this wicked man.

Jonathan stared down at his uneaten breakfast. He'd managed only a few bites. His stomach churned, and he couldn't concentrate on anything but the wordless, relentless dread that arose in his mind every time he thought of his father's impending dealings with Mr. Wickham.

Talk to Father, he told himself. Darcy was more plainspoken than most people; Jonathan found this easier to understand. (Mother spoke good sense as well, but her humor sometimes escaped him.) If his father told him not to worry, that there was no reason for this meeting with Wickham to prove anything worse than uncomfortable—then Jonathan could stop worrying.

Maybe then he could manage to converse with a pretty girl.

So Jonathan left the breakfast room and headed in the general direction of the library, which he judged his father's likeliest location at this hour. On a rainy day such as this one, where no riding or fishing was to be had and no visits would be paid, letters might be written or newspapers read. Donwell's layout was similar to other abbeys Jonathan had visited, so he made his way easily through the corridors toward the library—then stopped just outside Mr. Knightley's study, currently in use by two of his guests. Through the doorway, Jonathan saw two men in intense conversation: his father and Mr. Wickham.

". . . knows no bounds," Darcy was saying. "The impudence of coming here among these people to harass them—"

"To gain what is rightfully mine," Wickham replied.

Jonathan ducked against the wall so as not to be seen, giving way to the impulse to eavesdrop—he knew it to be against the rules of society, but every once in a while, such impulses were irresistible.

"My new wealth appears to disturb you. Perhaps you've always believed Pemberley and your ten thousand a year are what make you superior to others. Now that I have my own ten thousand, you're exposed as nothing so very special. Someone rather . . . ordinary."

Darcy sounded more frustrated than insulted. "Your hunger for the high opinion of others has never plagued me. It might have plagued you less had your behavior merited the reputation you have always sought."

If Wickham understood the remonstrance, he revealed no sign. "This matter does not concern you, Darcy. It is only accident that brought us to the same house at the same time."

"I stood by once and allowed you to do what I knew you should not," Darcy said, and now there was anger in his voice. "It cost Susannah her life. Never again will I permit you to harm others."

"You may dwell on the past all you like," Wickham said. "I look toward the future. Mine shall be a bright one. Do not think of interfering with me again."

"I meant what I said," Darcy said, low and even. "I will never let you cause another harm."

Wickham only strode out of Mr. Knightley's study—and almost directly into Jonathan. The knowing smirk Wickham gave Jonathan deepened his shame. Terrible to be caught eavesdropping; worse to be caught by someone who thought it meant you were no better than he.

It was this that kept him from going to his father. His father's disappointment would be much harder for Jonathan to endure than Wickham's mocking glance.

By eavesdropping I have learned only that which disturbs me, Jonathan realized. *And so by shaming myself, I have lost the chance to speak with Father.* There was nothing to do but walk away quietly, hoping he would not add to his father's worries and unable to be reassured about his own.

⁂

If Mrs. Knightley did not appreciate Donwell Abbey's magnificent library, Marianne Dashwood intended to do so for her. Greater ease might evolve as the house party went on, but Marianne intended to read her way through these next few awkward days. She stood at the bookshelves, selecting her volume with care. Cowper's verse she largely knew by heart, but revisiting it could not fail to bring her joy.

Or so she thought, before Mr. Wickham entered the library.

The others present—Mr. Knightley, Mrs. Bertram—possessed the self-control not to look up. Marianne, lacking it, had the misfortune of meeting Mr. Wickham's eyes, which spurred him to her side.

"Good morning, Mrs. Brandon," he said, all politeness. "It is a bit early for reading, is it not?"

"I am inclined to think it cannot be too early to read, should the choice of book be worthy." Marianne gripped the Cowper volume in her hand, oddly concerned he might try to pry it from her.

"Then you possess a most refined mind, ma'am." Wickham smiled so charmingly that, for an instant, Marianne wondered whether the others might be wrong about him. "Other ladies, I fear, allow themselves to be distracted by more frivolous pursuits."

Frivolous pursuits are nearly the only ones we are allowed, she wanted to say, but restrained herself. "If you do not read in the mornings, sir, then what has brought you to the library at this hour?"

"I must be somewhere, you know, and it appears I am unwelcome in certain quarters." The light, easy way in which Wickham spoke did not obscure the fact that Marianne's hosts, as well as the other guests, appeared to have very good reasons for not making him welcome.

"Perhaps you will find something to catch your interest

despite the early hour," Marianne suggested, as it would lead Wickham toward an activity that did not involve speaking with her. "There is so much here to choose from! Indeed, I wonder that Mrs. Knightley is not a great reader, with so much here to tempt her."

Wickham seemed not to have paid attention to her words. "Your husband, Mrs. Brandon—where is he?"

"At this hour I should imagine he is with the other gentlemen." Marianne clasped Cowper close to her bosom. "Why should you ask?"

"I thought I detected a certain . . . distance in him, an unwillingness to make my acquaintance," Wickham said.

Who *would* be willing to make any new acquaintance with someone described as Mr. Wickham had been? Marianne had manners enough not to ask. "Surely you are mistaken, sir. My husband has no prior knowledge of you to awaken any animosity."

"So it would seem," Wickham said. "Yet I wonder. And how careless of him, to leave so young and lovely a bride alone."

Marianne had sense enough to know when she was being baited. She simply walked away, took a chair, and opened her book of poetry. How proud of her Elinor would be, for such self-control!

Still, the questions Marianne longed to ask burned within her, hot as coals.

⨎

The dreadful weather had caused many to give up hope of any pleasant occupation on this day—trapped inside with George Wickham. But Anne Wentworth was determined to make the best of it. Wickham could not interrupt her embroidery, ruin playing the piano, or spring at her from the pages of a novel. By endeavoring to fill her hours with such simple, virtuous pursuits, she could perhaps even forget such an unpleasant man was in the house.

Soon another, even finer distraction offered itself: the Donwell Abbey servant who had managed to fetch the post had brought back letters not only for Mr. and Mrs. Knightley but also for Anne herself. She had given her destination to only a few friends, any of whom Anne would've been delighted to hear from. Yet none could have made her smile more brightly than the name she saw written on the outside: that of her former schoolmate and now one of her closest friends, Mrs. Smith.

Although normally a letter would've been read aloud to the entire company, the members of the house party were still unfamiliar enough with one another for such correspondence to be considered not of general interest. Clutching the letter, Anne took herself off to a quiet corner of the drawing room. Clouds had banished sunlight almost entirely, but the thoughtful Mrs. Knightley had seen to it that plentiful candles were lit.

> *Dear Mrs. Wentworth,*
> *To think of you reading this in Surrey! Such pretty*
> *countryside, I hear, and surely on the Knightleys' estate*
> *you will have plenty of room to walk, think, and*
> *explore, as you so love to do.*

Anne glanced at the window. The countryside was visible only as grayish shapes behind sheets of rain.

> *Truth be told, I'm considering making a journey myself,*
> *soon. Nurse Rooke says she is willing to leave Bath*
> *for a time, and she has always been as curious to see*

> *Cornwall as I am. My health has improved enough*
> *that I think the journey will do me no great harm—or,*
> *at least, none that cannot be cured with a brief spell at*
> *the Cornish seaside!*

This was what Anne most admired about Mrs. Smith: her indefatigable good cheer, regardless of the circumstance. Others unable to go about without a stick or a helper's arm might have bewailed their plight. Mrs. Smith simply delighted in what she could do instead of dwelling upon what she could not. Even when confined to her bedchamber, she had found enjoyments in life, whether in visits from friends or gossiping with her intelligent, lively nurse. She looked at the risks of her journey and thought first of how they might be cured. *If only others,* Anne thought, *had such inner reserves of strength and hope.*

Her eyes darted over to where her husband stood, making chitchat with Darcy. He seemed so much older than he had been at this time only last year.

> *My sympathies on the death of your cousin Lady*
> *Dalrymple. You would wish to know that I also called*
> *upon your father and sister in Bath to express my*
> *condolences in person. They received me with rather*
> *more pleasure than I would've expected—but I think*
> *it gratifies them to know that others understand their*
> *deep connection to Her Late Ladyship.*

Anne bit her lower lip to contain her smile. Her proud father and prouder elder sister did not think any "Mrs. Smith" grand enough for their inner circles. However, anyone would make a good audience for their show of desperate grief over a woman they hardly knew but whose title had, in their opinion, added to their luster.

Mrs. Smith, of course, understood all this and was tactful enough not to say so directly, while still making herself entirely clear.

> *Do you and Captain Wentworth expect to remain*
> *another season in Surrey? I know its proximity to*
> *London is important to you at present. Hartfield sounds*
> *a lovely house*

This reminded Anne that she hadn't yet written Mrs. Smith the tale of the collapsing staircase.

> *and it seems as though you are already making many*
> *friends in Highbury village. That Miss Bates sounds*
> *quite a character! I would say the same of the curate's*
> *wife, Mrs. Elton, but with perhaps a somewhat*
> *different tone.*

Apparently Anne's best efforts to remain tactful about Mrs. Elton had failed.

> *I would begrudge you no pleasure in this world, my*
> *dear friend, and so if it delights you to linger in your*
> *new county, you must by all means do so. However,*
> *I fear that you may be making your choice for less*
> *gladsome reasons.*
>   *Forgive me if I offend you with my next. Certainly*
> *I am transgressing against the boundaries of polite*
> *conversation, but I trust that you will know I do so*
> *with the most sincere desire to be of some service. And*
> *who can speak better to one in financial distress than*
> *one who has been in that situation herself? When I was*
> *impoverished, sickly, and without hope, you befriended*
> *me anew. You and dear Captain Wentworth made my*

concerns your own, and it was through his efforts that
my property was finally restored to me. How could I
fail to offer my help to you in return? I am powerless
to act against anyone so vile as that Mr. Wickham,
but I do not lack the power to aid you, if you will but
accept my help. It would be not only my pleasure but
also my privilege to assist you in some small measure.
Please know that you would only honor me by doing
so. This alone might lessen some small measure of the
tremendous obligation I feel to you and your husband,
though nothing could ever diminish my gratitude. You
need not answer now, but I beg of you to consider it
seriously, without any undue pride. There is no room
for it between such friends.

Ever yours—
Mrs. Ronald Smith

Anne carefully folded the letter so that Frederick would not glimpse the contents. He couldn't accept charity, not even when so humbly offered. Instead, he would be galled by the contrast (which, in truth, struck Anne herself somewhat) of the lowly widow they had once lifted from poverty now being the one to offer them assistance.

Those words—*without any undue pride*. In his present state of mind, Frederick would seize upon those. Even now, he still believed Anne carried some small crumb of "the Elliot pride."

Never could she make him see that the pride destroying his soul was his own.

❧

Marianne Brandon *loved* storms.

Great winds whipping through the trees, moody skies,

brilliant flashes of lightning accompanied by rolls of thunder—was not a storm, in its own way, as beautiful as any sunshine?

The others prayed in vain that the rain would lift, despite the gray gloom overhead. Marianne thought it more reasonable by far to hope that the rain would ripen into a proper thunderstorm. However, the weather took no note of either wish and continued to drizzle on interminably. When the mists were not too thick, the view across Donwell Abbey's grounds was suitably picturesque, so Marianne considered herself content . . . at least, in that respect.

Her disquiet instead directed itself wholly toward her husband. Colonel Brandon had become even more silent than usual. Though they had not been long married, Marianne had acquired enough of the instinct of a wife to realize precisely when her husband had altered from quiet to withdrawn.

It related to Mr. Wickham. Not his arrival—that Brandon had seemed to react to, but not as the other outraged members of the party had. No, the true shift occurred when Brandon had confirmed the man's full name. Wickham himself had picked up on it, which further awakened Marianne's curiosity.

Her sister Elinor, no doubt, would say not to pry. Marianne had grown to have a greater respect for her sister's opinions, but this didn't change the fact that sometimes Elinor got it wrong.

Deeper conversation was impossible in company, but when the Brandons retired to their room at noon, she took her chance. As Brandon changed into a coat appropriate for afternoon tea, she sat on the edge of the bed and ventured, "Mr. Wickham's presence here troubles you, does it not?"

Brandon paused mid-gesture, coat half upon one arm. "It need not concern you."

"Anything that causes you distress concerns me," Marianne insisted, busying herself with her handkerchiefs.

He gave her a look then that was not so far away—in that instant revealing how much her love meant to him. However, his gaze grew distant again immediately. "We need not discuss it."

"But I *want* to discuss it. Concealment of every kind is my abhorrence," said Marianne, rather huffily. "Surely between man and wife there should be no secrets."

Colonel Brandon replied quietly, "This is no accurate picture of the marriages I have observed."

Marianne barely held on to her temper. "And is that all you wish of me? To simper on about muslins or embroidery and to greet you only at breakfast and dinnertime?"

"No, it is not," Brandon said with real feeling in his tone. "But there are things you cannot hear."

"There may be things I cannot hear, in your opinion," she said. "That does not change what I already know. You have some prior acquaintance with Mr. Wickham. He pretends that you don't and that he has no conception what might provoke such an idea. You pretend, too, but you are not so accomplished an actor."

Brandon remained silent a moment before replying, "Then you have learned enough of the matter. Be grateful you know no more."

"I shall never be grateful for ignorance," Marianne insisted. That much had to be said. However, she was wise enough to know that such statements were unlikely to have the effect she wished. She must appeal to the best of her husband's nature, to something in him, and between them, that surely transcended whatever discord arose from Mr. Wickham. "If you will not speak with me now, so be it. But I ask you not to protect me where I do not require protection. You are my husband. If something has . . . has caused a husband harm, or troubled his spirit, then it is a wife's privilege to hear him as no other person in this world can do. To bear his pain along-side him, and in so doing leaven his suffering. Would you deny me this?" She stood up and began her own preparations for the afternoon, adding only, "Believe me capable of that courage, and believe me capable of more."

As she tended to her hair, the mirror on her dressing table revealed Brandon's face, showing how deeply he felt her words. But had she moved him enough to make him speak the truth at last?

❧

Fanny Bertram found the day less irksome than most. Candlelight had proved sufficient for her to read a volume of Wordsworth's poetry, which provided transport enough for any morning. Edmund had been absorbed in a London newspaper or discussing the new parliament with his cousin Knightley. She left them deeply rapt in such talk in order to go to her room for a brief rest before tea. Even a quiet morning like this one tired her when spent in company with whom she was largely unfamiliar. (The one acquaintance here Fanny trusted, the gentle Mrs. Wentworth, had been understandably occupied with a letter.)

As she reached the top of the first staircase, just steps shy of her room, she saw another figure descending the stairs from the second floor—Mr. Wickham, of course. No one slept up there but the servants. She nodded civilly, grateful she had not encountered him in one of the main rooms, where she might've been forced to converse.

To her dismay, Mr. Wickham stopped and gave her that ingratiating, unconvincing smile. "Why, Mrs. Bertram. What an unexpected pleasure."

"Mr. Wickham," she said in a tone that made it a complete, and closed, conversation.

However, he was not deterred. "Will you not take a turn with me? I believe the gallery features tapestries that date back to when the abbey was new."

"I—" Fanny's principles were firm, but her manner was not. "I beg your pardon, sir, I am rather fatigued."

"From sitting inside all day? Surely a walk would do you good."

A walk with absolutely anyone else might have sounded refreshing. "I must beg you to release me, Mr. Wickham. Really I am too tired."

"Not for this." A strange tone had entered Wickham's voice. "Please, Mrs. Bertram. I think ultimately you will be very glad you availed yourself of this chance to tell me more about your brother the sailor."

Who had told him about William? Fanny couldn't guess but supposed someone had been stuck with the man at breakfast and made what chitchat they could. She didn't blame them for that. Wickham's interest struck her as strangely pointed, however. So much so that it stoked the fear within her, making her tremble.

No. Nobody would've told him that. *Nobody knows in this world, except me.*

And his—his friend—but no one else—

Fanny summoned what courage she could. If this disreputable man was determined to have a conversation with her, better they should have it downstairs, nearer the others. "Very well, Mr. Wickham. Lead the way to the gallery."

The gallery at Donwell Abbey proved more richly appointed than most. Knightley's family had been in possession of the estate for almost three hundred years, and they had not only preserved the abbey's original treasures but also added greatly to the house's artwork through a fine collection of busts in marble and bronze—everyone from Shakespeare to Lord Nelson—and numerous oil paintings. These pictures went back to the days when Knightley's and Edmund's families were one. A bewigged gentleman of the seventeenth century bore such a resemblance to her Edmund that his descent was undeniable. Fanny smiled with pride and resolved to walk here again in the near future, more pleasantly, with her husband.

Wickham strolled alongside her in apparently polite silence until they were nearly at the far end of the gallery, then stopped, which meant Fanny had to stop also. Perhaps to disconcert her, he had positioned them directly opposite a large painting depicting a mythological theme. The ancients had been in the unfortunate habit of wearing very little clothing. Fanny hoped the shadowy nature of the hall hid her blushes.

"They say," Wickham began, "that Donwell Abbey has a fine armory as well, complete with weapons that go back to medieval ages."

Fanny confessed, "Such things are of little interest to me."

"How strange that you would be unconcerned with things military, given your brother's profession. Your brother, his name is William Price, is it not?"

She nodded. "Have you also an acquaintance in the navy, sir?"

Instead of responding to this, Wickham continued: "William must be very dear to you."

"I—I should hope all brothers would be dear to their sisters." Fanny could think of exceptions, starting with Edmund's two sisters, but would never discuss private family matters with any stranger, much less one who appeared to be of low moral character.

Wickham's smile had never seemed warmer or more genuine than when he said, "Your brother writes to you as if you are the one person in the world in whom he has full trust."

How could Wickham know that? Fanny wondered, but almost

before the thought had entirely taken shape, she knew—as he held the evidence before her, for one brief moment.

The night before flooded her memory: Wickham in her room by error, left alone with her writing-desk, William's letter unguarded in its drawer. *But the letter was still there after he was in the room!* Fanny had checked, more out of an abundance of caution than any real thought that Mr. Wickham—a person so wholly unknown to her—would have gone searching within her things.

Wickham must've come back. He had searched her writing-desk after all. She had kept many of William's letters, but only one had traveled here with her. It had the power of life and death over her brother.

Which meant that now Mr. Wickham did, too.

"Please," Fanny said, her voice breaking. "Please, give it back to me."

"Ah, Mrs. Bertram. There's no need for fear." Wickham seemed so comforting. So sincere. As if he were protecting her from harm, instead of inflicting it. "I fully intend to give the letter back—after proper recompense is made, of course."

Fanny shook her head. "We are not rich. Edmund is a clergyman, our parish is small—"

"Is he not the younger son of Sir Thomas Bertram of Mansfield Park? That great family is very well known, as is its wealth. If your husband requires a sum of, say . . . five hundred pounds, I feel certain it would be given him."

Five hundred pounds. Fanny and Edmund lived on scarcely more than five hundred pounds a year. How was such a sum to be got? Yes, if Edmund asked for it, Sir Thomas would agree—but he would want to know why. And Edmund would not make such a request in the first place without demanding that Fanny tell him why it was needed. "They will not give it without a reason."

"Certainly you can invent something," Wickham said, resuming his stroll toward the door. "I am forever astonished by the exercise of female ingenuity."

"I do not lie!" Fanny cried. Nothing but the greatest turmoil could've made her speak so to a near stranger.

"I find it helps not to think of it as lying," Wickham replied. "Think of it as a means to a more important end."

With that, he walked away from her and out of the gallery hall. Fanny stood there, trembling, wondering how—or if—she could save her brother's life.

Chapter Four

"This madness has gone on long enough," Knightley said. "If Wickham will not see justice, perhaps he will see reason."

Emma felt a small stirring of hope, the first that had visited her that day. By now it seemed apparent that the weather would not change in time for the roads to become passable by sunset. Donwell Abbey would therefore remain host to George Wickham for at least one night longer. That night could not be spent in comfort, but perhaps it could be made useful. "What do you mean?"

Knightley glanced toward the door of his study, which was securely shut. They were alone here as they could be in no other place in the house, save their bedchamber. "The considerable debt John owes to Wickham threatens us all."

To Emma this phrasing seemed overly dramatic and thus quite unlike Knightley. As much as it hurt them to see their siblings in such financial distress, Emma did not feel threatened by it, only very angry.

This passing thought faded as Knightley continued: "I fear Mr. Wickham is correct in one particular: his 'investment scheme' appears legally sound. He allowed many to invest borrowed funds in addition to their ready money, and thus he gained not only their initial investment but also debts in the hundreds or even thousands of pounds. It was presented as a great favor, a chance to double or triple their returns, and that chance was taken by many, including my brother. And as diabolical as all this is, none of it is against the law. Therefore we cannot hope for redress from the courts."

Always, Emma had thought Knightley would find some way out of the trouble, but she'd been deceiving herself. She never had been very good at hearing a final *no*. "Then it would seem Wickham already sees reason all too well."

"He believes that no gentleman would take him to court, both because of the futility of the suit and because of the natural unpleasantness of having one's personal affairs exposed before the public." Knightley sighed. "However, if John and Isabella are willing to brave the latter, then I think we need not concern ourselves with the former."

Emma frowned. "Why not? Surely if a suit cannot win, it is foolish to bring it. That means nothing but needless expense . . ." Her voice trailed off as the idea took shape in her mind. "Expense that would come to Mr. Wickham as well."

"Clever Emma! John is a barrister himself and can bring the suit at no cost save his time. They say an attorney representing himself has a fool for a client, but in this situation, John would not need to win. He would need only to keep the suit alive." Knightley thumped the desk for emphasis. "Every month the suit dragged on would mean more money drained from George Wickham. A judge might even cut off Wickham's access to the funds in dispute. It is possible for such cases to stagnate in the courts for years on end."

"So you will challenge Wickham with this," said Emma, her imagination already running ahead. "Tell him that if John and Isabella cannot have their money, nor the poor Wentworths, then he shall not have it either."

"Precisely." Knightley sighed. "I fear we will have to ask for less than anyone is truly owed; if there is no incentive for Mr. Wickham to avoid the courts, no profit at all to be made, he might brave the lawsuit out of pure spite. But even a partial recovery would vastly benefit those who fell prey to Wickham's schemes."

"I knew you would find a way!" Emma clapped her hands together, then dropped a quick kiss on her husband's cheek. "But—should you not write to John first, to make sure that he consents to such a suit?"

"I think not. It would be the properest thing to do, but we are presented with a rare opportunity here. Wickham is on our estate, unable to depart. He came to collect payment; perhaps he is in need of the money. This is the time to bargain with him." After a moment's consideration, Knightley added, "However, I shall speak to Captain Wentworth immediately. His consent, we *can* obtain, and the argument may be stronger for two instead of one."

Emma felt a wave of relief so deep that it seemed to her the matter had been resolved already. "I pray it may be true."

❧

After tea, people shuffled themselves about to fresh entertainments. Emma put together a game of cassino; Knightley led a few of the men to his wine cellar to choose vintages for the night. Darcy went with these. Elizabeth decided to take a turn about the house, which struck her greatly with its grandeur and antiquity. Pemberley was without doubt elegant and imposing, but it was only from the seventeenth century. The core structure of Donwell would've been built four hundred years earlier. What wonders might it hold?

This was her first chance to explore on her own, and she was not disappointed. Knowing that any room on the ground floor not reserved for the servants would be open to all, Elizabeth wandered freely through the halls. Although she longed to explore the gallery, her curiosity was first rewarded when she found the abbey's small armory around the corner. A true suit of armor stood near the fireplace, its cuirass showing damage from a mace wielded long ago. Such a mace hung nearby, somewhat precarious on its hook; she wondered whether it was the very one responsible. *Does this show how one of Mr. Knightley's ancestors died,* she mused, *or how he dispatched another?* Various helmets, shields, and banners sat on shelves and hung on walls. Elizabeth could spend hours in this room alone, in thrall of the history captured here.

Or so she thought, until someone appeared at the door.

"It appears we share our choice of amusements," said Wickham.

Elizabeth closed her eyes for a moment, summoned her strength, then turned to him. "Are our minds so similar? I have not been accustomed to think so. Perhaps it would be more accurate to say that where options are limited, coincidences will occur."

"So eager to distance yourself from me." Wickham sauntered toward her. "It was not always so."

Many years had passed since Wickham had last possessed the audacity to remind Elizabeth that they had once kept company—that she had admired him more than any other gentleman of her acquaintance. Briefly. "We all of us have episodes in our past of which we greatly repent," she said. "Some more than others. I prefer to be amused by them, when I can."

Wickham's smile tightened, a hint that the congenial expression he wore was no more than a mask. "I repent of very little."

Elizabeth knew she ought to have continued in the same light, bantering way. When she thought of Susannah, however, her wit failed her. "You believe, then, that you have caused no harm?"

"None I did not mean to cause."

His words struck Elizabeth's heart like an arrow, the pain so sharp and so real she would not have been surprised to look down and see her breast red with blood. Could even George Wickham be so unfeeling?

He was even worse than Elizabeth had imagined, for he had not been thinking of Susannah at all. Instead, he continued: "You were so proud to take up Darcy's side and reject mine. All the belief and trust you had once given me, you cast aside at the first sign of attention from a wealthier man."

Elizabeth gaped at him. More than twenty years later, Wickham was still aggrieved that she had believed Darcy's word over his—even after the facts had more than demonstrated Darcy's truthfulness and Wickham's lack of it. For all that time he had nursed that wounded pride, while conveniently forgetting that he had ceased to court Elizabeth long before any revelations from Darcy and that she had not mourned his absence. It was almost pitiable, this smallness within him that limited his world to his grievances.

Whatever pity she might've felt vanished with his next words: "I had thought to put an end to your matrimonial pretensions. My consolation is that those pretensions were answered only at a fitting price."

"You mean—" Her voice broke off, as though refusing to speak the truths now forming within her mind. "You mean that your elopement with Lydia had nothing to do with her? That it was only to spite *me*?"

"You think too highly of yourself," Wickham said. "You forget, madam, that my acquaintance with Mr. Darcy far preceded yours, and my grievances against him were much the greater."

Overcome, Elizabeth could no longer meet his eyes. She stared at the wall—at an ancient gauntlet, metal fingers still curled in a fist—as she struggled to believe the words she had just heard.

From the first news of their elopement, Elizabeth had wondered at it. Lydia had been foolish and headstrong enough to do nearly anything, but Wickham's motives had been elusive. Why *Lydia*? No one had previously detected much special affection between the two. Lydia had no dowry to make her eligible as a wife, but she was hardly without friends of influence, which made her a risky mistress. Elizabeth had decided it was proof of the thoughtless irresponsibility of both parties, no less and no more.

The truth had finally been revealed. With cold calculation, Wickham had seduced and very nearly ruined Lydia, only in the hopes of ruining Elizabeth, too. Had he not been forced to marry Lydia, the tattered reputation of the family would've ended any chances the sisters had of marrying—not only Elizabeth but also Mary, Kitty, and even dear Jane. The image of Jane torn asunder from her beloved Bingley stole Elizabeth's breath from her body. All this to hurt Darcy—and it would have hurt him terribly.

Worst was the knowledge that Wickham's plan had very nearly worked. Had Darcy not come upon Elizabeth at a moment when she was vulnerable enough to tell him of Lydia's plight, they would indeed have been parted forever.

"Contemptible man!" she finally said. "Cruel, false, irredeemable—you have proved yourself beneath even the contempt I have long held for you. *That* I would have once thought impossible."

"You forget, madam, that I have already been duly punished for my crime, for what else could one call so many years of wedlock with Lydia?" His smile was less cruel now, as though he genuinely expected her to share in the joke. Indeed, Elizabeth knew Lydia had been little better as wife than Wickham had been as husband.

But there were reasons for that, many of them not Lydia's fault. She had failed them, but had they not failed her, too—Wickham most of all?

Her silence provided Wickham with a chance for escape, which he must have been desirous of taking, as he said, "I should remain here no longer."

His footsteps echoed in the corridor outside, and she listened to him depart with equal chagrin and relief. Elizabeth was never sure whether he walked away out of a belated sense of propriety, or because he realized how close she stood to the mace.

Thunder rolled heavily through Donwell Abbey, setting some of the candlesticks wobbling. (A loud thump proved to be the falling of a mace in the armory, much to the alarm of Mrs. Darcy, who escaped without injury.) Marianne decided she could take pleasure in a proper storm, now that one was finally upon them. She settled herself in the abbey's small conservatory to watch the heavy rain ripple down the glass. Though no candles had been lit, in deference to the safety of the plants' leaves, her view was occasionally illuminated by lightning.

Marianne sat looking upward, rapt in admiration, until a voice interrupted her reverie. "I suspected I might find you here."

She turned to see Brandon emerging from the shadows. "Your suspicions were correct. I cannot resist a thunderstorm."

"Nor I," he said, surprising her. "There is a beauty in nature unrestrained."

"My feelings precisely." It was something Willoughby might've said, Marianne thought, then felt guilty for the remembrance.

Brandon took his seat beside her on the conservatory's metal bench. She could feel the weight of unspoken words between them, heavy and stifling—

Until, at last, he spoke.

"You wish to know the history of my dealings with Mr. Wickham," Brandon said. "There are none. To him I am a person entirely unknown. However, we have had acquaintance in common, and her fate was forever ruined by him."

The mere fact of her husband's openness was nearly as shocking to Marianne as the information itself. "Do you mean—" She hesitated. "You gave Elinor leave to share with me what you had told her about—about—"

"Eliza."

Brandon's voice roughened as he spoke the name of his long-ago love. Jealousy warred with concern within Marianne, but concern won. She placed her hand over his. "Was it Eliza who Wickham knew?"

"Wickham was the ruin of her." Brandon rubbed his forehead, only for an instant, but it revealed the weariness of many years. "Eliza was forced into a marriage she did not want, to a brute who mistreated her—but she remained respectable. She had a place in society. She was not yet entirely lost. Then a man who had made her acquaintance persuaded her to leave her situation. On her deathbed, she confessed that she had originally hoped for an annulment, however unlikely, and that she would resolve her elopement with a marriage. Instead her husband divorced her, which cast her out of all polite society. Only afterward did she discover Wickham was married already, that his every word to her was a lie. Every word except his name: George Wickham."

"It might not be the same person," Marianne ventured. "The name is not uncommon, surely."

Brandon shook his head. "No. This is the man. When she discovered he had a wife, she also learned her name, and it was Lydia. Eliza knew he had grown up in Derbyshire. One of the only other clues she could give was that his marriage had connected him to a very powerful family, but one that barely countenanced him. Surely that refers to the Darcys of Pemberley. And Wickham, too, was in the army."

It was convincing evidence but not absolute proof. Marianne considered arguing against it, then remembered the man's shameless opportunism, how he reveled in the trouble he created for others. Wickham was precisely the kind of man who would ruin a friendless woman for his own amusement.

A man, in other words, too much like Willoughby.

No, it could not be doubted that that Wickham and this were one and the same.

Brandon continued: "He abandoned Eliza, left her alone to suffer and perish from consumption. I sought him for years after her death—not to upbraid him for his role in her downfall and degradation but to inform him that he had a daughter. To see if he could summon some remnant of proper feeling for Beth, if for no one else. His career in the army was both lengthy and erratic. This I know because I would track down regiment after regiment, determining that Wickham had once been in their number but had been obliged to move on due to debt, scandal, or both. Eventually the trail became too broken for me to follow any further. I resigned myself to the mystery—or I thought I had, before Beth's confinement last year." He paused. "Your sister—I presume she informed you—"

"Elinor and I have no concealment between us, not in such matters." Marianne had long wished to speak with her husband on this subject but had found it too fearsome before. The time had at last come. "Beth's plight is known to me. I hope that you will introduce us one day."

Brandon's eyes met hers. At last, Marianne thought, there were no more walls between them, no more locks—

Thunder rolled. He drew back. "There is no more need to sully your thoughts by dwelling on the subject."

Marianne's spirits crashed, a wave shattering on the shore. There was nothing more to be said, except words that did not matter; the very idea exhausted her. He rose to go, and she did not try to stop him.

As he reached the door of the conservatory, however, a question came to her. "Do you intend to confront him?"

Brandon stopped and paused—but her only answer was silence as he resumed walking away.

⤮

The thought of retrieving less than what he had lost rankled Captain Wentworth. However, the thought of retrieving none of it rankled more. Therefore he acceded readily to Knightley's plan.

When he told Anne of it, she agreed with him whole-heartedly but insisted that she, too, should be part of the conversation. He attempted to dissuade her, saying, "This sort of talk—money and legal suits—hardly fit for a woman to hear."

"And yet I hear you speaking of them this very moment." A small, knowing smile played on Anne's lips. "What you mean is that you think it improper for Mr. Knightley and Mr. Wickham to know that I know."

She had a way of unfolding things sometimes. "All the same, it will be unpleasant, and I would spare you that."

"I would rather face unpleasantness than deny it," Anne said. "Do not doubt that I have the strength to stand by you. To defend you, even, if it came to that—though I know it never shall."

The fineness of her feelings impressed Wentworth so much that it was more than an hour before he realized she might have another motive for wishing to attend the meeting: to keep watch over his quick temper. He had to admit that her caution was just. Besides, by the time he'd perceived it, they were already in Mr. Knightley's study, and Mr. Wickham was at the door.

"You surprised me with your invitation, sir," said Wickham to Knightley. He acknowledged Captain Wentworth with no more than a glance, which left an impression of contempt. "I had thought you disinclined to my company, to judge by the coldness of your welcome to Donwell Abbey. Yet now you are eager to chat."

Knightley was not a man so easily provoked. "You wish to collect on a debt. We wish to avoid the ruination of our families." That stung—Wentworth knew Knightley would not have spoken so bluntly of "ruination" had it been himself in debt rather than his brother—but it would have to be borne. "There is, perhaps, a way for both of us to achieve what we desire."

"Impossible," Wickham said. "You think to offer me a paltry fraction of what I am truly owed and to scurry away at the first mention of the courts."

Wentworth tensed. How could Wickham have known what they planned to offer him?

Because someone else had offered it before. Some other wretch bankrupted by Wickham's schemes had tried to escape the trap and failed.

Anne stood in one corner, silent and watchful. Her placid expression revealed no hint of the contempt she must feel.

But was it Wickham alone she had come to despise?

How proud you were, snarled the voice deep inside Wentworth, the one he tried so hard not to hear but could never silence. *Her family convinced her to refuse you because you had nothing. You thought you'd proved them wrong. It was not enough to double your wealth—no, you indebted yourself in the hopes of tripling it, to make a sum of money you could scarce have spent in a lifetime. Instead, you have trapped Anne in the very life they warned her against: struggling, without security, debased in the eyes of the world.*

And it is not the only harm you have caused her—not the only loss she has suffered because of you—

Undaunted, Knightley pressed on. "I offer you more than you would collect should my brother choose to pursue the matter in the courts."

"Your brother the barrister. You believe it costs a man of the law nothing to bring a suit, because he need not seek counsel." Wickham strolled toward the cigar box and opened it as though it were his own. "But for a lawyer, time is the same thing as money. Any hours—or days, or months, or years— Mr. John Knightley spends fruitlessly litigating with me represent time he will not spend working for his usual clients. You would have him bankrupt himself twice over? To spite me, I suppose you would. But I am not inclined to spite myself, and your proposed settlement is therefore declined." Lazily Wickham rolled the cigar he'd chosen between his fingers, as though expecting someone to offer him a light.

It was this arrogant gesture that snapped Wentworth's forbearance. He stepped forward, to within mere inches of Wickham, using every one of the four inches he had of height over the man. "You think yourself above us all, don't you? Son of a steward—"

"I see Mr. Darcy has shared my background," Wickham said. "I have never denied it." But the words did not come out as easily as they were no doubt intended to. His face was that of a bilge rat seeking to abandon ship.

"Crooked liar and swindler, and you dare swagger about as though you were a gentleman—"

"Are you, sir?" Wickham lifted his chin, though he remained clearly intimidated by Wentworth's size and fury. "A gentleman? I had heard it was not a common thing, in the navy, for officers to be."

"Oh, we are both lowborn," Wentworth said. "The difference in us lies in how we have conducted ourselves."

"I have conducted myself wisely, I should say. You, on the other hand—"

Wentworth shoved Wickham backward, a push that sent him staggering. "You are a cheater and a coward," Wentworth said, "and the time will come when you will answer for it."

He would have continued—he had a great more to say on the subject of Mr. Wickham's shortcomings—had Anne not rushed to his side. "My dearest," she murmured in her low, gentle voice, "do not sully yourself in behaving so. He is not worth your abasement."

Always wise, his Anne. Always temperate and just.

Yet as Wickham departed and drew her attention, Wentworth spied something he would never have dreamed of glimpsing in his wife's eyes: a flash of pure hatred.

⌒

Jonathan Darcy had hoped that his uncle's untimely visit would not long disturb the events of the Knightleys' house party. The rain had already unsettled affairs quite enough, in his opinion. He longed for a return to orderly conduct and custom—for the party to settle into a pattern he'd be able to navigate.

Instead, as the afternoon went on, the house party became more disorderly, not less. Rather than remaining in only one or two larger groups in as many rooms, the hosts and guests were gathering in small, secretive pairings or even wandering off on their own. Dinner, he'd thought, would provide the necessary opportunity for correction.

Though dinner, too, presented difficulties. Would Wickham be seated or not? If so, tempers would remain frayed, and there would be an odd number at table, which was of course poor etiquette. If not, then a guest would be excluded, which was extraordinarily rude, even when the guest was uninvited.

As they assembled for dinner, Jonathan noted that the Knightleys had chosen to err on the side of inclusion. Wickham stood insouciantly at the very back of the gathering, accepting that he would walk in last without having to be informed. What would the others make of this? Careful to be subtle with his glances, Jonathan examined them one by one.

His mother: uncharacteristically silent and pale. His father: uncharacteristically flushed and restless.

Mr. Knightley: much the same as usual, albeit with a furrowed brow. Mrs. Knightley: not smiling, which Jonathan realized she had been doing every other time he'd seen her.

Captain Wentworth: glowering with ill-concealed fury. Mrs. Wentworth: looking up at her husband as though afraid he might do something rash.

Mr. Bertram: largely untroubled, if anything somewhat self-satisfied. Mrs. Bertram: flustered and frightened, even more so than before. Jonathan had already noted her unease with unfamiliar company, and sympathized greatly.

Colonel Brandon: not looking at Wickham, but decidedly so, his interest ironically made clear by his show of uninterest. Mrs. Brandon: openly watching Wickham with disapproval, unconcerned who saw it.

Juliet Tilney, who stood at Jonathan's side: studying all the others in turn, exactly as Jonathan had been doing himself.

She startled slightly when she realized he'd caught her at it, then lowered her head. But when their eyes met, he saw neither shame (at her lapse in manners) nor disapproval (at his own lapse). Often, Jonathan found it difficult to look into the eyes of another, but not at this moment. Their glance was almost . . . conspiratorial.

Someone else knew what he was thinking. Someone else felt apart from the gathering, enough to sense that it could be judged only from the outside, not from within. Someone felt as he felt. This was a sensation Jonathan had almost never experienced before. It was as though something tightly tied within him had finally been loosed—not much, just a bit, but enough.

He held his arm out to her with more grace than the night before, and it seemed to him that she took it more gladly.

Dinner proceeded normally enough at first. Wickham's chair was indeed wedged in awkwardly, between Mr. Knightley and Mother. Knightley was no doubt suffering, as any good host should. Mother was no doubt assumed to be able to tolerate the man, as his former sister-in-law, but Jonathan could tell how violently she wished to be anywhere other than in Wickham's presence.

Wickham seemed to take pleasure in making conversation, despite—or perhaps because of—the fact that no one wished to speak with him. His smile broad, he said, "Mrs. Wentworth, if I recall correctly, you have been to sea with your husband on more than one occasion."

"Indeed I have." Anne Wentworth's voice was as smooth and flat as glass, yet far less transparent. "Thus I am doubly grateful for our hosts' fine meal, for you cannot imagine some of the dinners we are obliged to have while sailing. I have even eaten octopus."

"Octopus?" Juliet Tilney managed to giggle and look disgusted at the same time, a reaction shared by much of the table.

Wickham, however, remained intent on his first line of inquiry. "Then you must be pleased to be ashore—permanently, I suppose?"

Captain Wentworth snapped, "Aye, indeed, when justice is done. No more will she be obliged to suffer at sea." His wife glanced over at him in apparent dismay, which Jonathan ascribed to the allusion to "justice." This must refer to Wickham's swindle in some way—and to judge by the twinkle in his uncle's eye, he had enjoyed reminding the Wentworths of it. Jonathan felt a wave of helpless anger. How shameful, to have a family connection to a man who not only continued to cause harm but delighted in it.

After this, at least, Wickham ate in silence. Everyone ate in silence, save for Mr. Bertram and Juliet Tilney. Mr. Bertram had thoughts on the proper deportment of young girls, too often recognized only in the breach in modern days. He seemed ready to approve of Juliet if only she would join him in disapproval.

Juliet surprised him by being not so easily swayed. "I do not see that fashions nowadays are so much more shocking than in years past," she said. "If they are surprising, surely it is in their newness, not their lack of modesty." Jonathan remembered how low necklines had been when he was little and silently agreed.

Mr. Bertram did not. "Once we drew our aesthetic ideals from the classical era. This is being lost, not only in matters of female attire but also in architecture and scholarship. Can anyone doubt that immorality would be the result?"

Jonathan wanted to help Juliet and thought perhaps he could. "My studies of the classics suggest that Christian morality was not foremost among the ancients' concerns."

The first genuine smiles of the night flickered through the room, and Mrs. Brandon even stifled a laugh. Had he actually said something witty? This was gratifying, especially when he saw Juliet's cheeks pink with pleasure.

His mother shot him a warning look, however, which meant that he should not, must not, begin talking about his favorite book, *The History of the Decline and Fall of the Roman Empire* by Edward Gibbon. Jonathan had read the first three volumes of this book perhaps one hundred times, could quote long sections by heart, and had done so regularly until his parents made it clear that most people's interest in the subject was regrettably less than his own. Jonathan restrained himself with difficulty, consoling himself that at least he had for once made a good joke.

However, Mr. Bertram was not to be so easily amused. "I speak of the classical virtues, Mr. Darcy. The ones written of by their highest thinkers, who were not at all—"

"Hypocrites?" Mr. Wickham said. The fragile bubble of good feeling in the room popped. Smiles faded. "I suspect there were as many hypocrites in those days as there are today. Enough, surely, to make up a house party—or at least to set a good table."

His words landed like a shell fired at Trafalgar. It was only a question of who would lash back first.

Wentworth found his tongue. "Hypocrisy? You, who claimed to be a trustworthy adviser on investments—you think to accuse *anyone* of hypocrisy?"

"He believes all others to be hypocrites," Mother said, "because he believes everyone else's nature to be as corrupt as his own. Mr. Wickham cannot understand that anyone's behavior might match their intent, because his own so rarely does."

At this, Wickham rose from his seat and threw down his napkin. "I see this dinner is meant only as an opportunity to chastise me. Therefore I shall take my leave. But those of you who despise me know, in your hearts, that I have bested you. Learn to endure it."

He strode out, obviously proud of his declaration. But as Jonathan studied the dark expressions around the table, he wondered whether Wickham had breached more than propriety—if he had destroyed something even more fundamental. Something, without which, no one could be truly safe.

Chapter Five

The weather, defying all hopes and even rational expectation, worsened yet more as the night went on. Rain hammered at the windows; lightning illuminated the trees and shrubs of the garden, twisting them into eerie shapes. None of the guests of Donwell Abbey could avoid the conclusion that the morrow would again be spent in the unendurable company of Mr. Wickham. Even Juliet Tilney, who had no history with the man, groaned at the thought of yet another day turned awkward and disagreeable by his presence.

Jonathan, too, sensed another restless night lay ahead of him. The social situation, disconcerting to all, was to him nearly overwhelming. He wished for something simpler to deal with, a scenario he might be able to resolve. When the thunder rolled, he thought of his horse, Ebony. She hated storms. If he could go to her, comfort her—he would be out of the house, and he would feel as though he were doing some good.

From earliest childhood, he had felt more at ease with animals than with fellow children, even more than with most adults. Jonathan's closest companions had ever been his father's hunting dogs, the barn cats, and the family's horses. His parents had much encouraged this interest, as it was entirely suitable for a young man (unlike, for instance, his fascination with the piano). Jonathan's favorite horse was Ebony, a black mare with a sweet disposition and intelligent eyes. She had been part of the team pulling the family carriage from

Pemberley to Donwell Abbey, and thus was currently kept in the Knightleys' stable.

Jonathan knew the horses well enough to have some sense of what they did and did not like. Ebony didn't like rainstorms.

He envisioned her in the unfamiliar stables, stamping her feet, wild-eyed with the endless rumbling of thunder in the distance. It felt important to imagine this in great detail, probably because it distracted Jonathan from the half-heard argument in his parents' room. Last night had been difficult enough to overhear, but then at least his mother's and father's anger had been a shared emotion, one directed at their common enemy, Mr. Wickham. Tonight, so far as he could tell, their wrath was for each other.

They had always been so happy together. Jonathan, like any other child, had taken comfort in the strong bond between his parents. Yes, they loved each other—but as he grew older, he'd recognized that his parents also shared something far more uncommon between married couples: they *liked* each other.

All such warmth and kindness between them seemed to have died with Susannah.

Their door shut hard—not quite slammed shut but close enough. Jonathan wondered which of his parents had stormed out of the room. (It seemed more like the sort of thing his mother would do, but everything was so mixed-up and contrary that anything was possible.) He wished he knew whether he should try to provide comfort or to continue pretending to know nothing. Above all, he wished his room was somewhere else, in a place where he could never have overheard a word.

∽

"House parties are overly frivolous," Edmund Bertram decided as he slipped into his nightshirt. "Granted, they may be the only way for friends and family to meet during the long summer months. But surely smaller, more intimate gatherings would better foster true friendship and goodwill."

Fanny sat on the edge of the bed, not preparing for sleep at all, though this was rather late for them to be awake. Dully she said, "The circumstances here are . . . are not ideal."

"You mean that no house party should be judged by this example," Edmund said. "I take your point, Fanny. Who can say how much more enjoyable our visit might've been had not Mr. Wickham chosen to make his appearance?"

She flinched. This was unsurprising. His wife was as timid as a mouse, deeply sensitive and fearful. In a woman, these were virtues, to be sure, though Edmund sometimes wished her a *little* sturdier.

"Fanny?" he asked. "Is all well?"

"Edmund, I—I—" Fanny clutched at the bedpost, as if trying to keep herself aright in a gale. "I need money."

How strange. His wife's wishes were modest, her household economy faultless. Then again, Edmund mused, it was only natural that attending a house party with so many elegant ladies might make a young woman long for finery of her own. As a common habit, such envy would be deplorable. However, this was so unusual for Fanny that Edmund found it charming, even a relief. Her spirits were too easily darkened. It was good to see her finally take an interest in something frivolous.

"Well," he said, "you have asked for so little throughout our marriage that I can hardly deny you some indulgence now. What is it? A few guineas for some fabric and trimmings, to make up a nice new dress?" Really, she needed one; even Edmund, no great scholar of ladies' wear, had noticed that a few of her gowns had gone shabby at the hem.

He expected Fanny to be quick and effusive with her

thanks, as usual. Instead, her eyes welled with tears and she shook her head.

"No? Not a gown, then?" He ought to have known better. Vanity was not one of Fanny's few faults. "Is it something for the house, then?"

"It is nothing," she sniffled. "Nothing at all, and forget I ever spoke of it."

"Fanny, are you quite well?" Edmund rested the back of his hand against her forehead. She was flushed—not unusual for her, with her quicksilver moods and uncertain health—but he found it worrying. "You need rest. The day has been too much for you."

She nodded and lay down on the bed. He tucked her in as though she were a little child. The moonlight frosted her hair an even paler shade of gold, which he found alluring, but Edmund pushed aside such thoughts. Fanny was in no condition for marital relations. She was a fragile creature, tender and unsure; and even after four years he was as careful with her as he had been on their wedding night.

Her request for money must have been about some passing fancy, no more.

Yet Edmund wondered nonetheless.

∞

As Jonathan lay sleepless in his bed, he wished for the sound of footsteps returning to his parents' door—evidence that their argument was forgotten, forgiven, and over. He did hear footsteps, more than once, but as soon as his hopes would rise, they would be dashed by the sound's disappearance. It seemed that many people were up and around tonight. No doubt the storm was keeping them awake.

No sooner had Jonathan thought this than he heard something new—or, rather, ceased to hear it. Raindrops no longer pattered against his window. The storm had finally stopped.

He went to the window to confirm this. Wind still thrashed the tree limbs, and the horizon continued to spark with lightning. This was not the end of the storms but a brief cessation. It was an opportunity Jonathan intended to capitalize upon. Quickly he tugged on his boots and overcoat, concealing his nightshirt and dressing gown almost completely. Although he would never be seen in company so attired, it would serve his purpose.

If he could not comfort his parents, nor himself, he could at least comfort Ebony.

Jonathan hurried downstairs. A small sound from the gallery made him turn his head—was this where his mother or father had taken refuge?—but when he glanced inside, he saw no one. Either he'd imagined the sound or whoever was within did not wish to be seen. No wonder, at this hour.

His first thought was to cut through the armory, toward one of the servants' doors, which he had noted when first entering the building. Would it be thought improper, were someone to awaken and find him? He was certainly not the only one awake. Best not to chance it.

He left through the front door and hurried through the mud toward the stables. A lantern burned there, which he thought careless until he entered and found one of the stable boys keeping watch.

"Oh," Jonathan said, embarrassed. "I shouldn't have come."

"One of these is your horse?" the boy said in a thick accent, perhaps Welsh. "Don't like thunder, do they? Figured I'd keep 'em company. Much the same as you, I reckon."

Jonathan simply nodded. At least in the stable boy's eyes, he had done nothing peculiar. With luck no one else would hear of it. As long as he was here, he might as well console

Ebony, whose eyes were wide with unease. He went to her side, clucking under his breath.

No sooner had he laid his hand upon her velvety muzzle than rain began to patter against the roof again. The stable boy chuckled. "Looks like you'll be stayin' awhile now, eh?"

"Looks like it," Jonathan agreed. It was something of a relief to be free of a house that contained so much strife. He looked out of the small stable window in an attempt to gauge the strength of the rain. The murky nighttime made such a task impossible—but he did glimpse in one window the outline of a woman in her nightdress, holding aloft a candle. Despite the darkness, he had the definite impression that it was Anne Wentworth. He had thought the Wentworths' room to be in an entirely different part of the abbey. Was she at the far end of the first-floor hall?

But he shouldn't think of such things. Jonathan had no more wanted to see Mrs. Wentworth in a state of undress than she would've wanted to be seen. It was best forgotten.

⁓

Marianne Brandon was not a sound sleeper. Her dreams were vivid and frequent, and the smallest noises could awaken her. Only a year or two prior, she had taken some pride in this, as it seemed to be proof of her exquisite sensibility. Yet she'd come to realize the disadvantages, especially now that she shared a bed with someone who was as light a sleeper as she.

Tonight, for instance, Brandon must have been awakened by something very minor some minutes ago. That was the most natural explanation for his absence from their bed.

She lay back, turned to one side, then to the other, restless and uneasy. Through the slit between the panels on their four-poster, lightning flickered.

He'll be back soon, Marianne thought. *Lie down and close your eyes. Pretend to be asleep.*

She did not tell herself to actually fall asleep. That seemed impossible.

Oh, Brandon, what are you doing? Where have you gone?

⁊

Juliet was awakened by a sound.

Precisely what sound, she couldn't have said—the noise had intruded into a dream, a foggy vision of silks and candles that dissipated before Juliet had even fully opened her eyes. She had no idea whether she'd been awakened by a knock on the door (unlikely) or a thunderclap (the most rational suspect). Propping up on her elbows, she attempted to recall it, then gave up, as it made no difference.

She had a more pressing concern, which was that she needed to answer the call of nature.

One disadvantage of very old houses: despite their grandeur, they did not allow for convenience in such matters. Groggily Juliet got out of bed and reached for the porcelain chamber pot beneath. She pulled it forward, accidentally knocking it against one of the bed's feet, and heard a clink and crumble that made her heart sink.

Juliet took up the chamber pot to see that, yes, she'd broken it. A chip had been knocked out of the side, making a hole almost the size of her thumb, rendering it unfit for its purpose.

Bad enough to have broken something that belonged to her hosts. But to have broken a *chamber pot?* The servants would find out, which was bad enough, but they would then tell the Knightleys, a thought even more appalling.

Worst of all was that Juliet now needed a chamber pot in the dead of night, quite badly in fact, and had none.

She could ring the bell for a servant. The housemaid look-ing after her, Hannah, had proved to be a good-natured, capable person. No doubt summoning her was the properest thing do under those circumstances. Yet that would require Juliet to talk about the unmentionable thing—or simply hand it over, which in some ways would be worse, as she would be seen *touching* this very everyday object that society forbade her to admit the existence of. Which was silly, to be sure. Juliet had thought so before. But such rational considerations held little sway at the moment. Because then the servant would have to go away and come back with another one, and give it to Juliet with the sure knowledge that it would imme-diately be used. What images that would awaken in the ser-vant's mind!

No doubt other images came to mind when the chamber pots were emptied every morning. That didn't even bear thinking about.

The only alternatives were to find some other object to use, or to go outside to the privy. It seemed to her that the rain might not have been falling when she first awoke, but cer-tainly it was raining now. Still, when she compared the nui-sance of getting wet versus the sheer horror of choosing a vase or a ewer—which would also be discovered by the servants, who would then not only know of her actions but, worse, con-sider her a boor—the privy was the clear choice.

If she was found wandering about the corridors at night, better she should preserve some measure of modesty; her che-mise alone would hardly suffice. Juliet took up a blue blanket and wrapped it around her shoulders to serve as a shawl. The candlestick had a handle for easy carrying, which was helpful, though she would have to leave it inside once she ventured out of doors, lest the flame be extinguished.

She opened her door slowly, without so much as a creak, and began hurrying down the hallway. Juliet's room was located at the far end of the corridor, which meant she passed both the Bertrams' and the Wentworths' rooms as she went. Light shone beneath the doors—from the fires in their hearths, no doubt, though it seemed to Juliet that both bedrooms were brighter than she would've reckoned at this hour. No doubt the storm had kept many people awake. She winced to think someone might hear her.

They won't know, she reassured herself as she made her way down the stairs, bare feet chilly against the naked wood. *The abbey is so old and so large, with so many corridors and stairwells turning this way and that—even if they heard something, they would scarcely know whence it came.*

Juliet reached the bottom of the stairs and paused. The labyrinthine nature of the abbey she had just been grateful for also presented difficulties, as she now realized, because she could not yet find her way around in the dark.

The side door had been nearest the privy. Did it open off of the armory or the conservatory? Juliet bit her lower lip as she tried to recall. If only it hadn't rained so much the past two days! Then she'd already have known the way, instead of using chamber pots all the while. Finally she decided to find the conservatory; it had a door that led outside, which was all she required. By this point she was willing to simply water the plants closest the house. No one would be the wiser.

She was encouraged when she found the entrance to the gallery. The conservatory lay just beyond. Only moments now.

Yet as she scurried into the room, she was struck by the sudden, palpable sensation that meant she was not alone.

Juliet hesitated, then held her candle up higher. Flickering light played upon the numerous oil paintings that covered the walls, the many busts in bronze and marble that stood atop pillars. Eyes, faces, profiles—they all surrounded her. No wonder she'd imagined somebody else in the room.

Or so she told herself. The feeling of another person's presence remained strong.

But nature would be denied no longer. Juliet carefully placed her candlestick on a small table near the door halfway down the gallery's length, braced herself, and dashed out.

Oh, misery, she thought as her feet splashed through the cold, sticky mud. At least she could spy the privy from here and thus perform her task without being rained upon all the while. Had the rain grown harder since she glanced through the windows last? It pelted down, plastering her thin chemise to her legs, and she could hardly see her destination through the downpour and the dark. A strange flicker of movement within the gallery startled her before she realized it must be only her own reflection, pale against the night.

At least the Knightleys' accommodations were very near the house and well kept. Juliet took a moment longer than necessary before hurrying back out again, simply to collect herself. *Get upstairs. Bathe your feet. Change into a new shift. Try not to wonder what the servants will think of you when they launder this nightdress tomorrow. And never break a chamber pot again!*

She ran back to Donwell Abbey even faster than she'd run from it, eager to complete her errand and return to the snug, safe confines of her room. Lightning crashed down as she dashed through the conservatory, so close that the bolt and the thunder were simultaneous, casting bright light into the gallery. The busts on their pillars cast sharp-edged shadows on the floor for one instant.

When the light was gone, one shadow remained, darker than the darkness around it.

She took up her candle and tiptoed forward to get a better look. Her eyes widened as recognition set in.

Who's screaming? Juliet thought, before realizing, *Oh, it's me.*

❧

Jonathan had just settled into a comfortable seat on a hay bale when he heard the shriek—so loud that it made the horses' ears prick up. He and the stable boy exchanged worried glances. The cry had come from within Donwell Abbey.

"I'll go," Jonathan said. Probably one of the ladies of the house had been startled or, at worst, injured. But if there was any danger, it was more appropriate to accept the risk than foist it upon a servant.

He took up a lantern and hurried out into the rain. Mud splashed beneath his booted feet, soaking the edges of his nightshirt and dressing gown beneath his sodden overcoat. The screaming didn't stop, as he would've expected for some minor fright; it kept on and on. Jonathan ran faster.

"Hello?" he called as he dashed into the house. By this point he could hear other footsteps and querulous sounds upstairs. At least some of the others had been awakened by the screams, which seemed to be coming from the direction of the gallery. "What's happening?"

The screams broke off. A voice cried out, "Help! Oh, *help*!"

Jonathan ran into the gallery. At the far end of the room stood Juliet Tilney, soaked through, shivering so violently that her candle rattled in its stick.

At her feet lay Mr. Wickham, blood on his face. He was staring blankly upward, quite dead.

Chapter Six

Juliet had been no more sheltered than anyone else from the fact of mortality, from being at her grandmother's deathbed to helping nurse a young friend through the final stages of consumption. Almost no one, rich or poor, male or female, reached the age of reason without confronting death.

Murder, however—that was another matter entirely. Her limbs felt weak, and dizziness threatened to claim her. Then she recalled something her mother had once told her:

Run mad as often as you choose, but do not faint.

It was enough to keep Juliet on her feet.

Jonathan Darcy hurried to her side. His hair was as wet with rain as hers, his boots even muddier than her feet. "What has happened?"

"I do not know," she said. Her voice trembled, and she attempted to steady it. "I found him here, like this."

Mr. Wickham made a pitiful sight. Blood covered the left side of his head, so much so that a pool of red had spread out from it on the floor, and his nose was badly misshapen. The blood seemed to be flowing from nasty cuts on his cheek and jaw. His eyes remained open but unfocused. If his face could be said to have an expression any longer, it was one of aston- ishment. Perhaps he had never truly expected to meet his Maker.

If he had, Juliet thought numbly, *he would surely have behaved better.*

Footsteps pounding on the stairs testified to the arrival of the others. The butler emerged first, but close upon his heels was Mr. Knightley and then Mr. Darcy. Anne Wentworth, too, appeared with surprising speed. Everyone was in varying states of undress, from Mr. Knightley missing only his cravat to Mrs. Darcy in a fine robe all the way to Mrs. Brandon, who came down no farther than the top of the stairs, wearing only her chemise. Most had dressing gowns or blankets tossed around their shoulders—Juliet belatedly realized that her thin, sodden blanket no longer provided much concealment, nor did her damp chemise. But nobody was looking at her.

"Dear Lord in heaven," whispered Mr. Knightley as he stepped to Wickham's side. His voice was flat, without expression, perhaps from shock. "The man is dead."

"Are you certain?" said Mr. Bertram, the upright curate, who showed less sign of disturbance than most of the others. His wife, who shivered behind him, had gone as pale as Wickham himself. As pale as death.

"He is most assuredly dead," Juliet said. "He has not drawn breath nor blinked since I came upon him."

When she spoke, the men all stared. Did they think her indelicate? Perhaps she *was* indelicate. *Have I read too many of Mamma's novels?*

Next to her, Jonathan Darcy went down on one knee and pressed two fingers to Wickham's throat. After a few seconds, he shook his head. "Miss Tilney is correct. Mr. Wickham is dead."

Elizabeth Darcy made a sound that could've been either a gasp or a laugh—though surely no one could laugh at such a sight as this. Juliet decided she had imagined that part of it.

"Did he perchance fall and strike his head?" Mrs. Knightley offered, with more hope than reason.

"No indeed." Captain Wentworth stepped forward to

regard the corpse. He appeared utterly unmoved. "I've seen men like this on deck after a shelling. This is the result of a violent blow."

"Agreed," said Colonel Brandon, who had been so much in shadow that Juliet had not at first seen him. Where had he come from? "A mere fall is incapable of inflicting such damage."

Everyone exchanged glances. Given the acknowledged evils of Mr. Wickham's behavior and history, it could be no great wonder that someone had disliked him enough to kill him.

And yet nobody was immune to the horror of discovering a murder.

⁓

Jonathan saw Juliet Tilney shivering. Should he offer her his overcoat, or would that be unduly familiar? And his coat was wet, meaning it was of dubious utility in the present circumstance.

This internal debate ended when Mr. Knightley broke in. "We must ascertain whether anyone lurks nearby. Greene, fetch me my hunting rifle as quickly as you can." The butler hurried off. "Young Mr. Darcy, you also are attired for the weather, if you would consent to join me in the search. Cousin Edmund, please see that all doors and windows are secured, and tell the housekeeper to light candles in every room. No one must be allowed to lurk in shadows."

Jonathan understood that these precautions were necessary to maintain calm throughout the household. But he felt no great urgency to search or check locks. It seemed to him obvious that Mr. Wickham's killer must still be in the house.

He looked for his parents, expecting one or the other to

object to his undertaking a potentially dangerous task. His mother must already have moved away with the others; his father, still present, said nothing. His expression was grave, even stricken. *He must have realized the same thing, that the murderer is no intruder,* Jonathan told himself.

He refused to countenance any alternate explanation.

So it was with little trepidation that Jonathan followed Mr. Knightley into the night. Between the patter of the rain and the frequent, distant roll of thunder, it was impossible to listen for anything as subtle as footfalls or heavy breaths. Nor could they see a great deal in a moonless night. Jonathan nonetheless attended to his surroundings as best he could. Although he expected to find nothing, he could not allow his expectations to guide him. Even the slightest threat of a criminal interloper required full vigilance.

Despite his thoroughness, neither he nor Mr. Knightley discovered any broken branches in the shrubbery, or any other indication of an unwanted presence outside. Knightley briefly brightened as they came closer to the stables. "Aha," he said. "Boot prints, thick in the mud—"

"I fear they are mine," Jonathan said, pointing at the deep tracks, which had already collected mud puddles within. "I ran from the stables to the house upon hearing Miss Tilney scream."

"So it would seem." Knightley sighed heavily. "There seems little for us to do. At daybreak, regardless of the state of the roads, I must send for the local magistrate."

Jonathan frowned. "It sounds as if you are reluctant to do so. Why? Surely a magistrate's presence is necessary."

"Oh, it is, it is, young Mr. Darcy. But why did it have to be *this* one?"

"Sir?"

Knightley shook his head in apparent chagrin. "You may

understand me better once you meet the fellow—magistrate Frank Churchill."

~~✺~~

The marriage of Emma Woodhouse and George Knightley had not been the greatest astonishment known to the town of Highbury. No, the character among the townsfolk who had provided the most surprise over the years was Frank Churchill.

After his mother's death during his boyhood, young Frank had been taken by his rich, haughty aunt, separating him from his loving father. This father, Mr. Weston, had never ceased to cherish his son and waited patiently for Frank to be old enough to declare his independence and come home on his own. Highbury had waited impatiently. Well past the age of reason, Frank Churchill had remained absent and therefore mysterious.

His sudden reappearance in his twenty-third year had shocked everyone, in the best possible sense. With his humor, charm, and zest for living, he had proved a welcome addition to the town. Why then, when never before? The timing of his return proved not to be a matter of filial duty (though his love for his father was sincere)—but the result of a secret engagement. Rather than choosing a bride from the upper crust of London society, as his late aunt would've preferred, Frank married Jane Fairfax, niece of the poor Miss Bates who eked out an existence in Highbury. Surprise enough for one lifetime, all might have thought, but more was in store.

Their marriage was a happy one. The Churchills spent more of their time in Highbury than in the grand estate Frank had inherited. Emma and Jane formed the beginnings of a true and deep friendship. Nothing but sunlight shone down upon them until their daughter was born; as the little girl entered the world, her mother departed it. Frank became father and widower in the same hour. All of Highbury strove to support him in his grief, but the common expectation was that he would soon leave the village his wife had so loved in favor of London, or at least his own estate.

Common expectation was defied. The greatest astonishment Frank had ever provided those around him was in his quiet decision to remain in Highbury; to cherish the memories of his wife; to raise their daughter, Grace, in the countryside; and to support her elderly aunts in their sorrow and destitution.

(Indeed, Miss Bates's adoration of Jane had been so all-encompassing that her friends had wondered whether she could survive the loss. But the heart Jane had broken by dying was restored by Jane's daughter, and within a few months Miss Bates was prattling on about the wondrous child and could not look on Grace without a smile.)

Frank Churchill's selflessness had won him the admiration of nearly all Highbury. Knightley alone still considered the man somewhat feckless, but even he honored Frank's goodness toward Miss Bates and devotion as a father. This general esteem had led to the selection of Frank Churchill as magistrate for the parish—the person responsible for, among numerous other duties, investigating a murder.

❧

For those staying at Donwell Abbey, it was a long and sleepless night.

Fanny Bertram wept brokenly, inconsolable. Edmund was accustomed to his wife's tears; she cried easily, at any excess of embarrassment or melancholy. Given her delicate nature, it could hardly be shocking that she was so devastated by a murder only rooms away.

Yet there was something in her crying that gave him pause. The sobs that racked her were deep, hoarse, uncontrolled—far different from her usual quiet tears. Edmund had never seen her like this, and the sight rattled him nearly as much as the murder.

"Fanny," he began, putting an arm around her shoulders. "My dear. It is most horrifying, but you must not fear for yourself."

"I do not fear." Her voice was thick with emotion. "I have nothing to fear any longer, except my own wickedness."

She was always declaring herself wicked for such vile offenses as failing to get the tea ready on time or riding her horse in hot weather. Often it made Edmund smile.

That night it did not.

As Frederick Wentworth paced the floor, Anne sat upon the trunk at the foot of the bed. Lying down in a state of such agitation was futile, a mockery of sleep. She had had not one moment's rest this night and did not anticipate any to come.

"He looked like a fellow who died upon the *Asp*. We lost control of the boom—swung across, struck him—the man was dead before he hit the deck," Frederick said, his agitation deepening. "How does such a villain die in exactly the same way as a fine young seaman serving his king? They even fell in the same posture. The exact same posture. Uncanny, really."

He so rarely talked about the war, and Anne thought it could not be good for him, but what could she say at this moment? Her throat felt choked with unspoken words. For now, silence must be her only response.

The Brandons, alone among the residents of the household, had gone back to bed. It was easier to do so than to speak of what had just occurred. Marianne had rarely felt so repressed and yet so unwilling to rebel against the repression. Instead, she lay utterly still beside her husband, back to back, each of them staring at a different wall. His wakefulness was as obvious to her as hers must have been to him, and yet she knew neither of them would acknowledge this until dawn.

She could not speak. She longed for Brandon to do so, and yet she desperately feared what he might say.

Inside her head, the same words repeated themselves, over and over: *He wasn't in bed. He was not here.*

Etiquette guides hostesses through any number of difficult circumstances. However, Emma was unaware of any such guidance pertaining to a murder on the premises. Yet all must be smoothed over to whatever extent could be managed. There was nothing to do but her best.

Her natural energy served her well, leading her to personally see to the lighting of candles and fires in every room. One of the footmen came with her, to ensure that no attacker would waylay her, but Emma was unafraid. No homicidal intruder lurked within. Of that she was entirely certain. Still, her guests and servants must be put at ease, insofar as was possible with a dead body lying in her gallery.

The butler had offered to move the corpse someplace less conspicuous, but Emma had declined. She would not have the constables saying that she had interfered with their work. Besides, where could it be put? The laundry? The scullery? Emma would never feel good about her linens or pots again.

When Knightley returned, muddy and distressed, she excused his valet and assisted him herself. He undressed in near silence, until the end, when he said, "This is a bad business, Emma."

"Is it?" The censorious look he gave her was such as she had not seen from him in many years. "Of course it is all very terrible, and there will be talk, but John and Isabella—they are now safe."

"Thus we benefit from Mr. Wickham's death," Knightley said. "And we are far from the only ones who will know it."

Darcy sat at the small desk near their bed, writing a letter. Elizabeth might have teased him about contriving to keep such even lines, were she not equally occupied with letters of her own.

On her way back to her room, falling in step with her fellow startled guests, Elizabeth had recognized certain important facts: Her family's connection to Wickham had been deeper than any others' present. The implications for themselves, and for their relations, were by far the greatest—as would the suspicion be. Thus it was critical that family members and close friends be informed immediately. Scandal was now inevitable, but it might perhaps be contained and controlled if those nearest to them had certain facts to hand.

Darcy, Elizabeth thought, was most likely writing his steward, a distant cousin of Wickham's. The steward would be more likely to support his employer than to mourn his profligate relation, and the man could be expected to give a reasonable accounting of events in Lambton and its environs. Elizabeth—somewhat to her own surprise—found that the family member she wanted to inform first was Mary. Though, of course, they would all have to know, and through Wickham's death they would each endure memories of both Lydia and Susannah . . .

A rap on the door startled them both. "Come," said Darcy,

and the door opened to reveal their son standing in the candle-light, dripping wet from his search of the grounds. "Jonathan. Are you well?"

"It is all most distressing," Elizabeth added. Did Jonathan need soothing? No doubt most would say he was past the age for such, but her son was not like most young men—sometimes sanguine where others were troubled, other times distressed over the most ordinary circumstances. She could hardly guess his reaction to an event so appalling as his uncle's murder.

Jonathan paused before saying, "No intruders were found on the grounds, nor any evidence that anyone approached the house from without."

Only then did it occur to Elizabeth that they should have asked about that. But she felt no fear, and it was beneath her to pretend.

Juliet Tilney, having recovered from her initial shock, found herself reacting in a most unfortunate manner.

Certainly that was what her father would say, though her mother might understand a bit more. Because as terrible as it had been to see the aftermath of such a gruesome killing, the event itself—a murder at Donwell—felt . . . intriguing.

Oh, I must be wicked, Juliet thought, but the reprimand had no sting. She had not enough knowledge of Mr. Wickham to either lament his death or take satisfaction in it. Therefore she was left with nothing but the fact that a murder had been committed, and that someone in this house—one of the genteel, polite people she had dined with by candlelight—had done it, but nobody knew who.

And Juliet felt as though sleep would be impossible until she found out the truth. But how?

Perhaps the magistrate would quickly discern the culprit the next morning . . .

Something caught her attention, though she could not tell what it was at first. Then she realized she perceived absence, not presence—that, at long last, the interminable rain had finally stopped.

∽

The duty of any proper young lady on such an occasion was to write her parents. Juliet might not always have fulfilled every one of propriety's many requirements, but this one she did not intend to neglect. Upon first awakening, on the morning after the killing, she turned to her task—but paused for a long while, pen in inkwell, unsure what next to write.

If she revealed that there had just been a murder at Donwell Abbey, her father would appear to fetch her home in the time it took for a fast horse to travel from Gloucestershire to Surrey. But Juliet didn't want to go home; as frightening as it was to be in the same house as a murderer, it was unthinkable to leave without even knowing who that person might be! She doubted her parents would see it that way.

Nor could she write home and simply omit the news of Mr. Wickham's death. The omission would undoubtedly become known to her parents sooner or later—most likely sooner—and when that happened, Juliet would be in serious trouble. (She had learned in early childhood that, in her mother's view, failing to mention something that needed mentioning was as bad as any spoken lie.)

What was she to do?

After a few minutes' consideration, Juliet wrote her letter, fully detailing the facts of the murder as she knew them. She folded and sealed the paper with wax. Then she wrote the direction for the letter—but wrote that direction abominably ill, her pen shaky and the ink blotchy, to the point that it could scarcely be read. It would be many days, possibly even weeks, before the letter made its way to the Tilney home. Her father would no doubt ascribe her scribbling to the shock occasioned by the murder and thus be none the wiser.

Mrs. Tilney, on the other hand, was of a more suspicious bent. She might have the penetration to realize what her daughter had done. If so, then eventually Juliet would have to answer for her stratagem.

But Juliet, like most of those who incur debts, resolved to think no more upon it until the bill came due. She rang the bell, gave Hannah the letter for posting, and considered her daughterly duty fulfilled.

Mr. Frank Churchill did not look very much like a magistrate, in Juliet's opinion. Summoned by one of the Knightleys' servants, he arrived during the final hour of a wan and silent breakfast, his open countenance and easy manner a marked contrast to the weary within Donwell Abbey.

"Gruesome business, this," said Mr. Churchill as he entered the main hall and turned to Mrs. Knightley. "Dear Emma, how dreadful for you."

"For all of us, though I suppose mostly for Mr. Wickham." Mrs. Knightley stopped herself there.

Juliet wondered—had that been a witticism? Could it possibly be acceptable to *joke* about such a thing? She felt as though she ought to be appalled, but she was not. How immoral a creature she was proving to be!

"We have left the situation intact," said Mr. Knightley, leading Churchill and the two constables through the house toward the gallery. He glanced over his shoulder to add, "Please, everyone, continue as though nothing has occurred."

What else was there to do? The subject could hardly be addressed in polite conversation, regardless of how obvious the event was to all. Society demanded that they all sit there and take breakfast while a dead body lay in a neighboring room.

Juliet stared down at her breakfast bread and jam, once against frustrated at what "society demanded."

As she had before, she decided not to listen to such demands.

She finished her food as quickly as was decent, leaving stilted chitchat to the others currently at table (Captain Wentworth, gray with fatigue, and Edmund Bertram, relatively unmoved). When she excused herself, she moved as though to go to the stairs—but then ducked through a hallway that would take her closer to the gallery. Eavesdropping was no doubt very unbecoming conduct for a young lady, so she told herself it didn't really count if she was in a situation where she couldn't help overhearing . . .

"Ghastly," said Mr. Churchill, his pleasant humor somewhat dimmed by what she presumed to be the sight of the corpse. "Definitely killed by a blow to the head with some heavy instrument. How long had he been deceased when his body was found?"

"Uncertain, but it could not have been very long," replied Knightley. "Our butler passed through the room late last night, on his way to check the wine cellar. Midnight, he thinks. No one else was here, living or otherwise. Miss Tilney awoke us with her cry of alarm scarce past one. So the crime must have taken place within that hour."

"Do you think it might have been Gypsies?" Mr. Churchill seemed to relish the prospect. "Not that our local travelers have ever given us much trouble, but such a crime as this—"

"No one intruded upon this house last night." Mr. Knightley spoke with great gravity. "Young Mr. Darcy and I searched thoroughly just after the discovery of the body, and I did so again this morning. The only footprints found were our own."

"One of the servants, then," Mr. Churchill said. "They must all be questioned."

A servant? Juliet frowned in consternation. Why should a servant wish to murder any guest at Donwell Abbey?

Then she realized—of course. Society would look to the lower classes first when it came to placing blame for such a crime.

Mr. Knightley seemed to be more in her own way of thinking. "I must tell you that many of our guests had prior acquaintance with Mr. Wickham—and none of us had any reason to favor the man."

A pause. Juliet wished she could see the expression on Mr. Churchill's face as he finally said, "Then I must ask that all guests remain in residence until this matter is settled. Merely as a formality, you realize."

"Yes," Mr. Knightley said distantly. "Just a formality."

I am in the same house as a murderer, Juliet thought, *and neither the murderer nor I will be allowed to leave.*

❧

Jonathan spent far too long debating whether he should go down for breakfast. He was hungry, but he could always ask a servant for a roll or a bit of cheese later, whereas if he went to breakfast, he could be trapped in polite conversation far longer than was expedient. Best, perhaps, to resume his investigation instead.

He went down toward the gallery, ignoring the murmurings and clinking from the breakfast room. At the gallery doorway, however, he saw only the constables engaged in the removal of the corpse. To them it must be a gruesome task, but at this distance, Jonathan could see only their awkward grappling with something heavy wrapped in a blanket.

Atop a horse for nearly the first time, holding on, listening to his uncle more closely than he ever had before or ever would again: "You can't be scared. The horse will know it. Show some courage and the horse is yours. Watch me, boy." Wickham then astride his own mount, riding ahead confidently, filling young Jonathan with envy—

The heavy, stiff bundle in the constables' arms had once been that man, proudly riding ahead into the sunlight.

Jonathan shook himself. The room of the murder could tell him only so much; a medical man might learn more from the body. He himself would learn more only from Mr. Knightley and the magistrate.

The distant murmur of voices told him these men were exploring the rooms nearest the gallery—a rational decision, as the killer would have had to pass through at least some of these rooms both before and after the crime. Jonathan followed the sound down a corridor, focusing on it so intently that he did not see the figure standing before him until they were nearly upon each other.

"Oh!" He stopped short. "Miss Tilney. I beg your pardon."

"No, no, I must beg yours." She moved as though to walk past him, then caught herself, then looked round the hall as though seeking something or someone. "I, ah, was looking for—for—"

"Knightley!" That had to be the voice of magistrate Frank Churchill. "By G-d, do you see this?"

That was the moment in which it became inarguably clear that a private and important conversation was taking place only a room away. The moment in which politeness demanded that anyone else nearby withdraw to a point where they would not overhear.

Jonathan didn't move.

Miss Tilney didn't either.

They stared at each other for one second longer. For one of the few times in his life, Jonathan knew someone else was thinking exactly the same thing he was.

Juliet Tilney was as curious about the murder as he. This was the sort of thing neither of them was ever supposed to admit out loud.

They didn't have to. Standing there was admission enough.

Miss Tilney seemed to make up her mind in the same instant Jonathan did. Together they leaned against the nearest door, eager to hear what came.

Chapter Seven

Frank Churchill talked loudly at almost all times, it seemed. This did not speak well of his discretion, but Juliet found it made him much easier to overhear through the armory door.

"Look at this," he said to Knightley, whom she believed was the only other person in the room with him. "Taken from its place, left on the floor, as deadly a weapon as can be imagined. Too heavy for any woman to lift, which tells us much."

"Yes, surely." But Knightley did not sound convinced. "However, I must tell you that it frequently falls from its mounting on the wall. We've been meaning to fix it."

What could they be speaking of? Juliet burned with curiosity. She glanced up at Jonathan Darcy, wondering whether he might know, but he remained intent on the conversation behind the door.

"Then the servants know of it," said Churchill. "That the mace is here, and that nobody would think much of its being out of place—"

"Why return it to the armory, yet not put it back in position?" Knightley countered. "Surely if it had been used in a murder, the weapon would be either put back where it belonged or hidden entirely."

This objection seemed reasonable to Juliet, but Frank Churchill would not so easily abandon his new theory. "Perhaps they tried, and it fell again. There must have been *some* disturbance in this room, Mr. Knightley."

"That I concede." From his tone of voice, it was clear that Knightley did so unwillingly. Why should he hesitate?

She had no time to mull over the question, because Churchill called out to the constables: "Cooper! Spaulding! Come and take a look at this."

Juliet would've been shamefaced about scurrying away so guiltily were Jonathan not right beside her.

The nearest and best room for their escape proved to be the billiard room. At this time of day, none of the men would be playing, and this was a space put to no other use. Jonathan closed the door behind them, and Juliet breathed out a sigh of relief.

It struck her that she was in a closed room with a young man, a potentially ruinous circumstance for any woman, particularly an unmarried one. But Juliet felt sure of Mr. Darcy's gentility, and also that they would be able to leave without being observed. Which was perhaps not a perfect rationale. She hoped no one would ever have to hear it.

"What do you think?" she began. "I do not believe Mr. Churchill's theories for a second."

At first, Jonathan seemed taken aback by her forthrightness. But his curiosity, like hers, quickly overcame propriety. "Nor I. It is alarming how quickly he has begun to suspect a servant. None of the Donwell staff is likely to have cause to harm Mr. Wickham. Nearly all the guests did have such cause. Churchill's distrust of the lower classes is a common one, but I consider it ill founded, particularly in the present case."

"I agree." They had admitted this much, so Juliet could see no further harm in adding, "If the investigation is left to Mr. Churchill, I feel there is no guarantee justice will be done. Instead, some poor servant will be hanged for another's crime."

She thought of Hannah being dragged to the gallows. It was enough to make her shudder. No, they could not allow lazy blame to fall upon those least able to defend themselves.

"The magistrate will hesitate to accuse any of the guests, due to his friendship with the household." Jonathan shook his head. "Yet the truth must be discerned, regardless of the constraints of civility. I myself have never been especially adept at—at so constraining myself. Thus I am fit to undertake that task, at least."

He seemed almost embarrassed. Juliet could not see why— he could be awkward, yes, but hardly offensive. Then she remembered that she herself had taken offense at his words, had in fact even suspected him of being a simpleton. Her ignorant assumptions now embarrassed her. Jonathan Darcy clearly possessed intelligence and a strong sense of right and wrong. These traits were the correct means of assessing his character, far more important than clever chitchat before dinner. Juliet resolved not to make such severe judgments in haste again.

Her sense of shame did not numb her to the possibility that Jonathan Darcy, like most other male persons, might make certain assumptions about her in turn—assumptions they could not afford were this murder to be solved.

"I shall help you," she said. Jonathan raised an eyebrow, but she would not be daunted. "You cannot do this all alone."

"Whyever not?"

"Do you not realize that women will have to be questioned as well as men? There are questions *I* can ask the women at Donwell Abbey that you absolutely cannot."

This was inarguable, but Jonathan Darcy remained dubious. "Surely investigating such a gruesome matter will be too shocking for you."

"It will not be more shocking than finding a dead body," Juliet pointed out, "and that I have already survived."

Most gentlemen would've ignored this fact (though fact it was) and dismissed her. Jonathan did not. Instead, he nodded slowly. "Quite so, Miss Tilney. Let us begin."

As the magistrate's visit drew to a close, Knightley found himself even wearier than he had been before. A not uncommon reaction of his when it came to Frank Churchill, but after the sleepless hours of the previous night, Knightley had believed nothing could sink him further into torpor. He had been incorrect.

Or, perhaps, he was further dispirited by the distant sight of the constables lugging their heavy, blanketed burden into the gaol wagon. *To think,* he mused, *yesterday that was a man, walking, talking, breathing—mocking, betraying—*

"Knightley?" Mr. Churchill held his hat in his hands. "Are you quite all right?"

How long had he been standing there, gaping at the corpse? Knightley collected himself. "Forgive me. It's difficult to think of it, and yet difficult to think of anything else."

Churchill finally asked the question he ought to have asked almost at the beginning. "What was your connection to the late Mr. Wickham?"

"My brother owed him a great deal of money," Knightley said.

"So I had heard," Frank Churchill said, confirming that gossip had indeed delivered to Highbury the news of the financial scheme and its collapse. "But why should that bring Wickham to your door?"

Knightley hesitated—but as it happened, Emma had just strolled out behind them, and it was she who replied. "Oh, John no doubt told Wickham of his family's wealth when he asked to borrow funds to purchase more shares. Wickham seems to be the sort to bully whomever he must to collect even a single shilling." She sighed. "John is my brother, and I love him dearly, but this—connecting us to this sad situation—it has further compounded his greatest error."

This was all true, so far as it went, and it seemed to satisfy Frank Churchill. Thus Knightley said no more.

Mr. Churchill continued, "I'll be back later, of course, once we've seen to the body. Your guests should all remain in Highbury until we get to the bottom of this. Their servants will have to be questioned as well as those of Donwell Abbey. Shouldn't be at all surprised to find that not every gentleman is as careful in choosing the members of his household as you are, Knightley."

Was this blithe assurance in a servant's guilt merely snobbery? Or was it simply that the alternative could not be spoken aloud without committing a social breach? Knightley found himself too tired to care.

As soon as Frank Churchill mounted his horse and rode away, Knightley turned to go back inside. Somehow he still had responsibilities as a host, and this continued to be a house party. The fiction of enjoyment must be maintained.

~

In the billiard room, Miss Tilney had taken a seat in one of the chairs lining the wall. Sitting was proper for conversation, as Jonathan well knew. Surely they should not abandon *all* propriety, even in their new endeavor.

However, Jonathan often found it difficult to sit still during periods of strong emotion or intense thought. It was as though being in motion helped him to think. His parents had urged him to curtail this uncouth habit, and he tried to comply—but at the moment, such constraint was beyond him. He paced the room, hoping Miss Tilney would not write him off as a boor. "It seems to me that you can have no possible motive for wishing Mr. Wickham dead," he began. "You had never met the man before two days ago, and so far as you know he has no connection to your family?" Miss Tilney shook her head. "No motive, then. And you would scarcely have raised the alarm in the manner you did, had you been the guilty party."

"Indeed not. Your innocence is also clear, Mr. Darcy."

"Yes, the stable boy can vouch for my presence during the time of the murder."

"There is that," she said, "but it is your current behavior that most convinces me. Were you the guilty party, you would support Mr. Churchill's theories about the servants, not seek to disprove them. Thus we two can be considered free from suspicion. Who else?"

"Captain Wentworth's dislike for the man was plain for all to see," Jonathan replied. "And Mrs. Wentworth—" Was it impolite, to say what a woman had been doing beyond her bedchamber in the night? No doubt. But where courtesy and investigation were at cross-purposes, and the stakes so high, surely he must choose the path of truth. "I saw her in one of the first-floor windows, which was certainly not the window to her room. This would have been very close to the time of the murder."

"That is more exculpatory than not," Miss Tilney declared. "Your information proves Mrs. Wentworth was not in the gallery on the ground floor at that particular moment . . . yet, still, she was afoot, and at such a strange time!"

Jonathan weighed what else he knew as he paced back and forth, back and forth. "I know of no connection between Wickham and the Bertrams," he said. "Certainly neither he nor they hinted at any such. Wickham has of course greatly troubled the Knightleys, and Mr. Bertram is Mr. Knightley's cousin, but a distant one. That seems unlikely to spur a man of the cloth to murder."

"I tend to agree," Miss Tilney said slowly, "though Mrs. Bertram's behavior has been somewhat peculiar."

Timid, delicate Mrs. Bertram seemed the unlikeliest human

on earth to commit a murder, but Jonathan saw no reason to be impolite by rejecting the suggestion out of hand. "Then there are the Brandons. While the colonel has not admitted to any knowledge of Mr. Wickham, he did make a point of asking Knightley his Christian name. As though, perhaps, the name was familiar even if the man was not."

Miss Tilney looked skeptical, but she said, "Then I suppose no one else among the guests can be excluded?"

Jonathan wanted to insist that his parents should be above suspicion. They were the Darcys of Pemberley, and beyond that . . . surely his parents could never commit such a sin. But would Juliet Tilney believe that?

He said only, "We must investigate everyone. Our conjectures are nothing without evidence."

❧

Despite its considerable size, Donwell Abbey felt, for the most part, like a warm, comfortable, and modern home. Rare was the room that let in no sunlight or did not offer at least one comfortable perch for reading or conversation.

Colonel Brandon had found one of those rooms.

Perhaps it had been a prayer alcove, back in its papist days. At any rate, it was small and gray, airless with only one small window looking out on the stables, not far from the guest bedrooms on the first floor. Brandon had discovered it the night before—and had been glad of it at the time, for reasons he would never have anticipated. He was even more grateful for it now, as it gave him the chance to remain alone and undiscovered. Even Marianne could not find him here.

He longed for both her presence and her absence. Both to share a great unburdening of the soul and to enshrine a silence that might last between them forever.

Yet *forever* was not a word Brandon could readily think, at the moment. Their marriage was imperiled—life itself was imperiled—and he found it difficult to think further ahead than the next few days.

Thinking back—that was easier, yet still painful.

I ought not to have married her, he thought, remembering his first sight of her as a vibrant young girl, so like his late Eliza and yet so completely, resolutely herself. *Willoughby was lost to her, but she would undoubtedly have found love with another man. Someone younger, more dashing, more able to share in her enthusiasms. But I would not abandon my foolish hopes, and they have led us here.*

The magistrate had only just left the house and would surely return soon to continue his investigations. What of the truth should Brandon reveal?

✑

Juliet found it strange, how *not* strange it was to be alone with Jonathan Darcy in a room. Surely with any other young man besides her brothers, she would be overcome with modesty (or, at least, she would be expected to be so). But he was no different with her than he was with anyone else. It was a new circumstance for her, to be taken so seriously by a man, even one nearly her own age.

His thoughts were more to the point. "We must address our inquiry in a more methodical manner." Mr. Darcy had begun pacing again. It was a peculiar habit of his, but Juliet found she did not mind it. His behavior was natural and unaffected. "We must impose order upon this confusion."

That was not how Juliet would have put it, but she agreed. "I shall write a sort of plan. Perhaps you could review it after dinner?"

He frowned. "Where?"

Juliet had already realized the location that would arouse the least suspicion. "Among the others, in plain sight."

*A Consideration of the Guests at Donwell Abbey
in the Matter of the Decease of Mr. George Wickham*

<u>*Mr. George Knightley*</u>—*his brother owed ruinous amounts
of money to Mr. Wickham, who intended to collect very
shortly*

<u>*Mrs. Emma Knightley*</u>—*the same as above, and it is to be
noted that her sister is wed to Mr. Knightley's brother, so
this is relation by both law and blood*

<u>*Colonel Christopher Brandon*</u>—*no known motive but
showed curiosity about Mr. Wickham for reasons still
undiscovered*

<u>*Mrs. Marianne Brandon*</u>—*no known motive but cannot
be wholly excluded until her husband's curiosity about
Mr. Wickham is explained*

<u>*Mr. Edmund Bertram*</u>—*no known motive*

<u>*Mrs. Fanny Bertram*</u>—*no known motive but cannot be
wholly excluded due to peculiar behavior before and since
the death*

<u>*Captain Frederick Wentworth*</u>—*had lost money to
Mr. Wickham and was deeply angered by this*

<u>*Mrs. Anne Wentworth*</u>—*her fortunes were compromised by
Captain Wentworth's loss*

<u>*Mr. Fitzwilliam Darcy*</u>—*brother-in-law of Mr. Wickham,
who was the cause of much family strife*

<u>*Mrs. Elizabeth Darcy*</u>—*sister-in-law of Mr. Wickham*

Juliet stopped writing there. From the way Mrs. Darcy had spoken of Wickham on the night of his arrival, she suspected that the man had pained Mrs. Darcy even more than he had her husband. Yet there was no point in speculating when Jonathan Darcy would undoubtedly have surer knowledge.

She sat in the drawing room, where the company had assembled after dinner. The mood was subdued, even grim, as would be expected. No music or games could be offered on such an occasion. Instead, people sat with books or newspapers, turning pages infrequently, their gazes unfocused. Juliet had commandeered the writing-desk to "compose a letter for her parents." (She had no intention of writing them again so soon, but no one in this room need know that.) Now she studied her work, wondering how best to get it to her newfound accomplice.

Simply handing it to him was out of the question—it would attract attention of the worst sort. Any more clandestine exchange had its own risks. No respectable young woman would ever write to an unmarried man unless they were engaged. To presume as much after meeting the younger Mr. Darcy only three days ago! Everyone else present would be shocked.

Perhaps she ought to be shocked herself. The most correct course of action would be for her to destroy this letter and pretend no such conversations had ever taken place between her and Jonathan Darcy. Certainly their current endeavor could not be described as proper.

Juliet looked down again at her letter. It would be so easy to crumple it, claim it was blotted with ink, and think upon it no more. The younger Mr. Darcy could continue on his own.

She kept the letter.

To her it seemed only rational that she take part in discerning the truth. Juliet was the lone guest at Donwell Abbey who seemed to be objective about Mr. Wickham, including even young Mr. Darcy. The magistrate was preoccupied with his own illogical theories about the guilty party. None of the servants could presume to take any steps to resolve the matter. That left Juliet.

What is more improper, she argued toward the imaginary versions of her parents, *pursuing the truth of a murder, or allowing the murderer to go free?*

Jonathan Darcy took a turn about the room, an unremarkable thing to do, but one that drew her attention. If he headed her way . . .

Swiftly, at the bottom, she added, *The armory at midnight.*

Juliet blew on the final line, ensuring the ink was dry, then folded the letter just as she would have to post it. The moment after she had finished, young Mr. Darcy's path took him directly by her desk. She pushed the letter to the very edge—where his fingers deftly snatched it. The paper had vanished into his pocket before he reached the corner.

I have corresponded with an unmarried man, Juliet thought. *How unladylike.*

How unfortunate for public morals that being unladylike feels so . . . exciting.

Chapter Eight

Jonathan would have set a meeting time well before midnight. Though the Knightleys were wealthy enough to keep many candles burning, allowing for nighttime activity, the guests of Donwell Abbey had not availed themselves of this opportunity this evening. No one was in a temper for cards; no one could concentrate on their books. Thus the entire party had returned to their rooms by ten at night, making for a long wait.

As he reached the armory, he glimpsed a pale flicker of candlelight through the open door. When he stepped inside, he was greeted by the sight of Juliet Tilney, taper in hand, wearing a thick wrapper over her nightdress. Jonathan, who had not undressed, flushed.

She would have required a maid's help to remove her dress, he reminded himself. *Miss Tilney has no choice but to conduct our investigation in her nightclothes.*

Should I wear them, too, in future? As a matter of courtesy, so that she will not be alone in such straits?

"There you are," Miss Tilney said. "I came down a few minutes ago, once I was sure all the servants were abed."

The servants! Jonathan had not considered the discrepancy between his hours and those of the staff. The midnight time had indeed been best. He said only, "Have you found anything?"

"I have been examining the mace."

"They did not take it into evidence?"

She shook her head. "It is suspected of being the weapon,

but they are not certain, which is lucky for us. It is the only one in the armory, and thus must be the one of which Mr. Churchill and Mr. Knightley spoke." She gestured with the candle. Its wavering light illuminated its surface. Though a medieval relic, the spikes of the mace remained brutally sharp. Miss Tilney said, "Mr. Churchill believed no woman could be strong enough to wield such a weapon, but he is in error."

Jonathan frowned. "It must weigh nearly twenty pounds."

"So does a year-old child, and women handle those often enough." To demonstrate, Miss Tilney took the mace in hand; though it was clearly heavy for her, she was perfectly capable of handling it. As she set it back in its tenuous place, she added, "Besides, women who work on farms haul pails of milk and swing scythes and do many things that ladies of higher classes are considered incapable of. But, as you see, we are not."

He had not considered this. "But would a woman turn to such a brutal weapon?"

Miss Tilney drew her wrapper more tightly about her shoulders. "That I am less certain of. She would have to be very afraid or very greatly angered."

However, Jonathan had begun to realize this line of inquiry would not avail them. "This cannot have been the murder weapon. The sharpness of the spikes—"

"Would've done far more damage than was done to Mr. Wickham. I believe you are right. This is another of Mr. Churchill's false assumptions."

Thus the murder weapon had yet to be determined. Had the killer kept it with them? Jonathan said, "We should search the gallery again. The constables were acting under Mr. Churchill's instructions, and so may not have looked as assiduously for a weapon as they should have, believing that the weapon had already been found."

"There seem few places for such a thing to be hidden in the gallery," Miss Tilney said, but she nodded. "Still, it is a place to begin."

The gallery smelled strongly of the soap used by the servants to scour the floor clean of blood. Otherwise, Jonathan noted, the room showed signs of a day's neglect—untrimmed candles, some dust on a few of the busts. He could not blame the maids for not wanting to spend time in this gallery, nor for assuming none of the guests would either. It jarred him to think of the dead body of his uncle lying here only hours before.

As Miss Tilney paced barefoot around the room, examining every corner, Jonathan had to concede that no weapon could be hidden here. Only a few chairs lined the walls, none of them upholstered, all bare of cushions. Nothing could be concealed in or beneath them. Although the gallery mostly displayed paintings, a few pieces of statuary stood upon pillars. They, too, offered no hiding places. And there was little point in shaking out the drapes, as he knew the constables had done this already.

Miss Tilney stopped short, stifling a small cry. Jonathan hurried to her. "What is it?"

"I merely stepped on something." She seemed embarrassed by her outburst as she bent to retrieve the object from the floor, just next to the wall. "Rather small, but it scraped my toe."

As she held it up to the candlelight, Jonathan realized what it was. "Part of a wax seal. Broken." Both of them leaned closer in order to study the marks on the seal. It might've been an anonymous sort of flourish—but it was not.

"It looks to be the letter *E*, but broken in half," Miss Tilney said. "No doubt it is Mrs. Knightley's. I understand her Christian name is Emma."

Jonathan shook his head. "Your thumb . . ."

Miss Tilney's eyes widened as she recognized what he had seen: flakes of what appeared to be dried blood.

"The servants here would have found and removed anything mistakenly dropped in the room before last night," he said. "Nor would Mrs. Knightley be likely to write her letters in this room. This, and the presence of blood—if blood it is—to me it strongly suggests this seal was left by either killer or victim."

"Perhaps the letter it sealed was the reason for the murder!" She bit her lower lip as she thought hard. It was an unexpectedly fetching expression. "Let us see. There is Emma Knightley. Is not Mr. Bertram's Christian name Edmund?"

"It is." Jonathan had a good memory for details. "And I believe Mrs. Wentworth's maiden name was Elliot. If the letter were from someone in her family, it might be sealed so."

"Is there anyone else?"

There was, of course, though Jonathan was loath to confess it. "My mother," he finally said. "She is Elizabeth."

Their eyes met. "Ah," Miss Tilney said. "Well. Then perhaps you know what her seal looks like—"

"This is preposterous." Jonathan turned from her. "My mother is no murderess. She would never stoop to such an act."

He had previously seen their names in Juliet's letter listing suspects but had assumed their inclusion to be a matter of form only. Apparently not.

Miss Tilney stepped into his line of vision, her chin raised. "We said that no one should be excluded from our inquiry."

"I wished only to establish my parents' innocence beyond any doubt. They cannot be guilty." This had to be true. Jonathan knew how much they disliked Wickham—far better than Miss Tilney did—knew they had argued—knew someone had stormed from their bedchamber—but none of that mattered. It could not matter. Jonathan recognized his reasoning to be unnatural, but he also felt his conclusion to be true.

"Be that as it may," she said, maddeningly assured, "their innocence *cannot* be established if you do not carry out the investigation to the fullest of your ability. There is no denying that your parents had the longest acquaintance with Mr. Wickham of anyone here, and the relationship seems to have been one of great strife. Your parents are the natural ones to suspect; the questions must be asked. You must accept that, or else you will never see true."

When Jonathan found himself in difficult, emotional situations, he often lost his composure. Not his temper, the way other men might; he would be overcome with a need for silence and solitude. Once alone, he would rock back and forth, back and forth, until his thoughts made sense again. Until he had done so, he could not speak.

So he turned on his heel and walked away from Juliet Tilney, the candlelight dimming behind him until he was again surrounded by the comforting, concealing dark.

Juliet didn't know whether to feel angry with Jonathan Darcy for his abandonment or sympathetic for the distress their investigation was causing him. It seemed her heart had room for both.

Either way, his behavior rendered him useless to her investigation. And it was hers now, it seemed, rather than theirs. She was on her own.

At first this loss only increased her determination. If young Mr. Darcy considered his family too high and mighty to be questioned, well, then . . .

Well, then virtually every person of gentility would agree with him.

It is fortunate for the servants of Donwell, Juliet decided, *that I am apparently not so genteel.*

Frank Churchill returned the next morning in good cheer—not unseemly but not the match of the somber mood of Donwell Abbey. "Well, well," he said, his voice too loud for the entry hall as he clapped his hands together, "let us get this business done with, hmm? Captain and Mrs. Wentworth, I had thought I might begin with you, as we have some prior acquaintance. Less awkward that way, perhaps?"

Nobody seemed to agree. Mrs. Wentworth, in particular, went rather pale; and her hand grasped for the nearby banister rather than for her husband's arm, though it was equally near. But no one objected either.

Mrs. Wentworth's distress suggested an opportunity. Juliet ventured, "If I might—I would be willing to sit with Mrs. Wentworth while she gives her testimony."

"Indeed," said Mr. Churchill. "Yes, a lady requires support during such vexing moments."

Mrs. Wentworth gave Juliet a timid, grateful smile, one that jabbed a splinter of guilt into her conscience. To stoop to such deception—was it not beneath her?

The alternative, Juliet reminded herself, was likely to be some innocent servant gone to the gallows. A life was worth a small deceit.

Mr. Churchill's interviews took place in Mr. Knightley's study, the most private place in the house and therefore the properest for such work. Anne Wentworth sat in one of the embroidered chairs with Juliet by her side. Befitting the status of a magistrate, Mr. Churchill took the seat at Knightley's desk. Although other chairs remained, Captain Wentworth paced the room—slowly, but still revealing the agitation he attempted to hide.

Anyone suspected of murder would be agitated, Juliet reminded herself. Were she herself among the suspects, she might faint dead away. Yet the particular disturbance of Captain Wentworth impressed upon her strongly.

"Really there's only one question to be asked," Mr. Churchill said. Even now he wore a smile. "Forgive the indelicacy. Did either of you leave your bedchamber between first turning in for the night and hearing Miss Tilney's scream?"

A silence followed—just long enough for excitement to crackle beneath Juliet's skin.

At length Wentworth admitted, "I did. I cannot say the precise hour, but not long before Miss Tilney raised the alarm. Perhaps fifteen minutes, or slightly less."

Mr. Churchill's smile had faded. "For what purpose?"

"Mere restlessness," Mr. Wentworth said as he continued to pace. Truly he was a restless man. "I did not wish to disturb anyone, particularly my wife. So I paced along the hallways. I doubt anyone heard me, as I did take care to be quiet as possible."

"And you heard nothing out of the ordinary?" Mr. Churchill asked. "No odd noises, anything like that? You saw no one else in the hallways?" He seemed still to think of the Wentworths as witnesses rather than potential suspects.

It took Wentworth a few seconds to reply. "Well, I heard a few footsteps. But I kept to the first floor. Anyone could have been about downstairs—as, indeed, someone must have been. I thought little of it until Miss Tilney screamed."

He could have heard the murderer, Juliet thought, *or he heard the final steps of Mr. Wickham—or it might only have been me, rushing to the privy.*

Or he could be lying, attempting to divert our attention to another.

Mr. Churchill then turned to Anne Wentworth; when their eyes met, she gave a small twitch. Juliet offered Mrs. Wentworth her hand. "And you, Mrs. Wentworth?" he asked. "What did you do during this quarter of an hour? Did you leave the room yourself?"

Anne paused a long moment before she shook her head. "Indeed not. There was some noise upstairs, but I saw no need to inquire upon it."

"Did you say 'upstairs'?" Mr. Churchill frowned. "Surely you mean downstairs."

"I mean upstairs, on the second floor," Anne insisted. "It must have been a servant, and probably the sound was unrelated to the gruesome happenings in the gallery below. Regardless, I remained in bed, trying to sleep."

But Jonathan Darcy had seen Mrs. Wentworth at the window. Juliet believed him to be telling the truth.

That meant Mrs. Wentworth was lying.

∽

Jonathan took his place in the hallway near the study, waiting for the others to emerge. He intended to offer himself as a sort of secretary to Mr. Churchill during the investigation—as the only male who could prove his innocence, he was in a good position to undertake such work. It would also give him access to all questioning.

But they'd started earlier than Jonathan had guessed, which meant he had missed this first chance. Regrettable—

Then the study door swung open, and the Wentworths emerged, each of them pale. After them came Mr. Churchill, who sniffed the air with satisfaction. "Who can resist the aroma of coffee?"

Emma Knightley, who stood near the door of the breakfast room, called back, "There is no need to resist! Come, Frank, and help yourself."

Apparently Mr. Churchill saw no reason to keep at the work of a public magistrate when coffee was to be had. He took himself off to the breakfast room just as Juliet Tilney exited the study. Somehow she had contrived to be present during the first questioning. Jonathan had to stifle a smile at her cleverness.

Miss Tilney appeared to have no difficulty not smiling at him. "Mr. Darcy," she said coolly. "I had thought you took no further interest in these goings-on."

"You have misunderstood me," Jonathan replied. "I did not intend—"

He broke off and glanced around the hallway. The Wentworths had gone up the stairs. Nobody else was close.

"Did not intend what?" Miss Tilney said. "To speak further of your parents?"

"They, too, must be considered. I realize this. But . . . it is difficult to think of." How could he explain himself? Jonathan had been taught many different ways of concealing or suppressing his stranger instincts. Yet he found he wished to tell Miss Tilney the truth. "When I am—troubled, or overwhelmed, I have a great need to move about. It's almost as though I cannot think properly until I have done so for a time. I do not know why, but it has always been so, for me."

Her frown was quizzical rather than disapproving. "You mean, to pace around? Like Captain Wentworth so often does?"

Jonathan shook his head. "It helps best to—to—" He felt his cheeks reddening. "To sit down and rock back and forth. As if in a rocking chair. Though any chair will do."

All his life, his habits had been a source of consternation to his parents. To others, they had been cause for contempt. Jonathan's ears still burned with some of the insults that had been hurled at him in school. Miss Tilney either would be bewildered or would laugh at him; his modest hopes were for the former.

Instead, she said, "You need not have left the room to accomplish that. I would not have minded it."

Jonathan wondered if she had misheard him. Or perhaps he was the one who had misheard her? "You would not?"

"It is peculiar, of course," Miss Tilney said, "but my mother has often told me that most people are really very peculiar, once you get to know them. The only difference is in how well we hide our peculiarities. Your habit seems harmless."

"I am well enough," Jonathan said. He did not wish to discuss the subject further at this time or perhaps ever. Welcome though Juliet's acceptance was, it was also unfamiliar. Nor was he certain he could trust it. She spoke without having seen him rock; if he ever dared to do so in front of her, Juliet's reaction might not be what she had expected or promised.

All the same . . . it was encouraging to think that she did not find him silly. That she was at least willing to try.

Dropping his voice, he continued, "Will you talk with me about the Wentworths?"

"Breakfast first," said Miss Tilney, "so that no one will note our behavior as strange, and so we shan't be hungry. It is always disagreeable to think on an empty stomach. After that, I shall reveal all."

❧

The other guests at Donwell Abbey might not have noticed, had Juliet and Jonathan not appeared for breakfast. The meal was not taken with all together at table, so the presence or absence of any individuals at any given moment mattered little.

For instance, no one took any particular note of the absence of Colonel Brandon and his wife.

In their room, Colonel Brandon was taking undue care of his coat, as though he were about to present himself to the king. Marianne, already fully dressed, sat on the edge of the bed weeping.

"You cannot," she pleaded, for the tenth time that morning. "Promise me you will not."

Brandon turned to her, and the pain he saw in her expression echoed within his soul. Even if Marianne did not—could not—love him as she had Willoughby, she cared more deeply for Brandon himself than he had realized. She feared for him so acutely that, for an instant, he considered not going, to spare her feelings.

But his sense of what must be done was even stronger than his compassion. "I must, Marianne. Honor demands no less."

∽

After breakfast, to Jonathan's dismay, his parents were to be the very next guests questioned by Mr. Churchill. His disquiet sprang from two equal sources: one, his natural discomfort with the thought of his parents' involvement in the crime; and, two, the fact that he could not offer himself to Mr. Churchill as a neutral observer. However, his mother unwittingly solved the latter by gesturing to Jonathan that he should come into the study with them, so that they might answer questions together as a family.

No one could solve the former, not until the true guilty party was identified. Jonathan dearly hoped he and Juliet would do this soon.

For the time being, however, he was obliged to take a chair in Mr. Knightley's study, a handsome room that smelled of cigar smoke, old books, and leather. His father sat beside his mother, with Jonathan slightly behind them and to one side. This allowed him to see the comforting hand Father lay on Mother's shoulder.

"It sounds as though the two of you have by far the longest acquaintance with the late Mr. Wickham," said Mr. Churchill.

Jonathan was able to control his fidgeting—barely—as his parents retold the tale. He had not heard it that many times, really, and almost never in the form of one united history. No, his uncle George's past had come in snips and whispers, a muttered aside from his father here, a bitter retort from Aunt Lydia there, a blush from Aunt Georgiana.

The worst of the interview was when they reached the part of the story Jonathan had never been told, because he, too, had lived it—the sad history of his cousin Susannah.

"We had always wanted a daughter, you see, and despite three sons, we were never so blessed," his mother explained. (Jonathan dimly recalled his grandmother insisting that she had been unable to have a son because Elizabeth had taken all the propensity for it with her upon her birth. This did not correlate with anything Jonathan knew of either nature or religion, but such absurdities were not unusual with Grandmama Bennet.) "Whereas my sister and Mr. Wickham remained childless for many years and apparently content to be so. Given their irresponsibility, I believed it a mercy. When at last Lydia was delivered of a little girl, neither she nor Wickham took pleasure in the limitations upon their liberty. At first Lydia made excuses for Susannah to visit us. Then I made the excuses. Her visits, intended to last for weeks, would stretch on for many months. I soon loved her as though she were my own."

Jonathan frowned. His mother had said *I*, rather than *we*. But had they not all loved Susannah?

For an instant he remembered her so vividly she might have been with them, sitting in the window seat, her feet dangling inches above the floor. She'd had a funny, crooked little smile, one that resembled neither her father's nor Lydia's; it had been Susannah's own. Jonathan had never seen another like it and would never see it again.

Grief tightened his throat, but Jonathan pushed it aside. He needed to support his parents in this. They had trouble enough without worrying about him.

Mr. Churchill had grown unusually grave. "But this child—is no longer with you."

"No longer with this world," said Darcy. Jonathan's father might have been carved of stone. "She died of a fever while in Mr. Wickham's keeping."

There was more to this story, but no one spoke the words aloud. Jonathan felt it unnecessary. Even so blithe a fellow as Frank Churchill could not fail to understand the depth of his parents' anger and pain. Reason enough, surely, for murder.

Besides—if Jonathan thought upon it any longer, the guilt would overwhelm him.

Churchill said only, "And were both of you in your bed-chamber on the night of the crime, throughout the evening?"

"Yes," Mother said. "We were."

"Naturally," Father said, endorsing the lie without quite joining in it.

Was Mother lying to protect Father? Or was it the other way around?

Had Churchill asked Jonathan whether he knew anything to the contrary, could he have brought himself to lie? False-hoods were difficult for him.

But Frank Churchill did not ask.

⁓

After hearing the Darcys leave the study, Juliet hastened toward the hallway, eager to intercept Jonathan. Or would he want to be left alone after such a discussion, the better to fidget or whatever it was he did? Juliet wondered whether it would be more polite to allow him the time. If one made allowances for peculiarity, it soon ceased to be peculiar and became ordinary.

Before she could make up her mind, however, she was startled by the sound of the Brandons emerging from the stairwell. Mrs. Brandon was pale, her eyes reddened from recent tears. Colonel Brandon looked scarce better, but determination rang in his voice as he called, "Mr. Churchill?"

Frank Churchill appeared in the study door. "Colonel Brandon, isn't it? I had planned to speak to the both of you later—"

"I would prefer to speak as soon as possible," Brandon replied. "I will conceal no longer my connection with the late Mr. Wickham."

Chapter Nine

Mrs. Brandon's state of agitation was such that Frank Churchill thought it inadvisable to question her. This connection was between Colonel Brandon and Wickham, after all, and young Mrs. Brandon looked as though she might fall down in a faint at any moment. Juliet had great compassion for her friend's distress, but this kindly feeling was sullied by an unseemly interest in Mrs. Brandon's unrestrained speech.

"It was so many years ago," Marianne Brandon said between sniffles, her linen handkerchief a sodden knot in her fist. "My husband wanted only to find Mr. Wickham to give him a chance to know his child—and, now, his grandchild. Who else would ever have been so generous of spirit? He could never have conceived of such a wicked act, not ever—he is too good a man."

"Surely you can absolve him," Juliet ventured. "You can attest that he did not leave his room last night, can you not?"

The pause that followed lasted one second too long. Juliet knew she had made a discovery; Colonel Brandon *had* left his room in the hours before the murder. What else might Marianne know?

Juliet had no opportunity to devise further questions, for Marianne's upset had only increased in intensity. "We are only just wed—are we to be rent asunder so soon? Fate cannot be so cruel, surely, surely—"

Sobs overcame her. Juliet put her arm around Marianne's shoulders, sincerely wishing her comfort. Yet Juliet's head buzzed like her father's beehives, thick with the conjectures inspired by Marianne's confession.

Colonel Brandon still honors his dead love, Juliet thought. *And he left his room on the night in question. But would he truly kill to avenge her now, when so much time has gone by?* According to Marianne, Brandon had never harbored murderous rage toward Wickham even in the past . . . but she could report only what her husband had said. Who could know what had remained unspoken?

Merely to distract Marianne from her woe, Juliet asked, "What was her name? This woman the colonel first loved."

Marianne gulped back another sob. "She was called Eliza."

Juliet remembered the broken wax seal they had found in the gallery. The one stamped with an *E.*

What if that letter had not been a monogram but a reminder? The seal upon a warning Mr. Wickham failed to heed?

❧

The suddenness of Colonel Brandon's revelation had left Jonathan no opportunity to offer himself as secretary to Frank Churchill. He took solace in the adroit way Juliet Tilney had led the colonel's wife aside—no doubt she would contrive to learn more without injury to the trembling Mrs. Brandon.

Jonathan needed to find other ways to occupy the rest of his morning. Although the skies had remained clear since the night of the murder, the grounds were still in a sorry state. Thus there could be no fishing, which was for Jonathan something of a relief. It was one thing to fish when his family ate what he caught—that was a simple matter of living off the land. But most gentlemen fished as they shot, merely to prove their ability. Jonathan could not kill another creature for no reason. Indeed, he found the desire to do so more perplexing than the murder of Mr. Wickham, for which reasons were abundant.

Nor could they yet readily travel into the nearby village of Highbury; the roads would be hard going for a horse and even worse for a carriage. And although the village was within an easy distance, such a walk would produce more mud stains than diversion. The party continued to be left to its own devices for amusement.

Jonathan strolled through Donwell Abbey, considering where to turn. In the library were the Wentworths—the captain on one side of the long, narrow room, and his wife on the other. *Why would two people seek to avoid each other in the same room?* Jonathan mused.

In the music room, his mother sat at the piano, idly plucking out a tune. If Jonathan entered, she would wish to speak with him. He could not imagine what they would talk about—given that he now knew what had gone unsaid to Mr. Churchill. His mother was intelligent and perceptive; might she not guess that he had overheard them in the night, that he knew they had lied?

Then again, his parents might have assumed he was already in the stables with Ebony. Or not. The variables were too plentiful, too disturbing. Jonathan could hardly bear to think of it.

Perhaps a walk along the paths surrounding the house would be diverting, and not too wretchedly muddy. But as Jonathan headed toward the gallery door, Mrs. Bertram dashed ahead of him, nearly running, as no gentlewoman would ever be seen to do. She didn't even appear to see him. He stood there watching as she raced across the damp grasses toward a small outbuilding the Knightleys had previously identified as the old chapel.

I need not fear my odd habits here, Jonathan decided, *for I am far from the only person behaving strangely.*

Edmund Bertram sought his wife throughout Donwell Abbey in vain, before realizing that she would, of course, have gone to seek comfort in the chapel. Fanny's faith shone from her, more constant than the sun, so strongly that even the pious Edmund sometimes felt shamed. A man of the cloth should not be second to his wife in his love of the Savior, but who could help it, if that wife was Fanny?

The chapel dated back to the abbey's papist days and thus was thick with ornament, from the elaborately carved stone walls to the stained glass windows. Edmund had no doubt his ancestors had reconsecrated it to the true faith, and so he could allow himself to enjoy its beauty. Fanny, too, had a weakness for chapels of great age. Surely praying here would have calmed her.

Instead, he found her on her knees, trembling, tears on her cheeks.

When she became aware of his presence, she startled. "Oh, Edmund—if you wish to pray in privacy, I can—"

"I did not come here to seek God but to seek you." Edmund was not a witty man, but he tried sometimes. "It is no great wonder that you should be shaken by the terrible crime that has occurred here. You are a sensitive creature, fragile before the bitter truths of this world. Even so, these past two days, you have been . . . at the point of collapse."

Fanny burst into tears anew. Edmund went to her side and took her hand.

"Tell me," he said. "Whatever it is that has made this particular event so devastating, I wish to know, so that I might better help you."

"Is it not enough that a man has died?" Fanny whispered. "Is it not enough that the mortal sin of murder has been committed?"

Her sobs overtook her, and there was nothing for Edmund to do but put his arm around her shoulders. Eventually he would have the truth of it, but insisting upon the point now would only shatter her further.

Though she had been nearly as upset the night before the murder—when she made that strange request for money—

Edmund folded his wife against his chest and prayed for her solace.

⁊

The servants had made a trudge into Highbury, the better to pick up necessary items and post the guests' many letters. When they returned, Juliet was surprised to see she had received one in return.

"Here you are, ma'am," Hannah said, depositing the folded paper on Juliet's small table. "I hope it will give you some comfort."

When Juliet saw her mother's handwriting, her heart leaped. "I'm sure it will. But they did not send *you* out in this dreadful mud, did they, Hannah?"

"No, ma'am. They sent one of the young lads still boy enough to think of puddles as good fun." Then Hannah's cheeks pinked; that was more than most servants would've shared in such circumstances.

So Juliet made sure to add, "I have brothers enough to know about boys and mud. It is good that he did not find it a chore."

"Indeed, ma'am." Hannah, apparently much relieved, curtsied and left Juliet to her letter reading.

Of course her parents could not yet have learned of the terrible event at Donwell Abbey—even if she *had* addressed her letter correctly—yet she took comfort in simply being able to read her mother's words. Despite her sincere eagerness to determine the killer, she did feel a little in need of comfort. Not that she had any intention of telling Jonathan Darcy.

Juliet read:

> *Dearest daughter,*
> *By now you will have an entirely new set of*
> *acquaintance—one almost entirely separate from your*
> *father's and my own, though I pray you will send*
> *Mrs. Knightley my compliments. You are a bright,*
> *capable girl, unlikely to be as overcome as I was on my*
> *first long trip away from home.*

Juliet had heard the story of her parents' courtship many times, though only recently had she been deemed old enough to know the full truth. They expected her to be scandalized or even wounded that her mother had once thought her grandfather Tilney capable of murdering her grandmother. In truth, Juliet's grandfather had always terrified her, and she'd had to pretend to be more surprised by their anecdote than she truly was.

The next paragraphs caught her up on the news of home, Theodosia's and Albion's doings, the death of an elderly neighbor, her aunt Eleanor's impending trip to Scotland—a place so far away it might have been the moon. But at the close, Catherine Tilney gave better advice to her daughter than she could ever have known when writing it.

> *When making new friends, pay less attention to what*
> *people say of themselves, more attention to how they*
> *behave. Truth is not in the telling but in the doing.*
> *Above all, I urge you to make this visit a study of*
> *human nature. It is the one tool of the novelist that is*

useful in day-to-day life—one that helps us interpret the hidden depths behind even the most ordinary circumstances.

Juliet believed her current circumstances to be rather extraordinary. But her mother's point remained true. This was what she and Jonathan were doing—not merely seeking out a killer but also learning how to look beneath the polite exteriors everyone presented to the world.

⁓

When Miss Tilney put this to Jonathan later, as they stole a moment in the billiard room, his first emotion was dismay. "I'm not very good at that. At reading people. You see, I keep expecting them to say what they mean. Mother insists almost no one ever does this, but I don't understand why."

"One cannot speak openly of *everything*," Miss Tilney said. "If one did, it would expose others to all manner of rudeness."

Jonathan frowned. "But many things we call *rude* are only so because it is supposedly wrong to speak of them. Thus we cannot talk about them because we cannot talk about them. It is a reflexive statement, no more, and I have never been able to discern any moral grounds for most such omissions." His parents had instilled manners in him, but they had been able to improve his behavior more than his comprehension.

"Yours is a valid point, sir, but not critical to our investigation. We must keep to our efforts. Perhaps we will learn the knack of understanding people's hidden motives through this exercise." Miss Tilney sighed. "We have both heard the tale of Colonel Brandon's past, and how it intersected with Mr. Wickham's. I feel certain from Mrs. Brandon's hesitations that her husband did, in fact, leave his room in the hour before the murder. This puts rather a different light on matters, don't you think?"

Jonathan agreed. "So far as I could see, the colonel spoke with measured civility, but even so, he was clearly distressed by the events of so long ago."

"Or of events not so long ago."

"Yet . . . I do not think him the killer," Jonathan said. "His motives are clear, but why confess them if he were guilty? No one present had any inkling of it, save for his wife, and thus he could have continued to elude suspicion. His action strikes me as one of great honesty."

Apparently Miss Tilney was a less trusting creature than himself. "What better way to avoid suspicion than to convincingly create the illusion of honesty?"

"Is that truly what you believe he has done?"

"I know not yet what to believe."

Jonathan found it easy to keep his thoughts upon the potential guilt of Colonel Brandon, to seek true conviction of that belief. Anything was easier than recalling how his parents had lied about their actions on the night of the murder . . . or what those lies might mean.

∽

Darcy observed his son walking through the corridors of Donwell Abbey with young Miss Tilney, a development he noted with interest.

Jonathan faced the same difficulty his father had during his bachelorhood, namely, a deluge of females whose ardor knew no bounds when it came to the Darcy wealth, while having little feeling for the actual man. Alas, Jonathan had no aptitude for discerning insincerity—but awkwardness had protected him as surely as discernment ever could. The greedy girls who swarmed around him at the beginning of a ball usually walked away afterward with expressions of either irritation or bewilderment. On the other hand, the rapport between Jonathan and Miss Tilney appeared genuine, and the girl did not strike Darcy as a fortune hunter. She neither flirted nor simpered. Yet what a time to have formed such a connection! Darcy hoped their shared interests did not run to the macabre. Young people could be so heedless—so headstrong—in their first romances. Georgiana had proved that beyond any doubt. Darcy profoundly hoped Jonathan would not take after his aunt.

It was as yet far too early to question his son on such a matter. He would withhold judgment on Miss Tilney . . . for now.

That, however, left Darcy alone with his thoughts of Mr. Wickham's fate. Those were thoughts he preferred to turn from, but they followed him as resolutely as a foxhound pursued a vixen.

He walked toward the music room and the sound of the piano. The tune was one of Elizabeth's favorite songs, played in her characteristic style. Always he had loved to hear her play.

Once she had loved for him to hear her. When Elizabeth had looked up from her music and her bewitching eyes would meet his—not once had that failed to enchant him, not in all their twenty-two years of marriage.

She never looked up from her playing any longer. Not since Susannah's death. His footsteps were something she pretended not to hear.

At the door of the music room, Darcy hesitated. He wanted to be with his wife. But he also wanted to feel that she wanted to be with him. If he went to her now, she would only pretend not to hear him again. He didn't think he could bear it.

So he walked away, listening to his wife's song as it faded behind him.

~~~

The Knightleys had decided to serve dinner as usual, and to continue as normally as possible henceforth. "We may not be as merry a party as we would wish," Emma said, with some degree of understatement, "but a house party we still are and shall remain. Let us console ourselves as best we can with good food and good conversation."

A house party we must *remain,* Juliet thought but did not say. The inescapability of their situation only testified to the wisdom of Mrs. Knightley's approach. If they could not depart, better to make the best of it.

Besides, she reasoned, as normal routines resumed, she would be better able to judge the behavior of those around her. One could not truly glimpse the extraordinary without the contrast of the ordinary as a guide.

Dinner did not yet fully conform to usual custom. While everyone came down appropriately attired, ability to engage as before was highly varied. Anne Wentworth made polite chitchat that Emma Knightley parried with real wit. Mr. Knightley, too, appeared to be only slightly less animated than he had been that first night. Was that a sign of their innocence? Or was it a proof that the murder had not been, for them, all that troubling?

The most obviously disquieted individuals were Fanny Bertram, Captain Wentworth, and Marianne Brandon. Mrs. Brandon appeared only slightly less heartbroken than she had that morning when Juliet consoled her. Her cheeks remained flushed from recent tears, and her eyes kept darting toward her husband, almost as if she dared not look away from him for long. Wentworth, on the other hand, seethed with a palpable anger. Had murder been insufficient to vent his rage? Yet even they presented a better front than did Mrs. Bertram. She trembled so that her fork clattered against the china enough that wine spilled from her glass. Her skin remained ghostly pale. Juliet wondered whether she should ask the Knightleys to call for a physician. Undoubtedly Mrs. Bertram's troubles were not of a physical nature, but at least a doctor might give her a draft of something to help the poor woman sleep.

Surely she cannot be the killer, Juliet thought. *Mrs. Bertram wouldn't say "boo" to a goose. But then why has this affected her so? Her husband seems to have no motive and is behaving in an ordinary manner—so why is she greatly agitated?*

She seems no more like a murderer than . . . than anybody else at Donwell Abbey. At least one of whom is indeed guilty.

"The ground is drying out at last," Mr. Knightley said. "I am informed that the roads will be passable within another day or two, should the fair weather hold. If so, we must go into Highbury. It is but a small village, with no more than the usual amusements, but surely you are all ready for some manner of variety."

Everyone brightened—save for Mrs. Bertram, who stared down at her plate with fresh tears in her eyes. Juliet glanced across the table at Jonathan Darcy to make sure he saw it, too. He nodded at her, then quickly raised his glass as though to take wine with her. She copied the motion.

How clever of him to disguise their interaction, so that if anyone noticed, they would think little of it! *He may be a very peculiar young man,* Juliet thought, *but truly, he is no simpleton.*

❧

Jonathan did not allow any valet to undress him beyond assistance with coat and boots. His father did the same, preferring his own ways of doing things; Jonathan followed his example mostly because he had no idea what else might be appropriate. It worked well enough.

As he untied his cravat, he thought of Juliet Tilney at dinner. She had hazel eyes of uncommon brilliance, perhaps because of the intelligence they communicated. She displayed greater powers of rational judgment than many of the young men he had encountered at university. It struck him that it would make more sense to educate her than half the members of his class, as there was a far higher probability the information would be absorbed.

A shout pierced the nighttime silence. Jonathan startled, crumpling the cravat in his hands. That had been a man's voice—but whose?

He dashed into the hallway, as did others—all the men of the party, with Mrs. Knightley and Miss Tilney quick behind. "What is it?" called Knightley. "Speak!"

The silence afterward lasted only seconds, but long enough for Jonathan to wonder if he and Juliet had been wrong, whether an intruder had killed here once and now come again. But then the reply came from upstairs. "It is Wesley, sir. Come quickly, you must see!"

"Wesley?" Captain Wentworth muttered as they all went for the stairs.

"One of our footmen," Knightley replied, "a solid lad. He would not raise the alarm without cause."

Jonathan glanced back to see whether the women remained with them. Mrs. Knightley had unquestioned right to investigate, as this was her home, but would anyone have stopped Miss Tilney? Nobody had. Though it struck him as odd how Colonel Brandon followed so slowly, behind everyone else, as if he did not wish to see what might be ahead.

Or did he already know?

On the second floor, their candlelight illuminated young

Wesley, who stood shaking in the hallway. He pointed to a door just off the stairs, one that stood ajar. "That was the room Mr. Wickham used," he said. "No one had disturbed it—in case Mr. Churchill should wish to look within, you see? But one of the younger housemaids forgot and opened the door and found this."

Mr. Knightley pushed the door wide open and held up his candle. There they could see the room in disarray, with clothes strewn on the floor, papers scattered across every flat surface, even the covers of the bed pulled back.

"There is no way to know what may or may not be missing," Mr. Knightley said. "But I suspect that if something has been taken, it was something very pertinent to Mr. Churchill's investigation."

Jonathan's and Juliet's eyes met with mutual chagrin. The motive for the murder might have been behind this door all along—and someone had beaten them to it.

Chapter Ten

Jonathan Darcy pushed through the group toward the front to get a good view of Wickham's room. Only after doing so did he recall that his status as an investigator was both wholly self-appointed and unknown to all the others, save Juliet Tilney. But no one stopped him or looked askance. Perhaps they were too caught up in their own reactions to worry about his.

Wickham had been assigned a room far less grand than any of the invited guests'. It was, in fact, one of the many rooms generally set aside for the servants of visiting guests. Although the servants' quarters at Donwell Abbey were better appointed than most, they remained humble. The room was long but extremely narrow, with a sharply slanted ceiling, and furnished with only a narrow bed and a capacious but battered wardrobe. One small window looked out on the back of the house—the stables, if Jonathan had reckoned rightly. The blankets on the bed were clearly not new, but they were thick enough to ward off any chill; and the small washstand was an amenity most servants would crave.

(Jonathan had talked more to servants than most people of his class because it had never occurred to him not to do so. His parents had finally convinced him to have such conversations only when those of his own station were not present, but this still allowed many opportunities to learn interesting things. Servants were refreshingly frank about many realities of existence, in his opinion.)

It did not matter that this room was an excellent example of its sort. At least, it would not have mattered to George Wickham. Jonathan knew his uncle well enough to understand that he would have been humiliated to stay here. Even enraged. The barest suggestion that he deserved less than any other man—regardless of that other man's status, behavior, or labor—had always incensed him. Aunt Lydia used to try to make jokes to jolly her husband out of such moods, which could be sparked by incidents as commonplace as someone riding by in a finer carriage, one with a coat of arms on the door.

My uncle may not have been entirely innocent in his final, fatal encounter, Jonathan realized. *There may have been an ugly incident of which he was the instigator.*

Certainly no one had offered any hint of why Mr. Wickham might be in the gallery after midnight.

The answer to that question might provide the answer to many others . . .

❧

Juliet envied the boldness with which Jonathan Darcy was able to work his way into the room. The same daring considered natural in a young man would be found bizarre for a young woman, so she had to inch forward more slowly. As she did so, she listened carefully, taking note of every word.

"The place has been ransacked," Mr. Knightley said. "Dear G-d, look at it. Every drawer emptied upon the floor."

"Nothing is broken," offered young Mr. Darcy. "This was not done in a wild rage. This was done with clear intent."

Mr. Knightley sounded more put out than shocked. "A robbery, no doubt. And there, I think, we must look to our own staff, loath though I am to suspect them. But none of you would have reason to steal from such a man."

Juliet, almost at the door, could keep silent no longer. "Perhaps the robbery was not one intended to enrich the thief," she said. "Perhaps it was intended to conceal the purpose of Mr. Wickham's murder."

That made Mr. Knightley startle—she could see him now, pale and tense next to the wardrobe—but almost no one else reacted. She had not been the only one to draw that conclusion, simply the one who spoke it aloud.

"We cannot know that," Mr. Knightley finally replied. "I would not wish to draw overly ambitious conclusions."

The elder Mr. Darcy spoke then, unexpectedly forceful. "Then let us search the room. It may be that something very obvious is missing—or that something is present which should not be. Any information would provide further insight to Mr. Churchill in his deliberations."

"Insofar as anything is capable of providing insight to Frank Churchill," muttered Mr. Knightley so quietly that only Juliet could hear. More loudly he added, "Yes, let us look."

Darcy, his son, and Knightley began searching the room immediately; Juliet started but a fraction of a second behind them. She was aware of the elder Mr. Darcy glancing at her most pointedly between his rifling through Wickham's papers. No doubt this was an inappropriate task for a young girl. But no rules of etiquette covered a situation such as this.

The wardrobe had been opened, and everything inside lay upon the floor. But the contents appeared to be old linen repurposed as cleaning cloths and a handful of unused servants' uniforms, sewing scraps like bits of lace and inches of gold braid—nothing of Mr. Wickham's, which made sense. "Mr. Wickham did not realize he would be staying overnight at Donwell Abbey," she murmured. "So he would have had with him only such possessions as he might carry on horseback."

"Naturally," the elder Mr. Darcy replied. His tone suggested that she must think him an idiot not to have realized as much himself. This meant he had missed her point.

Though it took great courage to speak again, given his icy demeanor, Juliet persisted. "That means the robbery must be connected to the murder, must it not?"

Knightley cut her off. "Perhaps. As yet, we do not even know that it *is* a robbery."

Jonathan Darcy took up the traveling case that had been his uncle's. The papers that had evidently been stored within it lay scattered about. Juliet saw several lists of what appeared to be monies owed to Mr. Wickham—debts he would now never collect. If money was the motive for Mr. Wickham's murder, then would not these have been taken or destroyed?

The group at the doorway had become restive. It appeared that the others no longer wished to stay but were waiting for some sort of cue that would allow them to leave. Colonel Brandon, who stood directly in front of the door, held up his candle like Diogenes, his expression grave.

Knightley joined the elder Mr. Darcy in examining the papers, sorting through them, unconsciously pushing her out. Juliet knew she had been unseemly, joining in this search, but worse was the thought that her action might have been futile. She began checking the bedcovers, which remained undisturbed; Mr. Wickham had never settled down for that final night's sleep. This was more to give Juliet some occupation than an earnest search, which was why it surprised her when her fingers found something small and hard between the bed frame and the mattress.

"What is this?" Juliet lifted it up, and her eyes widened. "A *ring?*"

Instantly Knightley and Darcy were at her side. Carefully Knightley took the ring from her. It was small and delicate, clearly a woman's ring. The smooth golden band was narrow, and at the center was a modest amethyst.

It is not the ring of a Mrs. Knightley or a Mrs. Darcy, Juliet realized. *It is a humbler ornament—unless, perhaps, it is from girlhood and has sentimental value.*

"This was not Mr. Wickham's," Knightley said. "Did he take it from one of you ladies?"

Nobody replied.

"Collateral on a loan, from one of his many debtors," the elder Mr. Darcy ventured.

Mrs. Knightley had moved forward, perhaps so that Juliet would no longer be the only woman in the room. Her attention was diverted, however, by one of the papers. "This is—my dear, this is your handwriting, is it not?"

She picked up one sheet from Wickham's papers and held it out for Mr. Knightley's review. Juliet sat close enough to read one of the larger words at the top: *Surety.*

"Indeed it is." Mr. Knightley squared his shoulders, clearly gathering strength. "Undoubtedly you all deserve to know: It was not only my brother endangered by Wickham's scheme. At John's request, I . . . I signed a surety guaranteeing his debt. Wickham had not yet enforced it upon me, but I have no doubt that he came here to do precisely that."

A few moments of silence followed, the air dense with unspoken words. Juliet glanced over at Jonathan Darcy, knowing his thoughts must be like her own: Mr. Knightley's motive to harm Mr. Wickham was even stronger than they had thought.

At the present time, however, the most murderous person in the room seemed to be Mrs. Knightley, who was looking *daggers* at her husband.

The elder Mr. Darcy, from either tact or a desire to preserve Mr. Knightley's life, spoke next. "What is missing from this room is likely to tell more than what is present. I propose that we leave everything in its place, close and lock the door, and allow Mr. Churchill and the constables to examine it in the morning."

No more searching tonight. Juliet could not deny feeling disappointed.

∽

We are becoming rather accustomed to seeing each other in our night-clothes, Jonathan thought. When he had been a small boy, and reluctant to wear clothing at all, his mother had suggested that if people outside the immediate family were to see them in anything but perfect dress, society itself would break down. Either she had been incorrect or the breakdown was even now in progress. To Jonathan, both seemed equally plausible.

"It has to have been a robbery," insisted Captain Wentworth, as the half-dressed group descended the stairs, destined for their separate bedchambers. "Regardless of what Mr. Knightley thinks—with respect, Mrs. Knightley."

Mrs. Knightley was holding on to her temper, but barely. "Our servants are honest," she said, her words clipped, "and none of us has any reason to steal from anybody, much less George Wickham."

"He had very little with him at the time," Jonathan felt obliged to point out. "There would be nothing to steal but records, which were not stolen—"

"So far as we know." Wentworth's voice had steel within it. This was a man used to giving orders that were instantly obeyed. Mrs. Wentworth glanced up at him, but in the darkness Jonathan could not read her expression. "But he seems to have believed some of his possessions had value. Otherwise, why would he have hidden the ring?"

This was an excellent point, one Jonathan wished he had

arrived at himself. A glance at Juliet Tilney revealed that she shared his chagrin and his interest.

Wentworth's conclusion is wrong, of that I am sure, Jonathan decided. *This was no robbery. But there is some strangeness regarding the ring yet to be deciphered.*

And Captain Wentworth is far too insistent. Why should he so badly want us to believe him?

✌

Sleep had understandably been a resource in short supply at Donwell Abbey since the night of the murder. Unfamiliar beds alone steal slumber from some. The far more troublesome events of recent days had proved more than sufficient to induce insomnia in all.

Who the most dismayed among the party could be, no one could say. (Well. One *could* say, but had not.) But it was most certain that Mr. Knightley would be the first to face the Furies. One Fury, in particular.

On many occasions before their marriage, and some since, Emma's husband had been angry with her. Civil as he was even when angered, she always found this difficult to bear, largely because his displeasure had always been richly deserved. Despite the inevitable frictions of marriage, Knightley had never truly angered her the same way. This she had attributed to his greater age and experience and to her own meddlesome nature.

Now, however, it felt as though she had saved every ounce of anger of which she was capable—all for this very moment.

"You signed a surety for John's debt?" Emma demanded as she followed Knightley into their bedroom and shut the door behind them. He would not be allowed to retreat. "Without ever telling me?"

"What would you have had me do, Emma?" His tone

suggested she was the one in the wrong, which made her even more enraged, a state of emotion she would have considered impossible only seconds prior. "Leave John and Isabella to be turned out into the street?"

"Hartfield is theirs! It is just on the other side of that grove! They were never in any danger of being thrown out upon the streets!"

Knightley did not acknowledge her point. "Their reputations were—and are—at stake. John's standing as a lawyer hangs in the balance, as does their very respectability as a family."

"So you gambled with our respectability instead?" Emma demanded. "You knew you should not have done it, because if you did not doubt yourself, you would have told me about it at the time. But you hid it. Secrecy is beneath you—or I believed it was."

She almost wished she had not said it, because for the first time ever, she saw shame upon his face. Her wife's heart felt that pain as if it were her own. Did she not understand why Knightley had tried so hard to help John and Isabella? Had he come to her, would she not ultimately have agreed that they must do all they could?

But he had not come to her. Though Emma's heart belonged to Knightley, her head remained her own.

"You scold *me* for meddling and matchmaking," she said. "For playing games with the happiness of others. Yet you played a game with our happiness—a game that, but for Mr. Wickham's death, might well have ruined us."

With that Emma got into bed, drew the covers up almost over her head, and stared at the far wall. After long moments of silence, Knightley followed. Her eyes pricked with tears as he blew out the candle, returning them to darkness.

⁓

"Jonathan seems greatly interested in these goings-on," Darcy said as he and his wife reentered their bedchamber. The flickering light from the candle she held did not fully reveal her countenance. "His interests tend to become all-consuming."

Elizabeth half turned. Her eyebrow arched in a way he had learned to be wary of. "Jonathan is hardly morbid. He has grown to be a kind man, even if he does not always know how to express his kindness."

Darcy inclined his head, acknowledging this. In truth his son was almost *too* kind—innocent, in a way, far behind his years—and he seemed likely to be taken advantage of, were he not eventually taught caution. Perhaps Jonathan's fascination with Wickham's demise would teach him more of the darker truths of the world. It would be unwise to object, so long as Jonathan's behavior remained proper.

Juliet Tilney had no such excuse, but Darcy might make allowances in such a young person whose parents could not possibly have thought to instruct her on this specific circumstance. These events would have unsettled persons far more stoic than the average seventeen-year-old girl.

Elizabeth ventured, "Have you written to Georgiana? To inform her of Wickham's death?"

Darcy had not. It seemed to him better to tell Georgiana in person. Not only could he then do so gently, taking his cues from her reaction, but that also meant no danger of her sneak of a husband finding the letter. If his sister had never felt the need to disclose her youthful errors in judgment to the earl of Dorchester, Darcy did not intend to reveal them now.

Wickham's death. The words returned to Darcy's mind as he lay beside Elizabeth. Her back was turned to him, as it had been too many nights these past eight months. Of late he had thought it was time to persuade her to his side; he'd even thought fondly of the way she slept with her head on his shoulder, when they were young and in the first raptures of married love. But this evening he could not concentrate even on so tender a matter as this.

Once again, George Wickham demanded his due from Darcy.

We played together as boys, Darcy had once told Elizabeth. Those words were a small, plain box for something large and complicated, an inadequate container for the whole of a childhood. Darcy's father, as good and wise a parent as could be imagined, had nonetheless had a large estate to run and no bent toward games or fun. Darcy's mother had gentled and warmed the interiors of Pemberley, an ideal contrast to her husband's noble bearing. Yet her health had never been strong. This meant that young Fitzwilliam had been left with far too much time to wander about, getting into trouble.

George Wickham was *so good* at getting into trouble! Darcy remembered laughing with joy as they stole down to the fishpond in the middle of the day. Wickham had been laughing, too. But while Darcy's happiness had sprung from the warmth of the sun and the sense of adventure, Wickham's had been entirely a matter of thinking himself smarter than their fathers or Darcy's tutor.

Or so Darcy remembered it. Perhaps that was not fair. Wickham's glee in deceiving others had been a cardinal aspect of his adult character, but as a boy—was it not possible that at least some small part of their friendship had been true?

It was the first time in many years, very nearly the first time at all, that Darcy had allowed himself to remember Wickham as his friend—to recall the time when Wickham had been very nearly as dear to him as his parents or Georgiana.

It was the first time he had thought of the dead body found downstairs not as that of his enemy but of the little boy who had shared his childhood.

Darcy turned over, closing his eyes tightly, willing back his unwelcome sorrow and guilt. As such, he did not see Elizabeth glance over her shoulder at him in gentle hope, nor witness that hope fading from her eyes.

Neither Anne nor Frederick Wentworth had come near returning to their bed.

"You left our room that night," Wentworth said, again pacing. "You say you saw nothing?"

"Nothing," Anne repeated, not for the first time.

His dark eyes burned into hers with an intensity—even an anger—she had not seen in him since he had returned to Uppercross that last winter before they reunited. "If you saw anything, anything at all, even if you do not understand it, I demand to know."

Demand. Anne's temper, generally placid to a fault, sparked near to anger. As he continued his endless pacing, she had half a mind to stick out a foot and trip him.

Then she wondered at herself. Did Frederick not need her kindness now more than ever?

Anne could scarcely blame him for having questions—or having guessed that she had lied. Nor could she share the truth of her actions on that night; the indelicacy of it all shocked her deeply and might be altogether too much for her husband to bear in his current state of mind.

"Nothing," she said again.

Either Frederick was finally satisfied or his mind had simply seized upon another source of anger. "The news of this will spread across half of England," he said. "It will soon reach Somersetshire, no doubt, if it has not already. How they will crow over our misfortunes at Kellynch Hall!"

"Indeed not," Anne replied, "for my family will be too concerned that *our* proximity to the murder may reflect poorly on *them*."

The truth of her words could not be denied, though they did little to calm Frederick's temper. "Their damnable pride haunts us even now."

It haunts you, Anne thought. *But it has so little to do with us. Why can you not see it?*

Yet she knew why. Despite the increase in her husband's fortunes during the war, which had given him greater acceptability as a suitor, Sir Walter Elliot and his other two daughters had never seen him as entirely their equal, nor would they unless fate somehow mysteriously granted Wentworth a title. The Elliots' snubs had been small but constant throughout the years. Anne, who had never been properly valued by her family, had long since numbed herself to their insults.

Frederick had not. She'd never blamed her husband for this; in truth, it warmed her heart that he would stand up for himself and for her. He had always been the more courageous of them.

What Anne had failed to glimpse before was the extent to which Frederick Wentworth's courage was supported by his fortune. Without it, his old self-doubts had returned, and worse for their reappearance. They nagged at him, ruined his temper, and sparked his fury.

He is not behaving like himself any longer, Anne thought, *not at all.*

Then again, nor am I.

⟋

Marianne Brandon lay in her bed, weeping brokenly. So she had cried herself to sleep ever since Wickham's death. Her husband was reminded of the first days after her cruel abandonment by Mr. Willoughby. Her misery was very nearly as complete now as it had been then—and then, her woe had broken her health and very nearly killed her.

This cannot be the consequence, Brandon thought. *Anything but this.*

"Marianne," he murmured. "You must rally."

The sound that emerged was neither laugh nor sob. "Rally. From this? I cannot. You know I cannot."

It was too much for her, sensible as she was.

If only he could comfort her! But Brandon felt himself well aware of his limitations in this area. His quiet temperament had not taught him how to handle a more tempestuous one.

No doubt Willoughby would have had better instincts here. Feckless and selfish though the man could be, his love for Marianne had been genuine. Their spirits had been more in harmony. Brandon knew himself to be Marianne's consolation rather than her prize. Was it enough for her?

He had convinced himself that it was enough for him. No doubt he had been wrong.

༄

He knew. She knew that he knew. Surely Edmund would speak. But he did not. They went back to bed without one word about the extraordinary circumstances that had roused them earlier. Every other night of their stay at Donwell, Edmund had opined at length about the dangers of unsuitable acquaintance, suggesting that all those entrapped by Wickham must share some part of the blame. Fanny had protested that this was unfair on that first night, before Wickham had found William's letter. Since then she had remained silent. Edmund generally accepted silence as an answer and did not press her. Before, she had considered this a kindness. Now it felt like torture.

He could not have failed to recognize the amethyst ring he had given her two birthdays past. It was so precious to her that she had kept it with her every single day since, wearing it more often than not, her most treasured symbol of their love.

Had Edmund believed Wickham to have stolen the ring, he would've said so immediately. Perhaps he had waited for her to do so. But she had not, which meant that Edmund must by now have realized the truth: Fanny had given the ring to Wickham.

And he would not ask her why.

What must he think of me? Fanny hid her face in her pillow, hot tears mixing with the cool damp spots left by her soggy collar. *Yet I must let him think it, or else—*

Or else she would have to reveal the full truth, a possibility too terrible to imagine.

❦

Juliet Tilney, alone among the company, felt energized.

If there had been nothing to discover within Wickham's room, she reasoned as she sat atop her bedcovers, *then the guilty person would not have bothered searching it and risking exposure.* But there was no saying what that important *something* might be, nor whether the ransacker had found it.

With real satisfaction she recalled holding up that ring. What might its meaning be? It was a fine ring, not priceless but too valuable for Wickham to have kept it purely for sentimental reasons. He did not strike Juliet as a man likely to sacrifice profit for sentiment.

Everyone had seen her searching. No doubt some of them disapproved, but they would be less surprised at her taking part in similar efforts in future. That would make her investigations easier . . .

Juliet's stomach dropped as she wondered—*Does the guilty party now know I am investigating?*

She did not think the murder of Mr. Wickham to be an act of purely homicidal madness. He had been killed for a purpose, and that purpose was unlikely to be furthered by any additional deaths, including her own.

But she locked her bedroom door, just in case.

Chapter Eleven

Jonathan preferred to be indoors rather than out, as a rule. One could predict what would happen indoors, to a reassuring extent. Nature was more capricious.

So he was surprised to find that the return of fine weather had lifted his spirits. He walked out before breakfast to check in on Ebony again. The sun shone down on Donwell's beautifully appointed grounds, and in the distance, on rolling fields thick with still-green barley. Although the day promised to be warm, it would not be uncomfortably so. For the first time since the Darcys' arrival in Surrey, summer made its presence known.

The roads look almost passable, Jonathan thought, assessing from the path on which he walked. Mud had kept the company from church on this fine Sunday, but it appeared this would be the end of their enforced confinement. *This means people will soon begin to travel into the nearby village.* It was a troubling prospect. The general (and, to Jonathan, inexplicable) hunger for variety would drive everyone out of the great house sooner rather than later. "Everyone" would include the guilty party. If that guilty party took along whatever it was that might've been stolen from Wickham's room, this item could then be discarded safely away from prying eyes. As the owner of one pair of these prying eyes, he wished there was some way to prevent this. None came to mind.

If breakfast provided the opportunity, he decided, he would ask Juliet Tilney. She possessed an enterprising mind.

As Jonathan turned the corner of the house that would lead him to the stables, he saw that he was not the only one in the mood for a morning stroll. Colonel Brandon walked slowly along one of the footpaths, dressed appropriately save for a battered, unfashionable hat with a wide brim, suitable for shading from the sun. Jonathan had such a hat at home himself, but his parents always discouraged him from wearing it, even when no strangers were present to witness. Thus he felt a moment of connection to the colonel, as well as an admiration for the man's practicality.

"Good morning, Colonel," Jonathan called out.

Colonel Brandon had been facing in Jonathan's direction, yet he startled. Apparently he had been so deep in thought that he had failed to perceive Jonathan not twenty-five feet away from him. Nonetheless, he answered civilly. "Good morning, Mr. Darcy. A fine morning, is it not?"

"Very fine indeed." Jonathan wondered whether it would be appropriate to compliment the colonel's hat. Possibly not.

"Checking the roads, I imagine." Colonel Brandon's smile was faint. "Young men are so often anxious to be coming and going."

This was no very accurate description of Jonathan's character, but such a contradiction would be rude. *When in doubt,* his mother always said, *be brief and polite. This may not always be the best response, but it will never be the worst.* So he said, "I am going to the stables, you see, to check on our horses. You are very welcome to join me."

The colonel gave him a look, and it occurred to Jonathan that stables—earthy, smelly reminders of nature in all its coarseness—were not generally considered polite meeting places. But then Brandon smiled. "I believe I shall. Our horses should be looked after, too."

Of course, the stable boys of Donwell Abbey had taken

exquisite care of all the horses. Their stables were clean and airy, and its guests were busily munching on their morning mash. Mr. Knightley's small black-and-white dog sat upon a small haystack, watching all with great interest. Jonathan went to Ebony right away, and she whickered at him in welcome. (His father dismissed such ideas, but Jonathan felt sure that Ebony greeted him from time to time.)

Colonel Brandon nodded toward Ebony. "She is a favorite, I take it."

Jonathan nodded. "My parents say I think of her too much like a pet." Was that admission too much?

Not, it seemed, for Brandon. "Do not be ashamed of caring for another creature. Would that the world contained more such feeling, rather than less."

This was encouraging. "Do you have a favorite among your horses?"

"Yes, but he is at home, resting a sore hoof. The groom says he will heal well enough." Brandon absently stroked the muzzle of his chestnut stallion. "Yet I worry. It is always difficult, leaving those we care for behind."

❧

Emma Knightley stood at the window of her husband's study, ostensibly watching for Frank Churchill. This was not the best vantage point in the house for sighting a rider approaching. It was, however, the best place to lay in wait for Knightley.

He had risen early this morning, before dawn, probably to meet with some of his tenant farmers. The weather had prevented such meetings for several days, and undoubtedly there would be much news of how various fields and crops had fared. Yet Emma suspected Knightley had taken even more care not to wake her today, in order to avoid a repeat of their last uncomfortable conversation.

She did not wish to repeat it either. Nor, however, did she wish to forget it. There was one point she had to make to him immediately. If Knightley heeded her—*for once*—then perhaps they might avoid the worst.

His footsteps approached the study door, and Emma turned to see him come in. As she'd expected, he'd been on the farms; his boots were muddier than a gentleman's should be. Despite everything, he smiled at the sight of her—a blessing, Emma knew, in a marriage of many years, particularly at such a time as this. However, she was about to put an end to smiles for a while.

Without preamble, she asked, "Are you going to tell Frank Churchill about the surety? Or have you already done so?"

"I have not," Knightley said. "I did not intend to conceal it, but . . . it was altogether too easy to think of reasons that it was not the right time to tell him."

"You must tell him today," Emma insisted. "Otherwise he will decide we are guilty, because we hid the truth from him."

Knightley scoffed. "Frank Churchill has no business scolding anyone else for hiding the truth. A secret engagement, of all the—"

"That was more than fifteen years ago, and no one will accept that as an excuse!"

"Dearest Emma, I do not intend to offer it as one." He paused then, more vulnerable before her than he had been in a while. "Such concealment was not the act of a gentleman. I told myself that—that I was only refusing to complicate matters further by introducing information that might confuse his deductions. Instead, I ought to have remembered how very easy it is to justify acting exactly as we wish. When Churchill arrives today, he shall have the full truth from me."

This was what Emma knew to be right and just. It was what she had come here to argue for. But now that it had been granted, she was not without some dismay. "Are there . . . other records of your surety?"

"I would assume so. Wickham was far too much of a blackguard to let anyone escape his snares too easily. Still, I cannot be certain."

Emma sighed. "A pity last night's thief didn't take that copy with him."

"My contrary wife, you cannot argue for justice in one breath and then hope for the disappearance of evidence with the next," he said.

"Indeed I can, if it keeps our home safe." After a second more, she added, with greater feeling, "If it keeps *you* safe."

"I only meant to tease." Knightley's smile was both kind and—Emma could tell—relieved. "I cannot blame you for wishing the debt gone by such convenient means, and I know you meant no harm."

She had not entirely forgiven him. But the larger danger hovering over Donwell Abbey forced her to see her husband's folly as only one part of a very complicated conundrum. Emma felt sure others saw the problems, and the possibilities. "Others might have had the same idea as I—and we were not the only ones present indebted to Mr. Wickham."

"To be sure," Knightley agreed. "Today, when Frank goes through Wickham's possessions with the constables, we may discover that particular truth for ourselves. You have surprised me, Emma."

She felt her cheeks flush with heat. "That I am so mercenary, you mean? To think of such a thing?"

Knightley shook his head. "No doubt that is how I should react. But I do not. Instead, I find you most . . . enterprising. I hope we are not mutually discovering our criminal natures."

Emma was unsure how to respond to this and was saved from the necessity by the person she glimpsed through the window. "Oh, and here is Frank now. In his carriage, no less—

the roads must be much improved. Thank goodness we shall soon be able to go into town!"

"Considerate of him to bring the constables along in his carriage," Knightley said doubtfully. Though his opinion of Frank Churchill had improved—marginally—in the years of their acquaintance, he still gave the man little credit for forethought and consideration.

"It is not the constables he has with him," Emma said, hurrying out to greet their visitor. "Someone much better!"

Juliet's high hopes for an early breakfast were dashed when she heard the carriage approaching Donwell Abbey. Of course, this meant she would also have a chance to talk with Frank Churchill about the investigation—as the finder of the amethyst ring, he would think nothing of her curiosity. But the opportunity to speak with him would have been lovelier had she been able to enjoy her coffee first.

Still, good fortune must be seized. Juliet hurried downstairs, tucking her curls back into her bun, and strolled toward the door as if she might just happen to find Mr. Churchill there.

Instead, she met a girl almost exactly her own age. The girl had Frank Churchill's fine coloring, with fair hair and vivid green eyes, which made Juliet unusually despondent about her own dark curls. And that dress! Such fine muslin and delicate braided trim were rarely the stuff of everyday gowns, more likely to be found in the trousseau of a newly-wed (like Marianne Brandon) or the wardrobe of someone extremely wealthy (like Elizabeth Darcy). For a moment Juliet felt almost shabby.

Then the girl saw her and lit up as though they were old friends. "Why, hello," she said. "You are Miss Tilney, are you not? My father said I should meet you—that you must be very lonely up here on your own."

Restored to good cheer, Juliet answered, "I am she. And you must be . . . Miss Churchill?"

"Grace Churchill." Grace inclined her head in a soft nod. "I'm so very sorry that such a dreadful thing should occur during your visit. Normally Donwell Abbey is the pleasantest place! Mrs. Knightley is such *fun*. Usually I visit often, but this summer, their daughter, Henrietta, has been away at the seaside with the Westons. So I have been negligent, you see."

"I am sure you are forgiven," Juliet said. Her new acquaintance seemed entirely charming. For all that she still considered Mrs. Brandon a potential friend, Juliet had to admit that it would be nice to spend time with another young woman who was not so deeply affected by Mr. Wickham's death.

Would friendship be more inconvenience than pleasure? Visiting Grace Churchill's home might be a welcome change from somber Donwell, but it would also take her away from the investigation in progress . . .

Frank Churchill walked in then, chatting happily with Mrs. Knightley about the finer weather. Behind him came Colonel Brandon in a most peculiar hat, and then Jonathan Darcy. Miss Churchill was presented to them both by Mr. Churchill with what seemed rather more enthusiasm than necessary.

Or so Juliet thought, until Miss Churchill looked into Jonathan's eyes and blushed.

Oh, she realized. *Her father is matchmaking with one of the most eligible young men in the country. Of course he is. Any parent would do the same.*

It is not as though Jonathan Darcy were paying court to me. Our connection is an entirely different matter. So I should not mind this at all.

So she told herself.

∽

"Mr. Darcy," Mrs. Knightley said, "may I introduce Grace Churchill, our magistrate's daughter. Miss Churchill, this is Jonathan Darcy of Pemberley, and one of our guests. I see you have already met Miss Tilney?"

"Yes, I have." Miss Churchill never glanced away from Jonathan's face. He generally found such scrutiny disconcerting, particularly from those he'd just met, but he must have been disguising it well, as Miss Churchill's smile only broadened. "You must be so tired of being cooped up in the house."

"I am not so restless as most," Jonathan said. "But the sunshine makes a pleasant change."

Miss Churchill paused only a moment before laughing. "You jest with me, I see. And look! Here is Pierre, come to greet me." She stooped down to pet the Knightleys' small dog, which had pranced out to her, tail wagging in a spiral of pure delight. "He and I are the best of friends. I hope you two have made your acquaintance as well."

Were proper introductions necessary for dogs? He didn't think so, but he gamely petted the little thing's head. "He does not bark when he should."

"And why should you bark, hmm? Why should you bark when you're so happy?" Grace Churchill ran her hands through the dog's fur. "You see, he thinks he is the true master of the house."

"Have you a dog, Miss Churchill?" Juliet Tilney asked.

"My father has hunting dogs, and they're lovely, but they are far fonder of him than they are of me." Miss Churchill looked up at Miss Tilney with just as much good cheer as she had given Jonathan. In his experience, young ladies attempting to attach themselves to him tended to look upon other young ladies as obstacles of some sort. This cordiality was far more pleasant. "But I have a cat who adores sitting in my lap."

Pets seemed to be as safe a conversational topic as the weather. Jonathan ventured, "What is your cat's name?"

Grace Churchill's cheeks turned pink. "I named her when I was much younger. I fear she is called Blancmange."

Even Jonathan understood the humor. But while they were still laughing, Miss Tilney had begun stepping away. "I feel the need for some fresh air—will you excuse me, Miss Churchill?"

"Of course." Already Miss Churchill had returned her attention to him. "I do hope we shall see each other more, while you are here with us."

"As do I." Miss Tilney's smile seemed genuine, yet she still left them. Jonathan didn't see the reason why and wished that he did. Had not the conversation between Miss Tilney and Miss Churchill been entirely cordial?

People were always difficult to understand. Girls his age were proving to be the hardest of all.

～

Of course Grace Churchill is taken with him, Juliet told herself as she eased out of the hallway and stepped outside. *He is not only eligible but also polite and kind. His person is certainly appealing. Her interest is natural.*

Insofar as Juliet had been able to tell in the brief moments she had witnessed them together, Grace's interest in Jonathan Darcy appeared to be more sincere than strategic. Pemberley might be one of the greatest estates in the land, but the elegance of her dress and her father's superb carriage suggested that Grace Churchill had no need to marry for money. She had simply met a handsome young man and was taken with him.

Juliet had absented herself because when two young women were making conversation with a young man, something in their talk often . . . *curdled.* Each girl would attempt to outdo the other with wit, admiration, or whatever else the young man in question seemed to like. Although Juliet thought such behavior ridiculous when the other girl started it, she found it very difficult not to respond in kind. Nobody likes to be outshone. So she avoided the circumstance when she could.

Grace Churchill had been truly friendly toward her, it seemed to Juliet. Better to leave the conversation there, before any strangeness had time to creep in.

A stroll will be nice, she told herself firmly, and it was true. Sunlight warmed her skin for the first time in days. Before, the general gloom had prevented her from fully admiring the beautiful grounds of Donwell Abbey, but now she could marvel over its splendid gardens and the softly rolling hills in the distance.

Nor was Juliet the only one who wished to enjoy the grounds' pleasures. At the far edge of the gardens, she spotted Mrs. Brandon.

Juliet hesitated for a moment, recalling Mrs. Brandon's distress the day prior. But surely, if she were still at such a pitch, she would not have left her room, much less gone for a stroll. Swiftly Juliet walked toward the hedges that lined Mrs. Brandon's path.

The sound of footsteps on gravel must have alerted Mrs. Brandon to Juliet's presence, because she looked up and managed a thin, watery smile. "Miss Tilney. You, too, have missed fresh air, I think."

"I have," Juliet said, realizing only after she'd spoken that it was true. "At home I am much out of doors. And this is my chance to see another part of England—it would be a shame to have viewed it only through glass streaked with rain."

"It will do us good." Mrs. Brandon sounded as though she wished, rather than believed, this to be true. "Nature is a kind of healer, I believe. And—and Cowper says grief is itself a medicine, so perhaps we are mending ourselves in more ways than one."

"I am sorry to know that you feel the need for such healing," Juliet said. "It is the murder alone that has discomfited you?"

Mrs. Brandon stumbled, perhaps from a stone underfoot. "Is that not sufficient cause? None of us are ourselves, I feel sure."

Juliet was entirely herself. She felt no grief for George Wickham, save for the conviction that almost no one deserved such a violent end. Why should Marianne Brandon grieve so?

Or was she feeling grief for someone else? For someone marred by a terrible act that could not be undone?

Furtively, Juliet glanced around for Colonel Brandon. Instead, she saw Fanny Bertram speaking with a few of the servants, clutching a kerchief evidently used to dab away tears. Even from this distance, it was apparent that she was flushed with distress.

"Mrs. Bertram appears to have very fine feelings," Marianne said. Her voice was shaky. "I admire such sensibility. To have such compassion for another that it brings her to weeping! Would that I were as kind."

Juliet was not so sure that it was compassion driving Fanny Bertram, but on this point, she remained silent.

⁓

Jonathan knew he should be making conversation with Miss Grace Churchill, but she was quite good at making it all by herself.

"Of course it would be unseemly *now*, given the unfortunate circumstance." Miss Churchill nodded slightly toward the gallery; her father had clearly informed her as to the location of the crime. "Later in your stay, however, we must have a dance. Not a grand ball, but at least an occasion where you may meet our local society. Are you fond of dancing, sir?"

"I am reasonably good at it," Jonathan answered. He liked the steps, the patterns, the rhythms. However, the subtler social demands of a dance had confounded him more than once.

Miss Churchill had an amiable smile. "Then it is settled. Everyone likes to do what they do well. It is a vanity universal to man."

This was true, in Jonathan's experience. Perhaps this was why—despite Grace Churchill's pleasant nature—he wished to leave this conversation and make his way upstairs. He was not good at lively conversation and doubted he would ever become so. As an investigator, however, he felt he was beginning to show promise. And he was sharply curious to know what Mr. Churchill and his constables made of Wickham's ransacked room.

Footsteps on the stair made him look up, but it was not the magistrate nor the officers of the law who approached. Mrs. Knightley came down alongside Captain Wentworth. The former looked determinedly cheerful, the latter anything but.

"We have been shooed downstairs like naughty children," Mrs. Knightley said.

"Are not naughty children usually sent upstairs?" Jonathan asked in all sincerity, which was why it was startling when the women laughed and even Wentworth smiled.

"You are too quick for me, young Mr. Darcy." Mrs. Knightley smiled at him with real warmth, which she then focused on Grace Churchill. "Now, let us leave the men to their own devices. The constables will not be so quick to exile them if we ladies are no longer present. Besides, you must see the orchids in the conservatory."

Within moments, Miss Churchill and Mrs. Knightley were walking across the grounds arm in arm. Miss Churchill gave Jonathan a smile over her shoulder as her only farewell. He supposed their introduction had gone well.

But where was Juliet? If the actual investigation could not be observed, he at least wished to share thoughts and impressions with her. Instead, it appeared he and Captain Wentworth were meant to entertain each other.

Wentworth did not look to be easily entertained. His glower had rarely been darker. "Madness," Wentworth said. "Sheer madness."

"To what do you refer, sir?"

"These wild theories of the magistrate's, about Gypsies and whatnot," Wentworth said. "Obviously it is the work of a servant. Who else had both access to the house and yet enough need of money to steal whatever pittance Wickham might've had hidden in his bedroom?"

It would be unwise to contradict the captain directly, Jonathan thought. Leading questions might have greater effect. "Surely none of those employed at Donwell Abbey would be guilty of theft, or else the Knightleys would have turned them out long ago. Given that, what possible reason would a servant have to murder Mr. Wickham?"

"Give Wickham ten minutes in a room with anyone, and they would find reason to dislike him," Wentworth retorted. "He would've insulted any maid alone with him, of that I feel certain."

These words jarred a memory of a trip many years ago to see Uncle Charles and Aunt Jane, the only one during which the Wickhams had also been present: Aunt Lydia shouting angrily at her husband across the table, not caring who could hear, "You are worse in a scullery than other men are in whorehouses!" Aunt Jane had spent much of the evening with the servants, apparently trying to convince someone not to leave that very night, while young Jonathan asked Uncle Charles what a whorehouse was. (The answer then given had been incomplete.)

Wickham, indeed, could not be trusted around servants. Could Jonathan and Juliet have been wrong from the beginning? Was it possible that a servant—either herself outraged or one of the men wishing to defend her—could've committed the crime after all?

He was startled from his reverie by a cry from the garden. "Mr. Knightley! Mrs. Knightley! Someone, come quickly?"

Jonathan and Wentworth exchanged glances, then rushed outside. Mrs. Knightley had answered the summons as well and was running toward an undergardener who stood near one of the topiary urns. The young man's face was white as fog, and he held something even paler: a linen handkerchief.

Even before Jonathan had reached the gardener's side, he could see the handkerchief was stained with blood.

"Begging your pardon, Mrs. Knightley," the gardener began, "but I come to find this in the planter. Tucked down in the soil, half-buried. Wouldn't be none of ours—"

"I believe we know why it was hidden," Mrs. Knightley said quietly.

Mr. Knightley, Frank Churchill, and the constables were hurrying out toward them now. Much of the rest of the party—including Juliet Tilney, Marianne Brandon, and Grace Churchill—were approaching as well. Knightley swore an oath not often heard in polite company. "What is this?"

"A handkerchief too fine to belong to any servant," Mrs. Knightley replied. "And it is stained with blood."

"It was dug deep," the gardener said. "With a trowel, most likely. And as it happens, the smaller trowel is missing from my kit."

"Stolen," Miss Tilney murmured.

Jonathan noted that the bloodstains were not droplets, as might fall from a nosebleed, nor wider blotches that might have signified an attempt to bandage a cut. No, the fabric was marked with maroon streaks. He murmured, "It was used to wipe away blood."

"I concur," said Frank Churchill. "The killer must have used this to wipe clean his weapon, then hidden it here."

"No intruder would have hidden it so," Jonathan pointed out. "Surely they would not have delayed here after committing such a crime, only to hide what might be more effectively hidden elsewhere, far from Donwell."

"Nor would any servant have chosen this as a hiding place," said Miss Tilney. The party stared at her—mostly in surprise, but Jonathan was eager to hear her deduction. "The servants clean the fireplaces, of course. Therefore a servant could burn the handkerchief and be able to sweep up the ashes afterward, discarding any remnants. But any of us would have feared to burn it, precisely because the servants could then discover whatever scrap might remain."

This was not necessarily so, Jonathan realized . . . but it was very likely. He saw the same understanding dawn upon the faces of all those present. Quietly he added, "And a servant would have had ample opportunity to return the trowel to the gardener's kit, surely. Any of us would have to wait for such a chance."

"We are not looking for a servant, then," Frank Churchill said. "Nor an intruder, who would have taken the kerchief away while escaping." His eyes met Mr. Knightley's, his demeanor grave. "I regret to say it, but—one of your guests must be responsible."

The others all looked at one another, and Jonathan imagined each one thinking, *Which of us killed Mr. Wickham?*

Chapter Twelve

Elizabeth Bennet Darcy did not suffer fools gladly, but that did not mean she lacked forbearance. For her husband's sake, she endured the occasional visit from Lady Catherine de Bourgh, from whom age had stolen neither vitality nor arrogance. For her eldest's son sake, she moderated her expectations and tolerated his eccentricities. And for her unfortunate hosts, the Knightleys, she had made the best of things during what had to be the worst house party in all England.

But forbearance could only stretch so far.

"What might they do with suspected criminals in Surrey?" Elizabeth asked as she walked along, about one hour after breakfast. "Should we inquire as to the state of the accommodations in the local gaol? Or is there to be no place of repose between accusation and the gallows?"

"Your humor has rarely been more ill placed." Darcy strode beside her, stiff as a starched collar. A few paces behind them was Jonathan. "We are accused of nothing, and there is no reason to think we will be."

Elizabeth laughed. "No reason! No reason other than that, of all those present, we knew Wickham the best and therefore liked him the least. Who could look at our history with this man and not wonder about our guilt?"

"Others here disliked Mr. Wickham very much as well," Jonathan pointed out, guileless and helpful, with as little feel as ever for the tension between his parents. "One could argue that, were we ever to commit violence against Wickham, we would certainly have done so long ago."

"That is not as persuasive an argument as could be wished," Darcy replied, but he gave his son the smallest echo of a smile.

Elizabeth had thought a family walk would do her good. All the guests must wish for some modicum of privacy at this time, or at least only the company of those they most loved. It was a fine, bright morning, one that promised to dispel the gloom of the past several days. But every step she took reminded her of how badly she wanted not to walk but to run—with all her strength—across the fields, away from Donwell Abbey, away even from her son and husband.

Where would you run? she asked herself. *To some country where you have no past, no connections, no burden of the spirit? That land has never existed, and never can.*

Jonathan said, "I have not noticed Mr. Frank Churchill taking any particular notice of us."

"Save for bringing his daughter to meet you, though no doubt she insisted upon that herself." Darcy remained convinced that any young woman intrigued by Jonathan was actually angling for the Pemberley inheritance. Sometimes Elizabeth pointed out that Pemberley had been insufficient to tempt *her* to matrimony, but Darcy believed her singular in that regard. (Caroline Bingley had had too strong an influence on Darcy's opinion of the gentler sex.)

"Still," Jonathan said, "he would not have brought his daughter to meet me if he thought that any of the three of us was a murderer."

"If he does not think it yet," Elizabeth said, "that is because he has only just given up on the notion of Gypsies. Before long, he will take more note of everything Wickham has done to us, then ask what we have done to him."

Jonathan remained guileless, even hopeful. "I do not think

Mr. Churchill would consider any events in the distant past to be a cause for murder, and most of Mr. Wickham's wrongs took place before my birth—"

"Except for Susannah." Elizabeth's voice was sharp enough to cut. She imagined she felt the blade herself. "Except for the death of a child who might as well have been our daughter."

Our, she said. But when she looked at Darcy's stony expression, Elizabeth was reminded that apparently the little girl had not meant as much to her husband. Not enough for love.

Because if Darcy had truly loved Susannah, it would be impossible for him to have gone on as usual, as he had these past eight months. It would be impossible for him to be so far away from Elizabeth now that even his love could not touch her.

Darcy said, "No court would hold Wickham liable for Susannah's death."

"Do you deny it?" Elizabeth had never dreamed her husband might think so. "Susannah was sick, and yet he insisted on her coming home to him immediately. She went out in a carriage, on hard roads, while still so frail—"

"Of course he is responsible," Darcy said sharply. "I mean only that the law could not hold him so."

"Then to perdition with the law." Elizabeth quickened her steps, the better to increase the distance between her and her husband and son. Whenever she thought of Susannah's death, of the actual reason for it—Wickham's pettiness and jealousy, the utter heartlessness required for him to insist on the child's traveling in such condition—

Eight months, she had borne it. And yet, every time this anger overtook her heart, Elizabeth wondered whether she could bear it even one minute more.

⌁

The mood in Donwell Abbey that afternoon was strange, Juliet thought. Before the discovery of the bloody kerchief, everyone had been troubled by the untimely demise of Mr. Wickham—but not afraid. At least, not afraid of being similarly dispatched; nobody here behaved in the same way that had led Wickham to such a bad end, and there was no reason to suspect a rampage was to begin. Juliet thought people were mostly worried about being suspected of murder, or that a loved one might fall under suspicion.

Why should the kerchief have changed everything? She wasn't certain, but perhaps that discovery had redirected everyone's worries. Before the fears had been only of accusations. Now people wondered whether someone they liked—or even loved—might actually be guilty.

Except for one person, of course: the one who feared being caught.

She herself startled when the door to the billiard room opened. But it was only Jonathan Darcy, arriving for their next discussion of their investigation—one they had agreed would now be nightly.

"I couldn't get a good look at the kerchief before Mr. Churchill took it away," he said, instead of a more civil greeting. Juliet found she preferred his frankness. "But I suppose had it been embroidered or otherwise marked, the constables would have said as much."

She nodded. "I agree that the kerchief told us nothing. But it has told the others in this house a great deal. They know now that the worst is true."

He seemed dubious. "Surely they realized before that no servant nor outsider did this."

"They suspected it. But they did not *know*. Knowing is different." Juliet tucked her shawl more securely around her shoulders. Beneath it she wore her simplest day dress. Were she found in a corridor, she could pretend she was merely investigating a noise; if she and Jonathan were found together, scandalous though that would be, she could forestall the worst by dropping her shawl and proving herself to be appropriately dressed—as long as no one noticed the clumsy job she'd done of redonning it without her maid's help. Juliet had thought this through in some detail. "What else have you learned today?"

"Very little, I fear. The discovery of the kerchief took precedence over all other concerns." Jonathan Darcy held himself rigidly upright, as though they were being presented at the Court of St. James's. Although Juliet wondered why, she kept her silence. "We should put the most effort where the greatest gain is to be had. Our attention should fix on those likeliest to be guilty."

"It is a risky strategy—but perhaps we should begin so. If we find no proofs of their wrongdoing, then we can turn to the other guests," Juliet said. "Who shall we include in our first group to be examined? Obviously Colonel Brandon must be considered. His motive may be distant in years, but he had only just encountered Wickham for the first time. That plus his absence from his room—well, he cannot be ignored." Her heart ached for poor Mrs. Brandon, so frightened for her husband, but Juliet took hope that perhaps their efforts would exonerate Brandon rather than condemn him.

"He did not stay in his room all night?" Jonathan looked startled. "How did you learn this?"

Juliet admitted, "It is only my surmise, but when I asked Mrs. Brandon whether he had left his room that night—it took her too long to answer. A pause can say much."

"Then that is certainly worth consideration. We must also look to Captain Wentworth," young Darcy said. "He, too, left his room for some time, and his temper can take a black turn. Wickham's scheme had already lost his prize money from the war, and the debt he owed Wickham would have ruined his family."

Juliet had less of a sense of Wentworth, but she would trust Jonathan's judgment. "Mrs. Knightley does not appear to have known just how severely Wickham's scheme would have impoverished her—but Mr. Knightley knew. And he would be more confident taking action in his own home, where all rooms and patterns of behavior are familiar to him. Also, I want to find out more about Fanny Bertram."

His disbelief was almost comic. "You cannot still seriously think of her as a killer."

"I know only that she is behaving very strangely," Juliet insisted. "There is a reason why, and I sense that it is connected to this terrible business in some way."

Although he was clearly not convinced, he said only, "Thus we have three principal suspects, and whatever fraction of a suspect Mrs. Bertram might be. We must both work harder at finding opportunities to ask questions."

"Yes, certainly." She had hoped he would not force her to ask this, but no such luck. "You realize that we cannot disregard your parents. Do you know whether or not they left their room?"

It took Jonathan Darcy a moment to say, "No, it seems they did not."

It seems was some distance from certainty. Juliet simply resolved that the Darcys, like Fanny Bertram, were a project she must undertake alone.

∽

Juliet was not the only one who knew that Fanny Bertram was not herself.

Edmund lay in his bed for a long time after the candles were blown out. Next to him, Fanny lay awake, too. He could tell because of her extreme motionlessness. Normally she tossed and turned for a bit before falling asleep. Tonight, she sought to deceive him so that he would not try to speak—or, perhaps, she was merely paralyzed by fear.

Fanny's terrors were usually such small things that it was all Edmund could do not to laugh at them. Tonight, however, he had fears of his own.

Suspense is no man's friend, Edmund told himself. *Speak.*

"Fanny," he said, his voice heavy, "we must talk."

After a long pause, she whispered, "I know, dear Edmund."

He sat up, readying himself to hear her out. "The ring Juliet Tilney found in Wickham's room—was not that your amethyst ring? The one I gave you for our first Christmas together?"

Fanny sat up, too, but she did not look him in the eye. "Yes, it was."

No further explanation came, forcing Edmund to say, "Then I must know how it came into his possession. I should not put it past a man of such low moral character to have stolen it . . . but were that the case, you would have claimed the ring as your own when it was first found."

Even in the dim moonlight, it was impossible not to see how pale Fanny was, as white as someone about to fall down in a faint. "I offered it to him for—for something that he had. Mr. Wickham took it, but he did not give me what I had asked for. He said only that he would consider it."

This answer only perplexed Edmund further. "What do you mean? What was it Wickham had that you wished to trade a ring for?"

She hung her head. "Mr. Wickham had stolen a letter from my traveling case. A—a letter from William."

"Why should the man want a letter from your brother?"

"I do not know how the idea first came into his mind." Fanny's eyes had welled with tears. "If only it had not! But when he had read it, Mr. Wickham knew that—that if the contents were ever known, my poor brother would be—" A sob stole her last words, and she covered her face with her hands.

"What on earth did William write?" Edmund had met Fanny's seafaring brother on only a handful of occasions; but on each, the young man had shown good manners, a sharp mind, a strong character, and the deepest love for his sister. Could Edmund's regard for him be misplaced? "Tell me, Fanny. It is wrong for us to have secrets from each other, especially in these dire circumstances."

It took her several moments to reply, and when she did, her voice was little more than a whisper. "William said—he said that he—that his friend Harris—"

Edmund had heard many of Harris's exploits in William's letters, and he'd even met the young man once in Portsmouth. He seemed as good-natured a lad as William himself, but had Harris led his friend astray? "What did they do?"

Fanny took a deep breath. "William loves him. He says it is as . . . as though they were married."

The truth took shape slowly in Edmund's mind, more grotesque to him by the instant. "Heaven forfend. Do you speak of—" It was difficult to say the next word aloud, even to his own wife—especially to her. "Of *sodomy*?"

She burst into tears. "They kill men for it. They hang them. I could not let William be hanged, not ever, not if I could prevent it. Already I was afraid he would be discovered, and then when Wickham threatened to expose him—yes, Edmund, I gave him my ring. I would've given him everything I possessed, if it would save William's life."

"You meant to shelter your brother from the consequence of his sins." Edmund could hardly think, so repulsed and astonished was he. "For this, you were willing to dishonor yourself by dealing with such a disreputable man?"

Fanny finally looked Edmund in the face. Her eyes were wide, disbelieving. "To stop William from being hanged? How could I not, Edmund? You—you would not have wished me to expose my brother in such a way. Surely you would not have."

He tried to collect himself. "I would not expect it of you, knowing your temperament as I do. But I would also not have expected you to aid your brother in the continuation of his sin."

"I did not! I only wished that he should not be found out."

"There is little enough difference between the two." When he felt uncertain, Edmund took shelter in doctrine, which was very clear on what was right and wrong. "Yes, men are sometimes hanged for it, but transportation or gaol would be more likely outcomes. That is what it means to see justice done."

"Even then, they put men in the pillory—the mob is allowed to pelt them with offal and refuse until they are injured as badly as any beating." Fanny stared at Edmund as though she did not recognize him. "William is my dearest brother. I could not abandon him to such a fate."

Edmund caught himself. While William no doubt deserved the strictest moral condemnation, Fanny had found herself caught between Christian virtue and her tender heart. Normally those two forces entwined easily in her soul and showed themselves in her every action. If this had confused her, she was not to be blamed. Probably Fanny had never even imagined such a thing possible between two men before. Even Edmund felt as though he needed more time to consider how best to act.

He patted her hand. "Your lapse in judgment was severe but, under the circumstances, perhaps not so surprising."

"No."

"We shall have to speak more upon this subject later."

"Yes. We will."

"For tonight, rest and know that at least honesty has been

restored between us." Edmund gave Fanny a little smile. "I am not angry with you."

When he lay back down, he could not immediately fall asleep, so full was his mind of wonder and fury at William's behavior.

Fanny could not fall asleep either. When her husband had said that he was not angry with her, she realized that—for very nearly the first time in her life—she was angry with him.

❧

The next morning, Jonathan again awakened early. Once more, the weather promised to be fair. Later in the day, he would take Ebony for a ride, one that would refresh her as much as him. He decided to descend before breakfast in order to give the groom instructions to have Ebony ready at the correct hour.

As he went down the stairs, though, he heard sounds that indicated he was not the only early riser.

From the library he heard a feminine voice say, "You do not think I should speak?"

A male voice replied, "You yourself have noted the risks. The rewards of silence are the greater, for now."

Jonathan recognized the voices, but still chanced a glimpse inside the library to confirm his instincts. As he had thought, the persons speaking were Anne Wentworth and Colonel Brandon.

Did they know each other? Had they met before the Knightleys' house party? Why should they meet secretly now—and what truth was it Brandon had urged her to conceal?

You cannot be certain that this pertains to Mr. Wickham's murder, Jonathan reminded himself. *It may touch upon another matter entirely.*

But, if so, what?

This was another matter to discuss later with Juliet Tilney. Already Jonathan was looking forward to having a nightly meeting with her. Not only would it add some routine to days which were far too unpredictable for Jonathan's taste, but it would also provide an opportunity to speak honestly—without pretense of any sort. He'd always known that he was not adept at the polite fictions used by everyone around him in virtually all conversations. What he had not known was how good it would feel to do without them.

When he spoke to Miss Tilney, he did not feel that he was strange. He did not have to pretend that he understood things he did not. Jonathan could be entirely himself. What a rare and exhilarating privilege.

‍♌

Had Jonathan traveled deeper into the house, he would've discovered that breakfast was in fact already laid out. The servants, noting the earlier risings of the guests and anticipating future visits from Frank Churchill, had set the dishes out earlier and prepared a larger quantity of toast and marmalade.

Instead, this discovery was made first by Juliet Tilney and only moments later by Elizabeth Darcy, who gave her a smile as she took up her plate. "Do not restrain yourself on my account," Elizabeth said, "as I do not intend to restrain myself on yours. Before men, we are expected to display only dainty appetites. Among each other, however, we may eat as we please."

Juliet grinned and took both a second scone and a cup of chocolate. "The food has been excellent at Donwell Abbey. Although the rest of us may be shaken, the cook has carried on brilliantly."

"Now, at last, we are able to enjoy her triumphs." Elizabeth took her seat and began to butter her bread. "I confess, for the first two days after—the unpleasantness—well, I could hardly taste a thing. Shock had stolen my appetite completely. Add that to the list of George Wickham's crimes. He denied me pleasure in strawberry scones."

It was shocking to hear her speak so flippantly. Juliet managed to say, "I had no difficulties eating, but then, I had no prior acquaintance with him, as you had."

"Indeed." Elizabeth sighed, and for an instant, Juliet glimpsed the weariness and vulnerability that hid beneath her smiles. It was not that Elizabeth Darcy took Wickham's death lightly; it was more than she found her way through difficulties by learning how to laugh at them. "But to know him was not to mourn him. Quite the opposite, in fact."

Time, Juliet thought, to press the point. "Do you think Mr. Frank Churchill's investigations will reveal the culprit?"

"Probably, as it has already revealed much else. The magistrate even insists upon knowing why my husband left his bedchamber in the night." Elizabeth caught herself, visibly horrified at her own slip—but for only the briefest instant. She resumed her former lightness of tone so swiftly that it would have gone unnoticed by anyone who was not actively investigating that same night. "Next he will ask us all to account for our dreams, perhaps, or what we dined upon the night before, in the hopes that a clue lurked upon the table, next to the seedcake."

Confused, Juliet turned her head and pretended to be very interested in dipping one of her scones in clotted cream. The Knightleys' small dog, Pierre, had suddenly appeared, apparently much intrigued by the aroma of breakfast, and he absorbed Mrs. Darcy's attention enough for Juliet to collect her thoughts.

Jonathan had said that his parents hadn't left their rooms. But if Mr. Darcy had done so, that meant his whereabouts were unaccounted for—and while he was gone, Mrs. Darcy has no witness for her movements either.

And now that Juliet thought back upon Jonathan's face as he'd claimed his parents didn't leave their rooms, she recognized the careful expression he had worn. It was the same as the one Elizabeth had worn in the moments following her slip of the tongue.

Jonathan lied.

And the only reason he would lie is because he's trying to protect them.

Their own son thinks they might be guilty.

Chapter Thirteen

Breakfast is the least formal of meals, which often makes it the most pleasurable. Precedence need not be observed overmuch, and foods can be taken from the buffet, or not, in the quantity one desires.

Granted, the breakfasts during the Knightleys' ill-fated house party had not provided as full a share of enjoyment as might have otherwise been the case. The first morning, there had been a general dread of socializing with Mr. Wickham; those who knew him could scarcely stand the thought, and those who did not had already determined they had no wish to make the man's acquaintance. After that, of course, the pall of the murder had fallen over the entire house. But at least at breakfast nobody had been forced to converse. Thoughts could be kept to oneself—the one wish nearly the entire party shared.

This morning, however, struck Jonathan as different, and in a most disagreeable sense.

First of all, when he arrived in the breakfast room, he found his mother and Juliet Tilney engrossed in conversation. On its own this would have been unsurprising, perhaps even welcome. But Miss Tilney did not look up to meet his eye. She sat rigidly in her chair and kept her attention on his mother alone.

Jonathan's initial fear was that his mother was telling stories from his childhood, in which he might seem ridiculous. He never wanted to seem ridiculous, and it felt as though

Miss Tilney were the very last person he wanted to see him thus. However, his mother was not overly mirthful, and from what he could tell from Miss Tilney's profile, no amusement appeared on her face either.

His second fear was far worse. Was she questioning his mother about the night of Wickham's death? If Miss Tilney learned of his father's midnight turn, she might assume the worst. The more Jonathan considered this possibility, the more likely he felt it to be.

It was his own fault that this was occurring, he decided. Last night, he had agreed that Miss Tilney should continue her lone investigation into Fanny Bertram's odd behavior. In doing so, had he perhaps tacitly encouraged her to investigate others Jonathan considered to be innocent—including his parents?

He had hit close to the truth, as he discovered when they rose from breakfast near the same time and wound up walking down the hall next to each other.

"You did not tell me that your father left his room the night of the murder," Miss Tilney whispered, never turning her head toward Jonathan.

His steps faltered, but he remained by her side. "I—I did not know it."

"You knew *someone* left, though, didn't you?"

There was no point in further denial. His head still spinning from the revelation, he admitted, "I heard someone leaving their bedchamber, yes. How did you—"

"How I figured this out is entirely beside the point. You lied to me. Do you think the Darcys of Pemberley are too good to be questioned in this matter? Or is it worse than that? Do you actually believe one of your parents might be guilty?"

"I would never believe such a false, terrible thing, nor should you." Jonathan could hardly bear the thought of accusation falling upon either his proud, noble father or his wise, witty mother. They were perhaps the last two people in the world he could imagine committing such a crime, unless Fanny Bertram were even less likely still. "I meant only to spare our attentions, that we might concentrate on more likely culprits. Why can you not accept my word in this matter? Why do you refuse to trust my knowledge of them as a guide?"

"It is precisely because you know and love them that you cannot see them clearly," Miss Tilney insisted. "Love blinds us more surely than anything else ever can."

Jonathan sensed that Miss Tilney had hit on a deeper truth. We forgive the faults of those we love so often, so deeply, that we sometimes convince ourselves the faults do not exist. The rest of the world is not so easily persuaded.

"You are wrong to suspect my parents," he insisted.

"You are wrong to deceive me," Miss Tilney retorted. "We cannot work together without trust. From now on, I shall undertake my inquiries on my own."

With that she turned down the hall leading toward the library. Jonathan wanted to follow her, to discuss this further, to make her see things as he did. But he could not think on anything so complex at the moment. He could hardly think at all. Instead, he went outside to ride Ebony, so to spend time with a creature far more comprehensible to him than Juliet Tilney ever would be.

Jonathan knew he had many flaws, but deceit had never been one of them. If anything, he was more likely to err by being too honest. He had always taken some pride in this: During his childhood, when he and his brothers were interrogated about small mishaps at home, his mother had often said, *If Jonathan tells me he did not do it, I know that is true*. His brothers would blush, their own boyish fibs thrown into stark contrast by Jonathan's candor. How he had congratulated himself on this rare difference from other boys that made him superior instead of inferior! Now Jonathan had lied to Juliet Tilney and been found out; he could no longer consider himself wholly honest. His mother would be so hurt, so disappointed, if ever she learned of it.

Meanwhile, his father's contempt for dissemblers had always been plain. One of the many issues Fitzwilliam Darcy had with his sister's choice of husband was that the earl of Dorchester could be rather selective with the truth, in ways that sometimes injured Aunt Georgiana. While Jonathan was somewhat more forgiving of his uncle—who could be great fun, and who seemed to delight his aunt even more often than he plagued her—he had always taken secret pride in being superior to his noble uncle in this regard.

It struck him then: one of Wickham's fellow conspirators, one of those who'd convinced so many others to risk and lose their fortunes, had been an earl. An earl who took liberties with the truth. Jonathan's father had reacted so sharply to that information. Was this because he suspected Wickham's partner was the earl of Dorchester himself?

Jonathan knew this merited further consideration. He also knew his attention to be too fragmented to consider it productively at the moment. Nor was it a suspicion he could voice lightly.

Assuming he had anyone to voice it to at all.

Which he wouldn't, if Juliet Tilney never forgave him.

✎

As it happened, Anne Wentworth was not in the library. She had gone back to her room before breakfast, thinking only of retrieving a shawl. (Though the weather was fine, Donwell Abbey could be a bit drafty and the summer heat had not returned to its intensity from before the rains.) Her belly rumbled with eagerness. Although her appetite had suffered since Mr. Wickham's untimely death, the body's needs could be ignored only for so long.

She thought it would be a brief interruption in her day, no more. That idea died as soon as she walked into her bedroom and found Frederick standing by their bed, a frown on his face and a creased sheet of paper in his grasp. The slanting letters upon it could only be by Mrs. Smith's hand.

Anne took a deep breath, stepped farther inside the room, and shut the door so no others would hear what was about to transpire.

Frederick noticed her presence only when he heard the closing of the door. Instantly his expression, already dark, became even more grim. "This," he said, his voice a low growl. "When were you going to tell me about *this*?"

"I was not going to tell you about it at all," Anne said evenly. "I knew it would anger you unjustly against Mrs. Smith."

"Unjustly! This woman—who so short a time ago was penniless, impoverished, in need of our help to even regain her own property—she considers us a subject of her pity now, does she?"

"She does not pity us. She knows we are in distress. Those are not the same."

"Oh, but they are." Frederick crumpled the paper in his hand and tossed it aside. "If even Mrs. Smith considers us fit subjects for charity, what will your father and sisters say? There we will find not even pity, and certainly not charity. There we will find only scorn and abandonment. Since your sister's illustrious marriage, they have looked upon us with greater contempt than ever. They will say that we disgrace them."

Anne had been putting off this particular conversation in the hopes it would never have to take place. It appeared she could delay no longer. She squared her shoulders and lifted her chin. "No, my family will not look upon us with pity, nor offer us charity. They are too proud for that. But why should you care so much for their good opinion? They have only ever granted it begrudgingly, and conditionally, to either of us. It has been many years since we troubled ourselves on their account."

"Their good opinion means nothing to me," Frederick insisted. "But I will not bear their contempt."

"What if we have to bear it?"

He stared at her, wounded by what he saw as betrayal. "Perhaps you saw this as inevitable. Perhaps you always suspected I would disappoint you. Fail to provide for you. You must have done, or else why would you have refused me the first time?"

"Enough!" Anne had not raised her voice to her husband ten times in their marriage, but she did so now. It startled him into silence. "My family's contempt is cheaply bought. It can be had for such sins as failing to recognize a coat of arms upon a carriage. For preferring congenial company to boredom in the presence of aristocracy. They have heaped it upon you for not being born to wealth, and on me for reasons I have never fully understood." In her youth, Anne had been haunted by not knowing, but it had been many years since that pain last ached. "We have never respected their opinions before. Why begin now?"

"Do we not have enough to bear?"

"Yes!" Anne cried. "We do! But it is not my family's pride that afflicts us. It is yours."

Frederick scoffed. "A man has a right to his own pride, where it is justly held, in good principles."

"In order to have one's own pride, one must believe oneself worthy of it," she replied. "True pride cannot be taken away, not by the contempt of the whole world. We cannot destroy the pride of others, only our own."

Doubt touched him then; she saw it in the clouding of his expression. "And you think I have destroyed mine. In my foolishness in trusting Mr. Wickham, in my greedy desire for even more wealth than I had won at war—"

"No, no." Anne went to his side then and clasped his hand. He did not squeeze back. "There is nothing ignoble in believing the word of your fellow man, not when you had been given no reason to think otherwise. Nor is there any evil in wishing to give even greater security to our family, a better dowry for Patience someday. You did nothing wrong. Mr. Wickham is the author of our evils, he alone."

"I wish I could believe that," Wentworth said quietly.

"Believe it." Anne could be surprisingly fierce when she chose. "I do. I always have. Since the first we learned of Wickham's wrongdoing, I have known exactly where to lay the blame. It is not at your feet. Less still does it belong to Mrs. Smith."

She had hoped this last might make him smile, at least for an instant. Instead, Frederick pulled his hand free of hers and stared out the window at a horizon she could not see.

❧

Unbeknownst to the Wentworths, the louder part of their conversation had been overheard by Juliet Tilney on her way to her room. Juliet continued walking, willing herself not to pay attention. But she could not forget what she had heard.

Families have their own pride, she thought. *Their own secret languages and inner laws. That includes the Darcys, too.*

Maybe what I have asked of Jonathan is simply beyond the boundaries his family pride will allow.

Still, I do not think I was wrong to ask it.

She also could not help musing that both Wentworths were capable of greater anger than she would have dreamed.

Donwell Abbey hosted many agricultural projects, each the result of its master's avid interest in progress. Knightley's curiosity had led to the building of beehives, the construction of a new type of waterwheel, and—most controversially among the gardeners—the planting of exotic, unfamiliar seeds. One such planting had finally borne fruit, literally.

"Hardly three weeks ago, they were so green," Knightley said. "And now look at this one. Red as an apple and even larger."

The head gardener stared at it with deep suspicion. "Is that what a tomato is supposed to look like?"

Knightley shrugged. "It has grown and softened from greenness, so one must assume the fruit is ripe."

"But is it safe?" This was the question that had long plagued the head gardener. "My gran always said they're poison."

"They eat them in the New World."

The gardener made a sound that suggested people in the Americas might do any sort of lunatic thing, whether making war against their Crown or eating poisonous fruit.

Knightley tried again. "Apparently tomatoes are becoming quite popular in London—used in soups and stews and all sorts of dishes."

"They're even crazier in London than in America," the gardener said, apparently considering the tomato absolute proof of this assertion.

But Knightley was not to be so easily dissuaded. This was the third year he had attempted to grow such plants, and the first any of them had survived to be fruitful. Besides, after the unceasing tension and gloom of the past few days, he wished to enjoy this one small, pure satisfaction. So he lifted it to his mouth, ignored the gardener's panicked expression, and took a bite.

His first thought was that tomatoes were apparently extremely messy.

His second was that it was *delicious*.

Knightley chuckled as he pulled away the juicy thing and grabbed a handkerchief to wipe his mouth and chin. "It's wonderful. Tastes like summer itself. But there must be some trick to eating them which I have not yet learned."

"As you say, sir." The gardener held his hands out slightly from his body, as though to catch Knightley were he suddenly to topple sideways in the grip of poison.

Such a triumph begged to be shared. Knightley turned to go into the house and find Emma, but then caught sight of two of his guests upon a nearby footpath. "Mr. and Mrs. Brandon!" he called. "I've grown a tomato from the Americas, and it's marvelous. Will you have a try?"

As soon as he'd spoken, however, Knightley wished he had not said a word. For he had seldom seen two people less in a mood for such frivolity than the Brandons were then.

≪⌒≫

The Brandons, warned as they were by Mr. Knightley, had handkerchiefs on hand when trying the tomato. So they were only slightly stickier for the experience as they walked away afterward.

Marianne said, "I liked it," her voice so flat as to make her statement almost comical.

"T'would be better cooked, I think," said Brandon in much the same tone.

When Marianne tried to imagine such an exotic dish at table, she could only see the plates draped in sauces that were bright red—redder than blood. It was not an appetizing prospect.

Would she soon have an appetite again? Sleep peacefully

next to her husband? Or be able to read Cowper or Scott without her mind numbing to the words until they were no more than black scars on white paper? The aftermath of this horrible crime was different than anything she had yet experienced, and she could not guess how long a shadow the events would cast.

She glanced over at Brandon. He had brought his military uniform for any formal occasions that might arise, and she wished for a moment to see him clad thus—in a scarlet coat trimmed with gold braid, smiling without a care, the way he had looked at their wedding only months ago. It had seemed like a new beginning for her, almost a kind of rebirth into a life where her sensibility would not drive her to melancholy but would instead open her to ever greater joy.

Now that day felt like an ending.

"I should not have insisted that we speak," Marianne began. She could not look at Brandon; instead she kept her gaze upon Jonathan Darcy, who was riding his black horse at a gentle canter in the nearby field. "Forgive me."

Colonel Brandon gave her a searching look. "You are already forgiven. I cannot blame you for wanting only the truth between us. There can be no true marriage without truth— as you yourself told me."

Marianne remembered passionately encouraging her husband to be open with her only days ago. It felt like the folly of another lifetime entirely. "What if we are sorry for the knowledge we possess?"

It took Brandon several moments to reply. "Then we should not be. The ugliest truth is more worthwhile than the most beautiful lie. Do you not agree?"

"Of course," Marianne said, though she was no longer at all sure whether that was the case.

Both Marianne and Colonel Brandon spoke in normal, con-versational tones. Probably they assumed that their voices would not carry over the sound of hooves and the wind in Jonathan's ears.

Had Ebony been traveling at a gallop or even a canter, this might have been true. At a trot, however, the horse made no noise Jonathan could not easily hear above.

It sounded like—very much like—Colonel Brandon had revealed something to Marianne, and that Marianne now regretted the revelation. Did their newly shared secret per-tain to the murder? There was no way to be certain from the content of their conversation. However, Jonathan thought the deathly pallor of Marianne Brandon's skin suggested that this could well be the case.

Despite the potential enormity of this realization, Jona-than's attention was at first more focused on what Brandon and his wife had said to each other, rather than what they had not.

If honesty was an irreplaceable virtue between husband and wife, must it not also be so for friends?

For a murder inquiry, it was *essential*.

Jonathan owed Juliet Tilney no less.

✍

That night, Juliet was in her own opinion doing an excellent job of ignoring Jonathan Darcy completely. As the house party had not fully resumed the usual gaieties of such an event, the group gathered in the library shared in no common concerns or amusements. Instead, several people read books (including Elizabeth Darcy and Anne Wentworth), a couple of the men wordlessly handed pages of the newspaper back and forth, and Emma Knightley was busily sketching a land-scape from memory.

She was also trying to do her duty as hostess in offering up topics of conversation, but none could easily be found. "I suppose this is not the ideal summer holiday. All of you must wish you had visited the seashore instead."

The silence that followed made it all too clear that, indeed, there was not a single person present who would not rather have been sea bathing far away from any murder or murderers. No one was so impolite as to say so, but it was difficult to say anything else either.

Hastily, Mrs. Knightley continued, "You know, our children are at the seaside now with our dear friends the Westons. Henrietta wrote us the most delightful letter about her first sight of the ocean—Knightley, do you have it in your study? We should read it for the company."

Hearing a congenial letter read aloud was generally a pleasure, and Juliet was especially interested because she had never seen the sea herself. Unfortunately, Knightley shook his head. "I believe I had it with me when I went to the Churchills' for their *Debrett's*. No doubt I stuck it in there to mark the page."

"Oh, dear," Emma said. "Well." Conversation sputtered out again.

Juliet generally preferred reading as a pastime, but she knew she would be unable to concentrate on a book at the moment. So instead she worked on her embroidery. The goal was a delicate collar for her aunt Eleanor; the result, so far, was anything but delicate. Embroidery frustrated Juliet no end, but she was determined at least to be able to stitch a simple cornflower at some point before her demise.

Jonathan Darcy strolled past her and leaned over, as though to study the embroidery. Juliet's cheeks heated. Must he observe her failures? Would it make him feel better about pushing her aside?

Then she realized a small, tightly folded piece of paper had been dropped into her lap.

Juliet waited several moments after he had walked on before turning her attention to the paper. Casually—as if she were checking an embroidery pattern, perhaps—she unfolded the sheet he'd given her and glanced downward.

> *Miss Tilney—*
> *Please forgive my indelicacy in writing to you. I most*
> *sincerely beg your pardon for my unworthy behavior.*
> *Our efforts required honesty, and I denied you that.*
> *Furthermore, my parents' character can withstand the*
> *most severe scrutiny. By lying, I suggested otherwise*
> *and therefore dishonored them.*
>
> *There is, I think, still a great deal to be discovered*
> *here. Certainly there is no one among the company I*
> *should wish to aid in those discoveries but you. If you*
> *will forgive me, please meet me in the billiard room*
> *tonight, as we have done before. The conversations I*
> *overheard today were potentially very enlightening.*
>
> *If you do not come to the billiard room tonight, I*
> *will understand your answer and press you no longer.*
> *Regardless, I remain*
>
> > *Very sincerely yours,*
> > *Jonathan Darcy*

Juliet refolded the paper and returned to her work. She held the embroidery frame higher so that it half covered her face—and entirely concealed the small smile that had just appeared.

Chapter Fourteen

"There is only so much entertainment," Emma said, "to be found in a tomato."

Knightley sighed as his wife splashed her face with water from the ewer. He remained in bed, not as a late riser but as a man who had learned through hard experience that it was best not to get in Emma Woodhouse Knightley's way in the morning. "I realize that my garden cannot stand as a substitute for all the other amusements we might have provided our guests. My point is that we can perhaps find diversions that are adequate to their needs without violating propriety."

Emma huffed as she began untwisting the curlpapers from her hair. (Like all married women, she wore a mobcap during the day, but she was not above letting a few ringlets peek out around the sides.) "*Propriety*, you say, as though there were a settled rule on how to handle a murder in the household. There is no such. Believe me, I wish there were."

"Then we must set the example," Knightley said in a tone he thought would sound patient. To judge by the angry flare in his wife's eyes, it did not.

"The example we are currently setting is far worse than you believe," Emma insisted. "To skulk about like this, why—it suggests we are guilty!"

It cost Knightley a great deal to answer, "One of us *is* guilty."

Emma would no longer look directly at him. "But most are not, and we should behave as though none of us are. To do otherwise risks the very respectability of Donwell Abbey."

Although Knightley was not as sure of this, he was willing

to concede. Certainly the gravity of their behavior in the first days after the murder should satisfy most wagging tongues, save for those most determined to wag. (Mrs. Elton came to mind unbidden.) Continuing to keep their guests confined, without any leavening of mood to be had, was all too suggestive of gaol—a suggestion he most ardently wished to avoid.

"As you wish, dear Emma," he said. "Let us talk to the assembled company tonight and see if they agree."

"They shall," Emma insisted as she pulled her wrapper on around her nightdress. Soon she would be off to her dressing room, where her maid would help her ready for the day. "Wait and see."

"I do not doubt you. I only mean that it will be best to ask." Knightley sighed. "After that, then, yes—the house party will resume."

They must, somehow, go on as though nothing had ever happened.

❧

Jonathan, meanwhile, absently ran a brush through his hair, his focus not on the small mirror upon his wall but on the events of his meeting with Juliet last night.

How profound his relief had been to find her awaiting him in the billiard room! "Of course you are loyal to your family," she had said, looking up at him with more trust than he would've imagined possible only the day before. "I know you did not mean to do anything wrong."

"But I ought to have told you everything." It had felt so important to impress this upon her. "From now on, I promise that I shall."

He had not yet told her his thoughts about his uncle, the

earl of Dorchester—but those were too tenuous at present to share. They might prove more distracting than dispositive.

Instead, they had next discussed the important conversations each had overheard. Captain Wentworth's anger came as a surprise to neither of them, but Jonathan had been as shocked as Miss Tilney to know that it was shared by his gentle wife, Anne. "She did not sound as troubled by the loss of money," Miss Tilney had explained. "Instead, she was angry at Wentworth for the extremity of his distress about it."

Jonathan had asked, "Is that, perhaps, because she fears that rage might have led him to act rashly toward Mr. Wickham?"

"I do not think we can discount the possibility."

"Colonel Brandon and Mrs. Wentworth are keeping some manner of secret—though I know not whether it pertains to the murder," Jonathan had added. "But I overheard them talking, saying they were not yet ready to reveal something with 'risk.'"

"How fascinating," Miss Tilney had murmured. "This is unforeseen! Do you think perhaps Colonel Brandon knows why she left her room that night? Might he have seen her?"

Jonathan had considered this. "Perhaps so. Yet they do not appear to have known each other before their time at Donwell Abbey. Surely two people who are no more than acquaintances would not have so easily conspired to such a crime as murder."

"I admit, that seems unlikely. But it is most intriguing."

She was even more intrigued by what he told her next: "It sounds as though Mrs. Brandon were regretting the honesty between her and her husband. She could not regret that unless—unless she had heard something she very much did not wish to hear. Although that was not necessarily a confession of murder."

"No. But that murder surrounds us all. What could seem

more horrible than that, here and now? What could be worse than a confession?"

Jonathan had shaken his head slowly. "I fear we will have to find out."

A knock on his door startled him back to the present. "Mr. Darcy, sir?" came the muffled voice of a servant, who would not try the knob without permission. "Shall you be needing a valet?"

"Yes, but not quite yet. Perhaps in ten minutes' time. Thank you."

Once again alone, Jonathan wondered precisely why it was so enjoyable to remember a conversation about such a grisly subject. Probably it had to do with the person with whom he spoke. Juliet Tilney was refreshing company. Sensible company. If she was not an entirely conventional girl, well, he was far from conventional himself. Certainly she was the only person he had met who considered his oddities in the most positive light.

He rather wished he could explain this to his mother and father. But they would take his interest in Miss Tilney as something very far removed from what it was.

At least, for now.

⁓

Today the servants were easily able to retrieve the post, and Marianne Brandon received a letter. She did not even look down at the note as she sought a private place to read, assuming it to be from her elder sister. Elinor was a faithful correspondent but not an overactive one: she never wrote for writing's sake, only when she had news or when she was responding to it. This letter had been sent express. Either something terrible had happened at home—*Oh,* Marianne thought, *please not Elinor's baby, she has but a few months to go*—or Elinor had received Marianne's missive sent immediately after the murder.

Yet the letter proved not to be from Elinor at all. Marianne sat a solitary corner in the armory to read in privacy, her eyes wide at the handwriting on the front—which, upon her first good look, was unmistakably that of John Willoughby.

> *Dearest Marianne,*
> *I may still call you Marianne, may I not? Do*
> *not ask me to refer to you by the despised words*
> *"Mrs. Brandon." Merely writing them has pained me.*
> *It will be a very long time before I can speak them*
> *aloud, and I hope it will not be very long before we*
> *shall be able to speak to each other once more.*

Marianne had hoped never again to speak to Willoughby in any but the briefest, politest sense, at such social occasions as could not be avoided. Nor had she expected to ever receive another letter from him. Her heart fluttered within her chest, and her breaths came quick and shallow as she read on.

> *Surely, by now, Elinor—her, I can call Mrs. Ferrars, as*
> *we shall never again be friends as we were, and in that*
> *case at least I can honestly wish her joy—she must have*
> *told you that I came to visit when you were ill. When*
> *I believed your life to be in danger, and thought, no,*
> *knew that my weakness and my wife's unkindness had*
> *led you to this pass—believe me, Marianne, the utter*
> *devastation I felt was punishment enough for my many*
> *sins, and for more sins even than that.*

"You call your wife unkind and yourself merely weak," Marianne muttered. "Perhaps you have suffered for your sins, but you have not learned from them."

Tell me the truth—did you choose Brandon to spite me?
Knowing that <u>he</u>, above any other man, would be the
last I would ever wish to have your hand? But then
there is no man I could wish to have your hand other
than myself, and now this can never be.

But that does not mean we must be parted forever,
my Marianne.

You are a woman of honor. This I understand
perfectly. Yet would you be so cruel as to deny us
even the chance of speaking together again? We had
such conversation, you and I. No other person of my
acquaintance feels so deeply about poetry, or landscape,
or any other refinements. Certainly my wife does not.

Marianne's heart was not so vulnerable to Willoughby as
once it had been. Yet she could not read those words again—
my wife—without wincing.

It would be no great matter for you to contrive to
visit Somersetshire. The Palmers, I am certain, would
welcome you at any time. But if you will not come
to me, I will come to Dorsetshire for you. My aunt,
having done the damage to our hopes through her small
cruelty, is more pleased with my marriage than I. Soon,
I will visit, alone if I can. Then we will surely have,
or find, some chance to speak. When that long-awaited
day at last comes—please open your heart to me. We are
done keeping secrets from each other, are we not?

"As though I had ever kept secrets from you," Marianne
whispered. The secrets had been his. The blame was his,
too—whether he knew it or not. It appeared from this note
that he didn't.

This mattered little, but she wished it mattered to her not at all.

She shoved the letter into the middle of a pile of paper rubbish set aside for the maid to take away; it would most likely be used to light a fire, which in Marianne's view was a good end to it. If the servants were so ill bred as to read anything found there, let them make of it what they would.

⁂

Meanwhile, in the library, Juliet was in search of a novel she had not read. Given her entire family's eager use of their subscription library, she had already devoured so many. She admitted defeat and took up a favorite by Maria Edgeworth—one she had reread so often that Juliet could give it as much or as little attention as she chose.

Others in the library were reading their own correspondence, or writing it, when the Knightleys walked in. Emma's expression was determinedly bright; Mr. Knightley was warier, but he stood by his wife's side as she said, "Well, as we have all seen, the weather is much improved, as are the roads. Our home remains under a sort of cloud of suspicion, but there is no reason for all to suffer because of one's rash actions. As of today, we hope to resume the house party in earnest."

People exchanged glances. Reactions varied widely—from Elizabeth Darcy's smile to Anne Wentworth's frown and much uncertainty in between. Juliet noted that Fanny and Edmund Bertram did not look at each other, and that they sat at opposite sides of the long library. Had Jonathan noted it, too?

It was Edmund who said, "Do you not think it indecorous? Engaging in such pursuits after a man has died under the worst circumstances?"

"More indecorous, I think, to suggest that all our guests are guilty or should be suspected as such," Emma replied firmly. "We must not be ashamed to show ourselves, nor afraid to carry on as we would have done had George Wickham never come at all."

Knightley interjected, "Tomorrow, we have decided to walk into Highbury. A simple walk to town, no more, no less. Any of you who wish to join us may certainly do so, just as anyone who wishes to remain is free to decline."

"You are kind to attempt to amuse and distract us," said Anne Wentworth. Her smile was soft and a little sad. "Under such trying circumstances, you have proven to be the most understanding and generous of hosts." A general murmur of assent ran through the company. Juliet silently reminded herself to think upon this event in the future, when she had a home of her own and parties to be nervous about. No challenge she would ever face as hostess was likely to rival this.

Emma's smile had become more natural. "I am so glad we are in agreement. Let us begin tonight! Let us have a musical evening, with display from all our ladies, if they will."

Fanny Bertram shook her head, but the others agreed. Which was when Juliet realized she would not escape without showing her own "accomplishments."

Oh, why didn't I practice my piano? The murder was so distracting. I doubt Mama will accept that as an excuse.

⁓

Fanny Bertram had never been coached in most of the accomplishments of fine young ladies. Though she had been brought up at Mansfield Park along with Sir Thomas's children, she had not been one of them—a point of distinction much emphasized by her aunt Norris. The lone decorative skill Fanny possessed was needlework, and she was ever grateful that this was not anything to be publicly performed. Merely getting up in front of the whole room and speaking to everyone present seemed terrifying; how much worse if she had to sing!

Normally she enjoyed hearing others perform, particularly when real taste and refinement were displayed. Tonight, however, seemed to her like one more torment to endure.

Every moment she spent without Edmund, without speaking of the terrible matter that lay between them, was torture.

And yet, speaking of that matter was even worse . . .

At her next opportunity, Fanny managed to excuse herself. Although she longed for the comfort of the chapel, she could not be certain Edmund was not there. Instead, she went to the nearest copse of trees, hoping to restore herself in nature. She noticed Juliet Tilney watching her go. Was her disquiet so obvious to others? Was she shaming Edmund even now?

No sooner had she entered the glade than she felt some of her anxiety fade. Here, in this leafy space, was quiet. Here was peace. Here was a place at which none would judge her save for the great Judge of humanity Himself.

Fanny would not kneel on the grass; she did not wish to trouble the Knightleys' servants with the resulting stains. Instead, she simply folded her hands and closed her eyes.

O Heavenly Father, she prayed, *forgive me, forgive me for all that I have done and what I have failed to do. I cannot be honest with anyone, not even with my husband, and I do not know how to bear the burden of these secrets alone. Please give me strength to endure what I must and to know what is right.*

On only one point did she feel certain: she would tell no one of what William had written. *What I was told in confidence is to remain in confidence. Edmund must be made to understand that, at least.*

Fanny opened her eyes, jolted out of her reverie by the

unfamiliar thought: *Edmund must*. She had always submitted to Edmund's judgment and will, first as his adoring cousin and then as his wife. Rarely had he given her any reason to doubt the justice of his views. Never before had she felt she had any reason to absolutely prevent him from doing anything.

Dare I contradict him, I who am so very weak and sinful? Am I failing in my duty as a wife, refusing to obey my husband in this matter?

Or is Edmund failing in his duty as a husband?

Rebellious, heretical thought! Fanny began reciting the Lord's Prayer over and over, in the hopes of abolishing such thinking from her sinful head.

Yet the idea lingered even longer than her prayers.

❧

Jonathan liked music a great deal more than a young man was meant to.

Oh, it was not unheard of for the sons of the gentry to sometimes take up an instrument, and a good singer was welcome in any company. But it was the job of the women in the house to provide such amusement; the men of the house were those to be amused. So daughters were trained extensively in musical arts, particularly if they showed some aptitude. Sons, by and large, were not.

Jonathan—in this as in so much else—was different. One of his earliest recollections was of being a very small child and reaching up on his tiptoes so his fingers could strike the piano keys. Both his mother and Aunt Georgiana had at first indulged his interest, then begun teaching him in earnest. All the adults of the household believed that Jonathan would abandon the instrument as soon as he was big enough for a hobbyhorse. Then they thought he would abandon it once he had a chance to ride a real horse. After that, Jonathan suspected, they had expected him to give it up at school. To this day, when at home, he played more days than he did not. However, his talents were employed only before his family; his family did not consider it fitting for a young man to play in front of company.

"For you, it is a fine entertainment," his mother had explained, her mischievous smile playing at her lips. "For the young women present, it is a matter of far more importance. They must be publicly seen to be accomplished. You, my dear son, do not."

"I only have to be rich."

Elizabeth Darcy had laughed. "We have higher expectations of you! But as for society in general—yes, that will probably suffice."

This was another way in which the Knightleys' house party had proved irksome. Not only had the weather been foul and his uncle murdered, but Jonathan had also no chance to play the piano for an entire week.

Jonathan folded his hands in his lap as Anne Wentworth played an Italian love song. Sometimes, when he heard others play, his fingers twitched, unconsciously finding the notes on an invisible keyboard in his mind; folding his hands thus kept him from embarrassment. Mrs. Wentworth's playing was delicate and fine, with technique he greatly envied. If only he could ask her for instruction!

When the song ended, everyone applauded. Mrs. Knightley cried out, "Who will be next? What say you, Miss Tilney?"

Juliet Tilney's cheeks pinked. "I am not very familiar with most of the songs you have," she said, gesturing at their written music, "and I brought none of my own. But there is one tune I think I can manage, if you will promise not to forgive my lack of practice."

"Of course we will," said Elizabeth Darcy, giving her husband a look. Jonathan knew his mother's "lack of practice" to be a sort of joke between them, for reasons he knew not.

Miss Tilney took her place at the piano and set one piece of written music carefully before her. After one deep breath, she began to play. Jonathan smiled—she had chosen an aria by Pasquini, one of his personal favorites. Then a fudged note made him frown. *She really doesn't know the piece yet,* he realized.

At least there was one kind of help he could provide. Jonathan quickly got to his feet and went to her side to help her turn pages. His reward was a quick smile from her before she concentrated anew on her playing, acquitting herself quite well.

He thought no more of his action until she had finished her performance. As the audience clapped, Jonathan straightened and saw them—all of whom were smiling rather more than he would have thought Miss Tilney's playing to inspire. Only when he noted his mother's broad grin did he realize the group's pleasure came from seeing him help Miss Tilney.

They believe I am interested in her, Jonathan thought. *That I wish to court her.*

Did he wish it? Did *she*? Jonathan glanced down at Miss Tilney, but she was folding the music and apparently thinking of him not at all. That was a relief.

Or was it?

Next to play was Mrs. Knightley herself. As she was a rather average player, Jonathan took the opportunity to duck out of the room. As long as he was not absent longer than required for a trip to the privy, nobody would ask any awkward questions.

A young man could show no particular interest in a young woman for very long without creating expectations in both the girl in question and the local society. To dance with a young woman more than thrice in a night, to visit her family, or to speak of her to others was very near declaring himself. So Jonathan had been taught and had observed for himself. So far as he knew, there was no general expectation arising out of investigating a murder together. But had Miss Tilney formed one? Would she, if they continued?

It was not that he *disliked* the idea courting Juliet Tilney. It was that society did not allow him to consider the idea for anything like an adequate length of time.

Why can men and women not be friends? Jonathan fretted. *We play together as children; why can we not converse together as adults? It would be much easier to tell whether I wish to be married to someone if I could form a friendship first.*

Polite manners, however, did not agree. And it was not as though he were any great expert at making friends.

Jonathan had been pacing along, paying little heed to his surroundings, so it came as a jolt when he realized he had wandered near the gallery. Most everyone had left this room severely alone since the murder, save only himself and Miss Tilney, and their time here had been brief.

Was there, perhaps, more to be found here?

His footsteps echoed slightly in the gallery as he made his way deeper down the long hall of portraits and statuary. It was not so dark as the night of the murder, so Jonathan was easily able to find his way back toward the place where Wickham's body had lain.

With no one around to judge him—even the understanding Miss Tilney—Jonathan felt free to try whatever came to mind, however morbid. Thus he imagined his uncle standing where he must've stood to fall on the floor so. One step back, then, and he stood where the murderer must have been. The blow had been to the left side of Wickham's face, suggesting that the murder had lashed out with the right hand. Jonathan turned to his right—and opened his eyes wide.

He stepped toward a small bronze bust of Lord Nelson just beyond his reach, which stood upon a Doric column. The base of the bust was not precisely aligned with the column; no one would have deliberately arranged it so. The marble base was also slightly chipped on one corner, strangely for something that would have been purchased within the last few years and that ought to have been properly cared for. And the column was stained with several small dark spots.

One of the spots was smeared, right beneath the edge of the bust.

It was too dark for Jonathan to determine the color. The spots were so small that he, and others, had walked by without noticing them. Yet he was certain these stains were blood.

Chapter Fifteen

As the women began to retire for the evening, Juliet left the music room with no small amount of relief. Her performance had not been exceptional enough to impress, but it had not been bad enough to disappoint. If she practiced a bit over the next few days, perhaps she would be able to do better before the party ended.

Juliet was walking to the stair when she heard a whisper. "Miss Tilney. May I have a moment?"

Jonathan Darcy stood in a shadowy place in the hall, near the entrance to the gallery. He seemed to be inviting her into the darkness beyond.

Does he intend to—to make a declaration? Juliet wondered. Or would he try to steal a kiss? Neither could be allowed. She wasn't sure whether that boundary provided more safety or disappointment.

Then he waved her toward him and added, "You must see this."

What relief—he was referring only to the murder.

Juliet let him lead her into the gallery, spooky though she now found the room; it stood to reason that there might be more important discoveries awaiting there. "What have you found?"

"The weapon used for the murder, I think."

Juliet gasped. "So it is as we thought. The murderer did not use the mace—it simply fell, as it had done before."

"So it seems," he said as they passed more oil paintings of

Knightley ancestors. "But let me know if you agree. It is not a certain thing."

She regretted that she had not taken a candle with her, but the skies were clear enough that the moonlight through the windows helped her to see. At first she squinted through the darkness as Jonathan Darcy showed her the bust of Lord Nelson. Her eyes widened as he explained how he had imagined the killing, then pointed out the damage to the base of the bust and the telltale spots of blood.

"It *is* blood," she said. "I feel sure of it. This is not a room where anything is likely to be spilled or scattered. There can be no other explanation for it."

The younger Mr. Darcy looked more doubtful. "There *could* be. But none of those explanations strike me as very probable."

The bust was heavy in Juliet's hands as she took it up to examine the damage more minutely. "The marble must have been chipped when the murderer dropped the weapon to the floor. And the terrible gashes in Mr. Wickham's cheek and throat—those could've been made by the sharp corners of the marble base."

"We know that the murderer wiped the weapon clean of blood, but if this was done after putting the bust back on its pedestal, he might have left a few drops on the marble and not noticed," he said. "It was a far darker night."

"Or she," Juliet said. When he frowned, she continued, "You said 'he' when referring to the murderer. We do not yet know to which sex the killer belonged." It seemed to her that men got up to a great deal more killing than women did, but Mr. Wickham had caused great offense to all.

He explained, "It seems that this crime was not a planned act. That it was instead the result of a moment of great anger. Men anger much more quickly than women do."

Juliet considered this for a moment. "I would say that men

reveal their anger much more quickly than women do. For them, it is not so strongly disapproved of. But anger that is hidden sometimes burns all the hotter. Like a pot with a lid on, you see?"

Then she flushed. She should never have admitted that she had set foot inside a kitchen in her life. The Tilney family kept a cook, of course, but Juliet and her siblings sometimes liked to spend time there chatting with her, not least because they might receive a sweet bun, too.

Jonathan Darcy, who had surely never been within the kitchen at Pemberley, did not catch the allusion, but he did not seem to mind it either. "I believe you are correct," he said. "A woman could be pushed to an act of great rashness. Even violence, were the provocation sufficient." His expression was grave. "My late uncle was a master of provocation."

⁓

The next morning, the Knightleys led all their guests into town—save for two.

"We hope to join you on your next excursion," Edmund Bertram said to his cousin as the party assembled at the door. Already, Edmund wore his riding clothes, and Fanny would shortly descend wearing the same. "But if Fanny does not have a regular chance of exercising, the effect on her constitution is very bad. Riding is by far the most congenial exercise for her."

If George Knightley thought a walk might be considered exercise as well, he was too polite to mention it. "Of course. We've all been cooped up too long indoors, have we not? Let your wife join us this evening, refreshed and in good spirits."

"Her spirits are very low indeed," Edmund replied. "The shadow of this crime falls over her greatly, I fear." He could not begin to explain the other reason for her dark mood.

Fortunately Knightley required no further explanation. "It does over us all, and we must each banish that shadow in whatever manner we find best. We should return before teatime."

With that the party set off: the older women in white gowns, the younger in dresses of pale blue and yellow and pink—the style was turning away from the purity and modesty of white, much to Edmund's dismay. They did not speak much among themselves, but the Surrey countryside would soon provide diversion enough. In truth, Edmund wished very much he had been able to take that walk with Fanny by his side. But until Edmund could trust Fanny to keep her composure in company, however, he considered it best to keep her apart from the others.

Fanny descended the stairs in her riding habit. It had been a wedding gift from his mother, lovely dark blue velvet, and normally it rendered her pale complexion almost brilliant. Today, however, Fanny looked . . . ghostly. Sick, Edmund would've said, had he not known the root cause.

"I am sorry to be late, Edmund," she said, her tone flat. "The grooms will be waiting for us." She did not meet his eyes as she walked toward the door.

For a moment Edmund did not follow her. He had been thinking of how best to tell Fanny that he was no longer angry with her. Yes, she had done wrong by not revealing William's sin to him and by dealing on her own with Mr. Wickham. If she was at first too tenderhearted toward her brother to fully condemn his evils, well, that was hardly surprising for one as gentle as Fanny. Soon she would see her Christian duty.

But Fanny did not seem to be worried that he was angry with her. For the first time in their marriage, he began to think she might be angry with *him*.

Edmund could scarcely give the idea credit. Fanny had

almost always deferred to his greater age, education, and wisdom; and the rare occasions when she had not, she had both apologized profusely and given her reasons. This flinty silence was wholly unlike her.

Perhaps it was not anger that motivated Fanny. Surely some other emotion underlay her current peculiar behavior. For she had nothing to be angry with Edmund about—at least, in Edmund's own opinion, which he was rarely inclined to doubt.

❧

Emma Knightley had made the walk from Hartfield to Highbury countless times in her life, beginning when she was just old enough to toddle alongside her beloved governess, Miss Taylor. Moving to Donwell Abbey after her father's death had changed that path only by making it a quarter mile shorter. She knew every field, every farm; she very nearly knew every cow. Some of the trees she had watched grow from saplings. So while the rest of her guests noticed and admired, and while Knightley served as their guide, she could chat with the highly inquisitive Miss Tilney.

"It is a pity we cannot enjoy the abbey's gallery as we might have before," Miss Tilney said. "Are your servants still avoiding it? I cannot blame them if so."

"Surely they are, but we must put an end to that," Emma resolved. "Cleaning and restoring the room is precisely the sort of task that becomes more difficult the longer it is delayed. If we let this go on, superstition will set in. Better to put it to rights again."

"So you are eager, then, for us to be able to walk there once more?"

Why should the girl wonder about that? No matter, Emma

decided. "We are still stranded together with precious little amusement. If the family art can provide any extra diversion, I feel sure it will be welcome to all."

That seemed to satisfy Miss Tilney. For the rest of the walk, Emma's mind was free to wander.

How good it would be to see her old friends again! The Westons, of course, were gone to Brighton with Henrietta, Oliver, and their own two children; they would not return for another month, sunbrowned and full of new stories. But all the other familiar faces were likely to be in the town square, and Emma longed to speak with each and every one.

It was not that she didn't care for her current guests. They had accepted the horrors of this house party with understanding and even good humor, and most were individuals Emma hoped to know better. But George Wickham's murder dominated their gathering; the man was a bully even after death, demanding more than his due. Emma was ready to think and speak of *something else*. Anything would suffice.

Thus, when they entered the outskirts of town, Emma was especially glad to see her friend Mrs. Robert Martin—who, as Harriet Smith, had been Emma's closest companion for a brief but significant time in her life. Harriet had married a farmer, honest and intelligent as farmers went but in a decidedly different class than the Knightleys. Inevitably their friendship had become more distant since. However, each retained fond memories of the other, and they always greeted each other warmly when their paths crossed.

"Harriet!" Emma called, waving gaily. "Good morning to you!"

Harriet Martin flinched so sharply that she nearly spilled her basket of peaches. "Oh. Oh, I—good morning, Mrs. Knightley." With that, Harriet briefly ducked her head and hurried away.

Emma could scarce believe it. Had Harriet Martin, the farmer's wife, just avoided her gentlewoman friend? Had Emma been . . . *snubbed*?

Both her shock and her certainty grew as the party walked farther into town. The merchants who normally welcomed her, the passersby who doffed their caps or nodded in her direction, all seemed incapable of even seeing Emma and her company. There could be only one reason for such a swift, complete change: the murder.

Do they suspect me? Emma thought, her mind awhirl. *Word must have spread that the murderer is surely a guest at Donwell Abbey. So either they think me a killer or they blame me for harboring one.*

Emma herself would have cast blame at the hostess in such a situation, before living it for herself. The walk into Highbury, the treat she had looked forward to for days, now seemed a misbegotten idea. She should not have shown her face before the culprit had been identified and the Knightleys had had a chance to repudiate them.

At last a friendly face appeared—one that Emma had not always been happy to see but was grateful for now.

"Dear Mrs. Knightley!" Miss Bates said. The old woman's smile was as open and unaffected as ever. "Mr. Knightley! And all your guests, goodness me, you must introduce me to absolutely everyone. I so look forward to making new acquaintances, for there are few to be had in such a small village as our own, and it is especially lovely to meet people who already friends of those I hold so dear. Then it is not like being strangers at all, is it? I do hope that you are all well pleased with Highbury. Little though we are, I daresay we dwell in one of the prettiest villages in all Surrey, and do not think that we lack for amusements! We all take it in turns to entertain and comfort each other, you see, with dinners or garden parties or dances—and, oh, what do you think, Mrs. Knightley! Frank Churchill is to hold a dance very soon, to which you will all be invited, I am very sure. Grace has been longing for a dance, and I cannot blame her, for I recall being as eager to dance at her age as she is. More, perhaps, if such a thing is possible! But then, I never could dance as well as Grace does. She is so light on her feet—why, it is almost magical to see. I do believe one could attend all the finest balls in London and never once see a dancer as talented as our darling Grace. Do you know, that is why we are out and about this morning? She wants to trim one of her dresses before the dance. I think it suits her very well as it is—then, most dresses suit her, I believe every color looks well on her—but she wishes to make it finer. And I dare say she can, for her needlework is so elegant! She can embroider and make lace and do every sort of thing, far better than I can for all my years with needle and thread, and I—"

"Dear aunt," Grace Churchill interrupted. She had stepped out of the nearby millinery shop and now shook her head in fond exasperation. "You should not go on about me so. There is nothing so tiring to hear as praise of another, just as there is nothing so enjoyable to hear as praise of oneself. So as much as it pains me to stop you, I must." She turned her pale eyes upon Jonathan Darcy, and her smile widened. "Besides, you will give them exaggerated opinions of me, and then I shall disappoint."

Miss Bates looked dumbfounded by the very idea that Grace could disappoint anyone, in any fashion. Emma seized the no doubt brief opportunity of silence to make further introductions.

The whole time she spoke, however, she watched Grace, who was watching Jonathan Darcy. She also watched Juliet Tilney, who was observing Grace even more closely than Emma herself. Was a rivalry brewing?

Well. Far be it from Emma to take sides. She'd learned her lesson about meddling, even if her husband had not.

But that didn't mean she couldn't enjoy watching it all play out. No circumstances could be so dire as to distract her from that!

$\sim$

"I am *quite* sure my aunt has already told you that Father is throwing a ball." Grace Churchill wound her arm around her aunt's, an affectionate gesture that gentled her mild teasing. "To which you are all invited."

Jonathan felt as though the invitation were more for him than for the rest of the company. Certainly Miss Churchill's gaze rested on him much longer than it did on anyone else in his party. He had learned enough to understand that this meant she had some interest in him, and that most young men would be flattered to be the object of interest to such a lovely girl. For Jonathan, however, such occasions were more worrisome than pleasant. Interest was likely to lead to more attempts at conversation. More attempts at conversation gave him more chances to get things terribly wrong.

Fortunately, this conversation was not his to uphold alone. Emma Knightley said, "Of course, we shall be only too pleased to attend! You are very kind to help me amuse my guests."

"Thank you so much, Miss Grace." Anne Wentworth's familiarity struck Jonathan as odd, until he remembered that the Wentworths had been resident in this area for some months. "It is good of you to include us." Next to her, Captain Wentworth did not seem very pleased to be included, but he was not so rude as to object.

"We shall be there as well," said Marianne Brandon. She had struck Jonathan as a vivacious young woman on their first acquaintance, one likely to enjoy dancing. But her acceptance was no more than polite. Colonel Brandon watched her and ignored everyone else around them.

"For my part," Mother said, her eyes dancing, "there is little I enjoy more than a country dance. My husband, I fear, rarely indulges."

Father looked at her—hopefully? There was a joke between them here, one Jonathan did not understand but one that connected them. After their strange silences these many months, Jonathan was heartened to see them share any moment of feeling. Darcy said, "I will of course be only too happy to dance on this occasion."

"There you have it!" Elizabeth declared. "Mr. Darcy shall dance. Your ball is already the social event of the season, Miss Churchill."

Juliet Tilney spoke up last. "I thank you for my share of the invitation."

"Good. I do hope we will get to know one another better," Miss Churchill said. She smiled at Miss Tilney as brilliantly as she had at Jonathan himself. Perhaps Miss Churchill was not so focused upon him as he had worried.

"Oh, yes, indeed, you must!" Miss Bates could be restrained no longer. "There are so few young ladies in Highbury of Grace's age and station. Of course, she and Henrietta are such friends"—she nodded toward Henrietta's parents, the Knightleys—"but Henrietta is gone away for such a long visit. Though who can blame any young person for wishing to go to Brighton? Not I, I am sure. So many exciting things to see and to do, and sea bathing as well! But how peculiar it must be, to always be out and about but surrounded by people one does not know. I have visited London twice and Portsmouth once, and on both occasions, I could not accustom myself to spending so much time with strangers. It is far nicer here, where everyone knows everyone and we are all such great friends, and—"

"And we will be very happy for our new friendships to grow," Miss Churchill said, interrupting her aunt with a smoothness that must have been created by much practice. "Papa will let you know all the details very soon. I hope you will all enjoy Highbury!"

With that, Grace Churchill and Miss Bates departed, heading back to the home Jonathan supposed he would see when the time for the ball came. Already he knew he would be expected to ask Miss Churchill to dance.

But he thought more upon the fact that he would also dance with Juliet Tilney.

ᴄ𝑜

Most young ladies, upon being invited to a ball, are immediately alive with interest as to what will be worn; what music will be played; what dishes will be served; and, most particularly, which other young persons will also be in attendance. Juliet was no less fascinated than the average girl of her age and station, but the subjects of her curiosity were very different.

It is one thing to carry on at breakfast and dinner, she mused as the group walked from store to store, largely ignored by the rest of the townsfolk. *It is quite another to do so at a ball. Can a person carrying the guilt of so terrible a crime truly be able to dance and laugh the night away?*

If so, then that person would be almost unspeakably cold-blooded—

"We should look in this next shop, I think," Anne Wentworth said to her. "Surely you will be wanting shoe-roses for the ball."

"Oh! Yes, of course. I am glad you thought of it, because

it had not entered my mind." Juliet hurried up the steps, and Anne kindly accompanied her. "I forget that you know a bit of Highbury already, including the best shops."

"It is a charming town," Anne said. "Frederick and I would have enjoyed our time here greatly had the cloud of Mr. Wickham's swindle not been over us all the while."

Juliet was at first surprised by Anne's frankness—but then, they had all been forced into a kind of intimacy that would otherwise have taken months or even years to form. She dared to ask, "Does Mr. Wickham's death change your financial situation?"

"I am not sure," Anne admitted. They stood now amid slippers and lengths of lace, unobserved while the merchant helped another customer. "The money is in Wickham's coffers. We could sue the estate for it, and with no one committed to defending the case, our chances might be very strong. But if it is spent, then it is gone." Anne's spirits seemed lower than before—no great surprise, except that the cause was not one Juliet would have anticipated. "In truth, I do not know if I want to see the money again."

"But—"

"Losing it hurt my husband's pride greatly," Anne said. "But his pride is a fault, both in penury and prosperity. The worst that happens to us if the money is lost—we return to sea. I never minded living on a ship with my husband. Oh, there were privations—illness, sometimes, and once a terrible storm that seemed the equal of Noah's. There was . . . there was a child that might have been, but was not."

Juliet caught her meaning; the admission was shockingly honest, but how could anyone not wish to unburden herself of such a terrible loss? "I am so very sorry to hear it."

"Thank you. But I do not dwell overmuch on what might have been—it is a lesson I learned too late in life but learned well." Anne sighed. "My husband still blames himself for exposing me to such risks. He should not. In truth, those were some of the most fascinating years of my existence. At sea, as a captain, Frederick is at his very best. On shore, with new wealth . . . less so." Then Anne seemed to catch herself. This, truly, was too much to reveal. "Please do not repeat what I have said. I ought not to have spoken so, but—"

"But we have been much cooped up, and none of us are quite ourselves," Juliet finished for her. Anne rewarded her with a grateful smile.

They were at that moment strolling past the butcher shop and toward the shop with shoe-roses. Captain Wentworth was several strides ahead of them, between Knightley and Brandon. A young man in a bloodstained apron walked out of the shop—the butcher's assistant, no doubt—carrying parcels wrapped in wax cloth and twine. It was an utterly ordinary delivery.

So why did Wentworth look at the young man with such intense anger? Why did the young man turn away, as if afraid of a scolding?

This is about something that passed before, Juliet thought before reminding herself, *That does not necessarily mean much. It could be some trifling disagreement. A late bill, even, given the Wentworths' indebtedness to the late Mr. Wickham.*

Still, what had been seen could not be forgotten.

Much later in the day, as the party returned to Donwell Abbey, Juliet's thoughts were still on her conversation with Mrs. Wentworth. *He is a man of dark temperament,* she mused as she absently set the new shoe-roses on her dressing table. *Anne Wentworth said that his pride is a powerful force, and I saw for myself his anger with Mr. Wickham. His absence from his room for part of the night remains unexplained. Could Wentworth be the one?*

A shudder went through Juliet. It was terrible to fix on any single person as the likeliest killer. Yet it was also terrible to doubt everyone all the time.

At least I need not suspect Mrs. Wentworth, Juliet told herself. *Such a gentle, soft-spoken person—she could not take a life. Of that I am sure. Yet . . . she loves her husband so. If she thought him endangered in some way, could that provoke her to an act otherwise unthinkable?*

A rap at the door startled her. "Oh! Yes, who is it?"

Hannah entered the room. It was not a time of day when her presence would be called for, and her expression was odd—almost afraid. "Miss Tilney? If it's not presuming too much—may I speak with you?"

"Certainly you may." Juliet wondered what had gone wrong. Maybe one of her dresses had been poorly laundered and was ruined. She hoped it was not the blue.

Instead, Hannah held out a scrap of paper, half-burned. The singe marks along the ragged edges did not entirely conceal the handwriting that remained. "A burned letter, ma'am." Juliet took it from her, and Hannah breathed out. "Found it in the hearth. Like as not it doesn't mean anything, but—what with everything that's happened—"

"You were quite right to bring it to me," said Juliet. "Where did you find it?"

It took Hannah a moment to get out the last. "It was in the Darcys' room."

Chapter Sixteen

Juliet took the singed letter from Hannah with both anticipation and regret. Impossible not to feel a small thrill at perhaps acquiring another piece of information regarding the murder of Mr. Wickham—but equally as impossible not to feel sorrow for Jonathan. He had such faith in his parents, honoring them as a good son should. Yet they appeared to be destroying evidence.

"Why did you not bring this to your mistress?" Juliet asked. She was grateful for this but could not help wondering at it.

Hannah replied, "Forgive the liberty, ma'am, but it seemed to me you was uncommon interested in what happened that night. Mrs. Knightley, she'd rather we all forgot about it completely. Maybe it's not to do with anything, but—most don't burn their letters—"

"Not unless they wish for the letters to remain forever unread." Juliet nodded. "Thank you, Hannah."

The truth had to be known. Steeling herself, Juliet gingerly pried open the brittle, burned sheet of paper to make out what she could. Only the first few words were perfectly clear . . . but they answered nothing. Instead, they made the puzzle even more complex.

༄

The group's trip into Highbury, so counted upon by Emma as a means of cheering her guests, had had the opposite effect.

Everyone had noticed their cool reception by the towns-folk, an impression that kindness of Miss Bates and Grace Churchill could not amend. Few things are more disagreeable than being considered guilty of a sin of which one is innocent; the usual remedy, self-righteousness, was available to none, for varied reasons. Doubt had of course been resident within Donwell Abbey for some time, but at least within the house, all present had understood that Mr. Wickham's murder, however unchristian, was no great loss to society. No such comprehension had softened the judgment of Highbury.

So that afternoon the mutual suspicion that had pricked its way into the minds of all at Donwell began to fester, like a splinter left too long within a wound. The mutual forbearance that had sustained them all since Wickham's death no longer stood at full strength. Shadows darkened, along with moods. Silences became more ominous. The grand abbey ceased to feel like a handsome country house and began to feel like a prison—never pleasant, but even less so when one or more persons involved has reason to believe a real prison could await in their very near future.

And yet! Magistrate Frank Churchill's command kept every single person there for days, possibly weeks to come. Beyond that, politeness would demand that nobody depart the very moment permission was given; to do so would be to slight their hosts for reasons beyond their control. (Unless one of the Knightleys proved guilty, in which case a hasty departure would be entirely understandable.) So the house party promised to stretch on, and on, no matter how badly anyone attending wished to escape.

The first signs of real trouble appeared at dinner.

Wine was, of course, offered at every civilized gathering. That night, however, the serving staff realized that bottles were emptying rather more quickly than was common. Women who might otherwise have indicated their glass should not be refilled were instead taking second or third helpings. Men, who would have been freer with their consumption in any case, went through the bottles so quickly that the butler was obliged to hurry down to the cellar and decant several more.

Where wine flows freely, so will wit—well chosen or otherwise.

"We seem to be making merry tonight," said Elizabeth Darcy as she watched her glass being refilled again. Across the table, Fanny Bertram frowned in ill-disguised disapproval. "Is it very improper of us, Mr. Bertram? As a clergyman, can you excuse our conviviality in the face of such tragedy?"

Edmund Bertram had been concentrating on his wife and as such had very nearly missed her question. He wished he had missed it entirely. "Were we celebrating the man's death, it could not be condoned. But this is merely dinner, as we would share on any other night."

Elizabeth pursed her lips, making a show of her doubt. "On any other night? It seems to me we have rarely enjoyed ourselves so well, even before Mr. Wickham's arrival, much less his demise. Not that we had much time before—such a pity."

"And why should we not enjoy ourselves?" Captain Wentworth's smile was fiercer than a beast's bared teeth.

This provoked Edmund to reply, "Whatever else Mr. Wickham was, he was a Christian and one of our fellow men."

"I am not so sure of the former as I would like to be," Elizabeth said. "I must concede that he was the latter. The resemblance is too strong to be mistaken. Too many of our fellow men are possessed of equally weak principles and equally strong avarice. Oh, come now, Mr. Bertram, do not look so sour with me. Would it not be hypocrisy, to pretend a grief for Mr. Wickham we do not feel? And is not hypocrisy itself a sort of sin?"

Emma, who sensed the evening getting away from her, interjected before Edmund Bertram could expound upon moral wrongs. "If there is one thing I am entirely certain of, it is that none of us wishes to devote any more time to Mr. Wickham. Let us speak about something else."

"*Anything* else," murmured Knightley.

Thus Emma sat smiling brightly through a few uncomfortable moments of silence. Her attempt to provide a topic was ill chosen, which she knew as soon as she spoke the words: "What did everyone make of Highbury?"

"It is a charming village," Darcy said, his words civil but his tone flat.

Elizabeth took another sip of wine. "I should rather wonder what Highbury made of us? Though I suspect we all know."

Juliet tried: "How happy that we came upon Grace Churchill and her aunt."

Captain Wentworth laughed, a harsh bark of sound. "You are the first person to describe an encounter with Miss Bates as 'happy' in quite some time, I imagine."

This, in turn, touched off the temper of Mr. Knightley, who had long been protective of the aging village spinster. "She is well liked in our local community."

"Indeed," said Anne Wentworth. "She has always been more than civil." Her eyes suggested that Captain Wentworth would regret any further attempts to say otherwise.

When silence fell again, this time the entire company was wise enough to let it lie, heavy as a blanket, covering them all.

⌘

On the whole, Fanny found this dismal dinner easier to navigate than most. (Aside, that is, from Mrs. Darcy's shocking indulgence in the wine. Supposedly the Darcys were one of the preeminent families of the English gentry; Fanny would have expected better, even from one so indelicate as Elizabeth Darcy.) The silence at the Knightleys' table this evening might have been oppressive, but she could bear that more readily than trying to make conversation with strangers. Her natural timidity made it easy for her to keep quiet and she was almost relieved when others remained quiet also, particularly on a subject she had no desire to discuss. However, the undeniable tension had taken its toll. As they went upstairs to bed, she felt a headache knocking at her temples, heralding its appearance.

"At last an early night," Edmund said. He had given her his arm to guide her up the stairs, and she had taken it, but Fanny felt they were acting by rote—that Edmund's gesture held no true feeling. "Pray we are allowed to sleep through it, instead of being awakened by yet another clamor."

"I do so pray." Real fervor animated Fanny in that moment, which drew Edmund's attention. But he attributed her warmth of feeling to the wrong cause.

Once they were safely in their room, behind a closed door, he began, "I sense that you wish to pray, Fanny—rather more than your usual bedtime prayers."

Fanny did not look at him, but she nodded slowly. "Yes. It will do me good."

Every night, she knelt beside their bed and whispered an Our Father. Her most heartfelt, personal prayers she usually reserved for church—either during services or in one of her frequent solitary visits. But sometimes, when she was at her most troubled or most fragile, she would pray by her bedside as fervently as an Evangelical in full froth. He expected as much this evening. Fanny would wish to plead for her brother's salvation from sin, and to be forgiven for her attempts to conceal that sin. Edmund had even—leniently, he supposed—decided that she should not be blamed merely for not wishing to speak of it. What could be more natural for such a delicate creature than to be silent on such an unmentionable topic? However, her actions in going to Mr. Wickham, to assenting to his blackmail . . . there, Fanny's repentance must be great indeed.

He kneeled down when she did, each on opposite sides of the bed, and waited for the soft sound of her voice.

"Dearest Savior," Fanny whispered, "most merciful King of Kings, please look down upon my brother William. Please forgive him. Please watch over him. He needs you now more than he ever has before. I need nothing—I want nothing—all my hopes and prayers are for William. Please grant him your infinite mercy, O Lord."

And more in this vein. None of it pleading for her own forgiveness; none of it asking for her brother's sin to end. None of it, in short, in any way resembling what Edmund had expected to hear from his wife.

It is only in how she phrases it, he told himself, and tried to believe this.

She was too gentle, too timid a creature to excuse sin. Scarcely anything could drive Fanny's pure heart to wrongdoing; in her entire life, Edmund had only seen her so moved by evidence of an even greater evil.

In the past few days, he had found himself reminded of the incident with the black cat.

Mansfield Park, home to his mother's beloved pug dog, housed no cats within. But any barn or stable attracts cats eventually, and a scrawny thing, its dark fur matted, found its way to them when Fanny was not yet twelve years old. She had taken pity and given it some milk salvaged from her own tea. However, Edmund's elder brother, Tom, was at that point very wild and not much given to pity. He took it in his head to torment the poor cat, throwing rocks at it as it yowled, entrapped in a corner of the stables. Edmund and Fanny came upon the scene just as Tom threw a larger rock, one that would surely have gravely injured the cat had it not missed its target by a fraction of an inch.

"What are you doing?" Edmund had said.

"Getting rid of a stupid cat." Tom had been laughing. "Once it can't scratch me any longer, I'll dunk it in the barrel and drown the thing."

"No!" Fanny had cried. Tom only laughed the harder.

Edmund had intended to tell his brother to stop immediately, but he never had the chance. Fanny flung herself at Tom, shoving him so hard he fell to the floor. Tom had of course reacted by howling at the injustice, which summoned their aunt Norris, who bandaged her favorite boy while scolding Fanny until she wept. The cat, meanwhile, took its chance and escaped.

Hours later, Edmund had gone out and managed to entice the little black cat back with a bit of fish from the kitchen. Upon taking it in hand, he had walked with it to a nearby tenant farmer's home, knowing they had recently complained of rodents at the grain. The cat had lived another seven years as both a great mouser and a beloved pet. Fanny had been so grateful, and even went to visit it from time to time.

But his parents had been very angry with Fanny for knocking their son down, angrier than they were at Tom's petty cruelty. She had been punished and lectured to a point a girl so fragile could scarcely endure.

But Fanny—who apologized for almost her every move— never said she was sorry for attacking Tom. The desperation that had come upon her in that moment was born of her fervent desire to protect the black cat.

Even Fanny, Edmund knew, had limits.

☙

Juliet was not one of the first to go up to bed. She hoped that the dismal, unstructured evening would allow her to simply remain downstairs until she and Jonathan had a chance to confer. The letter she had read earlier in the day burned within her mind as bright as flame. His thoughts on this fragment from his parents' hearth would be invaluable.

However, this pleasure was delayed, because she was not the only one who failed to retire early. While a few of the men took brandy and cigars, Juliet was trapped in the drawing room with a few of the ladies and seated next to Marianne Brandon.

Marianne's former vitality had vanished. Her fine coloring had faded to pallor, and her once-bright eyes now never met another's. She kept glancing toward the door through which Brandon would return; Juliet could not tell whether she was eager for her husband or dreading him.

"At least there is to be a dance," Juliet said. "You told me you are fond of dancing."

"I am." It seemed to surprise Marianne, this recollection that she had ever enjoyed anything. "In a few days, there will be music and songs as though on any other night. We shall dance as though none of this ever happened."

"So I hope!" Juliet tried to think of what else she might say, but no words seemed adequate to capture her companion's attention. The one question that she burned to ask—*Who do you think might have killed Mr. Wickham?*—was so far beyond the bounds of etiquette that it could not be spoken outside her clandestine partnership with Jonathan Darcy. No guest could be expected to condemn another with anything but absolute certainty.

So Juliet said nothing, and the silence stretched out between them. Marianne simply kept staring after Colonel Brandon as though there were nobody else in the world.

At that moment the door opened. Marianne tensed, and Juliet could not keep herself from staring. But the man emerging from Knightley's study was not the colonel but instead Mr. Darcy.

He went directly to his wife's side. Elizabeth Darcy, who had partaken of more wine than most on a night when much had been drunk, sat alone near the fireplace, staring into its light, leaning slightly to one side. Darcy held out his hand, more command than offer. "I have done my duty as guest. Now we will away to bed."

"You may go if you wish," Elizabeth said. "I like it here by the fire."

Darcy's jaw twitched. "You are not presentable."

"But I have already been presented, and therefore there is no more harm to be done."

"It is time for you to come to bed," Darcy insisted.

Elizabeth finally turned to her husband, her eyes narrowed. "Why should you care if I am there or not?"

Embarrassment flushed Juliet's cheeks. To hear such a spat between married people was mortifying. Even Mrs. Brandon, numbed to so much else, turned her head rather than witness it.

Jonathan Darcy—who must have been waiting for her in the billiard room already, oh dear—hurried past Juliet to go to his mother's side. "You are not yourself," he said quietly. "Will you please let me walk you upstairs?"

Elizabeth lay one hand on her son's cheek, then rose to go. Mr. Darcy did not follow. He simply stood there, as motionless and silent as his wife had been just minutes before.

There was much for Juliet to think about, but her first consideration was her most important: it looked as though she and Jonathan might not have a chance to confer tonight. The letter's secrets would have to wait until tomorrow.

Jonathan was greatly relieved that his mother raised no further objections to going to bed. Never before had he seen her take too much wine. He did not think her behavior had been grossly inappropriate, but his father seemed to disagree, and Jonathan knew he was not always the best judge.

"My head hurts already," Mother said as she walked through her bedroom doorway. "What joy tomorrow will bring."

"It will be all right," Jonathan insisted.

She smiled at him unevenly, then shut the door.

What next? Perhaps Miss Tilney could take advantage of the strange, unstructured evening to meet him in the billiard room earlier than usual. How stupid that a young man and woman could not openly spend time together unchaperoned and that they had to guess at each other's intentions. If only a third party were available—someone who could chaperone them but had no motive to kill Mr. Wickham—but sadly, no such person was staying at Donwell Abbey.

He still hoped to meet with Miss Tilney later that night, at least until he reached the drawing room again. She glanced up at him expectantly, but it was his father who drew his attention. Darcy stood at the fireplace, as downcast as Jonathan had ever seen him, save for the worst days after Susannah's death.

His duty as a son was clear. Jonathan went to his father's side. "Mother is safely abed. Should you not join her?"

"I think not." Darcy studied his son for a long moment. "Come. Walk with me."

Jonathan at first expected a nighttime stroll outside, but his father simply led him to the library. It was one of the few rooms that might be occupied at night, but they found it empty. Darcy sat down heavily on the nearest sofa, as though he had taken a much longer walk and were weary from the journey.

"Do you think your mother will ever forgive me?" Darcy said.

Never before had he spoken so to his son. To be confided in—almost as a friend—was both gratifying and intimidating. "To be forgiven for . . . what?" Jonathan had no sooner asked the question than he realized he might not want to know.

Certainly he did not anticipate his father's answer: "For Susannah's death."

This made no sense. Maybe his father had taken more wine than Jonathan had realized. "She died of a putrid fever."

"Because her father took no decent care of her. And it was I who sent her back to her father."

Jonathan's own memory of these events did not align with this. "Mr. Wickham wrote to us, insisting upon her return. We thought it could not be for long, that she would be back with us soon."

Darcy took no note of this. "Your mother said we should refuse to send her back. Wickham only wanted her with him to spite me—because she had begun to call me Papa." Jonathan winced at the memory; his father did not notice, simply continued speaking: "The man's vanity was wounded. No doubt at any other time, he would have returned her to Pemberley in short order. But it was not any other time. It was in the first stages of recovery from her illness. Elizabeth thought she should not be moved. The doctor believed it possible, however, and so I thought—I thought, better to have it over and done with, the sooner she goes the sooner she will return—"

Jonathan remembered Susannah more vividly than he had in months: her love of fairy stories, the way she would pop an entire strawberry in her mouth, her hearty laugh so surprising in a child that small. He had never reveled in rough games as a boy with his brothers, but with Susannah he had happily played horsey or chase. It was different—he was doing something to amuse her, not himself—and her delight had been reward enough for any effort or indignity. Susannah had become very near to a sister for Jonathan during the last years of her life. Was it any wonder that she had come to think of his parents as her own?

Should not Wickham already have understood that?

"What kind of a father fails to call a doctor when his child is ill?" Darcy got to his feet, unable to restrain restless energy. "What kind of father leaves a child of that age alone for hours, ill or not? But when so weakened—"

She'd been so frail when she left Pemberley that last time. Jonathan remembered how light she'd been in his arms. Her touch had never troubled him, not then, not once.

"If I had refused, Wickham would have created trouble," Darcy said. "If I had accepted that trouble, Susannah might well be alive. And now she would be ours forever, outright."

"Father . . . you could not have known what would happen. The putrid fever might well have taken Susannah's life no matter what we did."

"It might not have done. That is what your mother can neither forget nor forgive. How can I expect it of her? For I do not forgive myself." Darcy's expression darkened. "Damn George Wickham and his selfish pride. Damn him to hell."

Jonathan had never heard his father speak so. But the profanity troubled him less than the fury he heard, barely contained. His father's rage was not born of purely of hatred for Wickham; it was equally tied to his love for Susannah.

It was not shocking that anger might lead to murder. Jonathan had to confront anew the truth that love might have that same power.

Chapter Seventeen

"I think I shall go to bed now," Juliet said to the only other woman still in the room, Anne Wentworth. Already she had lingered so late that it verged on impropriety, and to no avail. Apparently the conversation between Jonathan and his father would be of some duration; no billiard room discussion was to be had. To bed, then. The tantalizing letter and all her speculations upon its contents would be just as interesting tomorrow. "The walk into Highbury is not long, but we have had so little exercise these past days that this short stroll has fatigued me."

It had not done so in the slightest; and her siblings—with whom she ran, jumped, and played at bowls on any day with good weather—would have convulsed with laughter had they heard her. But one had to give a reason for leaving another alone in such circumstances.

Anne nodded. "It has been a long night. I shall wait for my husband."

"Then wait no longer." Captain Wentworth finally returned to the room. He was the last of the men to return from brandy and cigars, having outstayed even his host, which was singular. Juliet thought she could still detect the scent of brandy on him, mixed with the tobacco. "Let us all three end this wretched day."

"It has not been wretched," Anne Wentworth said as she rose, and they headed for the stairs. Then she seemed to reconsider her words. "Not compared to the other days we have recently experienced. A small matter for satisfaction, I admit, but as it is the only one we have lately had, we should not forget it."

"We have other, greater reasons for satisfaction," Wentworth said. "Such as the fact that Mr. Wickham appears to have no heirs."

"That does not concern us," Anne Wentworth insisted.

Wentworth raised an eyebrow. "Does it not? You astonish me."

Juliet sensed she was no longer a part of their conversation—that they had forgotten her or would like to. There was nothing for her to do but to pretend to be as invisible until her companions again acknowledged her, if they did at all.

"When I invested with Mr. Wickham, I told him I had a family," Wentworth continued. "I told him about Patience, and how I hoped to give her a dowry that would allow her to choose any young man in the land. I told him about your family, and he was much impressed with the Elliot name. Never did he mention any family or child of his own. I ought to have known then that he would have no one to remember him. No one to regret his going."

It sounded to Juliet rather as though Wentworth *had* known that—and thus, had known his debt would likely die with George Wickham.

Anne said, "Why should you tell him of my family? He did not need to know, and certainly you have never felt any great fondness for them." When Wentworth did not immediately reply, Anne answered her own question: "You told him that they looked down upon you. That you wished to rebuke them with even greater wealth. In other words, you showed him just how vulnerable you were to his cheap tricks of deception."

Wentworth jerked his head back, as though he'd been slapped. "Is this what you think of me, then?"

"No—you know that I—" Anne looked skyward as though

for deliverance. "You are my husband and I love you, but when you close me out—"

"*I* close *you* out?" Wentworth retorted. "And which one of us has not told the truth about wandering around on the night of—" He caught himself then, remembering that Juliet was beside them, fervently as she wished not to be.

So she took the opportunity to hurry up the last few steps and go quickly toward her own bedroom. It would be difficult to sleep when she now had twice as much to reveal to Jonathan!

Anne Wentworth had, indeed, been outside her room on the night of Wickham's murder. Upon reflection, Juliet did not think Anne the killer; Jonathan Darcy had seen her on the upper floor, not down in the gallery or anywhere especially near it. Nor was she as angry with Mr. Wickham as Juliet had supposed—to her, the loss of money was more gift than curse.

But any wife might well lie if, by so doing, she was able to obscure her husband's guilty actions. Anne Wentworth herself thought the captain was hiding something—she who knew him better than anyone!

If his wife suspected Captain Wentworth, Juliet could do no less.

༄

Already Darcy wished he had not confided in his son. It was not the responsibility of a son to hear his father's intimate burdens, nor should Jonathan be privy to the secrets of his parents' marriage. At least Jonathan could be trusted to keep such matters private.

Darcy pushed open his bedroom door slowly, taking care to make no noise. As he had expected, Elizabeth was very much asleep. If he awakened her, she would still be uninhibited from wine but past its more congenial effects. Any argument that ensued would be terrible indeed. Although Darcy usually valued his wife's wit, he had discovered how sharp it could be on the few occasions it had been unleashed upon him. He wondered sometimes what she would be with just as much intelligence, eloquence, and humor but without the fundamentally good nature that rendered those qualities gifts rather than weapons. With luck, this question would remain forever unanswered.

While he undressed, he watched his wife sleep. Normally she woke easily—too easily—but tonight the wine allowed him to move about freely. This was one of the only occasions in their entire marriage at which she had drunk too much; the cause, he supposed, was sufficient.

She looked younger abed—vulnerable, with her bared, shorn head revealed. Elizabeth had cut her hair short not long after their marriage, when it was fashionable for both men and women to do so, and had kept it so ever since, though she insisted both then and now that her primary reason was simple practicality. "If my hair is hidden under my cap," she would point out, "it cannot matter to anyone else what it looks like—except, of course, to you. If you cease to find me beautiful with short hair, I shall let it grow all the way to my toes."

He found her beautiful with short hair or long. He had found her beautiful as a twenty-year-old with fine eyes and high spirits, and he did so now that she was forty-two, graying at the temples, with delicate lines on her face hinting at her countless smiles over the years.

Darcy had seen her smile so seldom these past eight months.

Forgive me, he wanted to say. *Forgive my foolish mistake. I wanted only to have things over and done with Wickham.*

But he would never be able to ask her that. Impossible, when he had not forgiven himself, and had no intention of doing so.

❦

Fanny lay still and sleepless, staring at the sliver of moonlight that filtered through the bed-curtains. Despite her many worries, she was by now so exhausted from emotion that she had thought she would dissolve into slumber the moment her head touched the pillow. So it might have been but for Edmund.

He was awake, too. Not only awake—alert and tense. Though he lay as motionless as she did, she could *sense* his watchfulness as though it were the heat from an unwelcome fire. Fanny knew, too, that he was unhappy. Before marriage, she had little dreamed how much a husband and wife could communicate simply from the way they lay beside each other in bed. Impossible to fall asleep with him in this state, so she had to hope that weariness would claim him before too long.

Her hopes were disappointed. "Fanny?" Edmund said, keeping up the pretense that neither knew of the other's wakefulness.

"Yes, Edmund." Fanny braced herself. This would not be one of the pleasanter midnight awakenings a wife could expect.

"They say never to let the sun set on anger." He sat up, pushing the pillows behind him. "Perhaps it is not anger between us, but it is a misunderstanding—and, I fear, a grave one. I will not rest easy until it is settled, and I suspect you will not either."

Fanny wanted to lie—to say she was not troubled, merely restless—but she knew it would be to no avail. As much as she feared confrontation, this one was inevitable; and she knew that sometimes the dread of a thing became worse than the thing itself. She rolled over to face Edmund. "Then speak to me."

He gazed down on her much as he had when she was only a girl, his shy little cousin come to stay: protective, considerate, all knowing. That look had always been dear to her, before. "Fanny, we can no longer put aside the topic of William's sin. It disquiets you, I know, as it does me. Perhaps you need guidance as to what you might do next."

"What would you have me do, Edmund?"

"Many would argue that you should immediately sever all bonds between you and your brother. But that is too severe for you, I am sure." Fanny's heart leaped, only to sink anew as Edmund continued, "You must write one final letter. Remind him of his Christian duties and explain that your own duty requires you to cast him aside until such time as he has repented and ceased his sin. William is yet young, and naval officers long at sea are known to—to behave as they would not at home. There is hope for his salvation yet, and by setting the right example, you will help lead him toward it. You will have every reason to believe that he may in time return to you as a good Christian."

Fanny could imagine a sister writing such a letter to a brother. But she could not imagine herself writing that letter to William.

"No," she said.

Edmund stared at her. "Pardon?"

She had surprised herself almost as much as she had her husband, but she would not lie. "William is my brother," she said. "My love for him is absolute, as it should be. God's first law is love, is it not?"

"Yes, but—"

"Then any preaching that tells me to repudiate my brother therefore cannot be the Word of God." Fanny sat upright to face Edmund evenly. "I am a good Christian. You know that I am. Sinful I am, and weak, but I work and pray to do better, to be better, and to know the Lord. When I imagine casting William out of my life—I do not feel closer to God but farther away from him. Thus it cannot be right."

Edmund had never been so astonished, at least not in Fanny's recollection. "Have you no regard for what the church says?"

"Are we to become papists? Only listening to dogma, never speaking to God ourselves?"

"Of course not!" The mere suggestion that he was behaving in a Roman Catholic manner seemed to have angered Edmund more than anything else she'd said that night. "But that does not mean that we surrender to our own weakness. Doing what is right is sometimes painful. This makes it no less right."

"Doing what is right may be painful *to us*," she said, "but doing what is painful *to others* is rarely right."

"William's pain is of his own making."

"He wrote to me in trust and hope. I will not abandon him."

"You refuse?" Edmund looked repulsed. Fanny felt miserable. No wonder he was surprised; she had refused him almost nothing during their many years together. Once she would've sworn that she never would, that her husband's guidance would forever be her light and her shield. Losing that confidence did not feel like liberation. It was more akin to the snuffing out of a candle in a vast dark room. "You take your brother's part in this? You agree with his actions?"

Of course not! Fanny nearly cried. She still could not think too much on what William and Harris did together. (Some aspects of it seemed wholly unworkable.) Yet—when she thought of how he had written to her of his friend Harris, of the warmth and real regard they shared . . . it did not seem so wicked. Certainly there were connections between men and women that were far more despicable.

Morality looked very different to her now than it had only days earlier. Right and wrong did not seem so absolute as Fanny had always believed. Her actions could not be governed by assumptions any longer. Each deed had to be judged on its own merits, in its own moment.

"I will say only this," she finally answered. "I believe that the smallest hatred is a greater sin than the most misguided love."

Edmund gaped at her. Fanny lay back down and turned away from him, ending the conversation for tonight.

But only for tonight? What would the future bring? If Fanny refused to repudiate William, would Edmund repudiate Fanny?

She prayed he would not. More than that, however, she prayed for William.

✧

At nearly one o'clock, a mere half hour after the final stragglers had gone to bed, Jonathan slipped out of his room and sneaked back down to the billiard room. He did not expect to find Juliet Tilney there; they had never met so late. But he hoped, enough so to wait nearly a half hour longer in dark solitude before deciding she was not coming.

Two options presented themselves: One, he could wait until tomorrow to talk with Miss Tilney, either at their usual meeting or if some opportunity arose earlier in the day. Two, he could rap on Miss Tilney's door and awaken her.

Option one was obviously the better choice. It was less improper by far. Yet Jonathan could not reconcile himself to it. His doubts about his parents weighed on him heavily;

worse were his memories of Susannah. He had forced himself to put those memories aside during the past months; it had seemed the only way to go on. Tonight, however, Susannah had come back into his heart, and he felt both the pain of losing her and the guilt of trying to forget her. This did not create ideal conditions for a good night's sleep.

Miss Tilney's conditions were probably more congenial, which meant she was unlikely to welcome any awakening. Even knowing this could not dissuade Jonathan. He had to talk to someone about his suspicions regarding Mr. Wickham, but even more than that—he simply needed to talk to someone. And Juliet Tilney was the only person he wished to talk to.

❧

Juliet had not even finished the final stages of undressing, so preoccupied was she with the day's discoveries, when the knock came at her door. "Yes, yes, what is it?" she whispered, just loud enough for the servant on the other side to hear.

Instead of a servant, she heard Jonathan Darcy's voice, no louder than her own. "You weren't in the billiard room."

She knew she ought to have found a way. "Wait, I'll be right there," she said, as she quickly tied her wrapper around her.

Juliet opened her bedroom door to find him still standing exactly there, rather than having gone down into the billiard room to wait for her. Did he expect her to invite him into her bedchamber? She blushed at the thought. Young Mr. Darcy's intentions were innocent—she had no doubt of that—but the scandal if they were found together! Bad enough if anyone caught them alone together at night in any corner of Donwell Abbey, but the bedchamber was beyond reckoning. So she hurried past him, waving for him to follow.

No sooner had they reached the bottom of the stairs than he began: "I am sorry to awaken you."

"I was not asleep. Besides, we have much to discuss." Juliet simply took her place on the settee near the stairwell. She was confident that none of the guests would be spying on them; they were all much too burdened with their own concerns. "Have you learned anything new? I have—and it concerns your parents." Jonathan's eyes widened. Hastily she continued, "No, what I found does not incriminate them. Or, rather, Hannah found it—she's one of the housemaids. It's a letter. Half-burned, doesn't make any sense—"

"But someone did not wish it to be seen." He took a step closer; the candle in his hand flickered. "Where was the letter found? What does it say?"

"It was found in your parents' hearth." When he visibly tensed, Juliet hastily added, "Yet the letter was not addressed to either of your parents. Look, I have it here in my pocket."

She handed him the fragile, charred paper, which he lifted almost to his face to make out the words by candlelight. From her day's studies, Juliet knew that very few of the words were legible, but the salutation was: *My dearest Fanny*.

His eyes widened as he took that in. "Why should Mrs. Bertram burn a letter in my parents' fire? And why burn this at all? What little one can make out seems ordinary enough."

"Just a bit about being on a ship, and someone named Harris is a friend of whomever the writer might be," Juliet said. "Nothing more can be read. So why make a secret of it? Why slip into your parents' room, if this has nothing to do with the murder?"

"It may have a great deal to do with it," he said, surprising her.

"Why?"

He flipped the letter over, which surprised her, as there was nothing readable on that side at all. "The seal. Look at it—it is mostly melted, but one can tell it had been broken before, and a little of the shape remains. Two arcs, side by side."

"You mean—the wax seal we found in the gallery, near where Mr. Wickham was killed." Juliet stood up to look at the seal anew. It was such a commonplace thing that she had forgotten to take particular note of it. Foolish, to have missed such a clue! She swore she would not again. "So the seal we found, the one we thought was an *E*, was instead a *B*."

He nodded. "For Bertram."

"But that is not likely—for her brother would seal his letter with a *P*, or perhaps a *W*."

"Look." Jonathan Darcy pointed to the overlapping dark marks around the broken seal. "This letter was opened and resealed more than once. The original seal no doubt bore William's mark, but Mrs. Bertram would have needed to reseal it with her own."

"So, unlikely as she seems, we cannot cease to consider Fanny Bertram a suspect. Though it is strange how either of your parents might possess this, I cannot see how it would connect either to the murder."

Jonathan's expression was hard to read at any time; by candlelight, it might as well have been a mask. "My parents—they would not have killed Wickham for any venal reason—but he had caused them very great grief, both in the distant and the more recent past. So much so that I fear it may have . . . impaired their judgment."

"Oh. *Oh.* Have you found anything definite?"

He shook his head. "I have only reconsidered their position, and thought more upon what forces might drive a person to act out of character. My father would never strike anyone out of anger or hatred, but out of love . . . for the sake of love, he might do much."

This made little sense to Juliet. "For whose love? I do not follow."

He remained silent for a long moment, so much so that she felt certain he was once again withholding information from her. Yet he surprised her by going on to explain: "Mr. Knightley mentioned an earl who was implicated in Wickham's schemes, whose recommendation led many to invest in the swindle. My aunt Georgiana, my father's sister, is married to the earl of Dorchester. So my father might have believed that she was mixed up in this business, too."

This hardly seemed to signify. "There are many earls in this country, surely."

"Yes, but—" Jonathan Darcy hesitated for a long moment, and Juliet found she was holding her breath. "You see, my aunt's marriage has apparently not been a peaceful one. My father has no great liking for the earl, nor much trust in him."

"And the earl of Dorchester and Wickham were connected, because they were both your uncles." This was a new lens through which Juliet could focus her thinking—and, indeed, much seemed clearer. "Still, why should a man with such power and fortune agree to be party to such a scheme?"

It took him even longer to answer this time. "I do not know the reason. But I have long suspected such a reason exists."

"Beg pardon?"

"We are never allowed to mention Mr. Wickham in front of Aunt Georgiana. His history with my family involves her, too, in some way, and that way must involve some terrible shame for not one person ever to speak of it." Hastily, he added, "My aunt is a woman of excellent character. I would not have you think otherwise. But even a good person may be compromised by a schemer."

"Mr. Wickham seems to have compromised many good people." Out of respect for Jonathan Darcy's aunt, Juliet refused to speculate on the particulars. They hardly mattered, compared to the existence of some root cause, and it appeared that had at last been unearthed. "So the earl and countess of Dorchester may have been under some—obligation, let us say, to Mr. Wickham. He might have been able to force them into endorsing his financial swindle. And if your father realized that—in order to protect his sister . . ."

Her voice trailed off. Jonathan Darcy, however, was strong enough to finish for her. "He might have done much, if he had learned her to be in danger. When he left their room on the night of the murder, he could've gone to look through Knightley's papers. Knightley had previously said the earl's name might be among them. So my father could have learned this on the night Wickham died."

The motive was all too clear. Juliet had always considered Mr. Darcy a suspect, but now he must stand at the center of their inquiry.

How much it must have pained Jonathan Darcy to tell her this! And he had held back that information about his uncle, at least for a while. Yet he had spoken. His commitment to the truth could not be denied; Juliet honored him greatly. Before she could say as much, he added, "We must of course learn the name of the earl in question for ourselves. But we cannot simply slip into Mr. Knightley's office. I believe Mr. Churchill has taken some of the relevant papers into evidence."

"We shall have to come up with another way."

"The trail must be followed," Jonathan said, his expression grave, "even if it leads to my father."

Chapter Eighteen

Unannounced guests are rarely welcome, least of all when too many guests are already present. So it was that Knightley looked out from his study before breakfast, saw a carriage coming up the walk, and breathed a heavy sigh. It had the look of a hired coach, not Frank Churchill's nor that of any other person known to him.

As the sound of hooves on gravel became audible, Knightley dropped his head in one hand and collected himself. The ongoing distress between himself and Emma had deprived him of sound sleep, tormenting him with dreams of her absence for various unreal reasons. Tossing and turning had, in turn, disturbed her and thus further darkened her mood toward him. How they would present a united front before their guests today, he did not know. Still, it would have to be tried.

He looked up again to see the carriage almost at the door and, in the far background, a figure on horseback that was unmistakably Frank Churchill. *Either he is especially zealous in his desire for justice to be done,* Knightley thought, *or he wishes to again invite himself for breakfast.*

Perhaps I am too harsh. Both motives may have force at the same time.

Knightley straightened himself in preparation for both visitors. He was entirely put to rights by the time his butler rapped on the door, and he believed he was ready to see anyone until the announcement came: "Mr. John Knightley, sir."

"John!" Before Knightley could even rise to his feet, his brother had entered the study. "What brings you here?"

"I had to know." John, a few years Knightley's junior, now looked far the elder. Gray streaked his hair, and his face was lined with care. This had not been the case until only months ago—only after George Wickham had entered their lives. "Wickham is truly dead? Murdered in this very house?"

"I wrote you as much." Yet Knightley did not wish to upbraid his brother for the hasty trip into Surrey. Impossible to hear of such a thing with equanimity, when so affected by it as John had been. "Come, come, sit down. Will you have tea or coffee? You must have left London before dawn. Surely you are exhausted."

John looked back at him with dark-circled eyes. "Promise me that you did nothing foolish on my account. Promise me that."

Knightley did not react with outrage. He *had* acted foolishly on John's account—so much so that it shamed him—but he did not intend to speak of it with his brother, least of all when John was so very much troubled. "I promise. Now, come. Eat. Rest."

∽

As little sleep as Juliet had had, she felt far more invigorated that morning than most of those staying at Donwell. She descended the stairs for breakfast in fine spirits, just in time to see Frank Churchill give his hat to the butler. "Mr. Churchill!" Juliet smiled. "How lovely to see you again, even under such sad circumstances."

"Miss Tilney. Today, the circumstances are happier than before." Frank's easy smile faltered for a moment. "There is of course the upcoming inquest to discuss—but I came merely to formalize the invitation my daughter made yesterday. A ball, to be held at my home, Friday evening. It is up to Mr. Knightley to tell me whether, as I hope, you will all come." He held up his hand, revealing the envelope that contained their proper invitation.

"I hope we shall, too," Juliet said. She'd been thinking about the ball with more and more interest, and had hit upon a clever plan. Eagerly she awaited a chance to tell Jonathan Darcy of her intentions.

Mr. Churchill misunderstood her enthusiasm. "Of course you do! I never met a girl of seventeen who was not longing for a ball. Well, I promise you good music so long into the night you will wear your slippers threadbare before we are done!"

"That sounds very merry." It did not take much to create more merriment than they'd had at Donwell Abbey these past several days, so Juliet felt anticipation to be entirely justified. "Will Miss Churchill be handling all the arrangements herself?"

"She will help, but I am quite good at such things, more I think than the average man." Mr. Churchill's smile was fond. "Ask Mrs. Knightley when you have the chance, and she will tell you what an old hand I am at hosting balls."

Juliet had half hoped to be asked to help Grace Churchill. Not that she wanted to spend too much time away from Donwell Abbey, and thus the investigation—but after so many days of being surrounded by the macabre, she longed for lighter diversion and less distracted company. Still, if Mr. Churchill was one of those rare males who took a great interest in the details of parties, there was nothing to be done for it. "Will you be staying to breakfast, sir? Not that I am able to issue an invitation, but I know how glad the Knightleys always are to see you."

"Perhaps not this morning," Mr. Churchill said thoughtfully, before continuing in a more conspiratorial tone. "The footman told me Mr. John Knightley has come to visit. Is this true?"

"I do not know, sir." Juliet glanced toward Mr. Knightley's study. She well remembered that John Knightley was the brother who had first, and most disastrously, become entangled with Mr. Wickham.

"Must be. The footman is scarcely likely to make such a mistake." Mr. Churchill seemed to be speaking more to himself than to her. "They wouldn't have invited him. Quite a time to make a visit, given these circumstances. Quite a time."

Juliet knew as well as Mr. Churchill that this was no normal visit. Did John Knightley suspect his brother of taking drastic action to protect him?

Was he here to question his elder brother—or even, perhaps, to thank him?

⁂

Elizabeth woke in no good temper. The headache she deserved throbbed, and Darcy had dressed and taken himself out on the grounds while she still slept. He was visible walking upon the lawns, at least when she could bear to look directly into the sunlight.

Her spirits were revived somewhat by the receipt of a letter in the post, delivered by a servant. Although Elizabeth had written to all three of her sisters after Wickham's death, she had always expected the promptest reply would come from her younger sister Mary.

In their youths, a letter from Mary would have been more the cause of irritation, or the increase of mirth. Mary then had been as much pedant as scholar. Her interest in theology, music, and history had been marred by too great a wish to display her accomplishments, often before they were equal to such attention. This habit had made her a figure of fun in the family and in Meryton. Disdaining balls and picnics, she met few eligible young men and therefore enchanted none. As Mary reached her twenty-fifth year, Mrs. Bennet had despaired of marrying her off to anybody of quality and begged Mr. Phillips to look among his clerks for someone who might do.

That summer, however, Mary traveled with her uncle and aunt on a tour of the Kentish coast. One Sunday they attended a local church in which the very long and lofty sermon was delivered by a Mr. Wheelwright, to the dismay of the rest of the congregation but to Mary's great interest. Afterward, she asked Mr. Wheelwright to elaborate on his remarks; he professed himself delighted to find a young woman of such serious mind.

Mr. Wheelwright was fifteen years Mary's senior, possessed of a reasonable fortune, a widower for three years, and childless. Never had he considered a second attachment, until fate provided a girl with a temperament he found most admirable. He had few pleasures beyond books and philosophical arguments, which suited Mary very well. They wed five months after meeting and had in the years since produced no fewer than six children as testimony to their marital harmony.

But Mary's situation improved in more ways than the material. Though Mr. Wheelwright could be pompous and dour, he had true affection for his new wife. Elizabeth had not realized how sorely their family teasing had tested Mary until she saw how much happier her sister was in a home where her intellectual strivings were praised rather than censured. Furthermore, Mr. Wheelwright was of superior mind and education. His library would've been the envy of any reader's home in England save for Pemberley itself. With such opportunity for learning, and a husband who provided her with informed conversation, Mary's understanding had greatly improved. She delivered pronouncements far less often; and when she did, those pronouncements were more worth the hearing.

None of this had accounted for much in Mrs. Bennet's initial view of the match. She was much relieved to have married off this final daughter at last, particularly given her longstanding belief that no man on this earth would gladly take Mary. But in the fullness of time this son-in-law became the favorite of them all when he was named the dean of Tunbridge Wells. This was a fine thing to boast about, but even more wonderful to Mrs. Bennet was that Mary's husband had become the very dean in authority over Mr. Collins! At this, all triumph was complete.

Elizabeth opened her sister's letter and read:

> *Dear Lizzie,*
> *Such shocking news as you have relayed gives rise to*
> *many emotions, yet bars many others. We cannot truly*
> *grieve the death of a man so immoral as Mr. Wickham,*
> *regardless of his connection to our family, but we cannot*
> *but feel the greatest revulsion for the criminal act*
> *committed. No doubt you, your husband, and your son*
> *are all still greatly distressed, and Mr. Wheelwright and*
> *I condole with you in your time of difficulty. We will*
> *pray nightly for the matter's swift resolution, so that*
> *you may be released from Donwell Abbey and return*
> *home. The sooner you return, the less time there will be*
> *for ill-informed talk to spread throughout Derbyshire.*

Elizabeth had not yet considered how gossip might bend the story outside of the tiny confines of Highbury. Groaning, she rubbed her sore temples and read on.

*Your account suggests that Jonathan is handling himself
well, despite the difficult situation and his own peculiar
temperament. What strikes me most forcefully is that
you scarcely mention Mr. Darcy at all—this, despite his
lifelong connection to Mr. Wickham, which suggests
that this event must be most troubling to him. If you will
forgive me for speaking of it, Elizabeth, I have noted
that you have written of your husband very little these
past eight months. If you are not talking of him, it seems
probable that you are not much talking with him either.*

*I shall not pry further into your most intimate
concerns, but as a clergyman's wife, I remind you that
it is the duty of a wife to cleave unto her husband—and
this duty is not only one for brides, but one we must
also maintain throughout our married lives. Most
importantly, as a sister, I urge you to be more open and
sincere in your dealings with your husband than our
mother and father have ever been with each other.
To be good wives, we have had to unlearn many bad
habits. Do not surrender your better habits now, in this
hour of travail, when they will serve you best.*

After that, Mary proceeded to detail the concerns of her
own home. With six children, this recitation went on for
almost an entire page. Elizabeth read it all, but it was Mary's
advice about Darcy that dominated her thoughts.

How happy Mary would have been, to know that one of her
pronouncements was being taken seriously at last!

⁓

"Two houses, and no bedrooms," Emma said as she fussed
over John. "I cannot believe we have no bed to offer you. Only

servants' quarters—and that is no fitting welcome home for you."

"It is quite all right," John said. His usual vitality was absent. He sat in Knightley's study, head hanging as if too heavy for his shoulders. "I can travel back to London tonight."

"Indeed not." Emma was indignant. "We will not hear of it. Perhaps the inn—"

"Better horseback than that inn," John said with a bit more feeling. The closest such establishment was not known for good food or fastidious housekeeping.

"Then stay here," she pleaded. "Please. Even if it is only servants' quarters, you will at least be dry and safe."

John's faint smile faded almost as swiftly as it had come. "We are now grateful for that which we once took for granted. But that is no reason for less gratitude. I will stay, Emma—not for long, but for tonight at least."

She breathed out in relief. At least she had accomplished that much.

Knightley returned to the study; Emma did not turn to look at him. John's gaze traveled from husband to wife and back again, but he said nothing.

"Well, John," said Knightley, "have we put your mind at ease? Now that you see Emma and I have not entirely lost our wits?"

John shook his head slowly. To Emma, he looked as weary as a farmer at harvest's end. "My mind will be at ease when Frank Churchill has found whatever vagrant is responsible for this mischief and your reputations are safe."

It was no vagrant, Emma wanted to say, but she restrained herself. John's low spirits would certainly not be revived by learning he was currently in the same house as a murderer. Her husband didn't mention it either.

At least his sense did not desert him permanently, Emma thought.

He only endangered the family home in a fit of madness. This was not great consolation.

"It was I who brought us to this pass," John said. "My foolish pride overcame the principles our father raised us with. My profession and my inheritance from our mother would have more than provided for my family throughout our lives. Instead, I became eager to make my own fortune. To prosper beyond those born to stations above me. Forgive me, George, but I even wanted to be that rare younger son with more wealth than his elder."

Emma did look at Knightley then and saw his most gentle smile. "It is not a rare younger son who *wants* to have more wealth than his elder. I believe it is an almost universal condition."

"Yet I pursued it. And to trust such a man as Wickham! If my principles alone were insufficient to discourage me, my profession ought to have. Had I been half so cautious as I advise my legal clients to be, I would not have fallen into such a trap." John's voice trembled as he faced his brother. "The worst of it all was asking you to sign that surety."

It was as though a tight knot that had been bound within Emma's heart for days suddenly loosened. Of course Knightley had not volunteered to sign such a surety; he had done so only because John had asked it of him. John asked for so little—he was so proud, so stubborn—Knightley would not have had the heart to deny him. She imagined that the same request had instead come from Isabella to Emma herself, and in the imagining, she realized instantly that she, too, would have agreed.

It was not that Emma had not surmised that these things would be true. But she had not *felt* them. Only now, looking at John so adrift and forlorn, did she understand the pain Knightley would have felt on his brother's behalf. Such pain might lead a person to do something far worse than signing a surety.

Of course, Knightley should have told her about it first—but if he had, Emma now realized, she would have urged him to act precisely as he did.

John shook his head sorrowfully. "At that time I thought the trouble was but temporary—that I would soon have the funds—"

"No," Knightley said. "You were no more foolish to ask me than I was foolish to say yes. Which is to say, we are both blockheads, just as Nanny always insisted. How vindicated she would feel if she could see us now."

John had to laugh at that, and Emma felt the tension within her begin to soften. Her husband might be self-righteous at times—perhaps he should consult her more and respect her opinions more thoroughly—but that did not change his good heart. She had to remember the best of him, even when facing the worst.

Emma took Knightley's hand. He kept his attention on John, but he squeezed her fingers, enough of a gesture to tell her that the breach between them was . . . not healed but healing.

⁓

At tea, Anne Wentworth listened with what interest she could manage as the party discussed whether or not to accept Mr. Churchill's invitation to his ball. Anne had been under the impression their acquiescence had already been given, but it seemed this was not the case.

"It ought not to be attempted," insisted Colonel Brandon. His wife watched him across the table almost warily. "We have seen how the local people doubt us. We can expect no better reception at a ball."

"Worse, perhaps." Elizabeth Darcy took another biscuit as she added, "If they disapprove of our merely taking a walk, what will their reaction be when we put on our finest clothing and perform the allemande?"

Anne saw a flicker of disappointed hope on Juliet Tilney's face, and her heart went out to the girl. To be seventeen was to want to wear lovely dresses and dance all night. Miss Tilney must have come to this house party hoping to meet others her own age, especially eligible young men. Instead, she had become entrapped in a grisly mess not of her own making, and in conditions not ideal for turning Jonathan Darcy's thoughts toward courting.

"Ridiculous business," John Knightley said. "This ball—for that matter, any ball whatsoever. Why should not everyone remain where they are most comfortable, instead of seeking out society?"

"We have already all but accepted," Emma Knightley pointed out. She sat next to her visiting brother-in-law. "It would be rude to refuse without good reason."

"If murder is not a good reason, then I do not know what is," said Frederick Wentworth. Anne glanced over at her husband, who was not watching her. She noted that Mr. Darcy flinched at the words.

Jonathan Darcy spoke up then. "Mr. Churchill does not consider it a good reason. If he felt that the murder made it improper for us to attend, he would not have invited us in the first place."

"Mr. Churchill may be the arbiter of fact when it comes to Mr. Wickham's death," said Edmund Bertram even more primly than usual. "However, that does not make him the arbiter of what behavior is appropriate in such a circumstance."

Anne generally let others speak their piece before she took her own turn. It seemed that time had come. "In my opinion, we should go. In fact, we must."

Everyone turned to look at her. When one spoke rarely, one's words were listened to more attentively. Anne had intuited this lesson long ago and wondered that so few people ever learned it at all.

She continued: "If we go, yes, there is a chance we will be censured. If we do not go, however, it will look far worse in the eyes of all Highbury. In the first instance, we are at worst imprudent. In the second, we will appear as though we have something to hide."

One among their number did, of course, have something to hide. But none of them could afford the appearance of it.

The others took in her words, seeing the truth of them. It was Knightley himself who said, "It is settled, then. To the Churchill ball we shall go."

⁓

After tea, Juliet Tilney and Jonathan Darcy managed to pass through a hallway together without anyone else walking especially close by. Miss Tilney whispered, "I am so relieved about the ball."

"As am I," Jonathan said. "We are fortunate that Mr. Churchill is not overly concerned with matters of propriety." Anne Wentworth's words were wise, which—Jonathan felt certain—was the only reason his parents had yielded.

Miss Tilney gave him a conspiratorial look. "Do you not perceive the opportunity we have been afforded?"

"What do you mean?"

"Your concerns about—about the mysterious earl named in Wickham's papers." She lowered her voice even further. "Mr. Knightley said he looked up the name of the earl in question in Frank Churchill's copy of *Debrett's*. Later he mentioned having left a letter behind in that same book as a marker. Meaning that if we can get away from the dancing and into the library—"

"We can then take up the *Debrett's*, open it to the marker, and discover which earl is named on those pages." Jonathan nodded. "Yes, of course."

It was, indeed, a splendid chance to investigate. Yet Jonathan could not be glad of it. He had thought any relief from his doubts about his father's innocence would be welcome, but now he had to reckon with the full dangers of certainty. If the *Debrett's* opened to the page about Harold Bellamy, earl of Dorchester, then . . .

It proves nothing, he told himself, *but it must be made known.* His father had always taught him to do what was right, as best he saw it; Jonathan would not betray his father's principles, even if his father had in a moment of madness forgotten them.

His disquiet must have been clear, because Miss Tilney added, now speaking in hardly more than a whisper, "It will be better to know, surely, one way or the other."

"It does not matter if it is better or not. It is what justice demands." Jonathan wondered if he sounded more sure than he felt.

Probably not—but Juliet Tilney mercifully took him at his word. She spoke quietly still, but more naturally. "Besides, Mr. Churchill may have other motives for his hospitality. He must determine which of us is responsible for Wickham's death. His interviews alone have not given him the answer. What better chance to study our characters than at a ball? He can observe our actions and interactions. Who among us will behave normally? Who among us will not? It is an invaluable opportunity for him to learn more."

Jonathan considered this. "I had not believed Mr. Churchill quite so . . . penetrating as to devise such a clever plan."

"Perhaps not." The doubt in her voice did not last long. "But even if he did invite us purely for fun, he is sure to soon realize that we will be on display at the ball in ways that will allow him to know far more about each of us than he did before."

At this, Mrs. Brandon came up beside Juliet, to talk about some feminine matter at which Jonathan could scarcely guess. He regretted their parting, because Juliet's theory was an intriguing one, worthy of further discussion.

And he had had no chance to ask her for the first two dances.

Chapter Nineteen

There is no plan so pleasant, no expectation so cherished, that someone cannot be found to disapprove of it.

So matters transpired for Juliet and the Churchills' ball. Her first flush of enthusiasm had been entirely due to the event's investigative potentialities, but she had awakened the next morning with entirely new reasons for delight, more in keeping with the traditional anticipation of such an event: the chance to dress her hair especially well; to don the prettiest dress she'd brought, a pale blue with braided trim that made her hazel eyes look almost emerald green—at least, in her opinion. And of course there was the prospect of dancing itself. Juliet was an active, healthy girl, one used to riding and walking and even a bit of archery from time to time. Their confinement at Donwell Abbey had begun to tax her. It would feel good to move again.

She fancied that the others in the party shared her enthusiasm. No one could expect those of three-and-forty to retain the full same measure of glee at the thought of a ball that they had possessed in their adolescent years, but at breakfast, Juliet detected a palpable change of mood. Anne Wentworth smiled more readily and chatted over her coffee, while Knightley took more than his usual satisfaction in describing the various personages of Highbury whom they might be expected to meet. Elizabeth Darcy asked her husband whether he would dance with all female guests in need, even those ladies slighted by other gentlemen. This struck Juliet as a strange way to phrase the question, but it must have had some meaning between them, because Mr. Darcy smiled more broadly than she had ever seen from him before.

"I take it you are as much in favor of dancing as I am, Mrs. Brandon?" Juliet ventured between bites of her Bath cake.

It took Marianne a moment to realize she had been addressed. "Oh. Yes, of course. There are few diversions so delightful. All are gathered together in true harmony."

This was true. Where there were not men enough, women would sometimes dance together. At more informal occasions, dancers might be no more than nine or ten, or people with more than threescore years. Choosing partners bore great significance for young persons of marrying age, but for the very young, or for those already wed, nearly anyone might partner happily with anyone else. In the same night, Juliet had once seen her father dance with both an eleven-year-old eager for practice and an unusually spry seventy-year-old woman of the parish, with apparently great satisfaction to all involved. She relayed this story to Marianne.

"Yes, that is gentlemanly behavior," Marianne murmured. Her eyes seemed to scan the room in search of Colonel Brandon, to no avail; he had not yet come down for breakfast. "To make all feel welcome, to share in the joy of the occasion to anybody who wishes it—those are the finest manners. Would that more men followed your father's example."

Knightley, who sat near them, turned toward the pair as though to offer his own thoughts on the matter. This turn afforded him a glimpse of the window, and that glimpse darkened his countenance. "I fear we are about to receive many more thoughts about 'setting examples.'"

"Why?" Juliet asked, turning to the window. There she saw a carriage, not in the newest fashion, coming up the walk. It was not one they had witnessed before. "Who has come to call?"

"Our vicar, Mr. Elton." Knightley sighed heavily. "And it appears he has brought his wife."

_✺_

Many years ago, Mr. Elton's first marital hope had been a match with Emma, then Miss Woodhouse. Emma had not shared in this vision of their future and had thus refused him. His hopes had been kindled by behavior on her part that, however indiscreet, had been entirely innocent. This was irrelevant to Mr. Elton, not a man to face disappointment philosophically. Instead, he had left Highbury in indignation as soon as the weather permitted, met a young woman of suitable dowry in Bath, and swiftly brought the new Mrs. Augusta Elton home with him in what he perceived to be triumph.

Mrs. Elton had come to Highbury in much the same spirit that missionaries went to the Indies: in the steadfast belief that the uninformed would be grateful for her superior knowledge and understanding. Also like the missionaries, she little anticipated that the local populace might have thoughts and opinions of their own. She had worn city fashions and instructed all and sundry on city manners and attempted to realign the social life of the community so that she stood at its center. As all new brides were afforded ample courtesies, Mrs. Elton had indeed enjoyed that privilege for a season.

Then both Jane Fairfax and Emma Woodhouse had married in short succession and enjoyed their own bridal seasons. Mrs. Elton had found she did not enjoy country balls near so much when she did not lead the first dance. The new Mrs. Churchill and Mrs. Knightley were naturally considered to be at the height of Highbury's social order—given the husbands' rank and wealth, and Emma's own considerable dowry, this should not have been as surprising to Mrs. Elton as it was. She had thought her husband's boasted friendship with Mr. Knightley would make her the natural third of a triumvirate. Instead, it soon became apparent that Mr. Elton's position within the highest set in Highbury was more marginal than had been suggested.

Instead, Mrs. Augusta Elton found that her position was solely that of the vicar's wife. Even with her dowry, she and Mr. Elton could not afford to live as richly as the Churchills or Knightleys; her dresses faded out of fashion more quickly than she could purchase new ones. No new-sprung societies or salons clamored for her membership; those she founded faltered even more quickly than her interest could fade. Even had her company been desired, a vicar's wife had duties to take up most of her spare time. Mrs. Elton was expected to visit the poor frequently and to make jellies, pies, and cloth goods that might ease their burdens.

This she did, but with little Christian feeling. Mrs. Elton preferred to express her piety through disapproval rather than charity. She was never more pleased than when finding a new thing to condemn, particularly when that thing could in some way be connected to Emma Knightley. The news of the murder at Donwell Abbey had made Mrs. Elton happier than she had been in many years.

"My dear Mrs. Knightley!" Mrs. Elton exclaimed as she and her husband swept into the house. Her hands were folded primly in front of her chest. "How very shocking this must have been for you. We have come to condole with you in your sorrows. I trust you understand why we could not come before—that of course a clergyman and his wife cannot be too careful of their reputations and must maintain a discreet distance from such events as—! Oh, you poor things. I do applaud you for bringing your party into Highbury. *Most* women would not have been able to hold their heads up under the shame. But you've never let shame stop you."

Emma Knightley had never yet lost her temper with Augusta Elton, knowing that to do so would be the only way in which she could be defeated. It took all her good breeding to reply civilly, "How good of you to call."

Mr. Elton said, "I furthermore wished to inquire whether you intended to attend church this week." This coming Sunday was to be the first that they could have gone to services. Barring a return of the wretched weather, they would of course be there—or so Emma would have said, before Mr. Elton added, "It might be more . . . discreet, perhaps, if you were to remain absent."

"You are forbidding us from church?" Emma stared at him. She was accustomed to Elton's snips and snipes by now, but this was an entirely new level of disdain.

"Oh, no, no, of course not. But I am sure that as a gentlewoman, you will see what good manners require." Elton seemed very satisfied with this pronouncement. However, his words attracted the attention of Edmund Bertram, who walked toward them. Emma introduced them hurriedly, in order to abandon her part of the conversation. She thought only of escape—but better was at hand.

The word *clergyman* had pricked at Edmund's ears, summoning his attention. At first he naturally thought someone was referring to him, but as he went to investigate, he found Mrs. Knightley in conversation with those who appeared to be the local vicar and his wife. Yet the words he overheard could not be allowed to pass unanswered.

Edmund said, "Mr. Elton. I have heard much of you. I myself have a parish in Northamptonshire."

Having spent many years insisting upon the respect due a clergyman, the Eltons could not snub another. Mrs. Elton put on what she believed to be her most charming smile. "Mr. Bertram. How good to have another man of the cloth present. Perhaps you will be able to lead a private service for those at Donwell Abbey. Much more appropriate, do you not agree?"

"I do not agree," Edmund replied. "The church should not be closed to those going through a time of travail. It is then that the comfort and wisdom of our Lord is most needed."

Mr. Elton was not a man of particular piety. He had chosen the church less from any sense of vocation, more from being both a third son and uninterested in the military. Rather than write his own sermons, he read ones from books sold to clergymen who wished to spend their time in other pursuits. Still, he had not drawn from this book for so many years without absorbing some of the information within. "One in your number may well be guilty of this heinous crime. It is this person we do not wish admitted to our church. The rest of you must abstain in order to protect the whole, who should not be brought into the company of such a criminal. As it is written in First Corinthians, we are not to associate with those who have committed sinful acts, even if they call themselves Christians. We are not even to eat with them, much less share a house of worship."

Edmund replied, "And yet in Luke, chapter six, we are told 'Judge not, and ye shall not be judged; condemn not, and ye shall not be condemned; forgive, and ye shall be forgiven.'"

Mrs. Elton gaped at him. It did not appear to have occurred to her that all Scripture was not in perfect accord. It took Elton a moment to summon his response. "But Ephesians, chapter five, is clear: 'Have no fellowship with the unfruitful works of darkness, but rather reprove them.' To admit a murderer among us, surely, is to have fellowship in such works?"

"I cannot agree," Edmund said evenly. "I would rather cite James, chapter five. 'He which converteth the sinner from the error of his way shall save a soul from death.' We are all sinners, certainly, which is why Romans, chapter three, reminds us, 'For all have sinned and fallen short of the glory of God.' Of course there is also First John, chapter one: 'If we say that we have no sin, we deceive ourselves, and the truth is not in us.' But now I am preaching to you, which is presumptuous. It is your parish, and you must do as you see fit."

Mr. Elton had no answer to this. Fortunately for his dignity, his wife could not long endure silence.

"Indeed," she said. Mrs. Elton understood only that Edmund had conceded and therefore assumed her husband to be triumphant. "Well. We will look forward to seeing you again once all this unpleasantness is no more, Mrs. Knightley, and your errant guest has been identified." (She considered it a mark of great Christian fellowship that she assumed the Knightleys themselves to be innocent.) "Come along, my dear. Other parishioners in greater need await us."

"I will show our guests out, dear Emma." John Knightley emerged from his brother's office. Though the man was still pale and haggard, he looked altogether better than he had upon his arrival. Edmund wished he had such fellowship with his brother, that a few days in his company could prove so restorative. "I am going to London soon, so this is my only chance to talk to the Eltons." Something in John Knightley's countenance suggested to Edmund that this opportunity was not one gladly seized.

Mrs. Elton, oblivious to such nuance, pounced. "How very good to see you! You must tell us all of your family's doings in London." Edmund, who knew the signs of a gossip at work, managed not to wince openly.

As soon as the butler had shut the door behind John Knightley and the Eltons, Emma shot Edmund Bertram a glance of profound gratitude. "You were very good to speak so. Both Eltons would no doubt have gone on at much greater length had they not met with informed resistance."

Yet Edmund managed to do no more than nod in response. He was much distracted. For as he had spoken the words of the Lord, he had also heard them with an open heart—more deeply than he had in far too long. Although he hoped he was no Elton, he wondered whether he had started down a road toward such smallness.

Everything in Edmund's teaching told him to condemn William Price, and to condemn Fanny for standing with him. But what if that teaching did not truly reflect the Word of God?

∽

It was a smaller group that made its way into Highbury that afternoon. Knightley had business to discuss with a local merchant and had asked if others would wish to ride with him. Captain Wentworth had agreed immediately—"Yes, we men of the navy can ride, when we are called to"—and Jonathan had joined soon after.

The discovery of Fanny Bertram's letter was certainly intriguing, but her shyness made her a difficult subject of study. Miss Tilney had some hope of speaking with her, girl to woman; Jonathan had none. Therefore he diverted his attention to another of their chief suspects. Wentworth's temperament and motives were such that he remained very much of interest. (Jonathan had caught himself hoping that the man was guilty, as it would mean Father was innocent. This was surely not the objectivity an investigator should possess.) The trip into town seemed an ideal opportunity to observe the man.

Besides, it was a chance to ride Ebony.

The day was punishingly hot. As though to make up for its absence a week earlier, the sun dominated a cloudless sky, bathing the Surrey countryside with warmth and light. On such days, Jonathan wondered why it was necessary to always wear coats, cravats, and hats. Would not a simple linen shirt and looser trousers provide enough decency? Apparently not, though neither his parents nor anyone else had ever provided a satisfactory reason why.

Upon their arrival in Highbury, Wentworth proclaimed, "Thirsty work, that. Let us have an ale."

Jonathan would've preferred chilled wine, but anything cold would do. Before he could agree, however, Frank Churchill—upon his own horse, halfway across the main square—raised his hand in greeting and had his mount canter toward them.

"Well, well, and how are you all this morning?" Mr. Churchill's smile remained steadfast.

"Well enough to confirm that we shall all be attending the ball," said Mr. Knightley. "Good of you to welcome us. Emma tells me Mr. Elton has made it clear not everyone in Highbury is of the same mind."

This did not daunt Mr. Churchill. "Wait until they have to decide between Elton's dusty aphorisms and the chance of attending a lively party, and see which wins out. Trust me, the town will be in accord soon enough."

Jonathan had been taught that God's Word was paramount, so he was somewhat surprised to see both Knightley and Wentworth nod and chuckle knowingly.

"I would've ridden to Donwell Abbey today, had we not met," Mr. Churchill continued. "The constables and I agree that the house must be searched. It is a great intrusion, I know, but I believe you will understand it is necessary."

"Indeed I do," said Knightley. "When will this occur?"

"We shall begin tomorrow morning if you have no strong objection."

Knightley simply nodded his assent.

The search would've been more to the purpose had it taken place immediately after Mr. Wickham's death, Jonathan thought. There had been too much time between the events—time for someone to bury a bloodied handkerchief, for someone to burn one of Fanny Bertram's letters in his parents' fireplace.

Yet it was entirely possible that more discoveries awaited, and would soon be brought to light . . .

⁓

Frederick Wentworth felt Frank Churchill's gaze upon him more steadily than he did the burning sun above. Knightley and the Darcy son might as well not have been present at all. This chatter about searching the house—it seemed mere pretext. Churchill's attention was for Wentworth alone, whether the others could discern it or not.

He was not a man to dissemble. Out with it, and done with, Wentworth told himself. "May I be of any assistance to you, Mr. Churchill?"

"Indeed you may. Yesterday I had a conversation with Sanders, the butcher's apprentice. He took the same stagecoach as you did from London but two weeks ago. As the stage was boarding, he overheard an argument between you and Mr. Wickham, who was there to see you off?"

Two weeks ago, Wentworth's biggest problems had been losing money he'd once scarcely dreamed of having and a collapsed staircase at his rented home. At the time it had seemed crushing. What he would give now for those to be his only troubles? "We had many disagreements concerning his mismanagement of my investment. I should not be surprised that one was overheard."

Mr. Churchill nodded. "Sanders said that you dared Wickham to challenge you outside London. That he would not be protected by his—I believe the phrase was 'foul hangers-on.' That you more or less goaded him to come here. When the carriage driver tried to end the quarrel, you shouted him down most vehemently. Your anger would allow no less. Is that a fair report of what was said?"

Wentworth had half a mind to go to the butcher's shop and tell the Sanders boy to mind his tongue and his own affairs. But it was not the lad's fault. It was Wentworth's own, both for what he had said and what he had done.

"It is," Wentworth said. "I do not deny any of it. I have no wish to deny it."

"Your candor is appreciated," replied Mr. Churchill, and for once his smile had disappeared.

Jonathan Darcy was staring at Wentworth outright now, but what was the point of upbraiding him? Frank Churchill had as good said that Wentworth was his main suspect, and for reasons not even Wentworth could deny.

The eye was upon him now, and it would not readily look away.

Chapter Twenty

Death is among the most serious of human concerns. Dancing is not. Therefore, it would be rational to conclude that the occasion of a ball could hardly provide diversion for those at Donwell Abbey, shadowed as they were by the unsolved murder of Mr. Wickham. But nothing about a ball is rational.

They were none of them frivolous people—not even young Juliet Tilney, however much she might ponder the correct choice of earrings. It was simply that they had come to Surrey in the expectation of some degree of enjoyment and thus far had experienced almost none. They had dwelled with the knowledge of a killer in their midst, borne the opprobrium of the townsfolk, and lived in suspense of being wrongly (or, as in one case, rightly) blamed for the criminal deed. This was not a state of being to be cherished, and it is no great wonder that the party took this chance to escape it. As the sun set on the date of the Churchills' ball, the entire house was lively with preparations.

Captain Wentworth and Colonel Brandon put on their uniforms, resplendent in coats of blue and red. Marianne Brandon's dress was one she had chosen to complement her husband's army regalia, trimmed with delicate braid, and her favorite of the wedding clothes she had purchased in such high joy only months before. Knightley, a man who did not normally relish formality and show for their own sakes, took extra care with his suit as Emma slipped on the ivory bracelet she saved for best. Elizabeth Darcy exchanged her mobcap for a turban of green velvet that set off her fine eyes. Darcy dressed simply, conscious that his well-made clothes and natural bearing were stately enough for any gathering.

Fanny Bertram put on the amber cross her brother William had given her a few years ago; it hung from a chain Edmund had gifted her for that very purpose. A few moments were spent in search of her amethyst ring before she remembered that it was no longer in her possession, nor likely to ever be so again, unless she confessed to actions she preferred to remain secret.

Jonathan Darcy found nearly all clothing to be restrictive and somewhat unpleasant; the sensations against his skin were sometimes difficult to ignore. So while some of the other men pretended to grouse about the stiffness of their collars or the tightness of their breeches, Jonathan considered his formal attire no more uncomfortable than any of the rest. As he examined himself in the mirror, he could see that he looked well. As Jonathan understood it, men were expected to look well but not to *notice* that they looked well; they had to take pains to make sure their appearance was its best while never acknowledging any effort expended thereby. It was all very strange, but at least he did look very well indeed.

It was Juliet, standing before the looking glass in her room, who felt uncertain. Her blue dress was her best, and very pretty it was, too. At least, it seemed so at gatherings in Gloucestershire. Highbury was hardly London or even Bath—it was smaller even than her own little town—but Juliet would be in company with far finer families, including the Darcys of Pemberley themselves. Would she look shabby by comparison?

She studied herself another moment in the mirror—black hair, hazel eyes, rosy skin—and decided she would not.

Besides, what did it matter? Dancing was her secondary concern of the evening. The Churchills' ball was also an opportunity to find out—finally—whether the elder Mr. Darcy had motive to be the killer.

Juliet prayed, for Jonathan's sake, that it would not be so. More than anything, however, she prayed for the truth.

❧

When Frank Churchill had first thrown a ball in Highbury, he had been a young man with no house of his own. Instead, he had hosted a ball in the Crown Inn, rendering it lovely with bunches of flowers and enough candles to light a palace. Sometimes he joked that he should use the inn again, as it had served them so well.

However, he now held all such parties at the house he had purchased upon his wedding, Medway Hall. It was a grand old place, but not in the best condition when Emma was growing up, as its elderly occupant was past caring about matters cosmetic. This occupant had very considerately perished just in time for Frank to fix the house up new and move in with his bride. Medway Hall was on the opposite side of Highbury from Donwell Abbey and Hartfield, a state of affairs Emma had much lamented and Knightley had silently been glad of. Still, it was scarcely a ten-minute carriage ride, as their guests all discovered that night.

Frank stood at the doorway to greet all comers, and there were many; he had to have invited nearly all of Highbury. Thus were many askance looks given to the Donwell guests as they emerged from their carriages. Frank grinned broadly and held out his hand to shake. "Good, good, you've come at last!"

Other smiles followed. All polite guests took their cues from their host, so whatever private suspicions might be held, publicly everyone would be made welcome.

Emma loved Medway Hall as much as it was possible to love a house not her own and was so familiar with the place she could easily have found her way to the scullery. It had been built half a century before Hartfield, and those fifty years had marked a great change in architecture. Where Hartfield was elegant and neat, with its symmetrical columns and tall windows, Medway Hall harkened back to older, more irregular days. A wing to the east had no counterpart at the west; heavy timbers supported the ceilings, still visible despite their whitewash. The broad fireplaces were made of rough stone rather than neat brick. Yet the dwelling possessed an undeniable kind of charm. It was the residence of a happy family, and where that is the case, no home can lack beauty.

ᗡ

Anne Wentworth's thoughts ran along similar lines as she moved through the hallway. Unlike most of the Knightleys' guests, she and her husband had some acquaintance in the town due to their short, ill-fated tenancy at Hartfield. Whether this worked to their advantage or against it was hard to determine.

She said as much to her husband, who murmured, "Against." Before she could ask him why, the answer came before them in the well-meaning form of Miss Bates.

"Well, well, good evening, Captain Wentworth, Mrs. Wentworth—how lovely to see you both!" Miss Bates's saving grace was her genuine happiness at even the smallest, most mundane pleasures in life. Naturally a fine ball had transported her entirely. "Is it not wonderful, how charmingly Grace and Frank have fitted up the ballroom? So many candles! Too many, really, they are so expensive and it is such an indulgence, but perhaps I am remembering the days when my dear late mama and I had to exercise much greater economy.

Only one candle at night, and how we were able to read and embroider by it, I am sure I do not recall. I declare, I think candles make the room warmer as well as brighter, do you not think so? Put all together, they give more light than any fire, so does it not follow that they should produce heat as well? Of course candles do produce some warmth, but heat such as this? I can scarcely credit it, not with all the candles in the world. But then, I do not know about such things, and it is probably only the excitement that makes it so warm. And once we are dancing, it shall be warmer still! Oh, no—you do not think we shall be too warm, do you? Perhaps Frank might open a window or two—"

Anne managed to interject, "I am sure we will not be over-heated. Mr. Churchill has made excellent arrangements."

To his wife's surprise, Wentworth spoke next. "Miss Bates, while I will of course be with my wife for the first two dances, will you favor me as a partner later this evening?"

Miss Bates's cheeks pinked with delight. "Oh, goodness. How kind you are to ask. Yes, of course. It has been too long since I danced!"

There he is, Anne thought as she saw him smile and bow his head in acknowledgment. *This good man who understands the feelings of others and wishes to do what is right. The man I fell in love with, the man I married. Beneath all the anger and strife, he is here still.*

❧

Fanny Bertram had had less of her share of dancing than the average young girl. Well did she remember the first ball ever thrown in her honor—how grown up she had felt, how special, how new. It was one of the few occasions in her life when she had been glad of attention rather than intimidated by it. The joy of standing up with Edmund had eclipsed all her fears.

After her season as a bride, however, Fanny had danced very little. Edmund felt that, as a clergyman, it was incumbent upon him to maintain a sense of decorum that was difficult to maintain while doing a jig. Thus, when they were invited to events in their small town, they watched others spin through reels and waltzes while watching decorously from the side. Every once in a while, a gentleman would kindly ask her to dance, but she rarely consented. Surely a clergyman's wife should dance only with her husband.

"There I think you may take dignity a bit far," Edmund had told her once in good humor. "If you wish to dance, dearest Fanny, by all means do so with those gentlemen whom you know and like well."

She had replied, "But I do not wish to dance. Not without you."

Edmund had understood this as Fanny's never wishing to dance at all. There was another interpretation, of course, but Fanny felt pointing that out would be too bold. It was not too great a sacrifice to make for the joy of being his wife.

So Fanny was much surprised when, upon their arrival in the Churchills' expansive ballroom, Edmund said, "Shall we stand up for the first dance, Fanny? Or will you need time to accustom yourself to the bustle of the gathering?"

"You wish to dance, Edmund?"

"I do miss it sometimes, you know," he said, surprising her. "One must think of appearances—yet here, however, we are not the vicar and his wife. We are merely cousins of Knightley's come for a visit. In fact, given the peculiar circumstances of our situation, it may be more seemly to dance than to refuse."

Fanny could see the sense of what he said. But the faint sensation of William's cross against her breastbone reminded her of all the things they both wished to forget.

"No," she said softly. "I will not dance tonight. Feel free to ask whom you choose."

Why, why must this lie between us? Fanny thought as she turned away from Edmund's hurt expression. But it was Edmund who had turned away from the principle of love, and thus Edmund who must change.

❧

Jonathan Darcy, resident of Pemberley, was not to be awestruck by the arrangements at Medway Hall. The candlelight looked well, he supposed, and the floor was commodious enough to welcome many dancers. What else was there to care about? Still, the others approved and complimented extravagantly, so he made sure to nod at appropriate intervals.

But there were *so many* dancers . . .

He felt it then: the flush of heat that made his clothing even more uncomfortable, the illusory swelling of sound that made it impossible for him to pick out any individual word, the feeling that too many things were happening at once and that he could bear it no longer.

Quickly he stepped into a corner, as though to let other arrivals greet the hosts first. However, his action was not one of politeness; it was to give him a necessary moment to collect himself.

The "too much" feeling, as Jonathan called it, came over him sometimes when he was in a crowd, surrounded by many people and great noise. When he had been a boy, this sensation had often overwhelmed him past the point of respectable conduct. Eventually his mother had hit upon the best solution, which was for Jonathan to take a moment away and inwardly prepare for the events to come.

It is but a ball like any other, he said to himself. *You will be touched, but only when etiquette or the dancers call for it; the touch will never be unexpected. You can always walk out again if the clamor proves overwhelming. Do not push beyond the point where you can excuse yourself with some dignity and all will be well.*

Once his spirits had been recollected, he rejoined the receiving line, braced for the touch of hands to come.

"Why, Mr. Darcy." Grace Churchill appeared, smiling sweetly. She wore a pale green dress and an ostrich plume in her hair. "Here you are at last. We had begun to despair of your coming."

"Are we late?" Jonathan said. He had thought them to be prompt; certainly other guests continued to file in and cast curious glances in his direction.

"Not a bit. But you know how it is, when one is eager to see another. The occasion cannot arrive too soon." Grace lowered her gaze, which he belatedly realized meant she wondered if she was being too forward. Which meant flirting.

Immediately Jonathan understood his duty. The host's daughter had presented herself to him; he had to ask her to dance. In point of fact, in politeness he had to ask her for the first two dances, a mark of especial attention. It was possible that Grace would already have a partner for those dances, but the attention she gave Jonathan made him think not. Really, he should have understood this from the beginning, but his hopes had obscured this basic social fact.

He had been looking forward to dancing with Miss Tilney . . .

The better to slip away, to find the Churchills' library and investigate, of course. But only now did Jonathan realize how much he'd been anticipating the dance itself.

Still, the forms must be obeyed. So he said, "Miss Churchill, may I inquire whether the first two dances are already spoken for?"

Grace's face lit up. "They are not, Mr. Darcy. Or I should say—they were not, until now."

Yes. He had handled this correctly. Jonathan was proud of himself until he caught a glimpse of Juliet Tilney out of the corner of his eye, just in time to see her face fall.

❧

Both Marianne and Colonel Brandon observed the interplay between the three young people. They said nothing, simply shared a knowing glance. In that instant, Marianne could pretend that nothing was wrong, could enjoy the night, could breathe again.

Willoughby's letter welled up in her mind—the words seemingly spoken by his voice, still so familiar to her—and the instant passed.

She murmured, "It seems so long ago that I was the giddy girl at balls, so conscious of those first two dances. And yet it was only last year."

"Imagine how distant it seems to me," Brandon replied. It was one of his rare attempts at humor, and for a brief moment she could smile back at him.

"Should we dance?" Marianne asked.

Brandon looked dubious. "It might appear improper."

"Indeed it may. But if we do not dance, we shall be obliged to converse with those around us." A shudder ran through her at the thought. "That I think is beyond me."

It felt impossible to speak to anyone any longer; even pretending naturalness with Brandon was difficult. Marianne thought she could pour her heart out to her sister, were she here, but in Elinor's absence, her tongue was stilled.

Colonel Brandon squeezed her hand. "Then we must dance. There, you will draw no comment save for admiration. You are a beautiful dancer, my love."

Marianne *was* a beautiful dancer. She could be a lively and gay conversationalist, especially now that she had learned to listen as well as speak. Such an elegant country dance as this ought to have filled her with raptures. Her true self felt so far away, and Marianne was not sure she would ever get it back again.

She looked up at her husband, tried again to understand him, and failed. As the musicians struck up a number, she took his hand and went to the dance floor, to trip along merrily on feet of lead.

∽

"You dance very well, Miss Churchill," said Jonathan.

He would have said this even if she were treading upon his feet every other second. It was one of the things a dancing partner was meant to say. Why dancing had to include conversation, Jonathan did not know, but he had learned the forms as surely as he had learned the steps.

"As do you, Mr. Darcy," Grace Churchill replied, precisely on cue. But then she deviated—eschewing the common phrases in apparent search of a real conversation. "Cooped up as you have been, I imagine you have done some reading at Donwell Abbey. Do they have any of your favorite books?"

"They do not have my favorite," Jonathan said.

"Which is?"

He had been warned not to begin talking about it. When he began talking about this subject, he found it hard to stop. Still, it would be rude not to reply at all. "*The History of the Decline and Fall of the Roman Empire* by Gibbon."

"No novels for you, I see!" Miss Churchill said in good humor. "Mr. Darcy, I am about to give you a rare opportunity. I will not admit that any history is as fascinating as a good novel. This is your chance to persuade me otherwise. What so fascinates you about this book?"

Surely it couldn't be wrong to talk about his favorite book if someone explicitly asked him to do so? Enthusiasm flared bright within Jonathan as he began, "We, in an empire, must heed the lessons of another empire—"

⁓

The lone consolation of the wallflower is observation. As Juliet had seen the Churchills' ball as a chance to study her fellow guests, she might have been expected to take more comfort in her state than is usually the case. Alas, not being chosen has a sting that is not so easy to soothe. Juliet watched from the side of the ballroom as Jonathan led Grace through Sir Roger de Coverley, talking more to her than he ever had to anyone else, at least in Juliet's short acquaintance. But she was steadfastly refusing to sulk. It did not help that Sir Roger de Coverley was one of her very favorite dances—

Unless you think Jonathan or Grace Churchill may be guilty, it does you no good to watch them, she told herself. *Apply yourself to observation until you have your chance at the library.*

Fanny Bertram—she whose letter had been burned—was seated at the very edge of the dance floor, watching the dancers with no more than polite interest. Her husband, Edmund, watched his wife with a sort of curiosity that Juliet found difficult to make out. Neither affection nor dislike was visible in his countenance. Instead, what she saw was . . . confusion. Uncertainty. Had his wife done something he could not understand, or did he at least suspect her of the same?

The Darcys—in whose hearth the letter had met its fate—were speaking with Frank Churchill. Animated though Mrs. Darcy was, Juliet could detect the wariness in both her and her husband. No doubt they were aware that Churchill was using this opportunity to make out their characters.

Anne and Captain Wentworth were dancing, as were Marianne and Colonel Brandon. The Wentworths seemed to be enjoying their dance rather more than would've been expected, given the captain's black moods. Was that unseemly glee a sign of some secret—even shameful—satisfaction? The Brandons, on the other hand, went through the motions joylessly. Was their lack of pleasure a sign, too?

Juliet breathed out in frustration. The ball was not proving useful as an investigative tool, at least not so far. Instead, it was just a dance—one where she was not dancing, which was of course the worst sort.

Still, she kept to her task. Mr. Knightley stood against the opposite wall, smiling and nodding as Miss Bates went on and on about something or everything. But where was Mrs. Knightley?

"Miss Tilney?" Juliet turned to see Emma standing right there, with an attractive young man by her side. "Allow me to introduce you to Arthur Cole, the son of some of our friends. Mr. Cole, this is Juliet Tilney of Gloucestershire."

Surely Arthur Cole had heard of the scandal currently surrounding Donwell Abbey, but he had allowed the introduction nevertheless. Juliet liked him already. So when he asked to be her partner, she accepted with pleasure. Any further observations could be made from the dance floor.

❦

"Oh, my," said Elizabeth. She and her husband had only just been released from Mr. Churchill's eager attention. "It looks as though Jonathan may have lost his opportunity."

Mr. Darcy cast a glance at the dance floor. "Miss Churchill seems well pleased with her conquest of the hour."

In truth, the girl looked somewhat dazed, but Elizabeth would not be distracted from her point. "You know quite well that I am speaking of Miss Tilney. The two of them have made such friends at Donwell. I had thought to see them together, but I suppose he had to ask Miss Churchill. Certainly Miss Churchill wished him to; and where that is the case, such things are difficult to avoid. Did you never teach him how you escaped the many snares of Caroline Bingley?"

"Jonathan could no more recognize a snare than he could fly," Darcy said. "Fortunately he is not particularly susceptible to them. Otherwise I shudder to think what sort of girl he might present to us as the next Mrs. Darcy."

"As do I, at times. All the more reason to hope he would look toward Miss Tilney."

"The girl has behaved strangely—"

"In strange circumstances," Elizabeth insisted. "Are any of us truly ourselves? All I know of her is that she is intelligent and spirited, and that her fondness for Jonathan seems unaffected. That is as much as we could hope. But now she is dancing with some other handsome young man."

Darcy said, "All the better for Jonathan. High time he learned that sometimes one must pursue what one wants."

"By, say, walking near her favorite paths in hopes of 'accidentally' meeting her there? I remember a young man who once tried that stratagem." A sparkle had returned to Elizabeth's eyes. "He met with success . . . eventually."

Darcy, too, had begun to smile. "Let us hope our son's path to matrimony is not so fraught as our own was."

"Do you know that once I swore never to dance with you? Not so long as I lived?"

"You are generally a woman of your word," he replied, "but I am glad that resolution was not one you kept. Will you break it again now and dance the next with me, Elizabeth?"

Rarely did Darcy use his wife's Christian name outside

of the confines of their own chambers. The surprise of it brought a flush to Elizabeth's cheeks. Surely all was not lost between them, she thought, not as long as Mr. Darcy could still make her blush. "Yes, Fitzwilliam. Let us dance."

And if Wickham's ghost were glaring down at the guests at the Churchills' ball, daring them to find joy when they knew what they knew—let him glare.

Even such a man as that had the right to glare when his killer spent the night dancing.

⁓

"Domitian's wise restructuring of the Empire might have had great effect, had that structure lasted longer—" Jonathan caught himself. "Are you well, Miss Churchill?"

It seemed to take her a moment to rouse herself; not only her attention but also her dancing moves had gone somewhat slack. "Oh. Yes. Very well, Mr. Darcy."

This was the point in conversation when she might add something, like *Pray continue.* Miss Churchill did not. Jonathan had learned, with difficulty, to recognize this sign that he was going on too long about one of his enthusiasms and should therefore change the subject.

But it was so difficult to stop talking about Gibbon's book! Whenever Jonathan had begun, he hated to end.

We are in the last form of the dance, he told himself. *You would have to stop soon anyway.* With almost physical discomfort, he forced himself to let it go. Jonathan used the phrase his mother had urged him to memorize: "I have gone on long enough."

Miss Churchill bit her lower lip but could not entirely disguise her smile. "I *did* ask, Mr. Darcy."

Was she mocking him, or inviting him to enjoy the joke

with her? Jonathan couldn't tell. He decided to trust in her apparent good nature . . . and resolved to speak on the book no more.

At least, not tonight.

⌾

During a first dance, it is customary to remark upon the other couples, to profess liking of the song (or lack thereof), and to find out some few basic facts about one's partner if not already known. Thus Juliet had told Arthur Cole that she was a vicar's daughter, visiting the Knightleys, and that she thought the Churchills' arrangements very elegant. She had learned that his father was in trade (and had liked him better for not apologizing on this account), and that he had two sisters and a brother, all younger. This was all in the normal way of such things, and, as Arthur was also an excellent dancer, it might have been supposed that Juliet had a fine time.

However, what was said between them had had less influence than what was *not* said. Arthur Cole was far too well bred to raise the subject of the murder at Donwell Abbey, but that meant he did not speak of Donwell at all. Juliet, too, found it impossible to raise that subject either. This meant they could not talk about their only common acquaintance, her hosts. Nor could he ask how she had found Surrey, what she had been doing the past several days, or any of the other ordinary questions of which such conversations are generally made. Awkward silences made for awkward dancing, and Juliet was more relieved than not when their second song ended and she was free. Undoubtedly Arthur Cole felt much the same.

But now she would be left a wallflower again, which was another form of awkwardness, and a far less pleasant one . . .

"Miss Tilney?" Jonathan Darcy appeared at last. "May I have the pleasure of the next two dances?"

She tried not to smile too broadly for gentility. "I would be honored, Mr. Darcy."

They took their positions for the quadrille. Juliet glanced over at Grace Churchill, but she seemed as taken with her new partner as she had ever been with Jonathan Darcy. Good—no one would be watching them too closely, either while they danced or when they afterward made their escape to the library.

(Or so Juliet thought, greatly underestimating the general interest of a wealthy young man standing up with a pretty young woman.)

"The ball is rather disappointing so far," Mr. Darcy said to her as they moved through the first steps.

"Do you think so? I find it rather lovely."

"I do not refer to the Churchills' home or arrangements. I meant, in terms of any investigation. I have not been able to make anything out from our fellow guests' behavior, nor does it seem that the magistrate has."

"Oh, on that point we entirely agree," Juliet said, holding out her hand. Their gloved fingers clasped as they slowly spun around. "I fear only the library will avail us."

He nodded. "When shall we make our search?"

Juliet had had ample time to consider this while sitting out the initial dance. "When dinner begins, there is always a bit of a crush, so much talking and activity—"

"That no one will miss us when we slip away."

❧

It is, of course, unthinkable to hold a ball without providing for the nourishment of the dancers. Such festivities are judged by the quality and quantity of food provided just as much as they are by the skill of the musicians. Some would even say the meal was more important than the number of gentlemen present; these would be the same souls who have, at one point or another, been obliged to dance for hours on a near-empty stomach.

Frank Churchill was far too generous a host to disappoint on this score. Late in the evening, the guests sat down to a fine repast, starting with a delicious white soup. Dining at such dances—though still governed by etiquette—was an easier, more convivial affair, and the earlier awkwardness of the evening largely faded away.

And, as anticipated, two guests were able to remove themselves from the festivities without attracting notice.

Jonathan Darcy and Juliet Tilney wordlessly separated from each other as they made their way to alternate sides of the crowd, the better to more easily edge away from the other guests entirely. Any person who observed the departure of one would be unable to note the departure of the other.

This they had done not by design but by mutual shared instinct, in which Juliet took great pleasure before reaching a darkened back corridor and realizing that she was now alone in Medway Hall with no idea where Jonathan might be.

Never mind that, she told herself. *We have the same goal in mind, and this is not such a great house that some diligence will not reveal the library.*

While Medway Hall's ballroom and foyer were brilliant with candlelight and loud with bustle, the rest of the house had fallen still and dark. Juliet wished for a lantern or candle as she edged along the long hallway. The silence was so complete that she heard even the footfalls of her slipper-clad feet.

Some doors were shut, and Juliet did not dare open them; the creak of a hinge would be enough to betray her, were any-

one nearby. But others were open, and the library was likely
to be among them. She peered through doorways, making
out a sitting room here and a drawing room there until at last,
at the end of the hall—"Mr. Darcy?"

He stood silhouetted at a broad window, a large book in his
hands. When he looked up, she hurried toward him, eager to
see what he held in his hands. At that moment she reached his
side, the moon emerged from behind a veil of clouds, revealing his disapproving face.

Juliet gasped. She had found the wrong Mr. Darcy—not the
son but the father.

❧

Jonathan Darcy had taken the time to ask a servant for a candle before heading to the library. This had been supplied with
haste and without comment, so he felt sure he was only a minute or two behind Miss Tilney. As he tiptoed down the long
hallway, he glanced in each doorway, sure that at any moment
he would find her. The last room must be the one. He called,
"Miss Tilney?"

"She is here," said a voice from this room—his father's voice.

Jonathan went within and found Miss Tilney standing
shamefaced in front of his father, who held a heavy book
in his hands. His father's expression had rarely been more
forbidding.

"What is this?" Darcy demanded, looking from one to the
other and back again. "Have I interrupted an *assignation*? Did
Miss Tilney convince you to—"

"It was not that," Jonathan hastened to explain. "Not that
at all, Father."

Darcy cocked his head, a gesture that accompanied only
his most piercing questions. "No? A young man and woman

slip away from a ball, unattended, unchaperoned, and you expect me to believe it was not improper?"

"It *is* improper," Miss Tilney said, so evenly both Darcy men were startled. "But it was not an—it was not what you suggest."

"What was it, then?" Darcy demanded.

Miss Tilney lifted her chin. "We wished to discover whether you had a motive for murder."

The following silence stretched on for several seconds. Jonathan realized that the book his father held in his hands was none other than *Debrett's Peerage*.

"You were looking for the letter Mr. Knightley left to mark the page," Jonathan said. "You were attempting to find out which earl had become entangled in Wickham's scheme— whether it might be Aunt Georgiana's husband. But if you did not already know, then . . . then this cannot have motivated you."

Darcy held out the book toward Jonathan. "As it happens, the earl in question has proved to be another man entirely." His father's voice was clear and sharp as broken glass. Sure enough, the page marked with the folded letter belonged to another earl, one from a very distant county. "Does this satisfy you? Or do you remain convinced of your father's guilt?"

"Do not misunderstand," Jonathan pleaded. "We did not begin this to prove you guilty. We wanted to prove you *innocent*."

Darcy turned his piercing attention to Miss Tilney. "What is it that you began? That you have been doing together?"

Most people found it difficult to stand up to Jonathan's father in his darker moods. Either Miss Tilney was made of sterner stuff, or she was much better at hiding her intimidation. She answered, "Jonathan was in the stables at the time of the murder and could not have done it. As I had no prior knowledge of Mr. Wickham, I had no motive. We knew our own innocence. We knew also that Mr. Churchill seemed determined to blame a servant or a traveler—that great injustice might be done."

"So you took it upon yourselves to determine the truth? To usurp the rightful place of the magistrate and the courts of law?" Darcy's tone told Jonathan that they might have been better off pretending this *was* a romantic assignation. "Your actions are as impudent as they are imprudent. Had anyone else found you together in this library, do you realize what would have happened? A young woman's honor would be forever ruined, and a young man's would be in little better condition. This would be a stain that would follow you both throughout your lives. As it happens, you need only answer to me. Jonathan, you and I will discuss at length the ways in which the reputations of young women are to be protected. Beyond that, I expect to neither hear nor see more of this. Am I understood?"

To Jonathan's astonishment, Miss Tilney shook her head. "We will not see a person wrongly hanged. So you must tell us—if you were not searching through Mr. Knightley's papers the night of the murder, then where did you go when your left your room?"

The clouds passed over the moon, deepening the shadows around them. Jonathan's candle, the only remaining light, was sufficient to show the alteration in his father as ire dwindled to something that might have been shame.

"I *was* searching through Mr. Knightley's papers," Darcy admitted. "He had signed the surety, and thus he must have seen some documentation of the scheme at some point. It was a dishonorable act, one I could never have undertaken for any less a purpose than my sister's protection. So I sought the name of the earl, just as you conjecture. But the name was not there to be found."

"You are innocent, then." Jonathan felt as though the sun were rising within him. "I always believed so—but we had to know."

The humility that had tempered his father's previous reply could not long stand against Darcy's anger. "The both of you forget your place. Jonathan, you and I will discuss this later, at length. Miss Tilney, I must consider whether or not to bring this to the attention of the Knightleys, who as our hosts must stand in place of your parents. They would most certainly send you home, which is undoubtedly where you belong, until such time as you have matured enough to conduct yourself with greater propriety."

Miss Tilney looked stricken, as well she might. When Darcy strode out of the room, Jonathan knew he was meant to follow, and he did, setting aside the *Debrett's* as he went. This was no time for further rebellion.

But he hated to leave Miss Tilney alone.

Juliet waited a few minutes before following the Darcys. This was mostly so that no one else would realize she had been in their company, but she needed the time to collect herself. Her cheeks blazed hot, and she could not bear to be seen blushing.

The worst of it all was that Mr. Darcy was correct. They *had* been presumptuous. They had risked their reputations, not once but many times. Their intentions were good, but intentions alone were not sufficient. Juliet felt as a lantern had been lit, illuminating her actions for the first time, and now she could not recognize them.

Arrogant! Naive! I am both of these things and worse. Oh, please, Lord, let Mr. Darcy decide not to tell the Knightleys. They would surely tell my parents, and then I would die of shame.

It did not matter that Jonathan Darcy had joined in with her; instead it felt as though she had urged him more deeply into folly.

When finally she came to the table, her absence had gone unremarked among the general hubbub. Juliet ate without tasting, nodded without hearing, and resolutely refused to look for Jonathan Darcy.

The dancing did not end after dinner, but for her, it no longer felt like a ball.

Chapter Twenty-One

The carriage ride back from Medway Hall felt more normal than any other part of the house party since Wickham's arrival. Although some were tense—Brandon noted that Wentworth, Darcy, and his son all seemed out of sorts—others were in higher spirits. Mrs. Knightley chattered away happily with Mr. Bertram, who although no great lover of balls nonetheless seemed to appreciate superior dancing.

Marianne joined in their conversation to some degree, though not as much as she would have once. She remained . . . burdened. Brandon wished he could deny that truth, but it became more apparent by the day.

They arrived home only a couple of hours short of dawn. Brandon escorted Marianne up to her room. Previously they had excused the servants from having to stay up so late; he was fully capable of helping his wife out of her gown.

"At least I can still dance until daybreak," Marianne said as he busied himself with the laces of her stays. "Even if not with the same gladness of heart."

Perhaps that gladness will return to you, Brandon thought. But he did not say it, because he did not truly believe it.

Now only in her chemise, Marianne went to the corner alcove to begin her nightly ablutions. (She traveled with so many creams and potions that one might have believed her a dowager desperate to hang on to youth, not a girl who had yet to reach her twentieth year.) Brandon sat in the chair at the room's small desk, untying his cravat, hopeful that tonight at least they would sleep soundly—and then he caught glimpse of a letter all but hidden beneath several pages of scrap paper on the desk. Brandon could make out only a few words. But he knew the hand well. One did not forget the handwriting in which a dueling challenge was accepted.

His wife had a letter from Willoughby.

Brandon reached out and carefully readjusted the book so that it covered the letter entirely. That way Marianne would not be tormented, later, by wondering if he knew of it.

There was no point in reading the letter or even in mentioning the thing. If Marianne had wished to bring it to Brandon's attention, she would have done so. He understood that she had not begun the correspondence—he knew his wife's character well enough for that. What Brandon did not know was how she might respond to the correspondence once begun.

He did not deceive himself about his wife's feelings for him: gratitude, honor, and liking. He also did not deceive himself about his wife's feelings for Willoughby. She had been as passionately in love with him as any woman Brandon had seen in many years—since his Eliza had, so long ago, loved Brandon himself.

A love like that did not die swiftly. In his and Eliza's case, it had never died at all. Brandon was not fool enough to think that it would be different for Marianne and Willoughby.

No doubt he wishes to meet with her on their next journey to visit his aunt, Brandon thought. A base yet natural part of him wished to rage against this, to forbid the very notion of it, to tell Marianne she was never to be alone with that man again. Yet Brandon knew better than most that love burns only brighter for having been forbidden.

Marianne's loyalty meant nothing if it were commanded. The decision must be hers alone.

He undressed and climbed into bed. When she joined him, he was able to smile for her.

The next day was one of peace, as it had to be following such an occasion. Dancers made merry until near four in the morning, and the next day all had to revive from their efforts. On the day hence, however, Frank Churchill made good his promise to search Donwell Abbey.

Emma bore this as best she could. The need was unquestionable; it ought to have been done even sooner; and if her entire house were to be turned upside down, at least the task would be overseen by someone she considered a good friend.

But how could one remain sanguine while watching two constables of the lower class going through one's nightclothes?

"Important evidence might be hidden anywhere," Frank attempted to reassure her as she stood in the hallway outside her own bedchamber, watching her garments being tossed aside. "The more unlikely the hiding place would seem to a person of gentility, the more likely an actual murderer would be to use it. Do you see?"

"I suppose so," Emma said. "But it is so very vexing to watch."

"Then let us not watch. Come along."

However, no consolation was to be taken from her walk through the house. Those guests who had already been searched—the Wentworths, the Bertrams—were obviously repacking in no good humor. Those who had not waited in even bleaker spirits.

And one of us, Emma thought, *truly does have something to hide—*

"We don't expect to find a weapon," Frank confided as they began toward the stairs. "Or, rather, we expect we already found it among your collection. The mace is by far the likeliest device used in the crime."

They were at that moment passing the room of Juliet

Tilney, who stood near her doorway. At Mr. Churchill's words, she opened her mouth as if to speak, then abruptly turned away. Emma wondered if the girl felt uneasy, and if so, why now. Nobody suspected her, obviously, and so far she had borne most of this quite bravely.

Besides, Miss Tilney ought to be feeling no small measure of triumph this evening. Jonathan Darcy had danced three dances with her, only two with Grace Churchill. Young people might pretend not to keep score, but Emma felt no such compunction.

Though come to think of it, they had not seemed so sprightly during the later part of the dance. Might they have quarreled?

She turned her attention back to Frank. "If your constables are not searching for a weapon, then what do they expect to find? It seems unlikely that the killer would have written a confession and left it lying about."

"They are looking for anything—markedly out of place, shall we say." Frank's knowing air would have fooled anyone who did not know him as Emma did; he saw his magistracy as largely a ceremonial position. This was one of the first cases he had taken a real interest in and had probably learned everything he said within the past few days. "The killer might have hidden bloodstained clothing, for instance, or some letter or object that demonstrated a link between himself and Mr. Wickham not otherwise known to us—"

"Mr. Churchill, sir!" called one of the constables. "Come and see!"

Emma and Frank exchanged glances of equal surprise, then hurried back together. The constables stood in the hallway, proudly holding out a gardening trowel marked with patches of dried mud. Its implications were immediate. The trowel was used to bury the handkerchief, Emma realized. The handkerchief was used to wipe away blood. There is no reason in the world for a trowel to be upstairs, so it must have been hidden here. And the person who would've hidden it must be the killer.

Did they have an answer at last? Was this nightmare over?

Frank Churchill beamed at his men. "Good work. Where did you find it?"

"The cabinet by the door right here," said Constable Cooper. "Found it as soon as we started looking in this room."

He pointed to the room in question. In the doorway stood a shocked, trembling Juliet Tilney.

⁓

"It is not mine," Juliet said. Astonishment had stolen her breath, and she could scarce more than whisper. Did that sound more guilty? What sounded guilty? She had been attempting to discern this for herself these past days, but only when studying others—never herself. "Please believe me, Mr. Churchill, I never saw this before in my entire life."

Frank Churchill looked as much surprised as suspicious, but he would not be so easily convinced. "You told us you had no prior acquaintance with Mr. Wickham. Was that the truth, Miss Tilney?"

"It was, indeed it was. I met the man only when he appeared here at Donwell Abbey, a day before his death. We hardly even spoke. Everything else I know of him I learned from others."

Juliet had thought the altercation with the elder Mr. Darcy at the ball represented the absolute depth of mortification possible. She had known nothing. This embarrassment—this terror—it was worse by a thousandfold.

Emma Knightley put a comforting hand on Juliet's shoulder. "Mr. and Mrs. Tilney made it clear that their daughter has hardly ever left Gloucestershire."

"There is no reason Mr. Wickham might not have had dealings in Gloucestershire," Mr. Churchill said.

By now others had appeared in the hallway: Colonel Brandon; Mr. Knightley; and, worst of all, Mr. Darcy. He would no doubt be pleased by her downfall. Juliet's shame was spreading wider and wider, like a puddle of water from a jug she'd dropped, no putting it right again . . .

But then Mr. Darcy said, "It seems unlikely that a young lady of good breeding—of any ilk, truly—could be easily moved to murder."

Her eyes met his, briefly. In his face she saw that she remained unforgiven for her presumption . . . but that the elder Mr. Darcy could still be just to her.

"Youth leads to many indiscretions, does it not?" Frank Churchill replied. "The young are quicker of temper, rasher in decisions, more prone to act without thought—young women no less than young men—"

"That is not proof, sir." Colonel Brandon's voice was sharp. "That is mere supposition."

Juliet's gratitude made her want to swoon. Or maybe her dizziness arose from the horror of this discovery. Or even the mere chagrin of discovering that one of the biggest pieces of evidence had been hidden in her own room, and she had not been the one to find it! Any of these on its own would be enough to disarm; all three together made her feel positively ill.

Mr. Knightley simply said, "It has been many days since Wickham's death. The trowel could have been hidden here at any time, by anyone. This is intriguing, and almost certainly connected to the murder, yes. But the connection to Miss Tilney is far more tenuous."

"Perhaps," Frank Churchill said, studying Juliet's face. She wondered what he saw there, or imagined, for if he could not see her innocence, then he was blind to much. "Perhaps not. But perhaps so."

⌘

The immediate aftermath of the search was somewhat anti-climactic. While the constables took the trowel away, Mrs. Knightley bid Juliet Tilney to lie down in her room and ordered that some hot tea be brought. The sudden end to the search left the rest of the household both surprised and uncertain.

"I cannot believe that Miss Tilney is responsible," murmured Anne Wentworth, watching out the window as the carriages rolled away. "Nor can I believe that anyone else does. Not even this Mr. Churchill."

She was not certain of that last. Ever perceptive, Anne had detected some note of scorn in Mr. Knightley's mentions of the man. Was Churchill not to be trusted?

Captain Wentworth had sat down in the room's one chair. He looked weary, displeased. "No one will believe it. Mark my words. The ridiculousness of it must be clear to all. No lasting harm has been done."

"Do you think so?" Anne did not agree. She was, however, reserving her conflict with her husband for much larger disagreements, many of which hovered near. "I do hope Miss Tilney is not overcome with the shock of it."

"I confess to being rather shocked myself," Wentworth replied. "That man Churchill has had me in his eye from the start. I know not why his suspicion bent to me, but it most certainly did. When he announced this search, I half expected it to be no more than a ruse, an excuse for him to pin all the blame on me. That was a misjudgment, it seems."

Anne studied her husband in the morning light. Sometimes

she could see hints of the younger man she had first loved; sometimes that person seemed entirely lost to her. This was one of the lost times. "Your anger with Mr. Wickham has been clear for all to see from the beginning, Frederick. It is no great wonder that Mr. Churchill fixed on you, if indeed he did."

"And why should I not be angry? After what Wickham did—stealing my pride, our future, our security—"

"He did not do that." Anne squared her shoulders to face him. "Wickham stole your money. No less, but no more."

Wentworth stared at her, uncomprehending. "They amount to the same thing!"

"No, they do not! Your pride is not your prize money, and I hope that it never was. It lay in your service to your country, and having discharged that service with merit and honor. Our future is not one of privation and want—my dowry alone sees to that. And our security lies in each other, the bonds of our marriage, and our love for our daughter. The money Wickham stole—wrong as he was to do it—it had nothing to do with any of these things. Consider to what extremes this loss has driven us!"

Her husband would not be so easily placated. "Your dowry cannot support us as we wish to live. You must realize, Anne, that if Wickham's death does not end our debt, I shall be obliged to return to sea?"

Anne could not help it. She smiled. "How I would love that!"

"But—the conditions in which you had to live—"

"Were nothing I could not endure, and a small price to pay for the many joys of that life. Seeing so many faraway lands—every day unlike the next—always new people to be met, new adventures to be had!" Anne did not consider herself overly adventurous, but who could not thrill to their first sight of the Mediterranean, their first glimpse of porpoises off the bow, their first footsteps on the coast of Africa?

Wentworth shook his head. "It was too harsh a life for a woman, and I often blamed myself for asking it of you. I recall when you were taken ill at sea—so seriously that we feared for you—"

"I did not fear for myself."

"But . . ." He struggled so to speak that she knew immediately what he would speak of; only one subject between them was so heavy with pain. "The child that would have been—"

"Our loss would have been equally as terrible had I been at shore." Anne would never again look at the ocean—not even after weeks or months at sea—without remembering that her first child had been sent to his rest there. "Nothing would have made that any easier to bear. But we bore it *together*."

"You do not think the rough seas caused this?"

Had he been blaming himself and his profession all this time? Empathy welled within Anne as she reached her hand out for his. "No, dearest. The seas were not so rough as that. Sometimes this . . . simply happens. We do not speak of it much, even among women, but it is not uncommon."

Had she gotten through to him? Maybe not, because Wentworth shook his head. "You deserve better than that, Anne. Better than a cabin smaller than a scullery, better than biscuit and salt pork to eat."

"What I deserve, in my opinion, is the chance to live by my husband's side. The best part of all those travelings was that I was with you. That we were never separated. We were one in spirit and thought and almost in action. How can you not miss those days, Frederick? I do. I miss them terribly."

Wentworth remained taken aback. She expected him to think this through for quite some time; and she would let him take what time he needed, as long as he finally considered these matters. At last he said, "I had no idea you thought so."

"You knew what pleasure I took in that life," Anne replied. "But you forgot it. All this while I believed you were blinded to it by the glitter of your prize gold. If that was not so—if you meant only to protect me—you must let that go. There is no protection against fate. We must build it together, as best we can, in the way that will make us both happy."

Maybe, she mused, they'd been wrong to be angry with Mr. Wickham at all. If Frederick could at last see her again, Wickham had actually done them a favor. If that change cost twenty-five thousand pounds, Anne considered it a bargain.

∽

Jonathan had been told, in no uncertain terms, to leave Juliet Tilney severely alone for the remainder of the Darcy family's time at Donwell Abbey. His father's temper had been such that Jonathan had said not one word in response—not even to point out the obvious impossibility of avoiding a person with whom they would be expected to take all their meals. Probably his father's dictum would gentle over time. But Jonathan had resigned himself to not speaking to Miss Tilney at any length for at least a few days.

That was before the household learned of the constables' discovery. As soon as Jonathan heard it, he knew his duty. Juliet Tilney would need support to bear up under such a burden. If that angered his father, so be it.

Having been chastised about the imprudence of knocking on Miss Tilney's door, however, Jonathan did not dare do so again. Thus he was obliged to wait to see her.

She made her first appearance many hours later, slightly before teatime. Miss Tilney looked pale, and she startled when she spotted him at the far end of the hall. "Oh! Were you waiting for me?"

"Of course. Since Churchill and his men left."

"But—that was hours ago." Her expression gentled; a smile

remained impossible, but this came close. "Have you been in the hall all that while?"

Jonathan nodded. "I came up with many plausible explanations for why I might be standing here, were anyone to see me and ask. No one did."

"I shall wish to hear these explanations for spending hours in a hallway," she said. "Someday. I had thought you would be forbidden ever to see me again."

"Not quite," Jonathan said. To tell her more would only be to distress her further.

Miss Tilney's mind remained on more critical subjects. "What is it you have to tell me? Have you learned who put that thing in my room?"

"No, that remains unknown. I wished only to tell you—it seems clear that nobody in Donwell Abbey believes you guilty. So if you have any concerns on that point, please dismiss them."

Her shoulders relaxed slightly, it seemed to Jonathan. She said, "One of them knows I am innocent, for it was that person who hid it."

"Undoubtedly. It might be worth asking the servants if anyone was seen entering or exiting your room. Anyone else, I mean."

"You are kind to concern yourself so. But in the hours since Mr. Churchill left, I have become more certain that I will not be arrested. That is not among my worries. However, I heard Mr. Churchill and Mrs. Knightley talking earlier in the search, and it has made me doubt our course of action."

"What did they say?" Jonathan hoped it was not persuasive. He did not want to stop investigating—nor meeting with Miss Tilney.

"They still think the murder weapon was the mace," she explained. "They do not know about the letter found in your parents' hearth. We had imagined presenting a solution to them, but by not sharing the information we have, we only make a solution less likely. We thought keeping it a secret allowed us to work more freely, but it is a secret no longer." She hung her head. "Now that I have tasted a little of what wrongful blame feels like, it makes it even harder to endure the thought of a person being wrongly accused. We cannot let it happen."

Jonathan could not deny the justice of her words. "Very well, then. We will tell Mr. Churchill about the letter and the bust. About all our efforts. Maybe he will let us work with him."

"I doubt it," Miss Tilney said. "But that does not mean we have to stop. No, Mr. Darcy, we must not stop."

Chapter Twenty-Two

In the end, Jonathan could not consent to speaking openly about their investigation until he had spoken to his parents about the burned letter in their hearth.

"Still I cannot bring myself to believe either of them guilty," he confided to Miss Tilney. "Especially after our discovery about the earl last night. But it appears there are difficult questions to be asked, and better that I should be the one to ask them, rather than the magistrate."

"That is reasonable and just," she said.

"If they were to—to admit anything of consequence, I would tell you."

"I know that you would," she said very simply, and it was one of the greater compliments he had ever been given.

Jonathan steeled his nerves for the coming confrontation as best he could. Yet his heart pounded in his chest as he went toward his parents' room, as strong and fast as it did when he had been out for a gallop on Ebony. Thus he startled when his mother opened the door in the instant before he could knock.

Elizabeth Darcy smiled, a strangely sad expression. "I thought you would be coming to see me soon."

His parents had been given the nicest guest room in Donwell Abbey, one with an ample window seat and a nook containing a writing-desk. Their mantel was as fine as the ones downstairs, carved of green marble with gold and ivory veins. Elizabeth led Jonathan to the window seat, which provided ample light to read by if needed—but if his mother had seen this before, she would recognize it instantly.

He drew out the fragile scrap of burned paper. "Mother, why was this in your hearth?"

"It was there because I burned it."

The straightforward answer made him blink in surprise. "Oh. Oh. But—why? And how did you come to have it?"

Elizabeth was as calm as he had ever seen her. "I found it in Mr. Wickham's things, shortly after his death."

"You mean that you were the one to ransack his room?" Jonathan had not dreamed of this. How badly had he misjudged his parents? What else might they have done?

"Not I." Then Elizabeth paused. "That is to say, I did search Wickham's quarters, and I am confident I was the first to do so. I slipped upstairs almost immediately after we were certain he was dead. But when I did so, I was quick and to the point. You see—in that first instant, when shock had overcome us all and none were thinking clearly—I wondered whether your father had, well, done something he should not." She bowed her head in apparent shame at having doubted her husband. "The enmity between them was so deep, so long-lived, borne of so many egregious wrongs by Mr. Wickham. I ought to have realized even that would not move your father to such a sinful act—though, at times, I was very near moved to it myself."

Jonathan asked, "So you went to Wickham's room to see whether your suspicion was correct?"

"No. I went there to see if there was any evidence that might condemn or endanger your father. I saw nothing in particular save one letter laid out on his bed, as though Wickham had been studying it shortly before his death. That I stole and hid beneath my shawl as I came back to the group, so as not to be missed."

That had been cleverly done. Jonathan realized they were lucky that his mother was such an upstanding woman, for she had wit enough to have gotten away with a great deal, if so inclined. "But the letter was not to or from my father. It appears to be a letter written to Mrs. Bertram."

Elizabeth brushed her fingers over the remaining legible words on the paper: *My dearest Fanny.* "Yes, it was. I read enough of the letter to recognize that it was not written by Mr. Wickham either. It was private correspondence of—of a nature that Mrs. Bertram would wish to keep private. In other words, I am fairly certain your late uncle was attempting to blackmail her."

This made little sense to Jonathan. "But Mrs. Bertram is a mild, pious young woman. What could she ever have done that would leave her open to blackmail?"

"Oh, my son." Elizabeth patted his arm. "Not all the secrets we keep are our own."

"So it was someone connected to her who had—"

"We must speak of it no more. I was and am confident that so gentle a creature as Mrs. Bertram could not be guilty of such an offense as murder. So I burned the letter—or I thought I did. Apparently I was not thorough enough."

"It is now impossible to know much of what the letter said," Jonathan replied, "only to whom it was addressed. Thus you were sufficiently thorough. Undoubtedly Mrs. Bertram would be grateful, if she knew."

Elizabeth looked doubtful. "She does not know, and thus I am sure she cannot rest easy. Perhaps I erred in not giving the letter back to her. That would have meant admitting that I knew about—well. That I knew. It seemed too much to confront her with, but upon reflection I think she might have preferred it so."

Jonathan believed his mother. It was clear that the letter served no more investigatory purpose. So he laid it in Elizabeth's palm. "You can give it back to her now, if you wish."

"I believe I shall."

❧

Juliet's experiences at that time were not as reassuring.

Still she labored under the weight of the discovery in her room. As ludicrous as it was to imagine that she herself the killer—a seventeen-year-old girl! Who had scarcely met the man!—surely nobody at Donwell Abbey could look at her in precisely the same way. Jonathan's reassurance and her own reason calmed her only so far. Even if the others present doubted what Mr. Churchill's constables had found, doubt must taint her as well. The stain of shame panicked her even more than had the thought of sharing a house with a murderer: the unknown killer seemed unlikely to strike again, whereas shame could stalk a young girl forever, ruining all her prospects and hopes.

She searched her room more thoroughly than even the constables had done. Where they had been looking for evidence pointing to the murderer, she was looking for evidence that might reveal who had put the trowel in her room. This individual wished to incriminate her, almost certainly to conceal their own wrongdoing. *A murderer slipped into my bedroom,* Juliet thought with a shudder. *That person stood where I am standing. That person knows where I sleep.*

A few odds and ends turned up, of uncertain import. One fading leaf from a shrub or flower lay under her bed—but might that not have come from one of the roses in the vase near her bed? It looked very much like it could've done. A snippet of slender gold braid was within the cabinet where the trowel had been found, ragged at the edge as though it had been torn away by the rougher paneling within the door—but that could've been there for days, months, even years. Had her stationery been rifled through? It seemed out of order to Juliet—but then again, when had she ever kept it in order?

She put one hand to her head and sighed. The mere knowledge of the murderer's intrusion had charged every single item in the room with a sense of dread. Would she ever be able to sleep here again?

Well, moping about it wouldn't help. Juliet took a seat at her desk and looked over the three pieces of evidence she had.

Paper and pen wiper out of place: well, that was nothing new. Juliet could not assess the likelihood of anyone's having searched her stationery, and thus worrying about it further would be useless.

The fallen leaf: almost certainly from the flowers in the vase. They were changed every few days, and it would be natural enough for a leaf to fall from time to time. And as the flowers would be changed as one of the very last tasks in straightening the room, the servants could very well not see it until the next day. Juliet was fairly certain her flowers had last been changed yesterday.

But the gold braid—that might mean something.

It is unlikely to have been left there by a servant, Juliet reasoned, *and the servants would go through this after every guest's stay in this room. So it would have been cleaned before my arrival. The braid must have been put there after my arrival. And it looks torn, not cut. Like the result of an accident had by someone in such a hurry she did not even notice she had torn her dress.*

They had all worn fine gowns to the Churchills' ball, but whose dress had been trimmed with braid?

She could not recollect it. Like many a young person at a ball, she had been too consumed with her own attire to take note of anyone else's.

How can I learn more? Because I must—as soon as possible.

Juliet had an enemy, and that person's identity must be established before the next act intended to incriminate her for the crime.

Finding Mrs. Bertram proved difficult for Elizabeth. The woman was quiet as a church mouse, and she scarcely seemed to appear save at mealtimes. Besides, it was important to find her in a place where they could be alone. For their next conversation—which would, in point of fact, be their first conversation—privacy was essential.

Elizabeth's searches were answered when she glanced out a window and saw a slim figure in lilac standing near the closest copse of elms. She had imagined Mrs. Bertram very much an interior creature—fond of riding, but otherwise to be found inside, kept from undue heat or cold, too fragile for the outdoors. It appeared her imagination had been in error.

Walking out to the wooded area took a few minutes, but Elizabeth was an excellent walker, unafraid of distance; she reached Mrs. Bertram easily enough. Elizabeth deliberately made noise as she approached, stepping on twigs and brushing against leaves, so that Fanny Bertram would not be surprised by her appearance.

And she was not, though she was not pleased either. "Oh. Mrs. Darcy. I had not thought you would . . ." Her words trailed away; she seemed uncertain of what to say.

To Elizabeth, conversation came more easily. "That I would appreciate the charms of nature? I assure you that I do. We might walk on together, unless you would consider it an imposition."

"Not at all." Fanny brightened, becoming more animated than Elizabeth had yet seen her. "Nature provides the surest solace, does it not? I am sure my spirit is never so at ease as it is when surrounded by green trees and blue sky."

"Indeed. It is one comfort that cannot be taken from us, save by a spell of rain, and even then the deprivation is but temporary." Elizabeth tried to conceive of a natural way to begin the next, thought of none, and decided to simply get to the point. "Mrs. Bertram, I must confess that I found something of yours a few days ago, which I have . . . damaged beyond repair."

Fanny's uncomprehending face froze in fear as Elizabeth held out the burned scrap of paper. "*Oh.* Oh, where did you—"

"Perhaps the question of where it was found should be left unasked," Elizabeth replied. "As will the question of what it contained."

Elizabeth had read only enough of the letter to comprehend why Mr. Wickham had it. That was enough. Shocking though the contents were, Elizabeth Darcy had a healthy understanding of what was and was not worth fretting over. The behavior of a certain William Price of the navy was not her concern and never would be. If his sister wished to protect him, there was no good reason not to let her do so.

Fanny remained doubtful. "You have not told anyone—you will not tell?"

"No one but myself knows what the contents were, and even I do not know all," Elizabeth said. "What little I did learn will never pass my lips. This I promise you."

"Thank you," Fanny whispered. Her hand clutched Elizabeth's for one moment with surprising strength. "Thank you so very much."

Elizabeth became more brisk. "I meant to destroy all evidence, but I made a terrible job of it, as you see. And I came to realize how worried you must be, not knowing it destroyed. So I bring you the remnants and the truth. Do with each as you see fit."

"You are very good," Fanny said. "I had not thought you capable of such delicacy." Then she caught herself, eyes wide with horror over her words.

Fortunately for both ladies, Elizabeth's wit was not to be dimmed by so slight a comment. "After the spectacle I made of myself a few nights ago, I can hardly wonder that you thought me devoid of proper feeling! Do not judge by that example, I beg you. We are of rather different temperaments, you and I, but our characters, I think, are not so very unalike."

"I see that now." With a small smile, Fanny further pledged, "I shall never forget it again."

⁓

Fanny had not been so grateful to another person in years as she now was to Elizabeth Darcy. All Mrs. Darcy's saucy words and sharp wit were forgiven in an instant. *I must not be so quick to judge,* Fanny resolved as she hurried back into the great house. *From now on I will not assume that such behavior is a mark of moral weakness. Do they not say that appearances are deceiving?* Surely only the greatest gentility of spirit could have motivated Mrs. Darcy to read what she had read, to know what she knew, and to respond with mercy.

It was a gentility of spirit Fanny's own husband had not yet shown.

Never before had she had to think about forgiving Edmund. Never had she assumed that her sense of right was truly better than his. Never had she found a point on which they differed where she was utterly determined not to budge.

Well. Edmund *had* briefly encouraged her courtship by a Mr. Henry Crawford, five years ago. It had taken him longer to understand the Crawfords. But even then, he had supported her right to make her own decisions in her own time.

Fanny did not want Edmund's forgiveness now. She did not feel she needed forgiveness. After weeks of terror for William and doubts about what she ought to do, both clarity and safety had arrived.

For an instant she recalled Mr. Wickham in their last conversation, in the gallery, not long before his death. She had offered him her ring, and he had taken it—but offered nothing in return beyond her broken wax seal, left over from one of the many times she had resealed William's letter in an attempt to protect his secret. She had not even managed to catch the wax seal when he tossed it to her, and it had been lost in the dark. How cruelly Mr. Wickham had laughed.

Was that the last time he had ever laughed—in malice rather than in joy? A sad epitaph for a life, saddest of all for Wickham himself.

The fires in Donwell Abbey were banked low during the day, at least during summertime, but embers glowed in the hearth of Edmund and Fanny's room. She knelt before the hearth and dropped in the last remaining fragment of William's letter and watched it turn to smoke and drift upward into nothingness.

∽

Mr. Churchill returned early Monday afternoon, somber and official. "I fear I must have a longer conversation with Miss Tilney," he said to the Knightleys.

Before their hosts could object on her behalf, Jonathan interjected, "A conversation is indeed overdue, Mr. Churchill. But we both should speak to you together."

Churchill stared at them. As did the Knightleys. As did Captain Wentworth, who had just come downstairs. Mercifully, Jonathan's father was elsewhere; otherwise, he might well have objected, preventing a discussion that dearly needed to take place. Juliet Tilney gave Jonathan a look that revealed the appreciation in her heart. It warmed him through. What a curious sensation . . .

"All right, then," Mr. Churchill said. "The both of you, in Mr. Knightley's study. Let's have it out."

He sounded very brusque when he said it. Jonathan had no idea what it was Frank Churchill expected to hear from them. Whatever it might have been, it was not what they actually said.

"Investigating a murder?" Frank Churchill looked at them as though they had proclaimed their intention to travel to the moon. "With no right of law? A young man hardly out of school and—and a *girl*?"

"We had to," Jonathan earnestly explained. "You see, your first assumptions about the case were entirely wrong. We feared that a servant or a Gypsy might be wrongly condemned if we did not step in."

Miss Tilney gave Jonathan a look that belatedly made him realize this was not the most tactful way to put things. Tact was often mysterious to Jonathan, but even he could see the problem.

Luckily, Frank Churchill was an amiable man. "I should be quite put out if I had not already realized myself to be on the wrong track at first. No, the killer is indeed one of the guests. But whatever gave you the idea that you could figure this out on your own?"

"I beg your pardon, Mr. Churchill, but we have learned some things that may prove to be of value," Miss Tilney said.

She went on to explain every point they had yet gained:

— that George Knightley had signed a surety for his
   brother's debt, involving his family in John's disgrace
   (a fact Emma Knightley had not known at the time
   of Wickham's death);

— that Mr. Wickham had been attempting to blackmail Fanny Bertram regarding the contents of a stolen letter that had since been destroyed but which had been in the gallery on the night of Wickham's death, as demonstrated by the presence of the broken wax seal;

— that both the Darcys had left their bedroom on the night of the murder, despite their protestations to the contrary (this pained Jonathan, but he did not object);

— that Mr. Darcy had been looking for information that might have given him motive to harm Mr. Wickham but had not found it and had subsequently discovered he had no new motive at all;

— that a woman—impossible to narrow down further—had put the incriminating trowel in Miss Tilney's room on the day of the dance at Medway Hall, as cover either for herself or for a husband, and had left a torn scrap of gold braid behind; and

— that the murder weapon was no medieval mace but instead a bust of Lord Nelson.

Mr. Churchill let them lead him to the bust, which he studied with great interest. "I say, you may be on to something here."

"We have determined the weapon," Jonathan said, "and many possible motives. What we have not learned is the identity of the killer."

"I ought to tell the both of you to stop meddling in matters beyond your years," said Mr. Churchill. "Still . . . there's no denying you've made real progress. Not in spite of your positions but because of them. They are all very careful around me, less so around you."

Miss Tilney smiled for the first time since the search of her room. "Then we are to continue?"

Frank Churchill held up a hand of caution. "In no official capacity, of course. And, needless to say, this must remain between us three. Whatever you learn, bring it to me. Then the law will act."

"So that you can arrest the murderer," Jonathan said. This made sense to him; anything that took place after such a discovery would be beyond his ability or Miss Tilney's.

"Well, yes," Mr. Churchill said. "But it is also a matter of your own safety. The guilty party has killed once. Knowing themselves on the verge of capture could be motive to kill again."

Jonathan and Miss Tilney exchanged glances. He saw fear there—but more resolution. "Trust us," he said to Mr. Churchill. "We will come to you when we learn more."

She added, "And we shall."

Frank Churchill grinned. "Do you know, I believe you will?"

Chapter Twenty-Three

As much as Juliet had learned of the arts of deception of late, she knew she was as yet not proficient. Thus it was a relief to practice her next stratagem on an entirely aware and willing target.

"Not that I *wish* to become practiced at deception," Juliet explained to the patient Elizabeth Darcy. "But in such a case as this—"

"Questions of right and wrong become more complicated," Elizabeth finished. "It would be lovely to think that absolute honesty served us best in all circumstances, but unfortunately it is not always the case."

Jonathan's interrogation of his mother regarding the burned letter had led to some understanding of the ongoing investigation—and Jonathan and Juliet's involvement in it. Juliet wondered whether Mr. Darcy had also informed his wife of their behavior, but, if so, Elizabeth did not seem to share his disapproval. Instead, when tentatively approached for help, she had responded with readiness.

She looked thoughtful for a moment, but before Juliet could inquire, Elizabeth had become her usual bright self again.

"Do you remember the dresses the night of the ball?" Juliet said. Elizabeth's memory for such flourishes might exceed her own; if she remembered the braid, then the entire inquiry might swiftly be concluded.

But Elizabeth shook her head. "I fear the only dress I recall with any clarity was one worn by a woman of Highbury, and that only because I disliked it so. So memory alone will not serve us. Perhaps you instead might begin by admiring my dresses and asking about some of the trimmings? A question which could then be put to the other ladies present."

Juliet thought this might come across as fawning, but it seemed the only alternative to snooping in people's rooms. She had no wish to compound the shame she had suffered during Churchill's search by being thought a thief. So, fawning it was. "Yes, that will be the quickest way."

"Many women would rush to display their finery," Elizabeth said, "but our company is more modest and reasonable. Still, I doubt anyone will refuse you. Certainly I shall not." She gestured toward her wardrobe, giving permission.

Hesitantly Juliet began going through Mrs. Darcy's things folded carefully on the wardrobe shelves. Her dresses seemed very simple but were rendered elegant by the luxury of their materials and the expertise of their tailoring. Some small bit of lace trimmed her finer gowns, and ribbon decorated others, but no braid was to be seen, gold or otherwise.

"Check the hats and caps," Elizabeth suggests. "I believe I have seen braid upon some caps—in fact, do I—"

"You do." Juliet took out the velvet turban Mrs. Darcy had worn to the Churchills' ball. "A bit of braid is looped around the base of the plume. But it is silver, not gold, and it is not torn."

Elizabeth smiled widely. "Then I am exonerated! Is it not remarkable how greatly we can be relieved at being pronounced not guilty, even when we knew ourselves to be innocent all the while?"

Juliet recalled the flush of shame she had felt when the constables confronted her with the trowel planted in her room. "I hope to know it very soon."

⁓

Never had Elizabeth doubted her son would marry; his good looks and his sizable inheritance would see to that if nothing else did. (Indeed, the former Caroline Bingley now had a sixteen-year-old daughter who was clearly being raised with an eye to accomplishing what her mother had not: becoming mistress of Pemberley.) But just as Elizabeth had wanted more than a material match for herself, she wanted that for Jonathan, too. Often had she wondered how best he might make the acquaintance of a young woman in such a way that this young woman could love him for himself, not for the wealth he brought.

As many tactics as she had devised, never had she conceived of Jonathan's cooperating with a girl on a murder inquiry.

Elizabeth caught herself. She sat in the library, a book open in her hands, but its pages might as well have been blank for all the attention she gave them. Her fancies were getting the better of her. *I must not behave like my mother, making matches every time an eligible young person comes within a mile. I will make myself ridiculous and accomplish nothing. At this rate I shall soon be sending Jonathan out on horseback in the rain in hopes he will catch cold!*

So Mrs. Bennet had done to Elizabeth's sister Jane, who had caught a very bad cold and—as Mrs. Bennet had hoped—had been obliged to stay at Bingley's home, Netherfield, for some days until she was well enough to return home. Elizabeth had gone to nurse her, scared that her sister would receive no proper care from Bingley's cold sisters. It was then that Elizabeth had made the better acquaintance of Mr. Darcy; and while this knowledge had had no great effect on her feelings, his had emerged very much changed.

Yet . . . if Darcy had not grown interested in her at Netherfield, he would not have proposed to her so disastrously on his first attempt. If he had not proposed so badly then, she would never have upbraided him for his treatment of Jane. If she had not upbraided Darcy, he would not have been more courteous to her later. Without that courtesy, she would never have confided in him about Wickham and Lydia's elopement. Without that information, Darcy would never have persuaded Wickham to marry Lydia. Thus Lydia, Elizabeth, Jane, and their other sisters would have been ruined. None of them would have married anyone. Trace it back to the beginning, and they had in fact been saved from this fate by . . . Jane's catching cold on horseback.

Mother was right all along, Elizabeth thought for very nearly the first time in her life. A laugh bubbled up within her, and she did not hold it back. The others in the library with her glanced in her direction, but none spoke. Darcy gazed at her longer than anyone, and on his face she saw the shadow of a smile. He found pleasure in her happiness, as he always had.

The distance that had widened between the Darcys since Susannah's death had never been easy for Elizabeth to bear. Only now was she willing to comprehend how much of it was her doing. Darcy was not wholly without fault in the matter—but she could not blame him for his mistakes without acknowledging her own. That way lay bitterness and discord. They were capable of better.

$\backsim$

"You are always so beautifully dressed, Mrs. Knightley." Juliet Tilney smiled up at Emma, all eagerness and sweet disposition. "I wanted to have one or two of my dresses trimmed up like yours—if I might be allowed to take a look?"

It was a peculiar request, but not an improper one, and Emma saw no need to refuse. No doubt the girl needed distraction after the horrifying discovery by the constables. "By all means. Come and see."

Emma led Miss Tilney to her room, grateful that her wardrobe was situated to the side and that she was not obliged to display anything so intimate as her marriage bed. *Though,* she thought, *after the many searches and late wanderings in our nightclothes, the entire house party is all but devoid of propriety.* "Here we are. Was there a particular dress you wished to see?"

"I should like to look at them all, if I might," Juliet replied brightly. "Your taste is impeccable, Mrs. Knightley."

Which, in Emma's opinion, was undeniably true. And had she not invited the young woman in hopes of giving her a broader view of the world, a larger acquaintance, more sophistication? Surely improving her clothing would play a role in that.

(Not that Miss Tilney was badly dressed—but simply so, and, having reached marriageable age, she would undoubtedly be adding a bit more ornament.)

Juliet began going through the dresses, praising each as she came across them. Although she skipped none, Emma noticed that she paid more attention to the finer ball gowns. That was no surprise. A girl of that age might happily wear sackcloth during the week if it meant she could have the dress of her dreams for a party.

"What beautiful cording," Juliet said, touching the peach-colored velvet at the neckline of one of Emma's older gowns. "Do you ever trim with gold braid, as well?"

Emma shrugged. "I have never been particularly fond of it. What slight glitter a lady can display should come from jewelry, in my opinion. Shiny braid can be no more than a distraction from that."

"Do you know, I think I agree." Juliet turned away from the wardrobe. "You have provided both an example and an education in matters of dress, Mrs. Knightley. Thank you ever so much."

What an odd girl, Emma thought after Juliet had departed. Not a killer—never would she believe *that,* trowels or no—but odd. Then again, who could blame her for admiring Emma Knightley?

Not Emma.

⁓

Edmund had never visited the Donwell Abbey chapel on his own, but he did so that afternoon. He had spoken too easily of the will of God; best to be absolutely certain of it before he talked to Fanny again. His prayers lasted long enough for the slant of the sunlight through the stained glass windows to sweep across a wide stretch of the wall.

At the very moment he opened his eyes, determined—as though a sign from above, the door to the chapel creaked. Edmund looked back to see Fanny entering for more of her own devotions. She was surprised to see him there, and the surprise was not a pleasant one, it seemed.

"Fanny," he said, rising to his feet. "Forgive me. I did not think you would come here again today. Please do not believe I lay in wait for you."

"That would be so unlike you. Surely we can pray together still, can we not?"

"Always, dearest Fanny." Edmund came to her, then. "We must speak again of your brother."

She paled but lifted her chin, determined to hold her ground. Had he ever seen her so resolute? "I will not abandon William. Not even for you."

"No longer will I ask."

Fanny looked as astonished to hear those words as Edmund would have been to speak them even a few days prior. It had taken much prayer and thought to bring him to this place—the place Fanny had apparently found almost immediately upon reading William's letter.

He continued, "I cannot condone William's behavior. Yet I cannot uphold the individual laws of God without honoring the spirit that underlies them. Religion must support the bonds of family and love, rather than work against them, if it is to symbolize God's love for man. Some must turn away their sinning family members for their own peace of mind and to avoid corrupting influences. But you, Fanny—if you have made your peace with William's actions, your good heart is as near incorruptible as any soul on earth can be. As long as you wish for William to be in your life, let it be so."

Fanny's eyes lit up with hope, but she remained wary. "I do wish for him to remain in my life. I will always so wish. It is not a thing I will be argued out of, so if you think to—"

"No, Fanny. I have preached at you as much on this subject as ever I will."

"And I may still visit William when his ship comes to port?"

"Of course you may."

She took a deep breath. "Will he be welcome in our home?"

This was difficult to countenance. Yet Edmund had allowed his sister Maria to visit the previous year, and were her sins truly less egregious? Love must conquer all else. "As you wish it."

His wife flung her arms around him, and Edmund embraced her tightly as she said, "How I prayed and prayed that you would come to see matters so—but I hardly dreamed—"

"That I might find sufficient humility? I do not blame you." For humility lay at the core of it all—the recognition of one's own self as a sinner, the willingness to surrender ultimate judgment to the ultimate Judge. "Besides, the New Testament makes it clear that Christ's sacrifice repeals some of the harshest tenets of the Old, does it not?"

Fanny beamed at him, tears of joy in her eyes. "Forgiveness is not contrary to faith. It cannot be."

Edmund had rarely felt so grateful for his wife's adoration, for her purity of heart. "Perhaps you should be the vicar, and I the parishioner, ready to learn."

"Oh, Edmund, we are all the students of the Lord together."

❧

Mrs. Knightley dressed very well, and Mrs. Darcy even better. Both followed fashion at a gentle distance, never looking either faddish nor out-of-date and always with the finest materials. Marianne Brandon, whose wedding clothes were not even a year old, wore the latest styles, and thus Juliet had decided to save her for last—the better to actually take her time admiring the dresses. But this meant her next targets were women whose attire was not so obviously of interest.

Fanny Bertram would be the most difficult, Juliet judged, and so she tried her luck with Anne Wentworth first.

"How kind you are to admire my clothes," Anne said, in the tone of one who is trying not to sound incredulous. "But, yes, of course, you may look if you like."

"Thank you." Juliet once again felt a bit ashamed to be using the trust of others so—especially now, when the constables' search had left her own trustworthiness in doubt. Still, she now had the magistrate's permission to continue, which was rather like being asked to enforce the law, if one looked at it at a certain angle, one Juliet was working very hard to see.

Anne Wentworth's dresses, though not so fine as the first two ladies', were still very well made. Juliet ran her hand along an emerald-green pelisse made of thicker fabric than seemed likely to be needed in the summer. "This is lovely, but would it not be warm?"

"It would be—but it is a favorite of mine, so I always have it with me in hopes it will be called for." Anne's smile was rueful. "Most often I wear it when at the seaside, or at sea itself, for the ocean cools the air very sharply."

"I forget that you have been to sea. How marvelous it must be to have seen so much of the world. I have never been any farther away from home than I am at this moment."

"It is a rare privilege for a lady," Anne agreed, "and one I am proud of. Though truly my pride comes from being the captain's wife, in knowing that my care for him helps him better serve our kingdom. Such is life with the Royal Navy." She hesitated, then added, with a widening smile, "We may return to sea after all. Perhaps within a few months. I should not mind seeing the Indies. At least, I would not mind the many wonders we are told of. But the practice of slavery is apparently much in evidence there, and witnessing the cruelties therein would be very difficult. Still, I should rather know the truth of the matter, the better to speak against it."

Juliet's family was also antislavery; her father had more than a passing acquaintance with William Wilberforce. So at any other time, she might have joined in a lively conversation with Anne Wentworth on the subject and would no doubt have learned much.

But Juliet did not ask, because she had stopped heeding Anne's words as soon as she heard "Royal Navy."

It is not only dresses that are trimmed with gold braid. So are military uniforms. And both Colonel Brandon and Captain Wentworth brought their uniform coats with them! Each wore them the night of the Churchills' ball, which has to have been the night someone went into my room . . .

"Excuse me," Juliet said. "I have just remembered—I must go. But thank you so very much!"

Anne frowned in confusion as the girl hurried away.

* birth*

Jonathan had been coerced into an evening game of whist, which was currently being very much regretted by the others at table.

"You cannot know which cards people hold after only one round," Captain Wentworth protested as Jonathan turned yet another trick. "That is impossible."

"To me it seems obvious," Jonathan said. Numbers and probabilities came easily to him and always had. With that knack, once one understood the rules of whist, and if one's fellow players were competent, the initial round told the entire story. "When I was younger, I didn't even understand that others did *not* know."

Emma Knightley looked cross, though she exaggerated her expression to make it clear all was in good fun. "I would think you a braggart, young Mr. Darcy, were it not for the fact that you have trounced us all yet again."

Jonathan's partner, Mr. Knightley, began shuffling cards for the next round. "As your triumph is my triumph, I should be pleased at your acumen. Instead, I am humbled by the proof of how much I have yet to learn."

Such reactions were common when Jonathan played cards, which was why he played seldom. He was never certain whether those at table were having fun or were concealing greater dismay. At least this time no money was at stake. Jonathan had once made the grave error of winning fifty pounds in a game at school, which had turned him into something of a social pariah for the rest of term.

Just beyond the doorway, he caught sight of Juliet Tilney. Her eyes widened, and she gestured toward him, clearly eager for a conference. Jonathan was not sorry to go. "I fear I must bow out of the next hand. If someone else might relieve me—"

"I can do so," said his father, who fortunately had not seen Miss Tilney at the door behind him. Mr. Darcy was no great enthusiast at cards, but he could play well enough to make up a fourth at any social occasions.

"Then we are *all* relieved." Mr. Knightley's play on words made his wife smile and slap playfully at his arm. Jonathan simply hurried out to meet Miss Tilney. They had not needed to exchange words for him to know she would be waiting in the billiard room.

Almost—she was just at that room's door when he caught up with her. So excited was she that she did not even enter before whispering, "There is another answer to the braid, one I had not considered before—"

"What do you mean?" Jonathan asked.

"Military uniforms." The truth of her words was evident to Jonathan immediately, though Miss Tilney continued on, "The dress uniform jackets of both army and navy are ornamented with gold braid!"

"Captain Wentworth," Jonathan said. He had been among their chief suspects from the beginning. "Of course there is the colonel to consider, too—"

"But you are right," Juliet interjected. "Brandon had no reason to confess knowing Wickham at all. Surely he would not have confessed that much if he were guilty. Whereas Wentworth—his temper, the depth of his anger toward Wickham, even the way he has spoken about the murder—everything points to him."

Jonathan nodded. "Then I must devise a way of seeing Captain Wentworth's dress jacket again." The simple pretense of admiration that Juliet had employed would not serve him. "Or we could simply explain to Mr. Churchill that he needs to request a viewing of such—"

"That will not be necessary," said a man's low voice.

They both whirled about to see Colonel Brandon standing only a few paces from them, his hands clasped behind his back. His face—never greatly expressive—remained utterly unreadable.

"Mr. Churchill may see my jacket if he likes," the colonel continued, "but it is beside the point. No longer will I engage in this subterfuge. I apologize for having continued it thus far."

Juliet shook her head as in disbelief. "What do you mean?"

"That I am guilty and must face my punishment," Colonel Brandon said. "It was I who murdered Mr. Wickham."

Chapter Twenty-Four

It is one thing to have a suspicion, quite another to have that suspicion confirmed. Juliet had felt nothing but an eagerness to investigate when she went to Jonathan Darcy—but now that Colonel Brandon stood before them, a confessed murderer, she felt a thousand other things: fear, shock, regret, even shame, as though somehow her looking for the murderer had been what made him a murderer. Nonsense, and yet she could not easily dispel her horror. She couldn't even move. She could only stare at Colonel Brandon, who remained as pale and impassive as a marble statue.

Thankfully, Jonathan was more collected. "I believe, sir, that it would be best for you to repeat your confession before one of our hosts."

Colonel Brandon nodded stiffly. "Indeed. I believe Mr. Knightley is playing at cards."

As indeed he was, though he quickly went with them to his study to hear more. Juliet stood next to Jonathan Darcy, watching, as Brandon repeated his former words verbatim. Blood drained from Knightley's face, until he looked very nearly as horrified as he had on the night of the murder itself.

Knightley did not speak at first. Then he leaned over and pulled the cord for the bell. When a servant appeared behind them in the doorway, Knightley finally managed, "Send someone to town immediately—Tom, perhaps. Whoever can be ready to go right away and at top speed." His gaze never left Brandon. "Bring Mr. Churchill here at once . . . and let him know that his constables should not be far behind him."

None of them left the study; none of them knew what to say. After several seconds of terrible silence, Knightley gestured to the chair. "You may as well sit. I hardly feel as if I could stand myself."

"Thank you," Colonel Brandon said, as polite as ever. (But how could one be both *polite* and a murderer? What was more *impolite* than killing someone? Juliet could not reckon it.) "Forgive me for these days of suspense, Mr. Knightley. I ought to have come to you at once."

"Yes, you ought," Knightley replied. "At least we can put things to rights now."

The younger Mr. Darcy crossed the room, and Juliet followed. She stood in the corner, making herself very small, so that nobody would tell her what a young lady should and should not hear. Jonathan Darcy, more assured of his welcome, remained near the center of the study. Why had he moved? Then Juliet realized that they were no longer blocking the door. It was a small act of courtesy on his part, indicating to Colonel Brandon that he was still trusted enough for no one to physically keep him from running away. It seemed to her that a murder should demolish all trust—but a confession had to be worth something. At any rate, Brandon made no move to run.

Frank Churchill arrived faster than ought to have been possible. "I was on my way here already," he explained, hurriedly handing his hat to the servant. "Tom found me halfway up the road. Colonel Brandon, it is you, then, is it?"

"Yes," Colonel Brandon replied very simply. "I am guilty and accept my fate."

Everyone exchanged glances. Churchill broke the silence: "Then tell us how this came to happen."

"You remember, I think, what I told you when first we spoke," Colonel Brandon said.

Jonathan remembered it well, and the memory prompted a question. But it was quite obviously not a good time for him to talk.

The colonel's profile was visible to Jonathan, and rare emotion was present there—but if Jonathan was interpreting that feeling correctly, he was not seeing anger or shame but a kind of tenderness that only deepened as Brandon continued.

"My Eliza died many years ago. Long had I known the role George Wickham played in her life; in the past I had even sought him not in anger but in hopes that he would wish to know his daughter. It all seemed very distant to me until Wickham's arrival at Donwell Abbey. When I discovered who he was, my anger returned to me as though—as though Eliza had died only yesterday. I told myself it would do no good to relive the past. My new bride deserves better." Brandon paused, perhaps gathering his strength. "Yet in the end, I came back to what his daughter would wish. If she could be united with her father, she and her child might find a substantially better situation in life. So I resolved to speak to Wickham on that subject, solely for those purposes."

"After midnight?" Frank Churchill demanded. "In the gallery?"

Colonel Brandon lowered his head, struggling for his answer. "I cannot explain it now. Had I met him in the light of day, this could not have occurred."

"What did occur, then?" Mr. Churchill dipped his pen into Mr. Knightley's inkwell once more, continuing to inscribe the details of the confession.

"We met," Brandon said. "We spoke. He scarcely even remembered Eliza—a woman who loved him, who bore his child, who lost her life because of his neglect! This, Wickham could forget as a mere trifle. When I told him about her daughter—*his* daughter—he said the child might be anyone's and insinuated that Eliza had been of low repute. At that I was incensed. I acted rashly and have committed a great wrong. It is only correct that I should pay the price."

Everyone in the room exchanged glances. The penalty for murder was death. Colonel Brandon had just condemned himself to the gallows.

❦

This cannot be happening, Marianne thought. *It cannot be so.*

She felt fevered, frantic, almost deranged. Marianne had not been so disconnected from her rational self since the first days after Willoughby had broken with her two years prior. Though she knew better, she could not stop *feeling* as though if she wished hard enough, with the right words, she could somehow make it so none of this had taken place. It made one understand why people had once believed in witchcraft—how one might believe pain and fear so powerful could give power to one's words and thoughts, could even reshape the world entire.

But we *do not believe in witches,* she imagined her sister Elinor saying. Her cool rationality would have been welcome. Marianne could not think, and she was divided—perhaps forever—from the only other person in her life who encouraged her to supersede her wildest, least-virtuous self.

"He should not have told them," Marianne whispered to herself as she sat in her room, tear-soaked linen handkerchief held to her flushed face. "If only he had spoken to me first— I could have stopped him, I know I could—"

Instead, the news of Colonel Brandon's confession was spreading throughout Donwell Abbey. The servants ought to have come by her room by now, but they had left it severely alone. How would the other guests react? Would none of them stand up for Brandon? But why would anybody defend a murderer who had freely confessed to the act?

"Damn George Wickham to hell," she murmured—rather late, as Mr. Wickham's fate in the afterlife had almost certainly been determined by this point. If there were any doubt, however, she wished God would hear her and decide the matter for good.

Soon her beloved husband would be dead, too.

I will not let it happen, Marianne thought. *I can make it as though this never happened.*

℞

As Marianne had divined, word was spreading through Donwell Abbey at tremendous speed. News such as this could hardly be announced to the entire company, but where information so shocking as this is concerned, it will find its own paths to being heard.

"Colonel Brandon?" Anne sat down heavily. "This cannot be."

"I have difficulty believing it myself, though I would scarcely have thought it of any one of us." Captain Wentworth bore the news better. "Still, he is an army officer, one who has seen action. I fear that I know all too well—as difficult as it is to first attempt to take another human life, even when that life belongs to an enemy of the Crown—the act becomes easier over time. Perhaps, for Brandon, it became too easy."

"But surely he could not have—" Anne caught herself. "Should I go to his wife? No—not yet—it is too soon. But tonight I will stay with her, if you consent."

"I would expect no less of your good heart."

Fanny and Edmund Bertram heard the news together. Buoyed as they were by both their faith and their newfound trust in each other, they were more sanguine than most.

"We must pray for Mrs. Brandon," Edmund said. "She must be terribly struck down. Some may wish to punish her by association, but such is unchristian. Yes, we should pray for her at once."

"Also for Colonel Brandon." Fanny's pale gaze had rarely been steadier. "He is more in need of God's love and forgiveness than ever."

Would she always have to remind him that faith required mercy? Fanny decided she did not mind it, not if Edmund always took it so well as he did now. He nodded firmly and gave her his arm. "Let us go to the chapel. Tonight, if Mrs. Brandon wishes it, she may join us. Until she is strong enough to pray, we will do it for her."

"Well!" Emma said. "Indeed. I can scarcely believe it."

Knightley nodded. He sat at his desk, heavier with sorrow for the murderer than he had ever been for the victim. "Nor I. Brandon hardly seemed the type—"

"To murder someone in another person's house!" Emma threw up her hands. "It is the height of rudeness! Can you imagine?"

It took her husband a few moments to reply. "Would the act be rendered less despicable if committed in the privacy of one's own home?"

"It would still be an outrage against God's commandments," Emma insisted, "but at least it would not draw others into fear and suspicion. That is worse, is it not?"

"By a rather marginal degree." Knightley gave her a look. "You do not mean what you are saying."

"No, I do not." Few saw Emma Knightley's more somber side, but it was in evidence now. "It is trivial. At such moments, it is a temptation to fixate upon the trivial, because that can be understood. Murder cannot."

Jonathan Darcy had been among the first to hear, but he had not yet accepted the news. Colonel Brandon's confession had been thorough, and he had made it, knowing that in so doing he consigned himself to be hanged. Was that not proof enough that he spoke truly? Certainly his motive made sense; it was one Jonathan and Juliet Tilney had both considered at length.

Yet an inconsistency worried at Jonathan, keeping him in doubt while all others had found certainty.

Mr. Churchill did not know of Colonel Brandon's connection to Mr. Wickham until Brandon confessed it soon after the murder.

But why confess the connection if attempting to conceal the crime?

☙

"I ought to feel more than this," Elizabeth said. She and Darcy sat together in the library, quite alone; every guest and resident of Donwell Abbey had sought a quiet place to reckon with the news. "Whatever else Wickham was, he was Lydia's husband and Susannah's father. I—I could see him in her features sometimes. Before, I always tried to deny the resemblance. Now I regret that I will never be able to glimpse her in his face, even for a moment."

Darcy's copy of *Sir Charles Grandison* sat forgotten in his lap. "I feel more than I thought I would," he admitted. "Since Wickham's death I have found myself thinking of him as I had not in many years—as my boyhood playmate. There was a time when he had all the wit and charm of his later self but had not yet lost his amiability. A time when George Wickham might have grown into a very different man, a far better one. I do not hold myself responsible for his alteration, and yet I cannot stop wondering how things might have been changed. It might have transformed everything, for all of us—even for Susannah—had his character been in the slightest measure improved."

His words surprised Elizabeth—not only in their content but more importantly in their character. Her husband had not been so open with her since before Susannah's death. It was time to repay him in kind.

You urged me to openness, Mary, she thought to her sister. *At long last I am taking some of your advice. When I tell you of this eventually, I hope you will not perish from astonishment.*

"I had thought—" Elizabeth's voice broke. She gathered herself and began again. "I had believed that perhaps you did not mourn Susannah as much as I did."

His pained look of reproof almost made her wish she had not spoken. "How could you believe such?"

"You never wept," she said. "Never lost heart. You went on as you ever had before. I did not know how you managed it. I still do not."

"I had to go on as I had before. Pemberley needed me. Our family—*you* needed me to remain strong. Else I thought we would collapse entirely."

Tears stung Elizabeth's eyes. "I did need you to remain strong. And yet I also needed you to condole with me. I felt as though I was suffering all alone, that no one else could ever truly understand, not even our children."

"You were never alone." Darcy's hand covered hers. "Forgive me if I abandoned you."

"Forgive me if I misunderstood you."

Though alone, they were in a public room, and thus despite the great emotion between them, it took the Darcys several seconds to surrender to the need for an embrace. Elizabeth laid her head on her husband's shoulder, breathed in the scent of him, and for the first time in eight months felt the tightness around her heart begin to ease.

"I should not have let her go." Darcy's voice shook such as Elizabeth had never heard it. "You were right—I ought to have forbidden the journey, told Wickham to sue and be damned—"

"No, no, no." She kissed his cheeks, his forehead. "The doctor said she could make the journey. You only wanted to get it all over with, so that Wickham might return her to us the sooner. You could not have known what would happen. None of us could have known."

"Yet I did it, and because I did, Susannah died."

Elizabeth shook her head. "Susannah died of a putrid fever. That is all. It is bad enough without any need for guilt."

Darcy studied her tenderly. "I used to wish I could give you a daughter. Then I began to think—perhaps it was better as it was, because if we had had girls of our own, we might not have been so quick to take in Susannah. For all the pain we have felt in her passing, I would not have missed a day with her."

A sob clutched at Elizabeth's throat. "Nor I. Not a single day."

It is perhaps best to leave them here, with the privacy of their feelings. Enough to know that the distance between husband and wife had, at long last, been bridged. This was not the last misunderstanding the Darcys would ever have—they were too different in temperament for perfect peace—but they would never be so far apart from each other again.

⁊

Jonathan finally decided that he had to put his question to Frank Churchill. Probably there was some solution, one of those obvious elements of human nature that everybody else could see while he could not.

When he sought out Mr. Churchill, however, he found him in front of the house talking with his constables. The gaol wagon sat in front of Donwell Abbey—a striking, unfathomable sight—its barred carriage waiting to transport a prisoner to prison, and then on to death.

"Mr. Churchill?" Jonathan began. "May I have a word?"

"No time, my boy." Frank Churchill looked past him to the doorway, where others were leaving the house.

Colonel Brandon stood next to Mr. Knightley, who was shepherding him along the way in what was surely the strangest duty of a host. Brandon appeared pale but he did not flinch, even when the constables walked toward him with irons in their hands.

"Are those necessary?" Knightley said, gesturing toward the cuffs. "You cannot think he means to break away or to cause any further violence."

Mr. Churchill gestured at the constables to step back again. "I suppose not. Whatever else Colonel Brandon is, he is a gentleman and will be treated as such."

"Thank you." Brandon inclined his head and walked toward the wagon—only to stop short when a call came from the doorway.

"Wait!" Juliet Tilney had hurried out onto the steps. "Forgive me, Mr. Churchill, but there is a question you did not ask Colonel Brandon."

"What else is there?" Mr. Churchill seemed more puzzled than annoyed. "What questions could possibly remain?"

Perhaps he could not fathom what remained to be asked after a confession. Jonathan could. And Miss Tilney—yet again, she had seen what he had. Had she learned to view the world through his eyes, or could he now see it through hers?

"There is but one," Jonathan said. "It is important, however."

He left the asking itself to Miss Tilney. "Mr. Churchill, you must ask Colonel Brandon with what weapon he committed the crime."

"Blast it, I know what weapon was used—thanks to you two—" Frank Churchill must have been caught off guard to say *blast* in mixed company.

"Yes, you know, and we know," Jonathan said. "The question is, does Colonel Brandon know? If he is truly the killer, he must."

As if by rote, fully expecting the obvious answer, Mr. Churchill said, "Very well. Colonel Brandon, what weapon did you use to strike Mr. Wickham?"

"I—" Brandon's eyes were wide, uncertain. "The mace, from the armory—you said it yourself."

Frank Churchill startled. Jonathan shared a glance with Miss Tilney. Why would a man confess to a crime he did not commit?

At that moment, from within the house, came the cry, "No! Wait—*stop!*"

Marianne Brandon ran out of the door, wearing no mob-cap, her hair half-loose from its bun, her cheeks still flushed from tears. Knightley went toward her and caught her before she could fling herself onto her husband. "Mrs. Brandon, I know this is hard, but—justice must be done."

"Yes, yes, it must," she insisted.

"Marianne." Brandon shook his head slowly at her. "Please, do not do this."

"I have to. Justice must be done, and it will not be if you take my husband to prison. He is innocent!"

Brandon repeated, more loudly, "*Marianne.*" She did not look at him. Everyone else did, however, appearing in the doorway or at the windows; even the Bertrams were just then coming back from the chapel to witness the entire scene.

Frank Churchill stared penetratingly at Mrs. Brandon.

"There are reasons to doubt your husband's guilt, but none from his own mouth, for he has confessed to the crime."

"He's lying," Marianne said. "He's trying to protect me. Because I—I—"

Jonathan took a step backward. He had considered this possibility but never seriously. And yet now he saw it all, as clearly as if he had witnessed the murder itself.

"I did it," Marianne finished. "I killed Mr. Wickham."

"Nonsense." Brandon's voice was sharper than Jonathan had yet heard it. "She is a mere girl. You cannot believe this, Mr. Churchill."

"I hardly know what to believe," Churchill said, glancing from one to the other.

Miss Tilney spoke then. "Ask Mrs. Brandon what was used to kill Mr. Wickham. The colonel does not know, but if she is guilty—she must."

Marianne stepped forward again, presenting her wrists to the constables. "It was a bust from the gallery. Of Lord Nelson, I think—it was hard to tell in the dark."

Jonathan and Miss Tilney shared a glance of terrible understanding. He had rarely been so unhappy to be right.

Chapter Twenty-Five

The drawing room of a house naturally lays the scene for any number of social interactions. Rarely does it host a confession of murder. However, on that day, the one in Donwell Abbey was pressed into such service.

Marianne knew that the entire party had gathered around her—Mr. Bertram staring in disbelief, Mrs. Wentworth projecting the greatest kindness—but it did not matter. None of them mattered. Her life was over, sacrificed upon the altar of her prized sensibility. Never before had she longed for a cooler head. But what was done was done. Her husband would not die for her crime. This was the only point upon which Marianne could ever imagine caring again.

Juliet Tilney very kindly took her hand and led her to a place on one of the settees. Marianne did not realize she was clinging on to the girl's fingers until Juliet sat beside her instead of going away. The small contact helped, and Marianne was grateful, for the only other source of soothing she could have expected would be to look into her husband's face—and that would be even more torment than comfort.

Mr. Knightley situated himself in a chair opposite her. Glancing about the room, he began: "Perhaps—it might be easier upon the lady were this not so public—"

The others were beginning to turn away before Marianne interrupted, "No. Please, those of you who will, stay. I have hidden the truth too long. You have all endured suspicion on my account. You deserve to hear all."

Did they understand how badly she wanted them to stay? Perhaps so, because nobody departed. As little as Marianne liked speaking of such personal and shameful matters in front of so many people, she was determined to find what redemption she could as her life drew to a close.

"Mrs. Brandon," said Mr. Knightley, "please tell us how this terrible event came about."

Marianne's words came slowly, then in a torrent, like a frozen waterfall come spring. "I had never met George Wickham before his arrival at Donwell Abbey. Nor had my husband. But they were indeed linked, as everyone here has come to understand, by Wickham's great unkindness to a woman my husband loved long ago. My husband wanted to confront Mr. Wickham, if only to tell him that—that there were matters he should know."

Very quietly, Brandon said, "They know about the child."

At least she had not had to speak *that*. Small consolation indeed. "I begged him not to speak to Wickham. What we all knew from the Darcys was enough to tell us that the man cared little for the life of a daughter he did know—what possible feeling could he have for a daughter he had never dreamed of? And my good husband agreed. For my sake, more than any other, Colonel Brandon refrained from speaking to Wickham about their shared past in any way."

From the corner of her eye she saw the Darcys turn to each other, no doubt recalling the dead girl. Marianne hoped they did not blame themselves for their frankness. This way, at least, Brandon had been spared a conversation that could only have caused him yet more pain.

Yet it was nothing compared to the pain *she* had caused with her rash, wretched act—

"But, you see, in my fear that Brandon would be drawn into such a confrontation, I paid close attention to Mr. Wickham, who greatly misconstrued my interest in him. He began attempting to charm me. To put it bluntly, to flirt with me. I ought to have upbraided him for the impudence at once, but at first—at first I did not even believe it, that even such a man as Wickham would behave so coarsely. When finally I did attempt to put him in his place, he believed it was only another form of flirtation. I do not know what honest man takes a woman's refusal as encouragement, but Wickham did."

How many times, in these past several days, had Marianne thought back to those first nights at Donwell Abbey, those first moments when Wickham took notice of her? She had imagined behaving so differently, so coldly, refusing even to look in the man's direction. If she had, surely Wickham would still be alive—and she would not be a murderess.

Time, finally, to speak the worst and the last. "On the night that—on that night I awoke and could not fall asleep again. In the past I had found that taking a short walk before returning to bed sometimes helped. So I threw my wrapper around me and went for a quick turn in the halls. My walk led me downstairs to the gallery, where I heard Mr. Wickham speaking. But he was not talking to my husband. He was with Mrs. Bertram." Marianne gave Fanny an apologetic glance. The worst of what she had heard would go with her to her grave; the only lie Marianne intended to tell that day would be told for Fanny's sake and not her own. "She was entirely innocent, asking only for something he had stolen from her—an amethyst ring, I think. I could not hear the entire conversation clearly. Wickham was being a brute, refusing to do so, and she was too frightened to confront him directly."

"Mrs. Bertram, can you confirm this much?" Frank Churchill demanded.

Fanny had gone so pale Marianne thought the woman

might faint. She felt rather as though she would faint herself. It would be such a blessing, to let the world go dark and far away—

"I can confirm it for her," said Anne Wentworth, unexpectedly stepping forward. "Or, rather, I can confirm what followed. I was awakened that night by the sound of weeping in the hallway and emerged, to give aid if I could. There I found Mrs. Bertram in a terrible state. Though she did not confide the reason for her distress, she allowed me to comfort her before she returned to her bedroom."

"Yes," Fanny managed to add. "It is true."

"I must further add," Anne said, "what I would have spoken of before anyone took the colonel away. You see, I knew he was not guilty. Colonel Brandon would have had no opportunity to kill Mr. Wickham. For when he was not in his room, he was speaking with me."

Everyone stared, most particularly Captain Wentworth. He said, "I beg your pardon?"

"We were so many of us restless that night," Anne said. "Shortly after I sent Mrs. Bertram to bed, Colonel Brandon and I came upon each other. We exchanged a few words to merely leaven the peculiarity of the situation—but then we talked at greater length about military life, both the costs and the blessings of it." She smiled at her husband, whose tender expression seemed to hint at a conversation between them, on this subject, not long ago.

At least one husband and wife are closer again, Marianne thought. Did it make up for one forever rent asunder?

Although Mr. Churchill looked as though he would like to ask more questions, his attention returned, as it must, to Marianne herself. "Continue, then."

Marianne wanted nothing more than to stop talking. But saving her husband required her to speak. "I hid behind the stairwell; I wished neither to see nor to be seen. I wanted to return to our room before Brandon awoke and missed me. Then there were footsteps on the stairs, and I believed both Wickham and Mrs. Bertram were gone. So I emerged and ran almost directly into Wickham himself. He—he believed I had come in search of him for improper purposes. I told him he was wrong—I slapped his hand away, and tried to get farther from him, which took me all the way into the gallery myself—"

Her voice had begun to tremble. She did not attempt to hide her tears. "I told Wickham I knew what sort of man he truly was. I told him I knew of his role in Eliza's downfall. And he—he *laughed*. He called her vile things—unspeakable things—"

Nothing better than a cheap little whore. You know what a whore is, don't you, darling? Shall I show you?

"And then I realized he had known who my husband was the whole time. Eliza had told him of her past, you see. Of the one man she truly cared for. The name was one Wickham recognized at first introduction. He thought it a fine jest that they should meet like this. He thought that—that importuning me made it all a sort of game—"

I had one of his women, and now you're here to give me another, aren't you?

"I could bear it no longer," Marianne said. "I lost my head entirely. I grabbed the nearest thing to hand—the bust of Lord Nelson—and I swung it at him with all my might. In truth I hoped to hurt him, but I did not think it would kill him. But when he fell, by the light of the candle I could see the animation leave his eyes. My father was the same way, when he died. That spirit within . . . vanishes. One understands that the soul is gone. It was then I knew I had murdered Mr. Wickham.

"Fear overcame me. I took his kerchief, wiped the bust clean, and put it back on its pedestal. My candle went out and I ran upstairs in the dark, trying to pretend none of it had happened." Marianne looked at Brandon then—she could not help it. He had awakened that night—had gone out in search of her during her absence—but had said little upon returning to bed to find her there, and nothing after the murder's discovery. There had been times she could *feel* the unasked questions burning between them, hot as flame, but neither of them had spoken. There had been one conversation when it was almost uttered, but not quite. He had understood her confession, she felt sure, and yet not one word confirmed that. On that slim basis, she was able to honestly say, "My husband did not know of my guilt. I prayed the crime might be thought the work of an intruder, someone who could not be found—but I always knew that if anyone else were legally accused, I would have to come forward. Otherwise I would have been responsible for a second death, even more despicably than the first. Little did I think my husband would confess in an attempt to protect me, but he did. So I have spoken."

After a long pause, Churchill said, "And the matter of the trowel?"

Marianne wiped at her eyes. "I went to bury the kerchief the next day, and one of the gardeners nearly caught me at it—I had to run off, and I took the trowel with me because otherwise I would have been seen putting it down. That would have raised questions I wished never to be asked. Then when you announced the search of our rooms, I knew I had to rid myself of it. Please forgive me, Miss Tilney—I put it in your room only because I knew you were the very last person anyone would blame for the crime. I would never have endangered you. That is, I swear to you on my immortal soul, the full and entire truth."

✑

Colonel Brandon had thought his heart past the point of being broken again. He had been so terribly wrong.

Churchill had left to speak with his constables; the others had departed to give Brandon a few last private moments with his wife. He sat beside her, clasping her hands in his.

He had suspected the truth from the beginning. When he had returned to bed that night to find Marianne back between the covers, trembling and all but unable to speak, Brandon had been sure *something* terrible had happened even before he knew what it was. He and Marianne had danced around that omission ever since—just enough to claim ignorance with some degree of honesty. Brandon had endured in the hopes that the truth might remain forever unknown to him and to the world entire. When he heard the young people talking, his worst fears had been confirmed—or what he then thought were his worst fears. Now even darker prospects lay before both him and his wife.

Why did you not let me take the blame? If you had but told me, I would have protected you. Wickham would not have gotten away with hurting another woman I loved. Brandon thought it all but said none. It would sound too much like remonstrance. That was not what Marianne needed now. He knew her good soul well enough to realize the depth of her remorse. Instead, he said only, "You have saved my life at a cost I would not have paid."

Marianne sobbed once. Her face was flushed with shame. "I am the one who must pay for this. No one else and least of all you. I have loved you as much as I have ever loved any person on this earth."

Such a tender confession should have pierced Colonel Brandon's heart. Instead, he felt only confusion. "We are but newly married—"

"Did you truly believe I married you without loving you?"

Brandon had. He still did. "You are fond of me," he said quietly. "More so all the time. This I have seen. But I know well that my best qualities are not those to engage the affections of a young woman. I am not the sort of man who could—whom you would—"

"You mean that you are not like Willoughby." Marianne spoke the name of the man she had nearly married with greater ease then he would once have thought possible. "No, and all the better. He is nothing to me now, compared to you."

"But—" The truth he had meant never to speak spilled out. "He wrote to you."

"Willoughby does whatever he wishes, heedless of consequence or right. Have we not both learned that much?"

He stared at her, still confused.

Despite her anguish, Marianne managed a crooked smile. "Always I longed to marry a romantic hero. Willoughby looked the part, with his passionate demeanor and beautiful horse and dashing clothes—but he possessed no truly deeper feeling. No romantic hero would ever abandon a woman simply because another had more money. But you, *Christopher*"— Marianne pronounced Brandon's Christian name for only the second time; the first had been at the altar—"you searched the world for your lost love. When you found her ruined and destitute, you did not abandon her; you nursed her through her tragic end. You raised her child to adulthood. And you defended that child's honor to the point of fighting a duel. What is that, if not the behavior of the most romantic hero of all? What I *believed* Willoughby to be, *you* truly are. It was a man like you I had dreamed of all along. Now we have discovered each other, but I have lost everything, everything, through my folly and my haste—"

As tears overtook her, Brandon clasped Marianne in his arms. The very words that once would have filled him with joy only added to his sorrow on the day his wife was lost to him, to the world, forever.

✍

Jonathan Darcy could not reconcile the difference in what was supposed to be the case and what truly was.

All along he had known that the killer had to be one of either the Knightleys or their guests. Juliet Tilney had convinced him it was possible that a woman had committed the act. Yet rational conclusions did not greatly aid him in fathoming that pretty young Mrs. Brandon, no taller than his shoulder, had killed Mr. Wickham.

Women were supposed to be of more placid temperament than men, so everyone insisted, despite ample evidence to the contrary. They were supposed to be above such terrible acts—at least gentlewomen were. So when Jonathan tried to picture the moment Marianne Brandon grabbed the bronze bust and struck Wickham a fatal blow with it, he failed.

The entire party was in disarray, seated or standing in various areas of the house with no eye toward what was proper or expected. Jonathan himself stood in the entry hallway, thinking of the prison wagon just outside. Soon it would contain Mrs. Brandon.

"It is terrible, is it not?" Miss Tilney appeared by his side; he must have been greatly distracted not to notice her approach. "We wanted the truth to be known, but I did not realize it would still be so wretched to know it."

"We wanted justice," Jonathan said. "Is this justice?"

"It does not feel like it," she answered, and he found he agreed.

✍

No sooner had Juliet begun speaking to Jonathan Darcy than Mr. Churchill emerged, his appearance more somber than she had ever seen it before. He marched back toward the drawing room where the Brandons waited alone. Juliet followed, almost not of her own volition. So, too, did Jonathan. The Knightleys and Mr. Darcy exchanged glances as Juliet walked by, then came behind. When Frank Churchill turned toward them, Juliet expected to be told to leave, but instead he called, "Everyone! Everyone of the house! A decision has been made, and it is right that you should all hear it."

Before long the entire party had gathered again in the drawing room. Mrs. Brandon looked even more wretchedly pale than before as she sat next to her pained husband.

Mr. Churchill began. "After hearing Mrs. Brandon's confession, my mind was quite made up. Yet I wished to discuss matters with Mr. Knightley and Mr. Darcy before I acted upon my convictions. As it happens, they are entirely in agreement with me—and as all of you heard her for yourselves, you will not be greatly surprised to hear that no crime has been committed here."

Juliet was caught short. She could tell some others were startled, too—the Bertrams and Captain Wentworth, at least. But some others—including Mrs. Darcy—nodded with a comprehension that had eluded Juliet herself.

It had eluded Marianne, too. "But—but I killed him. You know that I did."

"You *defended yourself*," Mr. Knightley said. "The law allows such."

Even with her salvation at hand, it appeared Marianne could not easily accept his word. "Mr. Wickham was not trying to kill me. Wicked as he was, I never believed he intended *that*."

Mr. Churchill cleared his throat. "Ah. What is—ah—less

commonly understood is that a woman who finds herself in—in such straits as you were—importuned—*forcibly*—has as much right to defend herself as she would were she threatened with death. You did so with the only means to hand." His cheeks were red at having to speak of such things, and he was not the only one in the room whose modesty had been thoroughly outraged. Yet Juliet felt it was Mr. Wickham who had outraged them by acting so, not Mr. Churchill by saying so. He continued: "Most of those here present were acquainted with Mr. Wickham; some had known him for many years. Do any of you doubt that Mr. Wickham was capable of such a vile act?"

"He was capable indeed, sir," said Mr. Darcy. "This was not the first time he had attempted mischief with a young woman. It is no great wonder that another might have to defend her honor as fiercely as she would defend her life."

Marianne's eyes widened. "Then—then it is over?"

"I ought by rights to fine you for hiding evidence," Mr. Churchill replied. "Under the circumstances, however, I cannot blame you for being frightened—and in the end, no further harm was done. Mr. Wickham was killed by the lawful action Marianne Brandon took in self-defense. And that is the end of the matter."

✑

The various listeners gathered around; all had their own opinions on what they had heard. Although they were all in accord as to the crucial point—Mrs. Brandon's story was true, and her behavior therefore lawful—each had their individual contemplations.

Edmund Bertram prayed for Mrs. Brandon, that she might be granted forgiveness, and further for others harmed by

Mr. Wickham, of which Edmund was certain there were too many to name. Fanny Bertram prayed for them both as well, though a small, guilty part of her mind wondered whether it was indecently early to ask Mr. Churchill for her ring back.

Anne Wentworth felt somewhat shamefaced to have been caught in a late-night conversation with a man not her husband—innocent as that conversation had been and valuable a role as it had played in fully establishing that man's innocence. Still, she preferred to have spoken the truth. At least she had done so at a time when every person involved had far more to think upon. Captain Wentworth wanted very badly to know whether Mr. Wickham's death erased debts owed to him and had resolved to consult with a lawyer soon—but not today. They had faced enough today.

The Knightleys were also interested in this point of the law, and Emma said as much to her husband as they finally left the drawing room. Knightley replied, "The question of Mr. Wickham's heirs has become rather more complicated. How it will affect the case, I cannot tell. We will have to learn more soon."

"I have learned one thing already," Emma said, "and will forever heed it."

"To what do you refer?"

"That house parties are more trouble than they are worth, and we shall never, ever have another one."

Knightley smiled. "On that subject, we are in complete agreement."

Jonathan's feelings on the matter were more complex than most. What care he had had as a boy for Uncle George was no more than a remnant of childhood, like the toy soldiers still kept in a wooden box in his trunk. Yet just as he occasionally took the soldiers out to look at them, he now called upon his few good memories of the man: his uncle sneaking

Jonathan a bit of cake well before teatime, riding with him on a foggy morning when the grass crunched with frost, holding out baby Susannah for her cousin's approval with what had been—at least for that moment—genuine paternal pride.

There were aspects to his character that might have made him a good man, Jonathan thought, *if that was what Mr. Wickham had wished to be.*

Instead, Jonathan had other memories, too: Wickham shouting at Aunt Lydia until she wept, his cold lack of feeling at Susannah's funeral, the sneering way he had addressed them all—even Jonathan—upon his arrival at Donwell Abbey. As difficult as it was to accept that this was the man Wickham had more wished himself, so it had to have been.

Jonathan wanted to talk this over with his parents, whose emotions were probably even greater than his own. As he turned toward them, however, he saw that they were holding hands as they walked along, looking into each other's eyes in a way that had not been seen since Susannah's death. There was joy there, understanding, too, their marriage a fortress that the troubles of the day could not pierce—even such a day as this one. It was, in short, as it had been before.

His parents' marriage was a fortress for Jonathan, too, and in that moment he felt almost secure again.

Yet they do not know everything, he told himself.

They knew that one of Susannah's cousins was responsible for betraying to Wickham that the little girl now called Darcy "Papa" and in so doing had unwittingly set into motion the events that led to her death.

They did not know that the one responsible was Jonathan himself.

Guilt pressed down on him again, as unbearable as it had been since the day he first realized that truth. If he told his parents, would they understand? Or would they blame him? Sometimes he thought they would place no responsibility upon him; at other moments, Jonathan imagined them casting him out of Pemberley, disowned, no longer loved.

The truth, probably, was between those extremes. Eventually, Jonathan knew, he would have to discover it for himself. He could not keep this from his parents forever.

But he had kept it for eight months, and he would keep it longer. It would be cruel to tell them today, when they had at last rediscovered some measure of joy in each other. The rest could wait.

Marianne Brandon could not feel delight for her escape from the gallows; any such mirth would be denied her for a long time to come by the gruesome memory of Wickham lying dead at her feet. But mortal terror gripped her no more, and in its wake, exhaustion claimed her. Colonel Brandon helped her up the stairs to the bed they shared.

"Is it impolite to take a nap in the middle of the day?" Marianne had scarcely slept since the murder, and days of weariness weighted her every step.

"Under the circumstances," said Brandon, "I believe our hosts will understand."

He put her to bed, drawing the covers over her before he lay down by her side. Brandon put his arm across her so that, as she slept, if her dreams caused her fear, she might feel him there and know that she was held. She was safe.

No one contested the magistrate's findings regarding the death of Mr. Wickham. The gossiping townsfolk were sufficiently horrified and titillated by the rumors of Wickham's "indecent acts toward a gentlewoman" to abandon their suspicions of the Donwell Abbey guests, which made future trips into Highbury far more congenial. There were, however, very few of these trips to be made, for as soon as Frank Churchill gave the guests their liberty to leave, all were in agreement that it was time for this ill-fated house party to end.

Juliet felt she had had an extraordinary experience, a far greater education into human nature than she would have thought possible. Furthermore, she had made the acquaintance of Jonathan Darcy—in rather a different way than their hostess had intended, but a more meaningful one, too. That alone made this visit worth its many travails.

However, almost all the others in attendance seemed to think that she had been greatly deprived.

"Young women have so few chances to get about in the world," fretted Emma Knightley as she helped Juliet pack. "It is most unfair that your first opportunity should be ruined in such a manner."

"It was not ruined," Juliet insisted. "Honestly, when it was not frightening, it was all very interesting."

Should she have admitted that out loud? Probably not. Emma's knowing look in response suggested *she* understood Juliet's true meaning . . . but not everyone would.

Emma said only, "We should very much like to have you back to visit someday. Or we may even spend part of the winter in London—have you been much to London?"

"Not at all." Juliet couldn't help brightening at the thought. London! It was the apex of all dreams, the font of infinite inspiration. Anything might happen to a girl in London. And if she could manage the investigation of a murder, surely the city had no terrors she could not conquer.

∽

"Already more invitations," said Knightley with a sigh, when Emma told him about this shortly thereafter. "If I had not already known that your appetite for society and liveliness was insatiable, this would have proved it beyond all doubt."

Emma leaned back in her chair, a posture no guest of Donwell Abbey would ever see. "You cannot claim we have done our duty by the girl."

"Under the circumstances, I think we did rather well." Knightley considered it for a moment. "That said, Miss Tilney showed great resourcefulness. More, really, than a young woman ought—but the effects were to the good. I should not mind knowing her better. She promises to become a formidable woman indeed."

"Then you join in my invitation?" Emma knew he did. She simply could not resist relishing triumph whenever it came.

Knightley understood this, which was why he smiled. "I do. But before we play the hosts again, and certainly before we spend any extended time in London, I wish to have the comfort, quiet, and solitude of my own home for many days. Weeks. Perhaps months."

This was where he expected Emma to object. Instead, she gave him a weary smile. "Perhaps I am turning into my father, because . . . that sounds like heaven."

∽

It would perhaps have been more prudent for Fanny Bertram to wait before replying to her brother's letter. She harbored no doubts about the Knightleys' character, no suspicions that they would stoop so low as to reading her mail—and their servants appeared honest and pleasant as well—but when it came to something so delicate, so dangerous, Fanny could not help but be afraid.

Yet she had come to understand that she let herself be afraid too often. It was a kind of impiety, a failure to trust in the Lord's providence. Fanny needed to live her faith in more than prayers and obedience. She needed to find the courage that true faith surely brought.

While Edmund made arrangements for their first postcoach, she took up ink and paper on the small table in their room.

> *Dearest William—*
> *Your letter surprised me very greatly, as you must have*
> *known it would. You asked for my understanding. I*
> *must admit, I do not understand,*

Fanny did not even comprehend how two men engaged in sexual congress, and she did not wish to.

> *but you do have my love, always, no matter what else*
> *may occur.*
> *You showed great trust in me by writing me so, and*
> *I want you to be assured that your trust was not ill*
> *placed. The only person to whom I have spoken of it is*
> *Edmund, who still welcomes you as a brother. Never*
> *again will any other soul hear of it from my lips, and*
> *the letter has been destroyed.*

One other knew—Elizabeth Darcy—and of course the story of the letter's journey over the past few weeks was one to raise fear in even such a stalwart soul as William's. Fanny thought informing William of all this would be more likely to alarm than to reassure. Whenever they might meet again, she would reveal the full story of Mr. Wickham's malevolence and demise. By then, William would already know himself safe.

Of course, this meant putting her trust in Elizabeth Darcy. Yet Fanny had learned that, for all Mrs. Darcy's fine gowns and satirical wit, she was at heart a good woman. Trusting providence seemed to lead to trusting people, as well. How differently the world appeared, when one stopped cringing away from it and faced it in the light.

> *I realize your duty near Saint Helena will keep you*
> *long from England. But whenever you do next come,*
> *rest assured that our home is welcome to you, our hearts*
> *are open to you, and you are as dear to me as ever you*
> *were—and that is very dear indeed.*
>
> > *All my love,*
> > *Your sister Fanny*

As she scattered sawdust on the page to blot the ink, Edmund returned to their room. "I fear we shall not be able to depart until tonight. That is the next coach we could possibly afford. The Darcys offered to convey us on the first leg of the journey, but we are significantly out of their way."

Fanny disliked traveling by night; she found it almost impossible to sleep in such a conveyance. Edmund knew this. However, he also had known she would more greatly dislike bothering the Darcys. She smiled up at him. "Then we have time for me to post my letter."

"Indeed." Edmund did not ask to whom she wrote, but he

must have understood. The warmth of his smile was both relief and promise. "Now for the good news. Mr. Churchill came to call, specifically to turn over the evidence in the case—one piece of which belongs to you." With that, he held out her amethyst ring.

"Oh!" Fanny hardly dared trust her eyes. "But did they not ask what it was that—why Mr. Wickham could—"

"They did not ask," Edmund said gently. "Both Mrs. Brandon and Mrs. Wentworth confirmed enough of your story that they had no need to know the rest. Your secret is safe, Fanny, and so is your ring."

Tears of gladness sprang to Fanny's eyes as she held out her hand. Edmund slipped this ring onto her finger as he had another, four years ago.

ↄ৴৶

With Hartfield still in disrepair, the Wentworths had as yet no home to return to. However, it was agreed between them that a short visit to London was in order. The final disposition of Mr. Wickham's estate would have a very great effect on their fortunes, and thus Captain Wentworth thought it prudent to keep even closer to the case, although it meant enduring the discomforts of the city in summer.

"Besides," Anne Wentworth reasoned that final morning at Donwell Abbey, "even the tumult of London cannot compare to the events of our past several days."

That made Captain Wentworth chuckle. Already he was smiling more easily, laughing more often. The wound to his pride inflicted by Mr. Wickham had finally begun to heal. "The city will seem an oasis of tranquility by comparison!"

Privately Anne doubted this; she did not like cities at all; and the larger they were, the less she liked them. London of course was the greatest city of all. But it would only be for a few weeks. Nearly anything might be endured for so short a span. Also, London would be a profound change in all ways, and change was something she thought they both needed.

"By the way," the captain added, "while in London, I shall have occasion to visit the Admiralty."

Anne hardly dared hope, but she asked, "Will you put in for another ship?"

How she had missed her husband's smile! "Aye, regardless of how the debts are resolved. The first one with room enough to take us, be it headed to Antigua or Antwerp or 'round the Cape."

"Anywhere in the world will be home, as long as you are with me."

*

Marianne stared into the mirror as the maid finished putting up her hair, then slipped on her lacy cap. It was precisely as it had been nearly every morning of her married life, and yet every moment seemed unreal. Could it really be happening? Or was it all a dream she was having while huddled in a cell, waiting to be condemned?

They all seemed to agree that her attack on Wickham was justified. Marianne remembered how frightened she had been but also how angry. Was it still self-defense when the action was borne as much of rage as of fear? Would Wickham really have attempted such an outrage with everyone just upstairs? Wouldn't he have thought she would scream?

But she had not screamed. Wickham had known she would not. And had the worst occurred—ever after, if Marianne had had the courage to tell a soul, they would have asked about her silence. They would have assumed that her silence meant complicity, that she had not been assaulted but seduced. That, Marianne did not think she could have endured.

Yet I am punished, Marianne thought. The memory of Wickham's dead body would never leave her. The guilt, remorse, and terror she had felt had left scars within her that would certainly never fade. *Someday God will decide if it is punishment enough.*

The maid's leaving the room coincided with Colonel Brandon's return to it. He smiled at her, as he did every morning, but there was a different quality to his affection now. The distance between them was forever diminished. Each better understood the love they felt for each other, and how much both were willing to sacrifice for that love. It was a test many marriages could not endure, Marianne thought, but one that had made their connection all the stronger.

How would Willoughby have handled a similar situation? Marianne could not imagine it. Moreover, she found she did not want to. It was of no moment.

Colonel Brandon put one hand on her shoulder, which she covered with her own. "Are you ready to depart, Marianne?"

"Almost. There is one person I must speak to first."

"Come to Devonshire?" Juliet Tilney's astonishment could not be wondered at. Marianne had gone from planting evidence in her room to asking her to stay within the space of three days. This would be reason enough to refuse, surely.

Yet Marianne pressed on. "I am ashamed of my behavior these past few days, and if you no longer desire the acquaintance, then I shall respect your wishes. Yet we were becoming friends, before Mr. Wickham's disturbance, and I should welcome the chance to get to know you better under more favorable circumstances. And I should so like to introduce you to my mother and to my sister and her husband. Do say you will come?"

"I—" Miss Tilney seemed to be struggling for words. "Already I have been invited to visit the Knightleys again."

"Right away?"

"No, for the London season. It is so very much! After never leaving home without my parents to having so many invitations . . ."

"Mine cannot be the most welcome, I know." Miss Tilney shook her head in denial, but Marianne persisted. "But I would welcome the chance to finally do you justice. To make amends for my behavior, if any such amends can be made. Will you consider it, at least?"

Marianne braced herself for a refusal, which was surely what she deserved. Instead, Miss Tilney began to nod. "I think I should like to see Devonshire."

⁓

"We ought to invite the Tilney girl to stay with us at Pemberley," said Elizabeth Darcy as she and her husband drank coffee in the breakfast room, temporarily alone. "She and Jonathan seem to have made a promising beginning."

Darcy had not made up his mind about Juliet Tilney. He had fully intended to inform the Knightleys about her snooping until suspicion turned upon her after the police search; he had not then had the heart to add to her burdens. As it happened, Jonathan's investigation with her—imprudent though it was—had borne fruit, preventing an innocent man from the gallows. So he no longer objected to Miss Tilney. However, it took more than the mere absence of disapproval to earn Darcy's full approval. It would serve all of them well to better understand this girl who had intrigued his son. "Then it shall be done."

Elizabeth could not entirely suppress her smile. Darcy knew his wife to be too sensible a woman to already imagine their son at the altar, but she cherished certain hopes. Time enough, he supposed, for her hopes to either realize or fade.

Indeed, with her next words, his wife wisely changed the subject. "I suppose we must wait some time, however, to ensure that all matters with Wickham's estate are addressed."

Darcy frowned. "Surely we are not further concerned with the situation."

"But if there is no heir to Wickham's estate, then it is possible that, as his wife's family, we may be the only persons capable of managing his affairs."

"You forget, my good wife—we now know that Wickham does possess living heirs: Colonel Brandon's ward and her child."

"How can this be? The young woman is only Wickham's natural child, and thus—"

"And thus she cannot inherit any property entailed upon him," Darcy said. "So far as I know, there is none such. However, illegitimate heirs can inherit other kinds of property, including debts owed. We must hope that the young woman's character is such that she will not deign to profit from the deception of others."

"Regardless, either Wickham's debtors or his heirs stand to benefit." Elizabeth could not help smiling. "Would you think me unfeeling if I said that this house party—crudely interrupted as it has been—may ultimately have caused more good than harm?"

"As long as we remember that harm was truly done," Darcy said, and it was censure enough.

"You know I do not regret Wickham's death, but I do not rejoice in it," she said. "He was our last tie to Susannah—and to Lydia, too. Perhaps to the folly of my youth, of which we should all be constantly reminded, lest we repeat it in drearier fashion. But I jest again." Elizabeth's expression became most tender. "Fitzwilliam, have you realized . . . this girl, Beth, is Susannah's half sister?"

While the fact of it had indeed occurred to him, only at this moment did Darcy's heart absorb the fullness of what she meant. If ever they met Colonel Brandon's ward, they might see something of Susannah in her face, her manner, her smile. He would give much to glimpse even such slight echoes of the little girl they had lost.

"We might ask to speak with her someday," Elizabeth said. "To tell her more of her history, if she wishes to know it. Surely Colonel Brandon would arrange that for us, if he can bear the memory of these unpleasant events."

"There is no joy to be taken from what has happened here," Darcy replied. "That does not mean there is not joy to be found in going forward."

Darcy lay his hand on her forearm briefly. After more than twenty years of marriage, such a touch still had the power to thrill them both. "Of this I have no doubt," he said. They shared a moment of mutual comfort and satisfaction—the simple harmony of marriage, which they had deprived themselves of for too long. "Once breakfast is done, then, we shall go—but where is our son?"

Elizabeth's smile could be very sly. "I believe he has some farewells to make."

$\mathcal{O}$

Jonathan found Miss Tilney alone in the library, her book in her lap, unattended. "Do I disturb you?" he asked.

The response was a smile. "Indeed you do, and glad I am of it. Reading is delightful, but—pretending to read, while one's thoughts are elsewhere—it is unaccountably tiring."

Sitting on the divan next to her would be too forward. Jonathan reckoned that the chair opposite would be suitable and took his place there. "Where are your thoughts, then?"

"On Devonshire. The Brandons have invited me for a visit. I can only imagine what my parents will say when I tell them I wish to visit a murderess." Miss Tilney shook her head. "I hope I can make them understand the true circumstances, so that I might go."

In her place, Jonathan would not have been so quick to accept. Surely Mrs. Brandon's actions, if not criminal, at least violated propriety. Then again, propriety had little to say about murder. "When will the visit take place?"

"Soon, I think. Within a few months." Thoughtfully she added, "I am homesick for my parents, but my first taste of new places has made me want more. They cannot all be this eventful!"

"Surely you deserve a more congenial visit than this." Jonathan wished to ask her to Pemberley, but that invitation was not his to give. Maybe his parents could be persuaded. He had a suspicion that his mother would not require much persuasion. "We are to depart soon. I hoped to say farewell."

"Oh!" The dismay on Miss Tilney's face gladdened Jonathan's heart, though he could not say why. "I suppose I am meant to say the same usual things about having the pleasure of making your acquaintance. The adventure we have undertaken together seems to require more, does it not?"

"Indeed it does," Jonathan replied. "And I am very glad to have taken the adventure with you."

The glow on her face then made him realize that, though his words obeyed no social protocol that he knew, he seemed to have said exactly the right thing.

∽

All the hopes of Wickham's debtors were jarred by the revelation that he did in fact possess heirs in the form of Colonel Brandon's ward, Beth, and her infant son. Brandon was greatly pained at the thought of pressing these people to pay their debts, villainously swindled as they had been. Such pains were all the greater now that he counted some of these among his friends. Yet Beth was a young, unmarried woman with a child. Generously though Brandon would provide for her, it was only natural that Beth should feel the need to ensure her baby's welfare to the fullest possible measure. When he told her of the events at Donwell Abbey, he made it clear the decision was hers, hers alone, and that if she chose to collect the entire fortune in the interest of her child's well-being, neither he nor anyone else would judge her.

This was a terrible conundrum for a new-made mother, freshly vulnerable to the worries and responsibilities of maternity. Many days did she ponder the decision. In the end, however, Beth's good conscience would not allow her to collect all the funds. "My father appears to have been a villain," she told Brandon, "and I will not be obliged to become one likewise, for the remembrance of a parent who never wished to know me." Beth looked down at her baby as she said this last, unable to fathom the lack of feeling necessary to abandon one's own child.

So it was that John and Isabella Knightley, the Wentworths, and all others who could demonstrate themselves victims of Wickham's financial scheme collected nearly everything they had previously believed to be lost. Yet Beth and her son still profited, as Wickham was revealed to have a large sum in addition to that pilfered from the scheme—its provenance unknown. As no debtors could there be identified, those funds were inherited by Wickham's daughter, and proved more than sufficient to promise an even better life for Beth and her child than Brandon could ever have provided alone.

The Wentworths had no more need to go to sea, yet as they still desired to do so, they set sail in the early autumn with Wentworth as captain of the *Manticore*. Thus Hartfield, newly repaired, was freed for occupancy by John and Isabella Knightley's family just as they were assured of keeping their London home forever.

Uncomfortable though many aspects of the Donwell Abbey house party had been, those who experienced it found themselves greatly connected to the others who had been there. Perhaps there is no surer ground for the foundation of a friendship than a shared time of trouble. Regardless, those families remained very much in contact with one another in subsequent years, their bonds connected through numerous letters and visits.

Only two members of the company could not contact one another directly: Jonathan Darcy and Juliet Tilney. Only for the sake of truth had they exchanged a note at Donwell Abbey; under no circumstances could unmarried young people of different sexes correspond without the greatest impropriety. So it was to their great fortune that the friends and families involved contrived, in unspoken agreement, through various invitations and visitations, to connect the two again.

Acknowledgments

Working on this book has been an absolute pleasure, for which I must first thank my wonderful editor, Anna Kaufman. She saw the potential in this story from the beginning, and through her work, she's made the book far better than it would have been otherwise. The rest of the team—Kayla Overbey, Martha Schwartz, Julie Ertl, Annie Locke, Zuleima Ugalde, and Lara Hinchberger—gave this their all, and I'm truly grateful.

Thanks also go out to my assistant, Sarah Simpson Weiss, who saves me from myself on a near-daily basis; my former agent, Diana Fox; cover designer Perry De La Vega; and my agent, Laura Rennert, and her team at Andrea Brown.

As ever, I am deeply grateful to my supportive parents, extended family, and friends. The first time I shared any part of this story was at a meeting of the New Orleans writing group Peauxdunque, and it was their enthusiastic reception that encouraged me to take this idea, which had been knocking around in my head for *years*, and finally turn it from a daydream into a novel.

Very special thanks go out to Kimberly VanderHorst, who provided a thorough and sensitive authenticity read centering on the character of Jonathan Darcy. The book is better for her insight and clarity; any remaining shortcomings are my responsibility alone.

Some years ago, I threw a Jane Austen party with several other Janeites I knew, complete with games, period food (syllabubs are *much* more alcoholic than I thought), etc. A male friend on the edge of my social circle turned out to be a Jane fan, too. He not only attended the party but also prepared a piece of period music to perform, the exact kind of entertainment Jane or her characters would have enjoyed of an evening. This man is now my husband. Paul supports me through all my writing, but in the case of *The Murder of Mr. Wickham*, he also helped me work out questions of characterization and plot as only another Austen devotee could. Thanks for everything, babe.

My final and greatest debt of gratitude is owed, of course, to Jane Austen herself. What would she think of the things her characters do here? I can hardly imagine. But I hope it would be clear to her—as I hope it is to the readers of this book—how deeply I love her books and characters. They've given me endless delight throughout the years, and they always will. So thank you, Jane, for all the joy you have brought to my life and to the lives of so many others.

The Murder of Mr. Wickham

Questions written by Claudia Gray

1. *The Murder of Mr. Wickham* features most of the principal characters from Jane Austen's novels, continuing their life stories after the original books. Which of the characters' "futures" felt most believable? Most interesting? Did any of these futures ring false for you, and if so, why?

2. Today, Jonathan Darcy would probably be understood as neurodivergent. How do the Regency-era characters—including Jonathan himself—understand him? In what ways do the differences between Jonathan's time and our own make his life harder, or perhaps easier?

3. Mr. Wickham deeply resents the other characters—above all, the Darcys. What do you think lies at the core of his resentment?

4. Many of the couples within the book struggle with keeping secrets from each other: George Knightley hides his entanglement with Wickham from Emma, Juliet Tilney becomes angry when Jonathan fails to give her critical information about his family, and Fanny Bertram is reluctant to reveal her brother's secret to Edmund. Which character, if any, did you feel was most justified in remaining silent? Which characters' silence could have been most damaging to their relationship?

5. Fanny isn't certain how to react to her brother William's romantic relationship with another man. How are her thoughts and conclusions influenced by the time and the culture in which she lives?

6. The Darcys' marriage has been strained in the months immediately preceding the events of *The Murder of Mr. Wickham*. How did each character express grief over the death of Susannah? How can differences in the ways we grieve cause problems within relationships?

7. Juliet Tilney is a conventional young woman of the 1820s English gentry in many ways . . . but not all. How does she deviate from societal expectations? In what ways do her differences make her life more difficult? More interesting?

8. The characters live in a world with very concrete expectations, rules, and schedules—an experience far less flexible than most of our lives today. Would you find this constrictive? Or would more definite guidelines make life less uncertain?

9. Through different characters' points of view, we learn a little about what happened to some secondary characters from Austen's six novels—such as Mary Bennet, John Willoughby, and Mrs. Smith. Which of these were you most eager to learn about? Which other Austen characters do you wish had been mentioned in greater detail?

10. Every principal character is either a member of the gentry—what we might now call the lower upper class—or related to nobility. To what extent do the characters consider the thoughts and needs of those with less money and lower social standing, from the servants at Donwell Abbey to the townspeople of Highbury?

ALSO BY

CLAUDIA GRAY

THE LATE MRS. WILLOUGHBY

Catherine and Henry Tilney of Northanger Abbey are not entirely pleased to be sending their eligible young daughter Juliet out into the world again. Particularly concerning is that she intends to visit her new friend Marianne Brandon, who's returned home to Devonshire shrouded in fresh scandal—made more potent by the news that her former suitor, the rakish Mr. Willoughby, intends to take up residence at his local estate with his new bride. Meanwhile, Elizabeth and Fitzwilliam Darcy of Pemberley are thrilled that their eldest son, Jonathan—who, like his father, has not always been the most socially adept—has been invited to stay with his former schoolmate, John Willoughby. Jonathan himself is decidedly less taken with the notion of having to spend extended time under the roof of his old bully, but that all changes when he finds himself reunited with his fellow amateur sleuth, the radiant Miss Tilney. Then Willoughby's new wife dies horribly at the party meant to welcome her to town. With rumors flying and Marianne under increased suspicion, Jonathan and Juliet must team up once more to uncover the murderer. But as they collect clues and close in on suspects, eerie incidents suggest that the pair are in far graver danger than they or their families could imagine.

Fiction

VINTAGE BOOKS
Available wherever books are sold.
vintagebooks.com